CONSUMED BY PASSION

"Diana."

His voice was quiet, yet commanding. Slowly she moved her arm and opened her eyes.

"Take off your chemise."

She drew a deep breath and very slowly lifted the chemise over her head and tossed it beside her. He began to caress her softly swelled woman's flesh and her desire flowed over him. She had never imagined such a feeling, such warmth. She wasn't the least bit afraid, not now. "I want you to remember this moment, Diana. This is the first time and it is magic. . . ."

Calypso Magic

Calypso
Magic

by
Catherine Coulter

AN ONYX BOOK

ONYX
Published by the Penguin Group
Penguin Books USA Inc., 375 Hudson Street,
New York, New York 10014, U.S.A.
Penguin Books Ltd, 27 Wrights Lane,
London W8 5TZ, England
Penguin Books Australia Ltd, Ringwood,
Victoria, Australia
Penguin Books Canada Ltd, 2801 John Street,
Markham, Ontario, Canada L3R 1B4
Penguin Books (N.Z.) Ltd, 182–190 Wairau Road,
Auckland 10, New Zealand

Penguin Books Ltd, Registered Offices:
Harmondsworth, Middlesex, England

First Printing, April, 1988
13   12   11   10   9   8

 REGISTERED TRADEMARK—MARCA REGISTRADA

Printed in the United States of America

To Sarah Butler,
who brings magic into my life.

London, England, 1813

Why should the Devil have all the good tunes?

ROWLAND HILL

Prologue

*Haversham House,
Richmond, England
March 1813*

Where the devil was Charlotte?

Lyonel Ashton, Sixth Earl of Saint Leven, strode through the wildly bedraggled Haversham garden.

Charlotte wasn't there, only one servant bent on finding enough presentable early-spring flowers for a bouquet. He silently wished her luck.

Lucia, his great-aunt, had suggested the stables. He sighed. Lucia didn't like Charlotte and barely hid her animosity toward Lord Haversham, whom she considered an ill-bred lout. She treated the entire Haversham family, he thought, with awful civility. He wondered why she'd insisted upon coming today. Her bland reason of the fine weather rang as false as the hairpiece she was wearing. He finally turned and walked past the drive toward the stables. Lord Haversham, as well as Charlotte, was hunting-mad and slate-roofed stables were in better condition than the house.

Lyon looked first at the pristine paddock. It seemed like all the stable hands and grooms were there, but not Charlotte.

He finally entered the cool stable. All of the horses were out being exercised. There was no one about. He frowned, but walked to the tack room. He paused a moment outside the closed door.

Charlotte was inside, he heard her voice. A smile on his face, he reached toward the doorknob, then abruptly drew back his hand. He also heard a man's voice, low, deep . . . caressing. Then Charlotte, a high cry.

Lyon felt the blood pound in his head.

As if he were another man in a dream, he watched his hand reach out for the door handle and slowly press down on it. The door swung open slowly, soundlessly.

Charlotte was on her back, her head resting on a Spanish saddle, Dancy Moressey, Lord Danvers, his buckskins pulled down to his knees, was between her widespread legs, pumping into her.

Lyon walked into the room. He very slowly picked up a riding crop. Charlotte saw him in that moment, and screamed.

He brought the crop down on Moressey's white buttocks. Dancy roared, jerking out of Charlotte, his face a study in horrified surprise and pain. Lyon brought the crop down again, then he threw it aside. He grabbed Moressey, pulling him upright, and slammed his fist into his erstwhile friend's face. Then again. Moressey struggled, but it was no use. Lyon hit him again and heard bone cracking.

"Stop! Lyonel, stop! You're killing him!" Charlotte jerked down her skirts and dived for him. She pulled at his arm, shaking him, screaming.

The dream came to an abrupt halt. Lyon stared into Moressey's battered face. He was unconscious. Slowly, deliberately, he released him and watched him crumble to the floor, his pants about his knees. Dancy could boast no rutting desire now, but his shrunken member was wet and glistening.

Lyon was aware of the smells of the tack room: linseed, leather, and sex. He turned to his betrothed.

He said in an unnaturally calm voice, "I trust that you will retract our engagement in the newspapers. When Lord Danvers comes to his senses, tell him that my second will be calling on him."

"Lyonel," Charlotte said, reaching her hand toward him. "Please, it's not what—"

"You may keep the engagement ring. Since it's new and not a Saint Leven heirloom, I will have no use for it." He watched tears pool in her beautiful eyes. "Perhaps," he said in that same calm voice, "you'd best see to your lover. I do believe I broke his nose." He turned on his heel and walked from the tack room.

"Lyonel! Damn you, come back here!"

He turned, his expression cold and forbidding. "I trust, my dear Charlotte, that you intend to marry Lord Danvers? He will need you, I fancy, to attend him after I put a bullet through his arm. A pity, really, I rather thought of Dancy as a friend. As for you, well, there is really nothing more to say."

His only clear thought as he walked back toward the house was, My God, what if we'd been married and I'd found her with another man?

He wasn't really surprised to find his Aunt Lucia standing by the carriage.

He looked at her.

"I'm sorry, my boy," she said, lightly touching his sleeve with her fingertips.

"This was the reason for our surprise visit?"

"Yes."

"The weather is very fine, as you said."

"I will not lie to you, Lyon. I am relieved that you have discovered the truth before it is too late."

"How did you know? You did know that she was playing me false with Moressey?"

"Come into the carriage. I will tell you on the way back to London."

He followed her, his face without expression. The carriage bowled down the wide drive.

Lyonel didn't look back.

1

There's a skirmish of wit between them.
SHAKESPEARE

Cranston House, London, England
May 1813

Diana Savarol hated London. It was May, and she was shivering, always shivering. She wanted to go home, back to Savarol Island in the West Indies, where it was always warm, the sky always filled with bright sunlight. She looked at Lucia, Lady Cranston, that old tartar whose tongue was as sharp as a snake's, and her mouth thinned. She wasn't at all certain as yet that she liked her. Even though she was small, she looked regal as a queen with her snow-white hair piled high on her head and her sharp chin always raised just a bit higher than ordinary mortals. "Call me Aunt Lucia," the imperious old woman had told her when she'd arrived. "I'm not exactly your aunt, not even your great-aunt, but it will do." And Diana had complied. Who wouldn't with those sharp pale-blue eyes staring at one with such command?

"I should like to have the fire lit," Diana said now, looking with undisguised longing at the empty grate.

"Really, my dear? I don't think so. Why don't you wear a warmer shawl?"

"I don't have a warmer shawl."

"Then you will have to accustom yourself. You've been here but a week, child." Lucia returned to her novel, a hair-raising gothic that was most improbable and excessively titillating. Diana had remarked on it, her eyes wide, and Lucia had said, "Well, I'm not dead yet, my dear child. I enjoy being wafted away from my fifty-six years, however temporarily. The heroine is such a wilting goose. Most enjoyable—yes, indeed."

"Has the heroine fainted yet in this chapter, Aunt?"

"Twice," said Lucia. "Once with the villain and once with the hero. She is quite accomplished at it. I fear it is her only accomplishment, unless one considers her eyes, which are described as blue as a cerulean sky—most improbable, I daresay—and large as fine China saucers. Wedgwood, I wonder? Oh, my dear Diana, we will attend a ball at Lady Bellermain's this evening. You will wear your new blue silk. It will make you look less tanned."

Diana liked the blue silk, but not because it made her complexion look fairer. It made her look as tall and narrow as a healthy sapling. A ball! She felt as if a thunderbolt had struck her. What would happen to her there, in front of a roomful of strangers, when it became obvious that she couldn't . . . "Aunt," she said somewhat desperately, "I must tell you that I cannot—"

Didier, Lucia's butler, whom she fondly called "that old monk," entered the drawing room, bowed slightly, and said in his deep voice, "Lord Saint Leven is here, my lady. As you instructed."

"Ah, Lyonel! Don't stand there like a block, Didier, show my nephew in." Lucia tucked the novel away under the seat of her chair, then gave Diana a look that she accurately translated as Mind your tongue or I'll skin you.

Who was this Lyonel person? A real nephew of Lucia's? Of course she would be polite to him. Why ever would Lucia believe she wouldn't? Diana could have easily answered her own query. She hadn't particularly pushed herself to be polite to anyone. She didn't want to be here, after all. I will hold my tongue, at least for the moment, she thought, and grinned at the thought of stuffing her hand into her mouth and wrapping her fingers about her tongue.

Lyonel hadn't wanted to see Lucia, at least not just yet, but he'd just returned from his estate near York. He'd spent most of his time with Frances and Hawk at their racing stud, Desborough. But he'd never in his life ignored a summons from Lucia, and besides, he rationalized to himself, he loved the old bird. She had, after all, saved him from a marriage that would never have seen the light of heaven. He thought briefly of Dancy Moressey, now Charlotte's poor fool of a husband. He'd shot him through the arm, and somehow, no one had found out about it. The good Lord knew that someone should have heard of it, for Charlotte had screeched like a banshee.

He strode into the drawing room and drew up short. There was a girl standing there, her shoulders hunched, shivering, in the middle of the room. She obviously wasn't a servant, for she was looking at him with rather arrogant curiosity, but her gray gown was not at all in fashion and was too small. Her breasts, he couldn't help noticing, were pressed so tightly against the bodice that he wondered that a seam didn't burst. She was well-enough-looking, he supposed without much interest, tall and slender, save for those breasts. Her hair was thick and a blond color mixed with various shades of brown and gold, and her eyes from this distance appeared an interesting greenish gray. He sent a look toward Lucia, a brow arched in question.

"Come in, come in, my boy," Lucia called. "I want you to meet your cousin, Diana Savarol. Diana, my dear, this is your cousin, Lyonel Ashton, Earl of Saint Leven."

"Cousin?" he said slowly, eyeing the shivering girl. "Do you have the ague?"

"No," Diana said sharply. "I'm bloody cold."

"Well, that at least shouldn't be catching. Cousin, you say?. I didn't know I had a Diana Savarol for a cousin."

"A cousin somewhat removed," said Lucia.

"I didn't know I had a Lyon for a cousin either," Diana said.

"All right," said Lucia. "Many times removed. Your grandmothers were first cousins, I think. Make your curtsy, Diana."

Diana gave a ghost of a curtsy.

Lyonel gave a mockery of a bow.

"Sit down, my boy. Didier, bring in the tea tray."

"As I recall from Father's family tree," Lyonel said, looking at Lucia, "my grandmother married a fellow from some ungodly place and left England."

"The West Indies are hardly ungodly," said Diana. "Well, not too much, not anymore. The pirates are long gone, but then again, so are the Quakers."

"Your great-uncle, Oliver Mendenhall, accompanied her, Lyonel, your grandmother, that is. He did well there. You are his heir, if you weren't aware of it."

"I fear to expire of excitement on the spot."

"So you are that Ashton whelp," Diana said.

"I beg your pardon?"

"Mr. Mendenhall refers to you as the Ashton whelp."
Diana raised her chin when he put his monocle to his eye.

Lucia hadn't known what to expect, but her precious
Lyonel, this Ashton whelp, was behaving most peculiarly,
and all because of that wretched Charlotte Haversham. He
was—rather used to be—urbane, exquisitely polite, particularly to females, and blessed with a wry wit that wasn't
at all malicious. This new Lyonel was regarding Diana as
if she were the possessor of three eyes and spots on her
face.

"That," said Diana under her breath, but not under
enough, "might be interesting to watch." So he was the
man that Old Oliver was being forced to leave all his
earthly goods to.

"What might be interesting to watch?"

"Why, your expiring on the spot."

"Ah," said Lucia, "our tea. Diana, my dear, would
you please pour?" Damn the two of them anyway. She'd
decided after three days that Diana was the girl for Lyonel.
She'd really had no intention of ever agreeing with Oliver,
who'd slyly suggested in his last letter that Diana and his
heir could make a match of it. She remembered Oliver as a
feckless lad with a big nose, a spotty complexion, and a
receding chin. Not only had he written to her, but Diana's
father as well. And now here they were sparring like two
ill-bred prizefighters. Both of them must have peasant
stock from somewhere. Not from her side of the family, of
course.

Diana poured the tea with little grace. "I suppose you
like to kill your tea with milk?"

Since she hadn't looked up as she'd spoken, Lyonel
said, "Who is the subject of your sentence?"

"Aunt Lucia doesn't kill her tea with anything. You,
my lord?"

"By all means, kill it," said Lyonel, who'd never had milk in his tea in his twenty-seven years. He watched her shiver, this time in distaste, and smiled. He rose and walked over to the sideboard. He poured himself a brandy.

"I changed my mind," he said, and gave a brief salute to Diana. "What are you doing here?"

"I live here for the moment. It's Aunt Lucia's sacred goal to polish me up and bring me out."

"You don't appear to be exactly first-season material," he said, and sipped at his brandy. It was good. Lucia had the best cellars in London.

Diana's teacup rattled. What was this awful man's problem? she wondered. He'd taken one look at her and turned nasty. Well, she wasn't one to lie down like a rug and be tread upon. She said only, "Just as well. I don't look good in white."

"No, you wouldn't," Lyonel said in bland agreement. "You'd look too sallow."

"I believe," said Lucia, eyeing first one, then the other, "that I shall send both of you back to the nursery to learn some manners. Come, my boy, it's been two months since that ghastly debacle."

Lyonel stiffened. Lord, he should have known that Lucia wouldn't keep her blasted mouth shut.

"What debacle?" Diana asked as if on cue. Had he fought a duel and killed somebody? Had he lost all his money in a gambling hell? Perhaps he'd been ill, perhaps . . .

"None of your business," Lyonel said. "Now, Aunt, why did you summon me here this fine day? I'm very busy, you know."

"At least you've come out of hiding," said Lucia.

"How are Frances and Hawk? I assume you licked your wounds at Desborough Hall?"

"Aunt," Lyonel said very quietly, "tell me what you wish or I will leave. Now."

Lucia knew when to retreat and when to attack. Now it was time for middle-ground cajoling. "My boy, I do have a problem. Abercrombie let me down. I need you to escort Diana and myself to the Bellermains' ball this evening."

He groaned, loudly. "I don't think so, Aunt."

"If you're afraid that Charlotte and Dancy will be there . . ." She let her voice trail off.

"I don't give a damn where Charlotte is or isn't!"

"Your language isn't proper," said Diana, sticking her oar in. Who was this Charlotte? Was she the debacle?

"As for you," Lyonel said, unable to resist her salvo, "why don't you go back to where you came from? Hopefully sallow women are more prevalent there and you wouldn't stick out so much."

"I am not sallow! I am tanned. Unlike you . . . dandies, I enjoy the sun on my face. Of course, here, in this ungodly country, you haven't the privilege of much sun, do you? You, for instance, look pale and unhealthy."

"Aunt, good-bye. Miss Savarol, do as you please."

"Lyon! I will cut you up in small pieces if you take one step!"

Lyonel wanted to spit he was so angry. Then, to his utter chagrin, Aunt Lucia burst into loud and rending tears, replete with low, guttural sobs. He cursed under his breath.

He saw Diana rush to Lucia and flutter about the old lady.

"Oh, for God's sake," he said, striding back, "let me give her a brandy. And stop acting like a hen."

Lucia peeked through her fingers at that comment. Diana was alarmingly stiff, staring at Lyonel, while he was calmly fetching a brandy.

"Here," he said, thrusting the snifter toward her.

Lucia drank just a bit, gave another mighty sob, then tried to produce some tears to wipe away. Wisely, she daubed her eyes with her handkerchief. "Diana, my dear," she said, her voice moderately shaky, "won't you please go to Grumber and ask her for my hartshorn?"

Diana wasn't a fool. Auntie was up to something, if she didn't miss her guess. And Auntie wanted her out of the way. So be it. She escaped the drawing room with alacrity. Maybe, Diana thought, Lucia would turn her blistering tongue on this rude far-removed cousin. That was her hope, in any case.

"Fine act, Lucia," Lyonel said, regarding her with his arms folded over his chest, his look ironic.

"Thank you, my boy. Now, tell me why you don't like your cousin."

"I don't even know my cousin, or whatever she is. What is she doing here, anyway?"

"If you will sit down, I will tell you."

Lyonel sat.

"Her father, Lucien Savarol, begged me to take her under my wing for one Season. I didn't at first wonder why the just one-Season stipulation, but I discovered the reason quickly enough. Diana refuses to stay here longer. I fear I won't find a husband for her. She's very prickly, you see, very proud, and at the moment she hates it here." She gave him one of her patented looks. "Then you come in and act like a fool. It is too bad of you, Lyonel. I had hoped that you would take the girl under your wing and sprinkle some of your consequence over her."

"She is ill-mannered," he said.

"Not until you baited her."

"Her looks are dreadful."

"Idiot! That blond hair of hers is incredible! And those high cheekbones? She's the picture of her mama, who, I am told, was a renowned beauty. As for her clothes, we've been shopping and her gown for this evening is most fashionable and lovely."

"Lucia, aren't there sufficient gentlemen in the West Indies? She is most certainly out of her ken here. Surely you don't really expect to find her a husband here in London?"

"She's also an heiress," said Lucia.

"Excellent," was his acid reply. "You let that be known, and you will be besieged by fortune-hunters and scoundrels." He cursed softly under his breath, aware that the net was firmly drawn over him. He threw up his hands. "All right. I'll escort the both of you to the Bellermains' this evening. I will introduce *little* Diana to all my hapless acquaintances. But, Lucia, if she sharpens her shrew's tongue on any of the gentlemen, you can forget—"

"Shrew's tongue! You insufferable dandy!"

Lyonel grit his teeth. "Did you bring the hartshorn?" he asked.

"Certainly. Here, Aunt."

"You must have raised your skirts and dashed up the stairs."

"Thank you, my dear," Lucia said, and tucked it under her handkerchief. "Lyonel didn't really mean exactly a shrew, Diana. He was just drawing comparisons about—"

"Ha!"

"You are not exactly soft-spoken and endowed with maidenly modesty," said Lyonel. "If you wish to go along at all here in London, I advise you to moderate your mouth and keep your more ill-bred opinions to yourself.''

Lucia rolled her eyes. Though she wanted to kick the both of them, she did find them, at least at this moment, more amusing than the hero and heroine of her novel. All that fainting did tend to get on one's nerves.

''I am not ill-bred! I am Diana Savarol of Savarol Island and I can say and do exactly as I please! And everyone would say I do it with good breeding.''

''I daresay that this Savarol Island has all the importance and civilization of a backwater barracks.'' Lyonel broke off. His many-times-removed cousin was regarding him with fury in her eyes, and a very flushed face. What had gotten into him anyway? He was baiting the girl, just as Lucia had said. He was not behaving as he should. He was not acting like the gentleman he was. Two months ago, more than likely, her prickly pride would have elicited nothing more from him than tolerant amusement. But now, he'd like to take her over his knee and thrash her. He cleared his throat and managed with a good deal of effort to moderate his voice. ''Miss Savarol, I apologize. I am certain that you have many fine attributes. Aunt, if you have no more use for me, I will see the both of you this evening.''

''I wouldn't go to the museum with you!''

''Which museum, my dear?''

Lyonel regarded her with his blandest expression. ''I didn't ask you, Miss Savarol, though the Tower of London is an interesting thought. Until this evening. Ladies.''

He bowed himself out, relieved that he wasn't the one to have to remain and endure Aunt Lucia's inevitable tirade. What an abominable twit the girl was. And conceited, and sallow.

"My lord," said the proper and sepulchral Didier as he handed Lyonel his cane and gloves.

Lyonel cocked an eyebrow. "Unfortunately, I shall return, Didier."

He thought he heard a screech from the drawing room as he swiftly passed out of the house. *I do not look pale and unhealthy,* he thought as he strolled down the street toward Piccadilly.

Nonetheless, he shortly found himself at Gentleman Jackson's Boxing Saloon. *I am not unhealthy,* he thought again as he looked down at bloody-nosed James Crockren at his feet.

2

Everyone must row with the oars he has.
ENGLISH PROVERB

Diana stared at her overflowing bosom in the long mirror. She grinned, then began to chuckle, just to see if her bosom would stay where it was supposed to. Amazingly, to her, it did. At least for the moment, she amended to herself. No wild and impetuous gesticulations for her this night. She tried hunching her shoulders just a bit, but that looked altogether ridiculous. Ah, well, there was nothing to be done about it; it was what her body was, and that was that.

Grumber came into her bedchamber at that moment, her perpetual look of indifference cracking just a bit. "Very nice, miss."

"Thank you, Grumber. What have you there?"

"Rice powder, that's all. Lady Cranston wants you to be the same color."

Diana was on the point of refusing, with a show of righteous outrage, then noticed that her tanned face did look a bit odd with the expanse of white shoulders and bosom.

Sallow, was she!

"All right, Grumber. Cover my face with it."

Once she was powdered up, Diana thanked Grumber again and made her way downstairs. Lucia was waiting for her in the drawing room, gowned in royal purple.

"Lovely, Diana, just lovely. Good heavens!" Lucia moved closer. "What in the world . . . You look dead!"

Diana touched her fingertips to her cheek very lightly. Her fingertips came away as white as snow, at least she assumed they were, for she'd never before seen snow.

Lucia dusted off her face with a handkerchief, telling her to close her eyes in the cloud of white powder.

"There, much better. I like your hair swept up with the thick curls over your shoulders. Very nice. Those close crops all the young ladies are affecting remind me of poodles who have been trimmed too closely." She was on the point of saying that the thick streaked blond hair reminded her of her own when she was young, but she didn't want Diana to become conceited. "Now, my dear, I have a little something for you." Lucia pulled out a beautiful strand of pearls from a black velvet case. She fastened them around Diana's neck, then handed her a pair of pearl earrings.

Diana looked helplessly at them. "They're lovely, Aunt, but my ears aren't pierced."

Lucia frowned a moment, then said briskly, "We'll see to it tomorrow. The necklace looks quite well on you. Now, where is Lyonel?"

"The necklace is beautiful, Aunt. Thank you. I don't know about the piercing, though."

"Nonsense. Just a bit of pain, then it's over. Don't be a coward. I won't let Grumber do it, she's a bit heavy with a needle when she's mending. No, I'll see to it myself."

Diana wasn't certain the experience would be m

improved, but said nothing. She walked to the mirror over the fireplace and studied the necklace. She looked very smart, yes, indeed. Then her eyes fell to her bosom, and she shuddered in embarrassment.

For the past four years she'd most rigorously kept her breasts well-covered, for she didn't care for the way men looked at her. She unconsciously tried to pull up the blue silk.

"Don't fiddle, Diana! You will shortly see that you are well in fashion, and, I might add, even on the modest side."

"But I'll pop out, Aunt, I just know it. I cannot believe it is modest—why, the gown couldn't be cut any lower."

"Nonsense. Ah, Lyonel, here at last."

Lyonel, who had heard this last interchange, took a good look at Diana's plentiful bosom. "You won't pop out, Miss Savarol. And if you do, I shall be certain to cover you immediately."

"Oh? With what?"

"With whatever I have available to me at the moment." He raised his hands, splaying his fingers.

"Lyonel!"

"Sorry, Lucia. Both you ladies are looking prime. My God—what the devil do you have on your face?"

"Rice powder," Diana said. "To make me all the same color."

"I wiped a goodly amount off, Lyonel. Do you still think it is too much?"

"Who cares what he thinks?" Diana stopped short, lowering her eyes.

"Well done," said Lyon. "I know, of course, that it is n affected maidenly pose, but nonetheless, it should pass strangers as the real article."

not that," she said, glaring at him. "I can't—
't dance!"

Lyonel groaned. "I thought you said you weren't from a backwater barracks?"

"Those were your ill-natured words! I was simply never interested in such things, and besides," she added, striving for a bit of honesty, "there was no one about to teach me."

"Now, now," said Lucia. "What is the time, Lyonel?"

"Just past eight o'clock."

"We have time, then. Didier!"

"Yes, my lady," said Didier but an instant later.

"To the music room. Lord Saint Leven will instruct Miss Savarol on the finer points of the waltz."

"Why the waltz, Lucia? She must have permission to dance it from a patroness."

"Sally will give her permission, you will see," said Lucia. "Besides, the country dances and the cotillion are too complicated for her to learn in a half an hour. Thank goodness that the waltz has finally been accepted."

When they walked into the small music room, Didier was already seated at the pianoforte, playing scales, looking every bit as distinguished as the leonine Beethoven.

Lucia seated herself in a comfortable wing chair and waved her hand at the two of them.

"Well, Miss Savarol, shall we?" Lyonel said, giving her a slight bow.

"Shall we what? I don't know what to do."

"First of all, you have to come closer and pretend to like it when I hold you. Now, you hear that Didier has broken into song with a strong three beats. So you will count, one, two, three, one two, three, emphasis on the first beat, and follow my lead."

Lyonel kept a respectable full foot between them. She was taller than he'd first thought, and it occurred to him that he didn't at all care for tall, bosomy women. Charlotte had been petite, coming only to his shoulder, her figure slight, her eyes a deep chocolate brown, not a gray green. Funny color, as if nature couldn't make up its mind. He pulled himself up short. In all honesty, he didn't like any sort of woman at the present. He counted aloud as he gently led her about. She was a natural dancer, he thought some moments later, grudgingly.

"That's it, don't falter, and don't step on my foot. Ouch!"

"Sorry," Diana said, her eyes on her own feet.

He whirled her about at that instant, and she fell against him. He felt a tingling of sheer lust and quickly eased her away from him. As for Diana, she was too embarrassed at her clumsiness to notice anything at all.

"Pay attention," he said, his voice sharp. That damned bosom of hers would drive the gentlemen mad.

Her eyes turned more gray and he realized he'd hurt her feelings. "You're doing fine. Just keep counting, but under your breath. Once you have permission to waltz, I'll claim the first two, then you're on your own."

"So gracious, my lord!"

"Yes, I agree."

Didier played three more waltzes, and toward the end of the third one, Diana had managed to look up at Lyonel at least part of the time.

"Once you get used to it, you will be able to converse with your partner. It is expected, you know."

"It feels odd to be close to a man," she said, more to herself than to him.

"Close? You're a good foot away from me."

"Considering you're a lion, a foot doesn't seem to be all that much."

He grinned over her head. "Shall I take that as a compliment?"

"It was just an observation. I do think this entire exercise is a bit improper. Why, even my father has never held me like this!"

"Men are just men, Miss Savarol. You will get used to it quickly. Just let your partner lead you—stop shoving at me!—and accept the fact that men are stronger, larger, and in all likelihood much more intelligent."

Diana came down hard on his foot. He yelped, and she gave him a nasty grin. "I suppose you could say now, with all honesty, that men are also slower, less coordinated, and the biggest babies with just the slightest amount of hurt."

"At least men keep their endowments well under wraps, as it were, and not hanging out and forced upward with the intent to draw attention to themselves. And don't step on my foot again or I will seek immediate retribution."

"I did not think that gentlemen were supposed to speak so outrageously."

"Excellent. You have spoken at some length now and haven't missed a beat. I am a marvelous teacher, am I not?"

"You, my lord, are an unprincipled rat."

"Is there any other kind? No? That certainly shuts me up, doesn't it? Ah, Didier is finished with his music. You will do, Miss Savarol." He released her, gave her a mocking bow, and turned to Lucia. "Well?"

"Well, indeed," said Lucia. "You make a marvelous couple, my dears."

Both members of the couple shot her a killing look, to which she showed no response. Lucia rose and shook out her bright purple silk skirts. "Shall we go?"

"By all means. Doesn't the chit have something to cover her up?"

"Certainly, a shawl matching the gown. Where is it, Diana?"

"I don't know."

Lucia sighed. "Didier, please have Grumber fetch the shawl."

"Very well, my lady."

"You are an excellent musician, Didier," Lyonel said.

"Thank you, my lord. One strives, to be sure." He left the room.

"Your perfume," said Lyonel, "is too strong. You come very close to smelling like an opera girl."

"Oh, and what does an opera girl smell like? What is an opera girl?"

"Lyonel, my boy, would you please keep your tongue behind your teeth?"

Lyon made a great attempt at an indifferent shrug. "Fine with me, Lucia, but have you sniffed her? She is rather overwhelming."

"Come here, Diana."

"She smells as if she's bathed in it."

Diana dutifully allowed herself to be sniffed at. "It is a bit too much," Lucia said at last. "But the evening air, and the time it will take us to reach the Bellermains', will reduce the scent."

"Is there anything else you would care to criticize, my lord?"

His eyes went again to her bosom, and he grinned. "I only remarked upon the obvious problems with your face and your perfume, Miss Savarol. The rest of you that is on display is most pleasing to the eye. The masculine eye, that is."

"Lyonel!"

"Forgive me, Lucia. Ah, your wrap, Miss Savarol. Shall we go, ladies?"

Lucia's grand old brougham was, if nothing else, blessed with a commodious interior. Still, Diana found that Lord

Saint Leven must stretch his legs out, and she was forced to move to the side. She was quiet, listening to him speak with Aunt Lucia, calmly, amusingly, and with not a single drawing remark. Why did he dislike her so much? Indeed, he had taken her into obvious aversion the moment he had walked into the drawing room that afternoon. He was rude. Perhaps English noblemen were all of a kind. He was well-looking this evening, she was forced to admit. He wore black evening clothes and his shirt was so white it reminded her of the rice powder. He laughed at something Lucia said and she saw the flash of his even white teeth. He used his hands a lot when he talked. She saw the flash of his emerald signet ring.

"Diana."

"What? I'm sorry, Aunt. I was thinking."

"'Something profound, Miss Savarol?'"

"No, actually, my thoughts and observations were quite boring."

"I said, my dear, that Lyonel has agreed to call you Diana. And you, my love, will call him Lyonel."

"It's a rather silly name."

"I shouldn't say that, Diana. Your namesake was, after all, the goddess of hunting, and, I might add, the goddess of virginity."

"That is not what I meant!"

"Can you claim prowess or, er, ownership, to either quality?"

"Lyonel!"

"Sorry, Lucia."

"I certainly shouldn't call you the king of the jungle."

"That would depend on the jungle, would it not? Now, for example, if you were to examine the social jungle, you might discover that I make my way well enough—"

"It seems that Charlotte brought you down."

"Diana!" Lucia exclaimed.

There was no flash of white teeth this time. She heard him suck in his breath. "May I thank you, Lucia, for this?"

"No, well, perhaps, my boy. Diana, your memory for names is most unfortunate. You will contrive to forget that one in particular."

"But who is she? Was she the debacle of two months ago? Did she turn you down?"

"That, you nosy chit, is none of your damned business. Thank God, we've arrived."

Because they were somewhat late, the line of carriages was not an excessive problem, and they were climbing the steps to the receiving line within ten minutes.

Lucia felt Diana's hand clutch at her sleeve. "It will be all right, my dear. Just be yourself. You are lovely and—"

"Be yourself, but keep your mouth shut."

Lady Bellermain, as awesome as the flagship in Macklin's fleet, greeted both Lucia and Lyonel with pleasure. "Such a joy to see you again, my lord. And who is this?"

"My grand-niece, Miss Diana Savarol, Belinda. Make your curtsy, my dear."

"Lovely. She is staying with you for the Season, Lucia?"

"Yes, indeed."

Lyonel said as they strolled away, "I suppose that Lord Bellermain is already in the card room?"

"Probably, the old fool," said Lucia with a snort. "It's fortunate that he's lucky, else he would have lost his fortune by the age of twenty."

They entered the ballroom and Diana felt a moment of sheer terror. She had never seen so many superb-looking people in all her life. All of them strangers. So much laughter and gaiety, and a fountain of champagne, she saw. A real fountain! And the jewels. And the very low-cut gowns on the ladies.

"Some of them even dampen their petticoats," said Lyonel in her ear. "Again, an example of ladies flaunting their endowments for the masculine eyes. See that lady? That is Lady Caroline Lamb. She looks positively naked, does she not?"

"Lyonel!"

"Forgive me, Lucia. Would you ladies care for some champagne?"

"Yes, take yourself off. I must find Sally."

Lady Jersey was located and professed herself delighted to meet Miss Savarol. Of course the young lady should dance the waltz. Vouchers to Almack's? Why, certainly. She would again be most delighted to assist her dear friend.

Lucia breathed a sigh of relief when they left the semiroyal presence. "Talk about perfume!"

"She reeked," said Diana.

"Ladies, your champagne."

Diana had drunk champagne once before. She accepted the glass, her fingers brushing Lyonel's. She gave a start and looked up at him. Her look of surprised awareness was not lost to Lyonel, and he frowned. He wanted nothing to do with any lady, much less this silly chit from the West Indies. He said, "Sip it, Miss—Diana."

"I know how to drink!"

"Not to excess, I trust. Ah, a waltz. Come, Diana. The sooner we begin, the sooner we can end. Then the king of this jungle will turn the wolves loose on your virtue."

"Lyonel!"

"Forgive me, Lucia. Diana?"

A fair-haired gentleman standing near a potted palm said to his friend, "Who is that with Lyonel? A lovely girl. He is so quickly over his bout of Charlotte Haversham?"

His friend, Lady Markham, laughed lightly. "I should trust so, particularly since she is now Lady Danvers."

"For my own part, I think Lyonel very lucky. This young lady looks like an innocent little flower, ready to—"

"Really, Edgar! You promised you would cease your poetry at eight o'clock. It is well past that."

"She is lovely," Edgar persisted. He saw Charlotte Moressey, Lady Danvers, from the corner of his eye, and raised his voice, "I hear tell that Lyonel is much taken with the girl. No wonder, I say. Why, just look at that beautiful hair and face, not to mention, well, her other remarkable assets."

Corinne, Lady Markham, wasn't at all stupid. Nor was she a friend to Charlotte. "I agree. Perhaps they will make a match of it."

Charlotte turned to her new husband and said in an overly bright voice, "Come, Dancy, let us waltz."

Corinne was a malicious bitch, Charlotte thought as she followed Dancy's rather erratic movements on the dance floor. Who was that wretched girl? She saw Lyonel smiling down at her, and winced. She knew he would have to marry, if nothing else, for an heir to the earldom. But so soon? If only, she thought for the hundredth time, he hadn't come to Haversham House that ill-fated day. If only she hadn't been in the tack room at that particular time, with Dancy. If only they'd been discussing Paulson's treatment for a swollen hock, if only . . .

Charlotte shook her head. She was honest enough to admit that she'd done herself in. She'd been greedy. She'd wanted both Lyonel, for a husband, and Dancy, for a lover. She'd heard that Lyonel had gone north and was in a way pleased that she had bowled him over so thoroughly. But here he was, only two months later, dancing with a dazzling girl and enjoying himself as if she, Charlotte, had never existed.

"You are a natural dancer," Lyonel said before he could censor the compliment.

She looked taken aback. "As you said, many times, my lord, you are an excellent teacher."

"You are supposed to say, Thank you, Lyonel."

"And assume my maidenly pose, complete with downcast eyes and perhaps a little blush?"

"You do learn quickly. Come along now, let me introduce you to some appropriate gentlemen. You will dance only with those of whom I approve. And no more than two dances with any gentleman, else it could cause unwanted gossip. There will not be a scoundrel, fortune-hunter, or philanderer among them"

"I am not stupid!"

"Perhaps not, but you are vastly ignorant. Do as I tell you or you will likely make a complete fool of yourself."

"I do not like you."

"If a gentleman looks overly long at your bosom, you will not dance with him again."

"Then I am not to waltz with you a second time?"

He grinned. "Since I am a relative—your only male relative in London—you may assume that my interest in your . . . Well, you may assume that my regard is in the avuncular vein."

Lyonel turned her over to Lord Donnovan, a young man with a delightful smile, who looked most worshipful at the succulent new vision. Diana felt her confidence soar and her lacerated sensibilities mend a bit.

"She will do just fine, Lucia, you will see," said Lyon to his aunt, "Donnovan is certain to feed her enough compliments to give her indigestion. And you can forget any thought of matchmaking between the two of us."

"The way you've been baiting her, I wonder that she still speaks to you."

"Diana Savarol, whatever else she may be, is not a submissive simpleton. She enjoys my baiting, I'll wager. She certainly has dished me up in my own sauce a couple of times."

"Only a couple?"

"Really, Lucia, by the time she's truly up to snuff, I'll be a doddering old man." He stopped cold, his eyes fastened on Charlotte, who was laughing somewhat immoderately at something Dancy had said. She looked achingly beautiful, just as beautiful as the first time he'd ever seen her at Newmarket, but his heart did nothing more this time than tighten, just a bit. Odd, how he'd only kissed her chastely even after they'd become betrothed. Then to see her on her back, her skirts tossed up, her head arched back, thighs spread and wrapped about. . . He drew a deep breath. Women, he thought. The whole bloody lot of them should be shipped off to Constantinople. Let them be lascivious in a harem.

"She was never worthy of you, my boy," Lucia said softly. "You closed your eyes to the truth, you know. She had snared you well and good, I'll say that for her. But it's over, and time for you to rejoin the world again. And, Lyonel, Diana isn't a bit like Charlotte. She's guileless, you know. Perhaps too much so."

He cursed under his breath. "There's Brandy and Ian. I think I will go speak to them."

Lucia sighed, watching Lyonel stride toward the Duke and Duchess of Portmaine. She grinned, wagering to herself that Lyonel would never in a million years draw attention to the duchess's bountiful bosom.

Lyonel, because he had no choice in the matter, escorted both Lucia and Diana to supper. He was not partic-

ularly surprised when two of his bachelor friends asked to
join their table. He saw that Diana was much enjoying
herself, but he quickly ceased listening or contributing to
the conversation. He wanted to leave; he wanted to return
to Yorkshire. He had spent some of his time with Frances
and Hawk, the Earl and Countess of Rothermere, until
their obvious adoration for each other made him so uncomfortable and unhappy that he couldn't bear it any longer.
Frances was nearing her term—this her second child—and
the thought of the child she would bear made him ache
more than he could have believed possible for what he had
lost, for what, indeed, he would never have had in the first
place. It had been difficult enough when little Charles,
Viscount Lindsey, had discovered his Uncle Lyon and
become his adoring fan. For a fleeting moment, he saw
Hawk's large brown hand gently caressing Frances' rounded
stomach. He blinked away the image.

Lyonel had been ready to marry, to raise a family, to
protect them and love them until he left this earth. And
then he had met Charlotte, so innocent, so shy and charming. God, what a fool he'd been! He sat back in his chair,
staring morosely into his glass of claret. He looked up at
the sound of Diana's bright laughter, and his eyes fell to
her breasts. He sucked in his breath. He would set up a
mistress as soon as possible. He had been too long without
sex, that was all.

Diana danced her second waltz with Lyonel at midnight.
She was mildly intoxicated from the champagne, and she
saw him through a very pleasant haze. "Why are you
being so quiet?"

"I haven't a thing to say. Unlike the weaker sex, I don't
chatter inanities and bore the devil out of my partner."

"I am not weak. I wager I could show a good account
of myself with you, were we to come to blows."

"No doubt an excellent talent for a lady to possess. I saw you dancing with that French idiot, DuPres. Stay away from him, Diana. He'll have you on your back and your petticoats up about your chin in five minutes."

"And you, I suppose, are a saint?"

"No, I simply have no interest in silly, overendowed little girls. Now be quiet, you lost track of the beat."

"I am sorry she hurt you so badly, Lyonel."

"Shut up, Diana."

She sighed, knowing that if she weren't vaguely tipsy, she would rip up at him at his galling rudeness. And all she was trying to do was to be sympathetic. When the dance ended, she said, "I must go to the ladies' withdrawing room."

"Too much champagne, huh?"

"Don't be crude."

It was odd, she thought as she made her way upstairs, weaving just a bit, but she would have dropped her jaw in utter horror had any of the other gentlemen she'd conversed with or danced with spoken to her as Lyonel did.

3

He who listens at keyholes will have his eye poked out.

ITALIAN PROVERB

"I hear she is from the West Indies."

"One can tell that she is from somewhere dreadful. Did you see that tan?"

"I do wonder if it's true what one hears—the dreadful morals of supposed ladies in that uncivilized place?"

"One mustn't forget that she is Lady Cranston's guest."

"But how could she walk about in the sun like that? I tell you, her face is the color of a berry!"

Oh, dear, Diana thought as she paused at the partially open door. Why would they care about me? She unconsciously touched her fingertips again to her cheek. No more powder. In fact, there was a light sheen of perspiration on her skin. Yes, she was probably as brown as a berry.

She heard the swish of silk, the buzz of conversation coming closer, and quickly moved down the corridor. Five ladies came out of the withdrawing room and walked away from her toward the staircase. Relieved, Diana pulled back her shoulders and went in.

There was but one lady there, seated in front of a mirror. Her mouth was open, her fingertip rubbing her front teeth.

Diana merely nodded to her and continued on her way. Once she had returned, she was surprised to see the lady still there, standing now, tapping her foot, her fingers out of her mouth.

"You are Diana Savarol, I presume."

"Why, yes. And you?"

"Charlotte Moressey, Lady Danvers. I understand that you and Lyonel are cousins of a sort."

Charlotte! This was the young lady who had severely ruptured Lyonel's heart? She felt a surge of envy and wondered at herself. It was doubtless the effects of the champagne.

"Yes," she said. "Of a sort."

"I also understand that Lady Cranston is to bring you out?"

Diana heard the tone of vexation in Charlotte's voice and wondered at it. "Yes, that is correct."

"Are you not a bit old to have a first Season?"

"Probably. I am nineteen, soon to be twenty."

"Dear me, I am only twenty, but, of course, a married lady."

"My congratulations, my lady."

Charlotte frowned, just a bit. Was this little twit being sarcastic? "Of course you know that Lord Saint Leven is not interested in ladies at the present time."

"I doubt that sincerely."

Charlotte gave a thin laugh. "Ladies, my dear, ladies. Gentlemen, you know, will have their little amours hidden away."

Little amours? Goodness, it sounded as if Lyonel was secreting away some sort of small rodent.

"Take my advice and avoid your cousin of sorts. He is not a nice man. In fact, that is why I broke off my engagement with him. He is most violent-natured. Really rather vile, as a matter of fact. I shouldn't trust him if I were you."

"He seems most mild-mannered," Diana said with great and instant untruth. "Quite the gentleman."

"Trust me, my dear." Charlotte patted her arm and said abruptly, "My, how very large you are! It is unfortunate that gentlemen prefer smaller, more gently endowed ladies. But of course, if you have a decent dowry, there will be some who will willingly overlook your—"

"My immense number of inches?"

"Well, yes, perhaps."

"Or perhaps hands, as in a horse?"

"Your humor is most odd, Miss Savarol. You will be thought rather fast if you do not moderate your opinions."

"It was not an opinion, merely an alternative so that you could be precise in your observations, my lady. Did you mean rather fast, as in a racing horse?"

"No! Rather fast, my dear, means loose."

"Goodness! Loose as in a saddle girth?"

"That is quite enough, Miss Savarol! I am not amused, I assure you. I do not find you at all acceptable."

"I am quite cast down," Diana said, eyeing this gorgeous lady with growing dislike. "Not cast off, as in a horseshoe, of course."

"Or cast off as in what a gentleman does to a loose girl."

Diana chuckled. "Yes, Lyonel told me about Monsieur DuPres. He was most explicit about what that particular gentleman did to the unwary of our sex."

"But of course you are quite familiar with his kind, are

you not? There is no society where you are from, no civilization, no refinement, no—"

"Not much of anything. Quite right, my lady. I cannot wait to return to my sort. Now, if you will excuse me."

Diana turned and walked from the room, knowing she'd made an enemy and not caring. Odious woman! If she had been the one to break off with Lyonel, why was she so concerned about Diana becoming involved with him? She had no reason to be jealous. Diana decided halfway down the wide staircase that Lyonel, whatever his faults, and they did appear to be numerous, didn't deserve that female, even at his most obnoxious.

Lucia informed a nearly comatose Diana that they would leave at three o'clock in the morning. Diana felt as though her feet would crumble and disintegrate, and she said as much.

"You did magnificently, my child," said Lucia. "Perhaps your slippers are a bit small. We will see to it in the morning."

"Morning, Aunt? I doubt I will be alive in the morning. I assure you my feet don't wish to see the light of day."

"Did you not order the largest of slippers for her, Lucia?"

"Lyonel! Mind your tongue."

"Sorry, Lucia. Ladies, shall we go?"

It was Lyonel who was silent on the ride back.

Finally, Lucia said, "My dear boy, whatever is wrong? I trust you are not blown?"

"No," he said, and that short, sharp word woke Diana up abruptly.

"Then what is wrong with you? Have you run short of nasty insults? Your shoes aren't too small, are they?"

"No. It is nothing. Go back to sleep, Diana. I am certain both of us would find that preferable."

"Will your gentlemanly sensibilities be offended if I remove my slippers?"

"There is no need to announce it. Simply do it and we will just trust that you do not have sweaty feet."

"Lyonel!"

"Sorry, Lucia." He sighed, leaned his head back against the soft squabs, and closed his eyes.

"He is in a snit," Diana said, her voice loud enough not only for Lyonel's ears, but also for the horses'.

"Miss—Diana, shut up!"

"I simply mean that I do not feel comfortable when you are not forthcoming, or rather, more accurate, obnoxious."

Lyon cocked an eye open. "Very well. Charlotte, Lady Danvers, was very busily shredding your character, your morals, or lack thereof, your impertinent mouth, and your lack of respect and deference for your London betters."

"That wretched bi—person!"

"My sentiments exactly."

"Oh, dear. Why is she doing such a thing, Lyonel?"

"I have a question first for Diana, Lucia. Did you speak to the lady?"

Diana shifted a bit uncomfortably. "Well, yes, perhaps. Do you remember when I went to the ladies' withdrawing room?"

"I remember very well. You had imbibed too much champagne and needed to—"

"Lyonel!"

"Forgive me, Lucia."

"She was there, waiting for me. She was the impertinent one! And I might add, I defended you, my lord. She was warning me about your vile character and your nasty temper."

That brought Lyonel upright. "She *what*?"

"She was warning me of you—"

"I heard you well enough. All right, you see, don't you, Lucia? My association with Diana can only hurt her chances now that Charlotte has decided to be petty."

"I dished her up in her own sauce," Diana said with great relish.

"She was the more ruthless. She dished you up in everyone else's sauce."

"Quiet, both of you," said Lucia. "I must think. In a sense, I am glad that Charlotte has shown her true colors immediately. I, as you know, Lyonel, am not without influence. I will not allow her to continue her malignant, very untrue, gossip. She is the one on the edge of social ruin."

"It appears she trusts my gentleman's honor not to betray her," said Lyonel, his voice as dry as Morgan's Island, a small bump of land in the Caribbean that sported not one tree or shrub.

"Betray her? What did she do? I thought she was the one who broke off your engagement? Why she told me that—"

"Shut up, Diana."

"No, my dear child, it was Lyonel who broke it off. I will make it clear to the chit that if she doesn't muzzle her mouth, it will become known exactly why he did it."

"No, Lucia. I forbid it."

Diana bounced forward on her seat. "Why? I do not understand you. You have done nothing but insult me from the moment we met, yet this woman, who isn't at all nice, you wish to protect. Do you still love her? Is that the reason?"

Lyonel sighed. "Lucia, try to find her a mute for a husband. No, better yet, he had better be deaf."

"You do still love her! You are so weak and—"

"Now, now, my dear. Let us hear no more about it. Ah, home at last."

"At last is right," said Lyon.

He assisted Lucia from the brougham, then held out his hand to Diana.

"You see, it is like this," Diana said, hanging back. "I cannot put my slippers back on. My feet are too swelled."

He cursed under his breath. "Oh, come here!"

To her surprise, he grasped her about the waist and lifted her from the carriage into his arms. "You will certainly strain my back."

Even as he spoke the words, he was very aware of her warm body against his, her breasts pressed against his chest, the very womanly thighs against his arms.

He said under his breath, "Tomorrow, the very first thing tomorrow, I will take care of this."

"Take care of what?" Diana asked, unconsciously leaning her face closer to his.

"None of your affair. Be quiet, else I might drop you. Lord knows you deserve it."

"Come, you have not been at all reticent with me before. Have you suddenly become a coward? Yes, I suppose that you have."

Goaded, he said, "Tomorrow I shall find a pleasant . . . companion."

"Ah. As in a little amour? To hide away?"

He pulled up short on the top step of Lucia's town house and stared at her, his face only an inch from hers. "What do you know of such things?"

"Your very nice Charlotte told me that you and all gentlemen have these amours hidden away. It sounded most odd to me, as if you were secreting rodents in your house."

He laughed, he couldn't help himself. "You, Diana, should be whipped."

"I think she should be whipped. She also informed me that you didn't like ladies, just these little amours, after she broke your heart."

"For someone who has been in London—out of society—for less than a day, you have dug up more dirt than I would in a year."

"Nonsense. She doesn't like me and—"

"And what? Are you the coward now?"

"You are standing still, Lyonel, the door is open, and it is quite cold out here. And you will strain your back with my great weight."

"All true. And—"

At last he entered the house. He eased her down, letting her slide against the length of him. Again, he saw the startled, bewildered look in her eyes and wondered at himself. His gentleman's code seemed to be tottering on the brink. "Yes," he said firmly to himself, "tomorrow." He sighed. "You are tedious, Diana. Go to bed. Soak your feet. Pop out of your gown. Just get thee gone."

"You, my lord, are a bore, a lout, a butcherer of Shakespeare, an obvious rake—"

"Rake! Surely Charlotte didn't go that far?"

"Well, no. I heard that wonderful word and wanted to use it. You gave me the opportunity, and well, I couldn't pass it up, could I?"

"No, of course not. Good night."

He patted her cheek, turned on his heel, and left. Didier appeared out of the shadows and nodded to Diana.

"Good night, Didier."

"Good night, miss."

She was relieved that he did not comment on her stockinged feet and her slippers dangling by their ribbons in her right hand. Had he seen Lyonel holding her?

It occurred to Diana as she snuggled under the covers some thirty minutes later that Lyonel had spoken about a companion when he was holding her. It was probably nothing more than an interest evoked by the close proximity of her bosom, she thought, depressed.

She touched her fingers to her breast and wondered why gentlemen were so very interested. Just because they were swelled up, like her feet . . . except she stuck out there all of the time. After all, her nanny, the sharp-tongued, black-as-night Dido, had told her quite specifically when she was but fourteen that "de melons be for de chiles." Dido had no use for men, so Diana assumed that she wouldn't include them in the "chile" category.

Or maybe she would.

She was suddenly seized with such a bout of homesickness that she caught a sob in her throat. She'd wanted Dido to come to England with her, but her father had been firmly against it. He'd said, "No, my love, there is too much feeling about slavery in England at this point. People simply wouldn't understand. You must trust me on this."

And so she'd traveled to England with strangers, an English planter and his family, from St. Thomas.

And she'd had to leave her father, Grainger, their overseer, her mare, Tanis, Dido . . . Her mind faltered as fatigue overtook her. Her last thought before succumbing was of Lyonel, her cousin of sorts, who had picked her up and held her close and made her feel so very odd.

Lyonel found his little amour the very next evening when he visited the theater. Her name was Lois, and she affected no French accent, for which he was profoundly grateful. She came from Birmingham, was fresh, quite pretty in a plump, plentiful manner, and, of course, had no means to support herself. He ignored three summonses, each more imperious than the last from Lucia, and plowed Lois until she finally said, in her light, breathless voice, "My lord, it's enough, I beg of you."

He drew up over her and felt like a rutting animal.

Lois ran her fingers over his beautiful face. "A long time without a woman, my lord?"

"Too bloody long," he said, and moved away from her. "Forgive me, Lois. I will not use you thus again." He began to dress, then turned to look down at her. He realized another reason he'd picked her was the size of her breasts. They were huge and round, her nipples large, a dusky color. He swallowed, knowing he was a fool, but not about to admit it, even to himself.

Lois regarded him as he dressed in front of the fireplace. He was magnificent, his body big and hard, and she knew from experience that this man would treat her well. There had been no perversion in him, merely immense hunger. The fire light danced in his chestnut hair, touching the strands with gold. Yes, she was indeed pleased with him.

He finally left her to make arrangements for a maid and a cook. Her small apartment was tucked just off Curzon Street. He discreetly left fifty pounds for her on the dressing table on his way out.

When he returned to the Saint Leven town house in Portsmouth Square, a monstrosity built by his grandfather, another summons awaited him. Too tired to do more than shake his head, he told his man, Kenworthy, to inform her ladyship that he had the ague. Then he chuckled to himself.

Kenworthy, a slight, bald man of middle years, and a valet of great capacity and loyalty, simply nodded, then watched with some concern as his master took himself upstairs to his bed.

"Ague!" Lucia muttered, studying the valet's stone face. "That is nonsense and you know it! Now, tell me what your master is up to, Kenworthy."

"The ague, my lady," he repeated with bland fortitude. "His lordship will call on you as soon as he leaves his bed."

"Oh, bosh!"

When Didier removed Kenworthy from Lady Cranston's august presence, Diana snorted. "Ridiculous! He is malingering and I don't care. We do not need him, Aunt. Let him take care of Charlotte's nasty gossip himself! Let him—"

"Hush, my dear. We do need him, at least we need his escort and his marvelous arrogance. However, I suppose he will come when he is ready to."

Diana nearly discovered the truth that afternoon when three old cronies of Aunt Lucia's were sipping endless cups of tea in the drawing room, shredding the younger generation with tuts, sighs, and headshakes punctuated with "deplorable," "such a shame for their parents," and the like.

"And of course when I heard what your dear Lord Saint Leven was doing, Lucia, I knew I must tell you immediately."

The seemingly reticent lady was a formidable dragon with tight gray sausage curls, a scrawny body, and a brain as tough as steel.

Diana, dismissed before these very interesting confidences were uttered, waited just outside the drawing-room door, all ears.

Lucia, who hadn't heard a word about Lyonel other than the ague, sat forward, willing to receive information even from the odious Agatha Damson.

". . . and so my maid heard it from her cousin's niece whom Lord Saint Leven hired to see to his, ah . . ."

"May I do something for you, miss?"

Diana could have spit with vexation, but she forced a smile for Didier. He knows I'm eavesdropping, she thought.

She looked him straight in the eye. "You have caught me, Didier, but you see, they are talking about Lyonel, and I want to know what is going on."

"You are a young lady," Didier announced in the repressive tones of an archbishop.

"You know and you will not tell me."

"Correct, miss."

"You are being most unfair, Didier."

"Yes, miss. Would you care for some tea?"

"No. I shall just have to find out for myself, won't I?"

Didier blanched and Diana smiled.

"I shall speak to my lady," he said. "You, miss, would be well advised to retire to your bedchamber."

Diana's eyes glittered. "On the contrary," she said, "I believe I shall go for a walk."

That sounded innocuous enough to Didier and he relaxed, just a bit. "I will fetch Jamison for you, miss. He will escort you. To the park, I think. Yes, that will be fine."

Diana did not disabuse him.

Jamison, a second footman with twinkling blue eyes and a wide smile, was delighted to escort the young Miss Savarol. Diana, on the other hand, plotted how to rid herself of him.

It turned out to be an impossible task. Jamison had his orders in no uncertain terms from Didier. One religiously followed the old monk's orders.

"I believe I should like to visit Portsmouth Square, Jamison."

"Uh? 'Tis a far piece, miss."

"Fine. Fetch a hansom cab for us."

Jamison, unfortunately, knew nothing about Lord Saint Leven's place of abode. He most willingly followed Miss Savarol into the lion's den.

Kenworthy just happened to be out when Diana firmly knocked on the Saint Leven brass town-house knocker.

Titwiller was not Didier's equal. He gawked, stammered, and fell back in disarray at Diana's imperious request to see her cousin immediately.

"Tell him," Diana added with a sapient eye, "that it is most urgent and that if he is not here in ten minutes I shall fetch him myself."

Jamison stared. He could easily picture Didier's reaction when he heard of this escapade. He nearly moaned aloud, knowing full well that the messenger of bad news usually had the misfortune to have his head bashed.

Titwiller lost what little aplomb he possessed as he took the stairs two at a time.

"What the devil!"

"It is Miss Diana Savarol to see you, my lord. She informed me, my lord, that it is most urgent."

Lyon was exhausted from oversatiation. He cursed long and fluently. "Get Kenworthy. He'll get rid of her."

"Kenworthy is not here at present, my lord. She informed me, my lord, that she could, er, come up here to fetch you if you did not come down."

Lyon finally reacted to the abject pleading in Titwiller's voice and Diana's threat, which he didn't doubt for more than ten seconds. He cursed again and threw back the covers.

Diana was getting ready to place her foot on the first step when Lyon appeared on the landing.

"Don't you dare!"

"Well, you have certainly taken your time!"

''The only reason I'm coming down is to toss you out on your ear, Diana!''

''Ha! Suffering from the ague! What is wrong with you? Don't you care that Charlotte has been—''

''Shut up!'' He reached her, took her arm, and pulled her none too gently into the library.

''Very nice,'' Diana said, looking about. ''I wager you haven't read a quarter of all these books.''

''Well, you'd be wrong. Diana, what the devil are you doing here? This is a gentleman's residence, a bachelor's residence as you well know, and it is most improper—''

''You look awful. Haven't you slept? Are you truly ill?''

''Thank you and no and no.''

''Then, what—''

He turned his back to her and fetched a glass of brandy from the liquor cabinet.

He tossed it down, drew a deep breath, and turned to face her. ''Oh, sit down. You have ten minutes, then you are leaving.''

''Such a gracious host,'' she said, and eased down into a leather armchair.

He merely looked at her, his face a study of irritation and long suffering.

''You must come to see Lucia. Charlotte has been spreading more venom and she is most desirous of having you aid her in a counterattack.''

''I will come this evening. I believe Lucia said she'd managed vouchers for Almack's. I will escort you. Anything else?''

''I want to know what is wrong with you. Why haven't you come?''

''I've been rather occupied.''

''Doing what, for heaven's sake? Ah, you've been at a

gaming hell, haven't you? Have you lost your fortune? Will you blow your brains out?''

He sighed and ran his hand through his already rumpled hair. ''Where, I dread to inquire, did you hear that term?''

''Gaming hell? I overheard Jamison—he's the second footman who accompanied me here—he was talking to Aunt Lucia's driver.''

''A foolish question. No, I wasn't at a gaming hell.''

''Then, where were you?''

''It is none of your damned affair, Diana.''

''Ah, I know. You were hiding from your precious Charlotte!''

Her tone was so insulting, so very nasty, he forgot his resolution, forgot that she was a young lady, and nearly yelled at her, ''I was with my new mistress, damn your impertinence!'' The instant the words were out of his mouth, he cursed.

Diana's eyes widened. ''Is she here? Upstairs in your . . . your bedchamber?''

Lyonel was without words. He turned back to pour himself another brandy.

He said over his shoulder, ''I fully intend to beat you, Diana.''

4

Nothing annoys a man more than not being taken seriously.

PALACIO VALDÉS

"You intend to do what?" Laughter spilled from her mouth, pure and loud, until she was hiccuping and holding her stomach.

He eyed her show of hilarity, then sighed. "I would like to thrash you, but I suppose you would do your female utmost to destroy my manhood, were I to try it."

"That, cousin, would be only the beginning of what I would do to you." She hiccuped again.

"Let us strive for some maidenly decorum, Diana. You really shouldn't know a thing about my manhood or how to bring it and me, as the natural course of things, low."

"I am not stupid, Lyonel, nor was I raised with horse blinders to protect me from the natural course of things around me." She had the gall to giggle.

"No, I suppose not," he said, his eyes narrowed, "but you are most certainly fast becoming a thorn in my flesh. But then again, I suppose a thorn is natural enough."

Diana ignored that provocation for the moment, harking

back to this mistress business. "Why are you so ill-looking?
Surely a little amour is for your, well, entertainment. Were
you outrageous to her? Did she hurt you?"

"On the contrary."

"You beat her?"

"Don't be stupid, Diana! Your ten minutes are up. You
may now take your leave."

"And you will go back upstairs to her?"

"Listen, you twit, a gentleman does not install a mistress in his home."

"She is hidden away, then."

"Not exactly. Well, just a bit. A gentleman is discreet."

"Not very if you make yourself sick with overindulgence."

He was forced to smile at that image, a very real one in
this case. "Yes," he said, "I did overindulge." He caught
himself in that instant, fully aware that this conversation
was most improper and that he was, at least normally, a
gentleman. "I want you to leave now. And remember,
little Diana—"

"*Little* Diana? That is most inaccurate of you, Lyon."

"Oh, just leave, Diana. I am exhausted and I will not
take you to Almack's this evening if I do not garner my
strength."

"What shall I tell Aunt Lucia?"

"That, you silly chit, is your problem. I do recommend,
however, that you do not inform her that you burst into my
home with only your footman in attendance and threatened
my butler that you would roust me out of my bed.'"

"Then what shall I say?"

"All right. Now that you have admitted that you are in
need of my superior intelligence and experience—"

"Lyonel, you are drawing dangerously close to drown-
ing in two inches of water."

"—I will send Kenworthy about again to inform her of
the plans. Come along now."

She rose, frowning at him, and walked beside him into the ornate entrance hall. She stopped a moment and stared around her. "This place is rather overwhelming."

"What you mean to say is that it is blessed with nauseating bad taste. You will have to take that up with the spirit world. My grandfather is responsible, not I."

"And now, of course, you have no time to redecorate."

She chuckled, unaware that Jamison was standing stiffly in the shadow of a very large, dead-white and naked Greek statue, eyes agog and ears at attention. "I trust you will be in a better humor by this evening?"

"It will tax me, but I shall try." He lowered his voice. "And, Diana, do remember that when I decide to beat you, you will be beaten, and most thoroughly."

"When? How certain you are of your own strength. I look forward to your howls of pain."

"That is ridiculous. Jamison!" He cursed again, and Diana, curse her, laughed. "Get thee gone. Now."

"More Shakespeare." She leaned closer and said in a stage whisper, "Surely you must now admit to the rake part."

"Yes, most thoroughly," he said through his teeth. He nodded to the now-present Titwiller, and the butler opened the door.

"Until tonight, Miss Savarol."

"I look forward to it with great interest, my lord."

"Impertinent chit," he said under his breath, and made his way back upstairs to bed.

Almack's on King Street, was a disappointment to Diana. She looked around, sighed even with her feet happily encased in new, larger slippers, and prepared to be bored. The place was drafty as a barn, the refreshments, she quickly noted, niggardly, but the company, the glitter of

jewels, the sound of the orchestra playing a country dance
. . . She rather hoped that Charlotte would be here. At
least it would enliven the evening when she wasn't dancing. Lyonel, in the requisite evening garb of black knee
breeches, looked lovely, at least that is what Diana thought,
forcing herself to utter objectivity. Odd how the black
evening clothes made his blue eyes all the more vivid.

Diana wasn't aware of the difference in the company
when they entered, but both Lucia and Lyonel were. He
knew that he must threaten Charlotte and make it believ-
able. He did not doubt his ability to muzzle her, and he
told Lucia as much.

"I don't know," Lucia said after a moment, thankful
that Diana's attention was elsewhere. "Why not let her
continue? No one is prepared to believe her, I think. If
there is a shift in the wind, you could always turn your
guns on Dancy. Poor man, even though he isn't a gentleman, he—"

"No, he isn't. I will think about it, Lucia. But stop it
will. Diana should enjoy herself . . . for the remaining
weeks she's here in England."

Lucia frowned a bit at that. She stoutly refused to let her
burgeoning plans fade into oblivion, particularly after Diana had taken herself to Lyon's town house. She'd said
nothing to Diana, but of course, Didier had pried it out of
Jamison and dutifully reported all to her. Diana, she thought
proudly, was no faintheart. She only hoped that her niece,
of sorts, would eventually come around and decide that
she wanted her cousin, of sorts. As for Lyonel, she believed he would succumb eventually if forced to be in
Diana's company long enough. Lucia would have succumbed to apoplexy before she admitted to either of the
two young people that she was delighted with Charlotte's
performance. Otherwise, Lyonel might just as well have
ignored Diana and gone his own way, stupid man.

Lyonel, with gentlemanly aplomb, took Diana's arm and led her to the four Almack's patronesses who held court that particular Wednesday evening. Diana was pronounced a sweet girl within Lyonel's hearing. He leaned his head down and said to her, "How much will you pay me not to tell the Countess Lieven the truth about you? Sweet, ha!"

But Diana wasn't to be drawn at that moment, for she'd spotted Charlotte in close knotty conversation with some of her cronies. She squared her shoulders, inadvertently increasing her bosom, much to Lyonel's interest. "I think," she said, her eyes turning green as the moss on an Irish stone, "that dear Charlotte is up to her old tricks again. I dislike being the subject of too many sentences."

Then, to Lyonel's surprise, she added, "I do not have too much powder on my face this evening, do I?"

He gave her face due consideration. Her arched brows and absurdly long lashes were a shade or two darker than her rich blondish hair, her nose was thin and neither too long nor too short, and her full lips were now slightly parted as she awaited his opinion.

"You will do," he said abruptly, his own lips tightening. "A waltz. Come, you have all the august permission needed. Remind me to teach you some of the other dances."

"That is too much hopping about for me," Diana said.

"You afraid that you will pop out of that gown?"

"Your memory is most tenacious."

"And your bosom, my dear Diana, is most attracting."

"Worthy of your exalted attention? Even now that you've got a little amour?"

"She, I venture to say, is even more well-endowed than you are, but no matter. I shall simply make do with what is available."

She called him a name, and he threw back his head and

laughed deeply. Heads turned toward them, Charlotte's in particular.

Lyonel took her in his arms and whirled her into the middle of the ballroom. "I've never been called that by a lady before," he said after he'd guided her expertly past an older couple.

"I am not questioning your antecedents, merely commenting on your character."

Lyonel realized with a start that he was enjoying himself immensely. The misery he'd lived with for the past months had magically disappeared. The betrayal was still there, making him wary, making him question any and all motives of the so-called weaker sex, but Diana . . . impertinent, burly-mouthed girl. . . He firmly tucked away further considerations and whirled her about in a large circle that made her breathless with excitement.

"I love that!"

"As I said before, you are a natural dancer."

"Oh, heavens, there is dear Charlotte, glaring at me. I do not understand it, Lyonel. Why should she so dislike me? Is it that she is still in love with you? Is she jealous?"

"Diana, I don't wish to speak of Charlotte or of my unfortunate, very brief engagement to that particular lady."

"I wish you would just tell me. You know I shall find out what—"

"Keep your tongue behind your teeth or your beating just might take place sooner than you expect."

To draw him, she said in what she thought an intrigued tone, "Ah, there is Monsieur DuPres. He is giving me the most . . . thorough inspection. I think I shall dance with him. Do you think he will try to seduce me?"

Lyonel didn't change expression. He was a very experienced old hand at verbal fencing. Usually, the fencing had been with his gentleman friends, not ladies, who tended to agree with him with nauseating regularity. It was most intriguing. "I shall take you to him when the waltz is ended. Perhaps you will be kind enough to tell me of his technique?"

"You are most provoking."

"True. Now, one more big . . . ouch! Diana, take care with my feet and your heels."

"Sorry."

"The devil you're sorry!"

He whirled her around so quickly that she had to cling to him to keep her balance. Again, that very discomfiting feeling assailed her, deep in her stomach, and she stared up at him, her hand tightening unconsciously on his shoulder. He would have sworn an oath on his favorite stallion's head that he would be immune, but he wasn't. Making love to Lois—Lord, he'd lost count—should have rendered him as uninterested as cold ashes in a summer grate, but here he was becoming as quickly aroused as a randy goat. He quickly pulled away from her, his mouth tight. He would hand her over to DuPres and damn the consequences.

But he didn't, of course. He steered her, eyes straight ahead, back to Lucia, who was surrounded by four gentlemen waiting for Diana to alight in their vicinity.

Lucia was congratulating herself on her brilliant strategy. She'd been the pleased recipient of several observations by other ladies, telling her that Lady Danvers' malicious gossip was all of a piece. "If she is not careful," Lady Ombersely had pronounced, "she will find herself *outré*. I, myself, will cut her!" Of course, Lucia had no intention of so informing dear Lyonel of the true state of affairs.

His look was a cool stare as he handed Diana over to the nearly drooling Sir Mortimer Dunlevy, the vacuous sod.

"I am going to the card room," Lyonel said, unwillingly following Diana with his eyes as she smiled up at the sod. "If I am not mistaken, Dancy will be endeavoring to lose his damned shirt. He believes himself the master of piquet. Indeed, I just might trounce him myself, then tell him in no uncertain terms—"

"No!"

Lyonel bent a sapient eye on Lucia. "Why the devil not?"

"I told you, my boy, that I should like to leave things just as they are. I wish to wait and see which way the wind is blowing."

"Unfortunately, my dearest Aunt, you are not making a whit of sense. I shall do what I think is appropriate." He raised a hand when he saw she would protest further. "I won't say a word until I deem it necessary, however."

Lucia had to be content with that. She watched him stride across the ballroom floor, stopping to chat with friends, nod to acquaintances. She saw young ladies' eyes follow him with wistful hope as well as older ladies with not so wistful looks in their eyes. Her heart no longer ached for him. Diana was fast bringing him back to life and perspective.

Unfortunately, Lyonel was still in the card room when Monsieur DuPres solicited Diana's hand in a waltz. Before she replied, she found herself looking over the group of people, searching for Lyonel. He wasn't there. She tossed her head, smiled at Etienne DuPres, and graciously gave him her hand. If Lyonel returned—and she prayed he would—he would have something to chew over.

Because she was continually looking for Lyonel, she merely nodded and agreed when Monsieur DuPres spoke. He, however, was most pleased and completely unaware of her mental defection. He was a bit surprised when she kept agreeing with him on his compliments to her, but all considered, it was an excellent sign. Lady Danvers had not led him astray. With years of smooth practice, he waltzed her toward the corner of the ballroom and drew her to a halt behind a large potted fern. A pity, he thought, that there was no balcony here at this dreary place.

Diana came to her senses when her feet stopped moving.

"Why are we stopping, *monsieur*? The music has not come to an end as yet."

He murmured something in seductive French and glided his fingertip over her cheek and down her throat. "So soft, so pliant," he continued in French, wondering now if the chit was so uneducated not to understand his beautifully turned French phrases.

Diana merely looked at him, a slight frown puckering her forehead. "Soft and pliant? That sounds like some sort of tropical flower."

"Ah, yes, pretty little dove, and your scent, so fragrant, so— so *séduisante*—"

"Sweaty?"

"No!" He muttered something in French again and Diana guessed with stunning accuracy that it was no compliment.

He splayed his hands in front of her, his fingertips but inches from her bosom. Diana took a step back only to feel the fern tickling her shoulder blades.

"You are ripe for the plucking, are you not, *ma petite*?"

"No," she said. "No, I am not ripe for anything except perhaps for a glass of that very bland punch."

DuPres frowned, then persevered. "Your body is ripe, for me. I will give you such pleasure, such—"

"Bosh. Excuse me, *monsieur*. I find you excessively tedious. I wish to return to my aunt." Thus annihilated, Monsieur DuPres, his face alarmingly red, had no choice but to escort the ridiculous girl back to her relative. His next stop was Lady Danvers. He had a few choice words to say to her, and since her French was excellent, he could unburden himself with potent accuracy.

"Why did you dance with that man?" Lucia demanded as Diana fanned herself vigorously with her hand.

"To spite Lyonel, but he wasn't even here. He is most provoking, Aunt."

Lucia smiled. She wondered what she would do if Diana weren't so appallingly honest. "Yes, he is."

Lyonel became more provoking as the night wore on. He did not return from the card room until the early hours of the morning to escort the ladies home. He said nothing, seemingly unaware of Diana's snit, until they reached Lucia's town house. After handing Lucia down, he merely looked at Diana and said, "I trust I do not have to strain my back? Your slippers are still on your feet?".

"They are too large and fell off."

"That is an impossibility. A girl of your size. . . Come along, Diana. I wish to seek out my bed without having a headache or an upset stomach."

"Still recovering from your bout of amour?"

"No," he said, his eyes glittering at her nasty tone, "I intend fully to continue with my bouting, just as soon as I've rid myself of you."

She again questioned his antecedents, adding a colorful description of his obvious relation to the braying cousin of a horse.

He laughed and whispered close to her ear, "Jealous, Miss Savarol?"

"Monsieur DuPres did say I was ripe for the plucking," she said. "That was when he took me behind a big fern."

His eyes narrowed, his lips thinned, and Diana, striving to look as demure as a vicar's youngest daughter, kept her own eyes down so he wouldn't see the drawing laughter in them.

"You disobeyed me."

"Oh, I am too fatigued," she said, yawning.

"I am adding that to my list. Your bottom will feel thé flat of my hand." His fingers tingling alarmingly from his own image, he strode off, not looking back at her.

It was difficult, but Lyonel managed it. He didn't leave Lois until the following morning, exhausted and rolled in a sleeping ball in the rumpled bed. But there was a smile on her face, he noted, quite pleased with himself.

At least with this bout of amour, he had given her pleasure, something he prided himself on. He was an excellent lover and found that a woman's moans and groans added to his own passion. The only fly in the ointment was the flitting image of Diana's face in his mind's eye as he caressed Lois' delightful breasts. He found himself wondering as he finally fell into his own bed if Diana would moan and groan, or even perhaps scream when he pleasured her.

Stupid fool.

She would probably yell at him . . . Yes, a rutting pig, that's what she would call him. She would probably slap away his hands when he would try to caress her, be disgusted at the thought of his tongue coursing over every inch of her body . . .

At least he was too tired, far too long gone from his bouts of amour to become aroused at the thought of thrashing her bare bottom with his bare hand.

Diana, innocent of bouts of anything remotely sexual, knew only that she felt more alive when Lyonel was with her. She realized, somewhat surprised, that neither of them knew much about the other. They couldn't seem to stop fighting long enough to just talk.

Talk, she decided, drifting into the sleep of the unawakened, was boring. Insults were more fun. And Lyonel was so baitable.

She felt only a slight twinge of homesickness as she drifted into sleep.

"You might at least pretend to like it!"

Charlotte dutifully brought her hands down to stroke her husband's back.

"Lord knows you used to beg for it! Are you already planning to cuckold me, as you did Lyonel?"

That brought her out of her plotting fog. She stiffened, feeling him probe between her thighs.

She started to say something, for she was furious at his carping, but he plunged into her at that moment, saying in a hoarse, angry voice, "You will bear me an heir before you take a lover, damn you!"

"Yes," she said just as he was on the point of spilling into her. "Yes, I will have your heir, then you will be out of my bed!"

He groaned, hating himself for being the biggest fool alive.

She waited until he was through and rolled off her. "I think, Dancy, that dear Lyonel will be my first lover. He is so marvelously large and well-formed, do you not think so? And his beautiful mouth and hands . . ."

"Lyonel would never come within a foot of you, Charlotte." He was tired, too weary of the farcical marriage even to be drawn. He had lost a man he considered a friend, and all for a woman who hadn't been real. God, that he could have been such a fool.

"We will see," she said, and yawned in his face.

'You are a bore, my dear wife. I fancy I will visit the theater tomorrow evening. I saw a lovely young thing there a week ago. She, I think, will be most accommodating."

"If you are thinking of that voluptuous sweet, Lois Braden, you can forget her."

He was thinking about the stunning Lois, and his wife's knowledge of her momentarily left him speechless. "How the devil do you know her and her name, for God's sake?"

"Men, my dear Dancy, are so naïve. It hurts me so to tell you that she is also now under Lyonel's protection."

Dancy sucked in his breath, but there was no anger against Lyon.

"Perhaps," he said, "Lois has a sister."

"They are all sisters of a sort, are they not? Cheap little harlots who—"

He laughed. "You are truly priceless, you know that, Charlotte?"

"Shut up, you pig."

"I just lost five hundred pounds this evening. You might consider a lover who would pay for your services. Help defray the cost of all your gowns and the like."

Charlotte, her tongue leaden in her mouth, at least for the moment, slid out of bed and grabbed her dressing gown.

"Why bother, my dear? I have already seen everything you have to offer."

"I would say the same of you, Dancy. Would be that I had seen you more clearly before I consented to bed with you."

"You have no idea how much in accord with you I am on that!"

5

Are you listening, or am I talking to deaf ears?

AESCHYLUS

"Diana, didn't you hear me?"

"I heard you, but I wasn't attending."

"Just leave, please, I should like to speak to Lucia privately."

"Why?" Diana demanded, lighting up like a Roman candle.

"Go to the park and play with the children, Diana."

"Yes, my dear," said Lucia, her eyes on Lyonel, "and take Jamison with you."

Diana didn't want to leave, but she saw no choice with both of them against her. She gave Lyonel a final frown and left the drawing room.

"Now, my boy, what is it you wish to say to me?"

"The most unfortunate event has transpired," he said. "A solicitor, a fellow named Manvers, came to my home this morning. It would appear that my great-uncle, Oliver Mendenhall, is quite dead, and I am, as you already know, his heir. He owns a sugar plantation on Tortola and I am now the proud possessor not only of the sugar and rum and molasses and whatever, but also of about one hundred slaves.

"He even wrote in his will about the Ashton whelp. You have told me the genealogy, Lucia, but I am still not certain that there is not a closer relative."

"And if there were?"

"I should dump the mess into his arms. Slaves, Lucia! One hundred of the poor souls. Damnation, I want nothing to do with any of this. What the devil am I to do?"

"You are his heir, my boy, just as you are also mine. Let me remind you that even if there were another closer relative, your duty would still be clear. There would be no dumping. Your responsibility is to carry out the wishes of your great-uncle."

"His wishes are, briefly put by Manvers once I poured a brandy down him to clear away his damned legal phrases, that I am to go to the plantation, look things over, and then decide, based on firsthand observation, what it is I wish to do."

"That sounds most reasonable to me." It is most unfair of me, Lucia was thinking, to be pleased at poor Oliver's demise. But, in all fairness to her own machinations, it couldn't have occurred at a more propitious time, and poor Oliver had been a very old man, a good ten years her senior. Lyonel, the dear boy, would escort his cousin back to the West Indies.

"It further appears that until I arrive, a manager by the name of Edward Bemis is running the plantation. Manvers intimated—and I doubt his sources, for after all he's had no time to inquire—that the man is something of a scoundrel."

Manvers was obviously a very astute man, Lucia was itching to say. He had observed Lyonel's doubts and, despite the brandy, applied pressure when he deemed it most useful. "I suppose that there are cases where slaves are terribly abused," she said, adding coals to the fire.

"That makes no sense! Why would a man abuse someone whose job it is to make him money?"

Lucia offered an elaborate shrug. "Don't be a nodcock, Lyonel. Think about some of your friends who allow their tenants' homes to deteriorate into shacks, who care not one whit if the children on their estate are even fed, the lords and ladies who treat their servants as things to obey their every whim without complaint. I can see no dichotomy in that. I think the world for the have-nots is a most cruel and unfriendly place."

He looked thoughtful. "You are right, of course. One wonders if their lot will improve once slavery is abolished."

"I doubt it. After all, dear boy, in England we have no use for black slaves. If we did, I doubt there would be such zeal against it."

"Again, you are probably right." He ran his hand through his hair. "It's just so damnably unexpected."

"But you will do your duty, my boy. Incidentally, why did you not wish Diana to know of this?"

He frowned. "I don't know. . . Well, actually, she would just stick her oar in and I would probably yell at her and—"

"I understand, my boy, indeed I do."

"There is another reason, of course. Diana has grown up with slavery. Doubtless it is a way of life with her and she accepts it without a qualm. As does her father. I would probably box her ears were she to begin to defend that dreadful institution."

Lucia, who had not discussed slavery with Diana, had no idea of her stand on the issue, but she had drawn some conclusions. "You know, Diana is most friendly to my servants. Indeed, perhaps too much so. Needless to say, they would likely kill to protect her. Can you really doubt that she would be cruel to servants who just happened to have black skin?''

"But they are owned, Aunt. They cannot leave a cruel master or mistress. They have no choice.''

"But they are given homes, medical care, and good food.''

Both Lucia and Lyonel turned at Diana's words.

"A very short visit to the park,'' said Lyon.

"I just took a stroll around the house.''

"They still have no choice,'' Lyon said.

"They would be helpless to make such a choice. If Father freed all his slaves, they would stand about looking helpless, which indeed they would be.''

"That is absurd! Just because you insist upon keeping them ignorant and uneducated—''

The fight was well on its way, Lucia thought, eyeing the two of them, now standing eye to eye, glaring.

To Lyonel's surprise, Diana said, her voice subdued, sad even, "I know. But you see, there are strict laws against education for the blacks. I think it is dreadful.'' She automatically raised her chin. "My father, however, is very fair, he—''

"So he is smart enough not to abuse people who make his money for him?''

Lucia wouldn't have been at all surprised to see Diana punch her fist in Lyon's stomach. However, she dropped her jaw when Diana said, her voice intense, even pleading, "You must live there to understand. You must see what it is like, for everyone, not just the slaves. Now, I shall go upstairs. We are still visiting Lady Banderson this afternoon, Aunt?''

"Yes, we are, my dear.''

Lyonel watched Diana hurriedly leave the drawing room. He felt guilty, damn her, for cutting up at her.

"Well," Lucia said, eyeing his stiff back, "I believe you have an answer of sorts."

"It still changes nothing."

"Fine, go to Tortola. Free all your—yes, *your*—slaves, Lyonel. Do what you believe best for them."

"I must find out more about the situation," he said more to himself than to Lucia.

"Then speak to Diana."

"I don't know . . . She probably does know this Bemis fellow and how the Mendenhall plantation is run. However—"

"Doubtless she does. Of course, she is just a silly young girl, probably doesn't really understand all the ramifications—"

"Don't be a bedlamite, Lucia! Diana is no fool, she—" He broke off, and his frown was ferocious.

Lucia smiled. Ah, Lyonel, she thought, your days with a mistress are numbered. Your warped belief that all women are like Charlotte is losing its grip.

Lyonel looked at his favorite relative. The old tartar was just that, but he knew that even though she ruled her estate in Yorkshire, only twenty miles from his, with an iron hand, it was with a velvet glove. She was never unfair. He didn't like the thought of having to step into her slippers. He never wanted Lucia to die.

"Have I told you, Lucia, that I am most fond of you?"

Lucia blinked and felt an overflowing of love so intense that for a moment even her sharp tongue was stilled. "Yes," she said, her voice soft, "you have, not recently, of course, but you have in the distant past."

"Allow me to apologize for my past relapses, and tell you that I am most fond of you."

"And I am equally fond of you, my boy. You really are a lot like your grandfather. He was quite a man, and a gentleman as well." She would have liked to tell him that she wished she hadn't been such a fool so many years before, that she would give everything now to have wed the fourth Earl of Saint Leven. Then Lyonel would be her grandson, not just her grandnephew. But life was filled with foolish decisions, and Lucia very rarely allowed herself to wallow in self-recriminations.

"How is your health, Lucia?" He'd blurted the words out and now looked appalled at what he'd asked, but Lucia understood. Death, even of an unknown relative, was a shock.

"I shall live to dangle your children on my knee."

"I should live that long," Lyonel said, acid back in his voice.

"Everyone makes mistakes, Lyonel. The trick is to accept them and continue on, not to condemn all of one's fellow men.".

"Does that also encompass one's fellow women?"

"Don't be an ass."

"I believe that is one of Diana's compliments."

"Then you must work on a cure for the malady."

"What I shall do, Lucia, is take myself off."

He paused, then strode to her, bent down, and kissed her parchment cheek. "You old martinet, do not overtax yourself."

She grinned at him and he saw that several of her back teeth were missing. Age, he thought, damnable, inevitable age and death. He didn't like it. The devil, he wouldn't accept it, at least not with Lucia.

Lyonel was sitting apart at White's, lost in a brown study, when the Earl of March, Julian St. Clair, came upon him.

"What you need," his friend said, quirking a brow, "is a good fight at Gentleman Jackson's. Come along, I shall see to it myself. And I shall be most careful not to destroy your beautiful face."

"Go to the devil, St. Clair," Lyonel said, but he went and all thoughts of death, responsibility for a hundred human souls, were temporarily shelved in his mind.

Diana had not a bit of interest in any of the five gentlemen who were assiduously sending her flowers, inviting her to drive in the park, and otherwise making nuisances of themselves, at least in her young eyes.

"I want to go home, Aunt," she said one evening, a rare occasion when they were not engaged somewhere. "I do not belong here. I am still cold most of the time. My tan is fading and soon I will look like a white lily, like all of those silly debutantes. They don't like me, Aunt. They think I'm some sort of oddity. They have no conversation, except to go on and on about Lord This or Lord That. And as for the gentlemen, all they wish to do is spew compliments at me, as if I wanted to hear their nonsense, and try in the most ridiculous ways possible to determine how much money I will have upon my marriage. And," Diana finished up, triumphant with disgust, "when they don't think I'm noticing, they ogle my bosom."

So does Lyonel, Lucia thought, but she didn't hark to that. Instead she said, "Lyonel doesn't whisper nonsense in your ears."

"No, indeed he tries to burn them off with his insults. Oh, very well, he isn't like the others."

"So you no longer believe him to be too pale and unhealthy-looking?"

"Perhaps not entirely," Diana said, thinking back to the evening when he lifted her into his arms out of the carriage. She had felt his strength. It still made her feel mildly alarmed.

"You promised your father that you would remain six weeks, my dear."

"I know, and there are still three more to go."

"I did not realize that you were still so very unhappy."

Diana caught herself, realizing that she had inflicted hurt where none was intended. It was all Lyonel's fault, damn him. She jumped from her chair at the dining table and rushed to Lucia's side, easing down to her knees. "Please do not mind me, or my stupid tongue. You know that you are my favorite person in all of London. Indeed, my very favorite female relative."

"I am the only one, you pert-mouthed chit!" But she laughed and gently patted Diana's head. "You are a good girl and you have been most patient with all my old woman's vagaries. Now, get back to your dinner."

"As Lyonel would doubtless say in his sardonic manner, 'Don't let your charms waste away.' "

"Yes, that is exactly what he would say." Lucia toyed with a bite of well-sauced chicken. "I have decided that Lyonel will escort you home."

"He will refuse."

"No, he won't. I see that you have already considered that possibility."

"No. . . Well, perhaps. It is a long voyage, Aunt, at least six weeks. Can you imagine the two of us cooped up for that period of time?"

"You will either kill each other or—"

"Or what?"

Lucia shrugged. "Well, you will just have to see, won't you? In terms of a chaperone, I am endeavoring to find a family who also plan to return to the West Indies. It will all work out, my dear, you will see."

"Ha!"

Lucia's expression was as bland as her vegetables. "Lyonel promised me he would come this evening to provide you with more dancing lessons."

"Lucky me."

Lucia merely smiled to herself, noting how Diana's hand immediately and unconsciously went to her hair to straighten any errant strands. She blurted out suddenly, "Aunt, he really doesn't like me, not a bit!"

"Bosh."

"He has a mistress and he sees more of her in one evening than he's ever seen us."

"I would imagine that he does," Lucia said, her voice dry.

"I didn't mean *see* precisely, I meant . . . Oh, drat the man, he is impossible! He will go to her as soon as he leaves us."

"I imagine you are right about that."

"I don't like him, Aunt, and as for him, he can barely tolerate my company."

"My lord Saint Leven," Didier said from the doorway.

"Good evening, ladies. Still dining?"

"As you see, Lyonel," said Diana.

"I shall enjoy your conversation, then. Perhaps I shall even improve upon it. Don't mind me at all."

"A glass of port, my lord?"

"Yes, thank you, Didier. Now, my dear Diana, what is all this about my being impossible? Am I not here to instruct you as I promised? Does not that prove that I can tolerate you and your feet well enough?"

Didier personally handed Lyonel a crystal goblet filled with Lucia's finest port.

"I don't really want your wretched instruction."

"In that case, it appears I was misinformed. Shall I leave, Lucia?"

"You move, dear boy, and I shall have Didier plant you a facer."

"Lucia, I am shocked! Such language, particularly in front of our innocent here."

"I will plant that facer if you do not at least pretend to gentlemanly behavior. And I am not an innocent."

"Are you not?" Lyonel toyed with the stem of the goblet, and Diana's eyes, despite herself, were drawn to his long, graceful fingers. "I shall have to keep that in mind."

"Why?"

"One never knows when such insights might prove advantageous."

"I believe, Aunt, that my feet hurt."

"You cannot find slippers large enough for her, Lucia?" He sighed. "I shall instruct you in your stocking feet then. At least when you tread on my toes, the agony shouldn't be quite as bad."

Diana struggled valiantly for a retort to put him in his wretched place. Unconsciously, her fingers tightened about the stem of her wineglass.

"Don't do it, Diana."

She blinked up at him.

"No wine on my clean linen, if you please. Kenworthy —my valet, you know—he would be most distraught. You wouldn't wish for him to take you into dislike. No indeed."

"Dandy."

"Thank you. Shall we drink to that?"

"Fop."

"Diana, my dear, I do believe it best to desist now. Lyonel, let us go to the music room. Didier!"

An hour later, Diana had mastered the cotillion and two country dances, and she was laughing.

Jamison knocked on the music-room door, then slithered in, his eyes darting toward Didier.

"Yes?" Lucia asked.

" 'Tis one of my Lord Chandos' men, my lady. He claims he must speak to Lord Saint Leven."

"The marquess's man?" Lyonel asked, releasing Diana.

"Yes, my lord."

"Excuse me, Lucia, Diana." He strode out of the music room, leaving the women and Didier to stare at one another.

"Who is this marquess, Aunt?"

"The Marquess of Chandos, my dear. A very old friend and the father of Lyonel's dearest friend, Hawk, the Earl of Rothermere."

"Hawk and Lyon? I begin to believe that English nick-names are absurd."

"Perhaps. Hawk's formal name is Philip and he is married to Frances. They own a huge racing stud near Yorkshire. I wonder what the devil is going on."

They found out not five minutes later when Lyonel strode into the room, saying, "I must be off, Lucia. It's Frances. The marquess just got word from Hawk that she is in labor, several weeks early, and is in a very bad way."

"This is her second child. I would have thought that it would go more easily with her this time."

"Evidently not."

"Poor girl."

"I am off. I will keep you informed—"

"Nonsense, my boy. I will accompany you."

"I as well," said Diana.

"Really, Lucia—"

"You are wasting time, Lyonel. Have your carriage back here within the hour. Diana and I will be ready."

*   *   *

They arrived at Desborough Hall the following afternoon, the horses blown and the two ladies exhausted.
Lucia got one look at the marquess's drawn face and felt
hope plummet.

"She is still holding her own," the marquess said quickly.
"Lucia, I am glad you came. Lyon, my boy. Go to Hawk.
He is in a very bad way. And who is this?"

"I am Diana Savarol, sir."

"Charmed, my dear. Come along."

"I wish to see Frances," Lucia said as she trailed
behind the marquess into the hall. "And speak to this
doctor of hers."

Diana's first glimpse of Philip Hawksbury, the Earl of
Rothermere, made her blink. He was of Lyonel's size,
dark-featured, his eyes a brilliant green, and he was
trembling, his large hands clutching Lyonel's shoulders.
"Nearly three days, Lyon, dammit! Oh, God, what am I
to do?"

Lyonel felt helpless and angry. He'd hoped. . . Oh,
God, how he'd prayed every cursed mile northward that
Frances would have delivered the child and Hawk, a smile
on his lips, would have yelled and clapped him on the
shoulder in delight.

"Diana, my dear," Lucia said quietly, "there is Grunyon,
Hawk's man. Tell him who you are and he will take care
of you. I am going to see Frances now."

Diana nodded numbly. She looked toward the short,
plump man, but he paid her no attention, his eyes on his
master, his own face pale and drawn. She slipped into the
library, unseen, and settled herself on a sofa. Until she
heard the scream. It was high, broken, and filled with such
agony that she sucked in her breath.

She heard pounding feet and rushed to the doorway. She

saw both Lyonel and Hawk racing up the stairs. "God, I shouldn't have left her!"

Lyonel happened to look back at that moment and saw Diana, white-faced, standing at the bottom of the stairs. "Stay there," he yelled at her.

The two men burst into the master bedchamber. Lucia was beside the bed, bending over Frances, the doctor and a midwife on the other side. The doctor was speaking, wildly gesticulating, but Lucia was ignoring him.

"Frances!"

"Hawk." Lucia looked briefly up at him. "Come and help me. Lyonel, get this idiot out of here, now!"

It was the marquess who took the doctor's arm and pulled him away.

"Now, I've managed to turn the child into the proper position, despite that fool of a doctor. I want you to press down on her belly, Hawk, now. Frances, child, look at me! Frances, listen! I want you to push down with all your strength. Do you hear me?"

Frances groaned. She heard the words, recognized Lucia's voice, and stared blindly up at her husband.

"Get those covers off her, Hawk. Now, push, Frances!"

The wailing, thin cries made Lyon tremble. He saw Hawk pressing down on the huge mound of Frances' belly. He saw Lucia motion to the midwife and the two of them lifted Frances' legs and parted them. He saw Lucia's hand plunge into Frances. He closed his eyes, a prayer on his lips.

"Push, Frances! Hawk, press down, harder!"

Lyon heard Frances gasping, her hoarse voice rending the silence of the room. "Oh, God, please," he whispered.

"The babe—I have his head! Again, Frances. Come on, girl, again, as hard as you can! Push, Hawk, 'tis the only way you can help her."

Lyon opened his eyes to see Lucia's hands receive a small, dark head. "I've got the babe's head. Stop pushing, Frances."

Lucia grasped the tiny shoulders, gently pulling the babe from its mother. "A girl, Hawk, 'tis a beautiful little girl you've got."

The room was chaotic for the next few minutes. A woman Lyon hadn't noticed rushed forward as the babe let forth a loud wail. Lyon saw Frances' head fall back against the pillow. She was unconscious. Hawk was just standing there, frozen.

"You've a girl," Lucia said again, her eyes on Hawk. But Hawk was bending over his wife, his hands gently cupping her white face.

"She will be all right," Lucia said. She motioned to the midwife and they rid Frances of the afterbirth. Lucia straightened and Lyon was so proud of her that he wanted to yell.

"Hawk, you may leave now. I will take care of Frances. She will be all right. Do you understand me? Lyon, take him out of here."

Lyon strode forward and grasped his friend's arm. "Come, Hawk. If Lucia says she is all right, she is. You need a drink."

Lucia said calmly, "Now, Mrs.—?"

"Miniver, my lady."

"Yes, Mrs. Miniver, let us get this bleeding under control, then we will bathe her ladyship and make her comfortable."

"What if she bleeds to death?"

"Stop it, Hawk! She will be fine. Lucia doesn't lie, you know."

Still Hawk didn't move.

"Let us find that damned doctor. You can personally boot his fat butt out of here."

"Yes," Hawk said, straightening. "I should like that."

Lyon could barely keep up with him. He saw Diana at the foot of the stairs and called out, "All is well, Diana."

The doctor, unfortunately for him, was arguing vociferously with the marquess. He turned when he saw the earl bearing down on him, and tactlessly, he said, "She is dead, is she not? I told you not to let that old woman near her, I—"

Those were his last words for five minutes. Hawk's fist struck him squarely in his jaw and he crumpled to the entrance-hall floor.

"Excellent, my boy," the marquess said. "Just excellent."

Hawk rubbed his knuckles. "You're a grandfather again. A girl, Frances has given me a girl this time."

Another young man emerged from the nether regions.

"Champagne, Carruthers," Lyonel called out.

They left the doctor on the floor, the servants merely stepping over him and around him.

"Who are you?" Hawk asked Diana. "I haven't seen you before, have I?"

"I am no one important, my lord," she said. "My congratulations." She stuck out her hand, and Hawk, with automatic courtesy, took hers.

"I have a girl," Hawk said, and Diana watched his mouth slowly widen into a big smile. "I have a beautiful little girl." He pulled up abruptly, his eyes staring upward. "Frances won't be pleased. The infant has black hair, just like Charles."

"Frances is a trooper, Hawk. She will be all right. She is all right. I trust your little girl will have the look of Frances, though, even with your black hair." Diana watched the two men grin at each other.

Diana turned toward the long open windows in the drawing room at the sound of loud cheering from the outside.

"Everyone loves Frances," Hawk said simply.

"Where is little Charles?" said Lyon.

"I sent him to Alicia and John two days ago. Grunyon! Have Lord Lindsey fetched, immediately!"

"Yes," said Lyon. "The viscount has a little sister."

6

A filly who wants to run will always find a rider.

JACQUES AUDIBERTI

"It will be a while before she is on Flying Davie's back," Hawk said. "And on her own back," he added under his breath in his wife's ear.

"Hawk!" Frances buffeted him on his shoulder.

Diana smiled at the two of them. Frances was beautiful, she thought without envy. She was sitting on her husband's lap, her head leaned against his broad shoulder. There was a smile on her pale lips and she was saying, her voice thin and hoarse from her travail, "I am delighted to be surrounded by old friends, and my new friend, Diana. Hawk has been driving me absolutely distracted."

"Just wait until your father arrives from Scotland, sweetheart. Then you'll see distracted."

"Papa?" Frances arched a brow. "You know he will spend all his congratulating you on *your* fine part in everything, just as he did when Charles was born. He just might spare a kiss for me and a pat on the head."

"Not if he'd been here while—" The earl's voice broke off abruptly.

"You scared the devil out of the boy," said the marquess.

"That," said Lyon, his eye on Hawk, "is impossible, the devil part anyway."

Both Hawk and Frances grinned at Lyonel. " 'Tis all too true," she said.

"I understand, Lucia," the countess continued, "that you saved my life, and my daughter's life. I remember you speaking to me, but not too much more. I am in your debt."

"I am glad you don't remember all that much, my dear," said Lucia.

"I am in your debt as well," the earl said.

Diana saw his hand tighten about his wife's waist as he spoke. To be loved like that, she thought. Some people were so very lucky. "We wish you to be our daughter's godmother, Lucia, if, that is, you don't mind sharing the responsibility with my interfering father."

Lucia grinned at the marquess and said, "This old man will do as I tell him. You, my boy, just haven't yet learned how to deal with him."

"Hurrumph," said the marquess. "Mixing up my stew with this old shrew. Come here, Lucia, and let me hug you."

"Philandering old goat," said Lucia, and hugged the marquess.

Lyonel said in a low voice to Diana, "The marquess is a wily old devil, but he has met his match in Lucia. I'll never forget how he got Hawk and Frances together, why it was—"

"Telling tales, Lyon?" Hawk said. "She'll never believe you."

"Very well, I'll hold the tale and wait for a boring winter night. Diana will particularly enjoy the part of your, er, former mistress, saving the day."

To Diana's surprise, Frances Hawksbury laughed, a grating, hoarse sound.

"Lyonel can tell Diana all about it when they are traveling to the West Indies," said Lucia with great complacency.

This announcement brought all eyes to Lyonel and Diana.

"Lucia," Lyon began, "I would that you not—"

"Nonsense, my boy."

"So that is the direction the wind blows," said the marquess. his green eyes, so like his son's, glittering.

"No!"

"No!"

"Sounds just like my poor stubborn Hawk here and my stubborn-as-the-devil Frances. Let's leave the young people to themselves, Lucia, and discuss matters."

"First," said Hawk, "we must name my daughter."

"*Our* daughter," his wife said. "And we've already decided. Arabella Lucia. What does everyone think of that?"

"The child has much to live up to," said the marquess.

"Excellent name," said Lucia. "The child's a fighter. She'll do just fine with it. Now, you old goat, let's leave the young people alone."

Diana watched the two old people leave the bedchamber, arm in arm.

"Damned old man," said Hawk.

"True," said the countess, putting her arms around her husband's neck and burying her face against his throat.

"Diana, 'tis time for us to take our leave," said Lyonel.

"You may go admire our progeny," said Hawk. "Then take a walk in the garden. Just go away.'

The countess smiled. "Thank you, both of you, for coming."

Diana, looking among the three friends, merely nodded and headed for the door, Lyonel on her heels.

"They love each other so much," she blurted out when they were in the corridor.

"Yes, they do," said Lyonel, his eyes straight ahead.

They remained at Desborough Hall for four more days. The early-summer weather held mild and sunny. Diana spent most of her time riding, a spritely bay mare named Glenda, admiring the racehorses, and watching their training with Belvis, a wiry old man who took an instant liking to her.

It was odd, Diana thought on the morning of their third day, that Lyonel never went into the stable. He avoided it, and the magnificent tack room, like the plague. "Do you not wish to pick out your own saddle?" she asked him finally.

"No," he said, his voice curt.

"Why not?"

"Leave it, Diana."

"But the grooms are having to carry out all these saddles for you to make your selection."

"Leave it, Diana."

"You, my lord, are becoming boring and repetitious in your conversation."

"At least I'm not a pushy, mouthy chit."

"No, you are an arrogant, selfish—"

He turned on his heel and left her standing by the paddock, Belvis staring after him.

"Most peculiar," said Belvis. "Pardon me, miss, but he wouldn't come near the stables when he stayed with his lord and lady several months ago."

"Hmmm," said Diana, frowning after him. "He visited here after his broken engagement with Charlotte Haversham?"

"Aye," said Belvis. "Now, ye go along, miss, else his young lordship might just clip my ears for speaking so bluntly to ye."

"All right. We are returning to London, you know, early tomorrow morning. I shall miss you, Belvis, and Desborough Hall."

"Ye mind yerself, miss, and his lordship."

"And you take care of Flying Davie."

"He'll take all comers at Newmarket this summer. Oh, indeed he will."

Diana didn't doubt that for a moment.

Leavetaking was difficult for Diana. So many new friends she'd made. And, she discovered, somewhat to her surprise, she'd fallen in love with the Yorkshire countryside. It was wild and desolate on the heather-covered moors, and free. It made her feel most odd, as if she had come home, which was, of course, quite ridiculous.

"Cannot we not visit your estate, Aunt?" she asked Lucia as their carriage bowled down the long drive.

"Not this time, my dear. We've too many engagements in town. Did you know that Lyonel also owns an estate here in Yorkshire? Quite near to mine, just five miles from Escrick."

"No, he didn't tell me." Damn the man! She had told him she much admired the countryside when they rode together, she recalled. He had merely grunted in that indifferent way, making her want to box his ears.

Their journey back to London was at a much slower pace and Diana saw much more of England. Lyonel spent not a minute inside the carriage, but Diana stoutly told herself that she was quite happy with his defection. She was a bit taken aback when they neared Grantham when Lucia said calmly, "I want you to know as much as possible about birthing a child, Diana. Even with a doctor—the bloody old fool—and midwife—cowering creature—present, Frances could have died, the child with her. I would imagine that women dying in childbirth is not at all uncommon in the West Indies. Now, you will listen to me carefully."

Diana listened.

What she did not realize was that Lucia had trapped Lyonel that same evening after Diana had taken to her bed, and told Lyonel the same things. "When you take a wife, my boy—and don't frown at me that way!—you will doubtless get her with child. You must know how to take charge if it is needed."

"Lucia, really!"

"'Shut up, Lyonel, and listen. It is not uncommon for a babe to be turned wrong in the womb, or even have the cord about its neck. You can feel the position of the babe and turn it if necessary."

"I shall never marry, Lucia, never."

"Don't be more of a fool than your father was. Now, your hands are quite large, so you much be as gentle as possible . . ."

Lyonel groaned, but he did listen. He had no choice. Not with Lucia. "However," Lucia concluded, her voice as bland as the roast beef they'd had for dinner, "Diana is no small, delicate female. Frances isn't either, but she had the misfortune of having the child in a breech position. Hawk now knows what care she will need with any future children. Now, in the normal course of things, Diana should not have much difficulty, but one never knows, and it is wise to be prepared."

"That is quite enough," Lyonel said, very softly. Lucia, who was familiar with that particular tone, retreated.

Lucia rose and kissed his cheek. "Good night, my boy. Do not drink yourself into a stupor. You will be most unhappy with your aching head in the morning if you do."

Lyonel silently agreed with that and took to his own bed not ten minutes later. Unfortunately, his dreams were fraught with images of Diana, her belly swelled with child, his child. He ground his teeth in his sleep.

He cursed fluently when he awoke the following morning.

He said to Lucia over the breakfast table, "I have decided not to visit Tortola as yet. I will go next spring, perhaps."

Diana dropped her fork at that announcement, the eggs falling onto the tablecloth. "You cannot wait! I will tell you, Lyonel, that it is most unwise to leave a plantation in the hands of an attorney. They are all opportunists. As for Mr. Bemis, I don't know him personally, but I doubt he is any different from the others. You cannot leave him to make decisions. I cannot imagine why Oliver Mendenhall left him in charge. Why, my father says— "

"I am going to check the horses," said Lyonel. He dropped his napkin, thrust back his chair, and strode from the small private dining room at the Wild Goose Inn.

"Why are you smiling, Aunt? He is the most arrogant, the most offensive, the—"

"Yes, all of those things. But he is fighting battles, Diana, and the poor boy just hasn't yet realized that—" Lucia broke off, eyeing Diana. She saw that the girl was bewildered, and held her peace.

She would simply work on Lyonel, dear boy, and he would be on that ship, indeed he would.

*   *   *

The wind was blowing in an ill direction when they attended a ball at Renfrew House in Grosvenor Square the second evening of their return to London. Charlotte had been quite busy, Lucia quickly realized, her lips tightening. Lord, were all her friends and acquaintances absolute fools? They'd been gone less than two weeks and here things had deteriorated alarmingly.

Diana was cut dead by Lady Marian Braverman. Lucia met the woman's eyes, and Lady Marian had the grace to blush.

Lucia kept Diana close until she could find out what had happened. It was really quite simple. Charlotte and that wretched Monsieur DuPres had busily spread the gossip that Diana Savarol and Lyonel Ashton had traveled together to his estate in Yorkshire, the journey there in the company of Lucia, of course, but the two young people had supposedly left her at her estate and gone to his. Alone. Obviously to disport themselves in improper, if not lewd, activities.

"I am going to kill her," Lucia said between her teeth. Knowing that this pleasure would be denied to her, Lucia immediately told a notorious gossip, Lady Gladstairs, in confidence, of course—the truth of the matter.

Lyonel was unaware of the situation until he strolled into Renfrew House near to midnight. He had not intended to come—no, he hadn't, it was just that . . . Damn. He shook his head at himself. He was met with a leering Monsieur DuPres and several cronies known for their salacious behavior.

He couldn't believe his ears. What made him more furious than the ferocious innuendos was the knowledge that DuPres was saying that Diana, the silly chit, had seduced not only him, but also Lyonel. She was, after all, from that ungodly West Indies, and equally as obviously, anything but a lady. She had taken Lady Cranston in.

He said nothing to either Diana or Lucia. He found Dancy in the card room. "I should like to speak to you. Now."

Dancy, no fool, paled. His arm still pained him occasionally from the bullet Lyonel had cleanly shot through it at their duel.

He rose from the chair, aware of many eyes watching, and followed Lyon into an antechamber. Lyon firmly closed the door.

"You know, do you not, what Charlotte has made people believe? Along with DuPres, of course."

Dancy nodded. "I have heard some things," he said, his voice wary. Damn, he had told Charlotte to keep her mouth shut!

"Have you so little regard for your hide, Dancy?"

"Look, Lyon, what do you expect me to do? Sew her mouth together?"

"Charlotte is your wife, Dancy, thus your responsibility. Either she halts all this malicious nonsense or I will let the truth be known. I will tell everyone that I found her on her back in the Haversham tack room, her skirts tossed up to her throat, with you between her legs. She will no longer rely on my honor as a gentleman. Do you understand me?"

Dancy Moressey swallowed. Lyonel hadn't raised his voice, not even a little bit. He looked as calm as if he were discussing the weather. But Dancy wasn't fooled. He'd known Lyonel Ashton since they were schoolboys.

"Do you understand, Dancy?"

"I—I, yes, I understand, Lyon."

"Have you the guts to speak to her, or shall I?"

"I will fetch her to you."

"Damned coward," Lyon said under his breath as he watched Dancy flee from the room. He waited for ten minutes before the door opened and Charlotte entered, alone. He noted that she was an ethereal vision in pale-blue silk, her face and figure stunning. She was the picture of innocence and soft vulnerability. He remained unmoved. If only he had seen her objectively before he'd made an abject fool of himself . . .

Her chin was up and her eyes glittered. "Yes, my lord?"

"You are a miserable human being, you know that, Charlotte?"

"And you are a miserable bastard! Don't you dare speak to me like that!"

"And a whore—"

"I will not stay here and listen to your filth!"

Lyon very calmly took her arm and drew her forward. He pressed her gently into a chair. He stood over her, his arms crossed over his chest. "I will tell you what I told your husband. I will tell the world everything if you do not immediately cease and detract all the filth you have spread about Diana Savarol, and me."

"You would not!" She looked scared, for the first time. Had she always viewed him as such a weak excuse for a man? A gentleman without a spine? Evidently so.

"Oh, yes," he said very softly. "I will tell the gentle-men about your lovely white legs, how they were wrapped around Dancy's flanks, how you made such pleading little mewling noises when he was pumping into you—"

"Stop it, damn you!" She clapped her hands over her ears.

"What is wrong, Charlotte? I have offended your sensibilities? Your modesty? Surely society will believe it most offensive of you to have taken a lover before you were married to me.''

"It is you who will be laughed at! And no one will believe you, they will think you are trying to protect that little slut from God knows where!''

"Charlotte, you make me forget that I am a gentleman and do not strike women.''

"No gentleman would threaten me as you are doing.''

"And no lady would spread such filth. Tell me, Charlotte, why are you doing it? Why do you wish me to suffer for what you did? And Diana Savarol—she's done nothing to you.''

"I know all about your little mistress, that Lois girl, an opera girl, that you are keeping. What would your precious Diana think about that?''

To Charlotte's chagrin, Lyonel threw his head back and laughed deeply. "My little amour, you mean? That is priceless, Charlotte. You continue to amaze me. You also cannot imagine how I thank God each and every night that I discovered what a whore you were before I married you. Dear God, to believe that the future Earl of Saint Leven could have easily been another man's child.'' He stopped abruptly, his eyes cold and narrowed. "Listen well, Charlotte. It will stop, now. If you continue, you cannot believe how sorry you will be. Actually, I am tempted to tell the truth in any case. Dancy's estate is in Cornwall, you know. I imagine you will adore living there. Think of all the local men you could pleasure. Ah, yes, it is a seductive thought, is it not?''

If looks could have killed, Lyonel would have lain dead at her feet. Looks didn't kill. But words and gossip did.

"Well?''

Charlotte was made of stern stuff. She cursed him in fluent French. Lyonel laughed and repeated, "Well?"

"Damn you, Lyon! A man can have a mistress, but a woman cannot have a lover! It is not fair."

"Ah, Charlotte, it is true that I have a mistress, but you see, I am not promised to a lady. Had I married you, my dear, I would have been like a faithful hound. There lies a vast difference between us."

"I do not believe you. You are a man! Why, my father took every female on our estate, under my mother's nose. All of you are the same."

"I cannot speak about your father, but it is a pity that you do not believe me, for I am telling you the truth. Now, what will you do?"

"You haven't given me much choice, have you?"

"No, none at all. Will you do as I demand?"

Finally, she nodded, and he saw that it was abhorrent to her to bend to his will.

"And DuPres? Must I kill him, Charlotte?"

Charlotte paled a bit. She was fond of Etienne DuPres, who was now her lover. She shook her head. "No, I shall speak to him."

"Wise of you. Do tell me, Charlotte, before you leave this room and my sight, for I am truly interested. Why did you play me false before our marriage?"

She rose and automatically shook out her skirts, her hand going to her beautifully coiffed hair to straighten it. She met his eyes and shrugged. "I was stupid," she said. She turned, head held high, and left the room.

Lyon stared after her. It was odd but he felt an unwonted pang of pity for her. No, he told himself firmly, she wasn't worth a moment's pity. He would speak to Lucia, then tell Diana to keep her mouth shut.

*   *   *

Diana quickly moved behind a huge potted fern when Charlotte swept from the antechamber. She was trembling with what she had heard. She turned to slip away when she felt a strong hand close around her throat.

"Well! So, along with all your other sterling qualities, you are also an eavesdropper. Very charming, Diana."

Diana turned slowly to face Lyonel. His hand remained about her throat. He was enraged, but she didn't at first realize it. How could he have come up to her so very quietly?

"I am sorry," she managed, wishing he would release her. "It is just that I saw you accompany Lord Danvers, then Charlotte came here. I had to—"

"Had to hear every gruesome detail, my dear? I assume that your ear was pressed against the door?"

She nodded, swallowing.

His fingers were following the lines of her throat—quite gently, really.

"Are you going to strangle me?"

He gave a glimmer of a smile, an evil smile to Diana's eyes. "Here? I fancy if I did you would yell the ballroom down upon my head."

She remained quiet.

His fingers continued to caress her throat. "You know, Diana, you have finally pushed me over the edge, as it were. Your childish behavior has gone beyond what I can accept." He paused, and he looked down at her, his eyes a dark blue in the dim light.

"I did apologize," Diana said, unable to meet his eyes. She wished she had never followed Charlotte. She had been wrong, very wrong, but once they had begun talking, once she had learned the truth, she simply had been unable to pull herself away. "Please, Lyon, I am sorry."

"Words," he said. "They are easy to say, are they

not?'' He abruptly released her. Her hand went unconsciously to her throat.

''I shall speak to Lucia. Then we will leave.''

His voice was light, normal again to Diana's ears. If she
had looked into his eyes, however, she would have seen
that his voice had nothing to do with anything at all.

''All right,'' Diana said, relief in her voice.

He followed her, his mind working, tossing aside one
idea only to quickly replace it with another. Oh, yes, he
thought, she had gone too far. What he needed now was
the opportunity and privacy.

His fury remained unabated until the next morning.
Then he smiled. He rose from his bed and pulled back the
window curtain. The day was bright and warm. Yes, he
thought, today was the day.

7

We put our revenge at risk if we post-pone it.

MOLIÈRE

Diana, who hadn't heard a single word about anything, was delighted when Grumber, in her unique disinterest, informed her that his lordship was downstairs and wished to speak to her.

She felt a happy lurch, frowned at herself, and quickly straightened her hair. Could it be that he had finally for-given her?

Lyonel was in conversation with Lucia. Upon Diana's entrance, he looked at her and smiled. "Hello, Diana."

Relief flooded her. He had forgiven her. What she had done had cost her a goodly amount of sleep the past night. She had even found herself thinking of her mother, the magnificent Lily, dead when Diana was six years old, and wondered whether her mother had ever scolded her, partic-ularly about eavesdropping. She couldn't dredge up one memory about such an occurrence, and sighed. Could she blame her motherless state for her lapse in doing the right thing? No, there was Dido. "You say dat word agin, Missie, and I smack you, but good!"

"Hello," she said now, smiling at the memory. She couldn't seem to remember the forbidden word.

"It is a beautiful day," Lyonel said, wondering about that small secret smile. "Lucia has given us her permission to ride to Richmond. I think you would much enjoy it. Can you be ready to leave in say thirty minutes?"

He really had forgiven her, he wasn't just being polite. She nodded. "Twenty minutes," she said, and left the drawing room with more speed than grace.

Lyonel looked after her, a thoughtful expression on his face.

"What are you planning, my boy?"

"I?" A thick brow shot upward and a long finger brushed an invisible speck from his coat sleeve. "Why, not a thing, Lucia. Merely a day of pleasure for your little charge."

"You forget I know you quite well. The look in your eyes. . . Well, I should like to know what you are up to."

She did know him well, curse her, Lyonel thought. He quickly got to his feet and poured himself a cup of tea.

He managed to turn the conversation to Hawk and Frances.

Twenty minutes later, Diana entered the drawing room, pulling on her York tan leather riding gloves. She was wearing her new royal-blue velvet riding habit, a jaunty hat upon her head with a matching blue feather sweeping beside her cheek.

"You look lovely, my dear."

Lyonel secretly agreed with Lucia, then quickly quashed his agreement. The little hussy was going to get her comeuppance today. Oh yes she was.

He smiled easily. "A lady who can tell time," he said. "Come along, Diana. I brought along a mare for you."

"You took my acquiescence for granted?"

He said, drawing her just a bit, "Why, certainly, my dear. It cannot but add to your consequence to be seen with me."

"Do not provoke me, Lyonel. I am vowing not to argue with you today."

"I hope that you can adhere to it," he said, "though I doubt that you will. Lucia, we will return in the afternoon." He kissed her and straightened. "Come along, Diana."

"Enjoy yourselves," Lucia called after them. She felt very good. Lyonel was shaping up. Or was he? She was frowning when Didier entered to remove the tea remains. "You know, Didier, Lord Saint Leven is up to something."

"More than likely it is true," said Didier mildly. "But his lordship is fair."

"What does that mean, you old monk?" But Didier just gave her his patented oblique look and she shook her head. "How many years now, Didier?"

"Twenty-one, my lady."

"A deuced long time."

"Indeed." He added as he balanced the tea tray on his arms, "As I said, Lord Saint Leven is a fair man."

Lyonel was patting the bay mare's nose. "Her name is Venus. She is spirited, but I assume you can handle her with ease." He waited until Diana had spoken to the mare, letting her sniff her hands, then he tossed her into the saddle. He gracefully mounted his own stallion, Lazar, a black brute with a white mane, a terror to those in the Four Horse Club.

Diana, who had decided to put that awful evening behind her, chatted happily, admiring the scenery, praising the mare, praising Lyonel on his excellent idea for their outing.

Lyonel responded well enough. He wished she didn't look so damned beautiful. No, it wasn't exactly her beauty that bothered him, he realized, it was her shining eyes, her very open happiness.

They were nearing Richmond when Diana asked, somewhat diffidently, "Lucia hasn't let me out of the house. Have you heard anything?"

"DuPres, I understand from Kenworthy, is leaving on Friday to visit friends in Berlin. He, ah, plans an extended stay. As for Charlotte, I will know about that soon. I would imagine that her husband just might take her to visit his estate in Cornwall. I doubt there will be further problems."

"Goodness," Diana said, her eyes dancing. "You are most convincing, Lyon."

"You should know," he said mildly. "You heard it all."

She flushed and toyed with her mare's reins. "Yes, and please, I do apologize. I shall never speak of it to anyone, you may be certain."

"No, you won't."

"I just don't understand!"

"What don't you understand?" He turned in his saddle to look at her.

"How she could do that to you. Why, if I accepted a man's proposal of marriage, I should also be a faithful hound, just like you told her and—"

"You will strive for amnesia, Diana. I do not wish to discuss what you heard, ever again."

"But—"

"Enough!"

"You needn't yell at me! I just wanted to agree with you."

He said nothing more, merely clicked his stallion into a gallop, leaving her to frown at his back.

"Come along, Venus. His lordship is in a snit."

They had luncheon in a small inn just outside Richmond, The King George.

When Diana sat back in her chair, replete with cold chicken and warm crusty bread, Lyonel said, "There is a particularly charming place I want to show you."

"Kew Gardens?"

"No. It is a special place. A place I fancy that you will long remember. Are you ready?"

She smiled at him. "Lead on, my lord."

He did, and twenty minutes later they were in a small, very isolated glade that bordered on a narrow stream. Lyonel dismounted and tethered his stallion. He walked to Diana and lifted her down. He was very aware of her scent, of her softness. He quickly moved away from her.

They walked to the edge of an incline that led down to the water's edge. "Not too close," he said. "The grass looks slippery. It must have rained here earlier."

Diana drew in a deep breath. "Thank you for bringing me here, Lyon, 'tis beautiful. It is so different from home, you know."

"Are you still cold all of the time?"

"Rarely now. I think it is because Aunt gives me that you-are-a-weakling look if I say anything."

"You don't like to be thought a weakling, do you, Diana?"

"Does anyone?"

"A man doesn't. As for a woman, who can say?"

"You will not provoke me, my lord."

"Excellent. Come here." He had seated himself on a large rock and was smiling at her.

Diana walked toward him, her face filled with honest enjoyment, damn her. "Truly, thank you for bringing me here. I am pleased you wanted to show it to me."

"Oh, there is much I intend to show you."

He grasped her suddenly about her waist and in one graceful movement hauled her over his thighs. Diana, stunned, was quiet, but just for a moment. She arched upward, turning her face upward. "Lyonel! What are—"

"Listen to me, Diana Savarol," he said, holding her down. "I told you once that I would beat you. What you did deserves more, but a good thrashing will just have to suffice, for the moment."

Her jaw dropped. "You mean you planned this?"

"Exactly. Quite well, as you now realize."

"But you cannot! It is ridiculous. Let me up at once!" She lurched wildly, and he realized he had quite a job cut out for him. He applied more strength, halting her wriggling. "Go ahead, yell, curse me, whatever you wish, you damned chit. It will do you no good."

It was no easy task, but he finally managed to pull up the heavy velvet riding skirt. Lord, she was strong, he thought, now using all his strength to hold her down. He got the skirt and petticoat up to her waist and stared down at her flailing stockinged legs: the white garters that held them up were just above her knees, the smooth expanse of white thighs above. Her only covering was a thin cambric chemise. He brought the flat of his hand down on her buttocks.

Diana yelled and cursed him, and he laughed, bringing his hand down again. "Never again will you do such a despicable thing. Do you understand me, Diana?"

"I will throttle you, Lyonel Ashton! I will! Ow!"

He growled and jerked up the chemise, tearing it. He brought his hand down on her bare buttocks.

Diana felt the cold air on her bottom, realized that she was bare as the day she was born, and howled, in fury, humiliation, and pain. She arched her back up and kicked with her legs. His grip didn't loosen. "Stop, you damned bastard!"

Again he brought his hand down. Suddenly, his hand raised, he looked at her, really looked. Her bottom was beautiful, soft, and very white, save for the red imprints of his hand. He brought his hand down again, but this time he didn't hit her hard. His fingers rested against her soft flesh, then caressed her, cupping her and gently easing inward between her slightly parted thighs. His fingers brushed her woman's flesh.

Diana froze. Then she twisted frantically, a frightened cry bursting from her throat.

Lyonel came to his senses. He saw his hand, as if it were another man's hand, caressing her buttocks and thighs. He cursed, pulled down her chemise, and hauled her upright. He was breathing hard.

He jerked her around to face him. Her face was white, her eyes mirroring both confusion and outrage. She was furiously yanking her riding skirt down her legs.

"Damn you," he said, and pulled her against him. He kissed her, hard, then immediately gentled the pressure against her lips.

Diana didn't know what she felt. Pain from her burning bottom, a strange swirling sensation low in her belly, and a spurt of something she didn't understand as Lyonel's tongue pressed against her closed lips.

"You are a thorn in my side," he said. "Enough. I trust you have learned your lesson."

He released her suddenly, and she stumbled backward.

They stared at each other.

"You looked at me. You touched me."

He felt swamped with guilt, but he refused to allow her to see it. "I beat you first. You deserved it. And don't get up in your maidenly arms, Diana. I have seen many ladies' bottoms. Yours is quite acceptable, but nothing—"

Diana, quick as a snake, brought up her knee and kicked him in the groin, hard.

He sucked in his breath, knowing that the agony would come, and dropped to his knees like a stone. waves of pain and nausea flooded him. He clutched his arms around his belly.

Diana stared down at him, breathing hard. She'd never before kicked a man there, and she was shocked at the result. His face was white with pain.

"I hate you," she said, whirled about, and ran from him.

It took Lyonel a few more minutes to control the pain and clear his head. He was furious, so furious he could throttle her. He rose to his feet, saw her struggling with the mare's reins. He smiled and whistled. The mare perked up her ears at the sound, reared onto her hind legs, and calmly pulled away from Diana.

Diana whirled about and yelled, "Damn you!" She saw him coming toward her. She'd wanted to mount the mare and ride away, taking his stallion with her. But it wasn't to be. "I was born under an unlucky star," she said, and releasing the recalcitrant mare's reins, she fled in the other direction.

Lyonel was quickly gaining on her. She turned, lost her footing on the slippery grass at the edge of the incline, and went down on her aching bottom. She rolled and slid, crying out, trying to grab at something, anything.

Lyonel watched her roll into the stream. There was a loud splash and a fan of water sprayed outward.

He wasn't at all worried. The water was only a couple feet deep. He stood at the edge of the incline, his arms crossed over his chest, and watched her thrash about.

Diana felt so angry, so very humiliated, she wanted to cry. She finally managed to pull herself upright. Her velvet skirts were like heavy weights, and her riding boots were squashing in the thick layer of mud at the stream bottom. She looked up and saw Lyonel standing there, legs spread, hands on his hips. He was laughing.

She yelled the most vile curse she could think of at him.

He laughed harder.

She swiped away a slimy water weed that was falling over her face, and struggled back toward the shore. She quickly discovered that her heavy skirts had an affinity for the slippery water grass. She fell to her knees, trying with all her strength to pull herself up the incline. She was nearly there. Then she felt her feet slipping. Once again she slid back into the water on her stomach.

And all she could hear was Lyonel's laughter.

She was making an amazing fool of herself. Stop, you idiot, and think! She did. Without hesitation, she unfastened the heavy velvet skirt and pulled herself out of it. She rolled it into a ball and threw it onto the bank. Her riding jacket followed the skirt. Then her riding boots. Clad only in her petticoat, chemise, and thin lawn blouse, she managed to crawl out of the water and up the incline.

She remained on her knees a moment, her head lowered, panting with exertion.

She looked up to see his riding boots. She reached out to grab him by his ankles. But Lyonel was faster and beyond her reach in an instant.

"You try that again, dear Diana, and I will throw you back in the water." His groin still ached. He meant every word he said.

"I hate you."

"Talk about being repetitious. You begin to sound like a half-wit. Of course, but you are a woman."

"I will get you for this, Lyonel Ashton. I swear it."

"Perhaps you will try. First, my dear, why don't you get dressed? You do look rather ridiculous, you know."

Actually, he thought, she looked endearingly pitiful, if such a thing was possible. Her thick hair was streaming down her back and over her shoulders. Her bountiful bosom was clearly outlined against the thin material of her blouse, her nipples taut from the cold. He felt a stirring in his still-aching groin. Damn her.

He gave her a mocking bow. "I shall give you privacy to, er, compose yourself. I will await you by *my* horses."

He heard her say something, but couldn't make out her words. Curses at him, he imagined. He turned his back and walked away from her. She would try to do him in, he knew, and a smile touched his lips. He wondered what she would try next. She'd very nearly caught him. He supposed that if she had, he would have thrashed her again, in the water.

Five minutes later, Diana emerged, sodden and bedraggled, but clothed again.

"I wish I had a blanket, to protect Venus. I do hope she doesn't get ill from having you wet on her back."

Diana said nothing. She had cursed herself out. She just wanted to go back to London, retreat to her bedchamber, and plan how to bring this damned scoundrel to his knees again.

That thought made her smile.

Lyonel, accurately guessing what caused that smile, said, "Any further attempts to destroy my manhood and I will beat you silly."

Her chin went up.

"I will tie you down and beat you silly."

Her eyes glittered murder at him.

"I will take off all your clothes, tie you down, and beat you silly."

"You, my lord, are a loudmouthed bully."

"Indeed, I shall much enjoy seeing your breasts. Comparisons, you know, are most interesting. But trust me to ensure that you are not cold. I wish to see if your nipples tauten with me looking at them.''

She gaped at him, shocked to the soles of her wet riding boots. Her eyes flew to his face, more green than gray now.

He felt so guilty at his unmeasured words that he quickly said, ''Get onto your horse. I wish to return to London and relieve myself of your damned company.''

Diana tried to mount Venus, but her wet boots slipped. Finally, after her third try, she leaned her face against the mare's neck and burst into tears.

She heard Lyonel curse, but she didn't care. She felt his hands close about her waist, and stiffened, trying to pull away.

''Dammit, hold still.'' He lifted her onto her mare's back. ''Lord, you're heavy. Those ridiculous skirts must weigh two stone. So women are weaklings. You can't take your medicine, huh? You must shower me with tears.''

Diana didn't wait for him to mount his stallion. She turned Venus and slammed her heels into the mare's sides. She wasn't really surprised to hear Lyonel's whistle.

Venus came to an abrupt halt.

''You hurt my horse and I will thrash you again. Now, pretend you're a lady, for once.''

Diana looked at him. ''I hope you are worthless to your mistress.''

''A little harder kick on your part and I just might have been. I shall tell her the story tonight when I see her.''

''See her?''

''Yes, indeed. Comparisons, you know. She very much likes for me to stroke her buttocks.''

Diana could find no words. No one had ever spoken to her like this. No one. She stared at him.

"Come along," Lyonel said. He had never in his life known another person who could make him lose all control. This damned twit made him say the most outrageous things, damnation, *do* the most outrageous things.

Diana got many curious looks. She kept her eyes straight between her mare's ears. Her back ached from holding herself rigid. She was aware that Lyonel was riding beside her, his face a study in calm disinterest.

When they finally reached Lucia's town house, Lyonel quickly dismounted, lifted Diana down from the mare's back, and said, "I can't wait to hear from Lucia what tale you tell her. Get inside. And good-bye, Diana. I trust you have learned your lesson well. A lady doesn't eavesdrop."

He didn't wait, merely mounted his stallion and rode away, leading the mare.

To his chagrin, Lyonel found himself worrying about her. Her lips had been nearly blue when they'd reached London. He winced at the ache in his groin and forced any more worries about her from his mind. He didn't visit Lois that evening.

He brooded.

"Most odd," Titwiller said to Kenworthy, casting his eyes upward, ostensibly at the earl's bedchamber.

"None of your affair," said Kenworthy. "Leave his lordship be."

But Kenworthy himself wondered and worried. His lordship was behaving most peculiarly. Yes, indeed. He knew, knew in his innermost thoughts, that his lordship was thinking about that Miss Savarol. He had taken her to Richmond today, Kenworthy had gotten that much from his lordship's groom, Teddy. What the devil had happened?

Lucia didn't screech at the sight of her bedraggled guest. She stared. She happened to be walking down the corridor when Diana was opening the door of her bedchamber.

Diana didn't want to see or talk to anyone. She wanted to dry herself, hide, and plot Lyon's downfall.

"My dear," Lucia finally managed, "whatever happened?"

The truth, at least some of it, Diana decided. "I fell into a stream near Richmond."

"I see," said Lucia, who didn't see anything. "I shall have Betsy fetch you hot water for a nice bath. Quickly, child, get out of those wet clothes. Where is Lyonel?"

Diana tensed from head to toe. "I haven't the faintest idea."

"He is not waiting downstairs?"

"Perhaps he is lying dead this moment, run over by a carriage. Or shot dead by a person he has hurt."

"Diana!"

Diana shivered, and Lucia quickly said, "Go, child. We will speak of this later."

She immediately sent Jamison with a message to Lyonel.

There was a reply, a very short note that said only, "Speak to Diana. Certainly she will tell you a tale."

But Diana told no tale, no matter how Lucia prodded. She was too humiliated. That evening she and Lucia attended a ball at Lady Marchpane's.

Although the evening was warm, the ballroom stifling, Diana was chilled. She dismissed the weakness.

She danced and flirted, and each compliment from a gentleman was balm to her miserable soul.

Lyonel strolled in with the Earl of March near eleven o'clock. His first view of Diana made him grind his teeth. She was laughing like a damned coquette at a doubtless inane comment from Sir Harvey Plummer.

"Lovely girl," said Julian St. Clair, Earl of March, following Lyonel's grim look. "Why don't you introduce me?"

"I will kill her first," Lyonel said.

The Earl of March merely chuckled. "She is very lively, is she not?" he asked, his look goading in the extreme.

"She is a miserable thorn in my hide," said Lyonel. "Come, let us have some of Lady Marchpane's dreadful champagne punch."

"As you like, old man," said the earl. "I do believe old Plummer just kissed the young lady's wrist. Can't imagine why she would allow that. Perhaps you should speak to her, Lyon."

Lyon wasn't a fool. He knew that Julian was well aware of Diana's name and her relationship to him and to Lucia. He said nothing, refusing the earl's dangling bait.

The earl found himself grinning not a half-hour later when he saw Lyon intercept Diana Savarol. His friend was furious, no doubt about that. Interesting, the earl thought. Yes, indeed, very interesting.

8

If fortune turns against you, even jelly breaks your tooth.

PERSIAN PROVERB

"Your face," Lyon said, glaring down at her, "is as red as a poppy. What was that ass saying to you?"

"Good evening, my lord. Which ass? The one over there or the one now speaking to me?"

"Push me, Diana, and you will feel my hand on your bottom again, I swear it."

"Push you, my lord? I am merely trying to make my way to Aunt Lucia. What is it you want?"

"I want you to stay away from that fool, Plummer, and his wet mouth. My God, why did you let him kiss your wrist? The inside of your wrist?"

Because I knew you were watching and I wanted to enrage you.

"His mouth isn't at all wet."

Lyon briefly saw red. "As for your gown, you are in danger of falling out of it. I can't imagine that Lucia would let you out of the house looking like that."

His eyes were on her bosom and Diana drew herself even straighter, even though it hurt to do so. She ached all over. Oddly, there were two of Lyon standing in front of her, each blurred. She blinked rapidly, clearing her vision, but now aware of a growing pain over her left ear. She shivered. What the devil was wrong with her? She'd never been ill a day in her life, save for that brief fever she'd had as a child. She remembered now the awful chills and how heavy she had felt, how helpless.

"So much of you is on display," Lyonel continued, warming to his subject, "you will surely take a cold."

"Will you keep me here in the middle of the dance floor, my lord? Displaying myself?"

"Damn you," he said, grasped her wrist, the one that Plummer had kissed, and led her in a waltz.

Diana admitted now that she was ill. She was feeling very hot now, but she knew that soon she would feel so cold her teeth would chatter. Her head hurt, her throat felt scratchy. And her body felt so very heavy, just as it had felt when she'd had that fever as a child.

Lyon looked down into her glittering, overbright eyes and was suspicious. "You do know that you cannot knee me in the middle of a waltz," he said.

"No, I shan't do that." She must find Lucia and leave before she disgraced herself.

He whirled her about at that moment, and Diana felt the room spin. It didn't right itself and she fell against Lyon. "What the devil is the matter with you? Are you trying to start the tongues wagging again?"

She heard his voice as if from a great distance. "Lyon," she said, "please, I don't feel well."

For the first time in her life, Diana fainted.

Lyon stood in the middle of the ballroom floor, holding her against his chest, his face a picture of chagrin.

Oh, God.

He hauled her into his arms, all too aware of the surprise and growing consternation surrounding them. He saw Julian St. Clair and called to him. "Tell Lucia that Diana is ill. Have her carriage fetched immediately."

Lady Marchpane was aghast and titillated that such a dramatic event took place in her ballroom. She fluttered about Lord Saint Leven, offering no assistance, just disjointed comments on Miss Savarol's pallor.

"Lady Cranston and I will see to her," he said over his shoulder. He was acutely aware of her limp body in his arms, of the poppy-red cheeks that now he realized meant a fever, not coquettish behavior. God, it was his fault. All of it. He was frightened and could feel himself shaking.

"She told me she fell into a stream," Lucia said. "Dear God, I thought she was all right. She was so excited about the ball, so insistent that we come. Quickly, Lyon, let's get her home."

Lyon didn't release her once in Lucia's carriage. He held her close, instructing Lucia to throw the carriage blanket over her. He tucked it firmly around her.

Diana moaned and he froze, his eyes meeting Lucia's.

"I should never have let her talk me into this ball," Lucia said. She swore like a trooper but Lyonel wasn't even tempted to laugh. "It was that fall into a stream. How did it happen, Lyonel?"

"She is burning up," said Lyon, his hand pressing against her cheek.

"It is my fault," said Lucia, her face parchment pale in the dim carriage light.

"No," Lyonel said, "none of it is your fault. Who is your doctor, Lucia? We will send Jamison for him immediately."

Diana burrowed into the warmth, but she couldn't stop the awful cold. It was deep inside her, and it hurt so badly. She realized she was being carried, but she couldn't make herself react. She heard voices, one of them Lyon's, and he sounded so very curt, like a general giving orders to his soldiers.

More voices. Was that Didier? No, he never raised his voice, never did anything that would reflect poorly on his dignity.

Hands were on her, pulling off her clothes, and she fought them, instinctively. Soothing voices. Lucia? Grumber?

She forced herself outward and stared up into the face of a strange man. He looked like the painting of a bird she had seen once, so thin, his neck ridiculously long. She said aloud, very clearly, "You are a stork?"

Dr. McComber laughed and patted her cheek. "No, miss, I'm just a fellow who is going to try to make you feel better. Now, you just hold still."

"I hurt," she said, and knew that her voice sounded like a confused child's.

"Yes, I imagine that you do. Tell me exactly where you hurt."

But she couldn't seem to speak a complete thought, just words. The stork nodded, as if satisfied.

"Lyon," she whispered.

"You want another animal with the stork?"

"Lyonel," she repeated.

Dr. McComber turned in question to Lucia.

"I'll get him," she said. She found him striding up and down the corridor, his head lowered, his hands thrust in his breeches' pockets.

"Diana wants you."

"Is she all right, Lucia? What does McComber say?"

"I don't know as yet."

Lyon walked very quickly toward the bed. McComber rose and blinked at him. "How is she?"

There was a small cry from the bed.

Lyon didn't wait for an answer. He eased down gently beside Diana and took her hand. Her eyes were closed, her breathing labored.

"I don't understand," he said. "She cried. Why did she cry?"

"She doesn't know she's crying, my lord. She is unconscious."

"What is wrong with her?"

"I should say that she could move into pneumonia, but we will hope not. Her ladyship informs me that she fell into a stream near Richmond and rode all the way back to London in wet clothes."

Lyonel cursed and McComber stared at him. "What are you doing for her?"

McComber shrugged. "There is nothing much to be done, my lord. Hot cloths on her chest, alcohol rubs to keep down the fever. Laudanum periodically for the pain."

It had to be asked. "Will she survive this?"

"She's a strong girl. She will have excellent nursing. I don't know."

To Lyonel's shock, Lucia, the indominable old tartar, began sobbing.

He enfolded her in his arms, soothing her.

Suddenly, from the bed, "Lyon! No!"

He spun about and rushed back to the bed. She wasn't conscious but she was thrashing about, her hair becoming wildly tangled about her head. "No! Don't you dare! I hate you!"

Lyon grasped her hands in his. She was staring at him, her eyes wide, but she didn't see him. "Diana," he said, leaning close to her face, "listen to me. You will be all right. Do you understand me? You will pull through this. Damn you, you will get well again."

Dr. McComber said in a lowered voice to Lucia, "Is Lord Saint Leven her betrothed?"

Lucia knew Lyonel could hear them. She said clearly, "Not as yet. They are quite close. They much enjoy arguing."

"More like brother and sister," Lyonel said, his voice loud and harsh. He turned back to Diana. "Listen to me, you little twit, you will be all right. I will thrash you but good if you are not."

She laughed, he knew it.

It sounded to Dr. McComber like an odd moan. He stared at the man who had just threatened his patient with a beating. Little twit! Not at all a brotherly remark.

"You look awful."

Lyon started and come awake in an instant. Diana was gazing at him, her eyes clear, her voice a low croak. He grinned at her. "You should see yourself, my girl."

"What are you doing here? Goodness, I am in bed. Surely this is most improper, Lyon."

"Shut up, Diana. You have been very ill, for three days. Your fever broke last night. If you ever scare me like that again, I will—"

"Beat me?"

Mrs. Bailey, the nurse, stood all ears near the fireplace. It was quite too much to have a gentleman camped in the young lady's bedchamber, but to have him sitting on her bed, trading insults! She quickly moved forward. "I shall go fetch Dr. McComber for Miss Savarol."

"You do that," said Lyon, not looking at her.

"Damned interfering besom," he added under his breath.

"What is a besom?"

"Well, actually it means a broom, you know, an old one made of twigs tied together. I meant it as a witch."

"You need to shave."

"You need to do other things, but not shave at least."

She smiled. If her nose didn't lie, she much needed to bathe. "Have you stayed here?"

"Yes, every bloody hour." It had been horrendous, particularly the second night, when he was certain she would die, her breathing was so labored, her fever so very high. "How do you feel, honestly?"

Diana was silent a moment, querying her body. "It hurts just a bit to breathe. I ache and my voice sounds odd. Other than that, I am ready to waltz with you."

"Let's wait for a week, all right?"

"Well, how is my patient?"

"Who are you?"

"I am your doctor, Miss Savarol. Name of McComber. Now, my lord, if I could get you to move aside, just a bit, I would like to examine my patient."

Lyon moved, just a bit. Diana held to his hand as if it were a lifeline.

He watched the doctor's hand move beneath her night-gown to her chest. Odd how that angered him. It shouldn't, for God's sake. I am becoming a half-wit, he thought, and shook his head at himself.

As for Diana, she was too shocked to move. Lyon quickly said, "It's all right. Just hold still. Dr. McComber will be through in just a moment."

Dr. McComber leaned his head against her breast and listened. "Clear," he said, smiling. "At last. You had me worried, young lady. You are very strong and didn't go into pneumonia as I had feared. But you must rest." He shot a look toward Lord Saint Leven. "You will see to it, my lord?"

"Certainly," said Lyon. He realized at that moment that he was committed. To what? He drew his hand away from Diana's and stepped away. "If she is all right now, I shall take myself off. You will do as the doctor tells you, Diana."

With those words, he left the bedchamber, not looking back.

"I don't believe I understand," said Dr. McComber, frowning at Lord Saint Leven's retreating back.

"He feels guilty," said Diana. "That is all. Just guilty."

"Why should he feel guilt?"

He thrashed me and I kicked him in the groin and I tried to escape on the mare and when I couldn't I fell into the stream.

"He was with me when I got wet."

"Not his fault, I don't suppose."

"Certainly not."

Dr. McComber rose. "You will sleep now, Miss Savarol. Have you any more pain?"

Diana shook her head, suddenly exhausted.

The following day Lucia sent a message through Jamison to Lyonel's town house. There was no reply.

Lucia was angry. Damn and blast the stupid boy! Diana was being stubborn, recalcitrant, insulting to Mrs. Bailey, and altogether a miserable patient.

"Take her to the country, my lady," Dr. McComber said after a trying interview with Diana. She'd refused to let him touch her. The girl was a handful. He was pleased that she was so much better.

But when approached with this suggestion, Diana said to Lucia, "I want to go home. I will be strong enough in a couple of days. I want to go home."

Lucia, seeing that she was growing more and more upset, patted her hand, murmured soothing words, and left. When Lyon did not show himself that day or evening, she sent another message the following morning. This one, she thought, pleased, should get him here quickly enough.

She was smiling when Lyonel was announced some thirty minutes later.

"She is ill again?" were his first words.

"She will be if you don't do something."

"I do something? What is this about, Lucia?"

He still felt off balance at Lucia's cryptic message: "Diana is urgently agitating."

"She insists she wants to go home. Within the week."

"Don't be absurd," he said. "She is weak as a nearly drowned kitten—"

"How would you know?"

He cursed and Lucia merely gave him her patented gimlet-eyed look.

He left her and headed upstairs to Diana's bedchamber. Mrs. Bailey, the dragon, was there. Lyon said in his most imperious voice, "You may leave us now."

Mrs. Bailey knew what was proper and what wasn't, and drew herself up for battle.

"Now!"

That was a voice she couldn't bring herself to object to. "Very well, my lord. Ten minutes. Then Miss Savarol must rest."

Diana eyed Lyonel. When Mrs. Bailey had left the room, she said, "I must learn that tone. It is most effective."

She was still very pale, he thought, coming toward the bed. But she looked wonderful. Her thick hair was brushed and plaited in a fat braid over her shoulder. Her eyes were clear, her look baleful.

"I hear you are urgently agitating."

Diana blinked, then laughed, but it came out as a hoarse rasping sound.

"I also hear you are being a complete and utter idiot."

"How could you hear anything? You haven't been here."

"Lucia sent me a message through the ubiquitous Jamison that you were at death's door again, or rather profoundly agitating. So you want to go home, do you?"

The chin went up. "Yes."

"Well, you aren't going anywhere, do you understand me, you silly twit?"

"You have no say in the matter, do you hear me, you damned arrogant dandy?"

"The next time I thrash you I will ensure that you aren't so clumsy that you fall into any water. Indeed, I will make certain that there isn't any water within ten miles."

Lucia, listening at the door, smiled. Had her proud and gentlemanly Lyonel actually thrashed her? Excellent, she thought. Now she just had to keep Mrs. Bailey away.

"You try that again and I shall make you useless to your damned little amour!"

"Oh, yes? You are so weak you couldn't even give a decent showing of yourself. You would probably start weeping and wailing and faint on me. Again."

"I hate you, you miserable—"

"Don't start that old refrain again, Diana. Leave to go home!" he added in disgust. "Haven't you an ounce of sense?"

"I do not weep or wail."

"Well, you surely faint, and you chose your setting with maximum exposure. In the middle of a ballroom."

"I wouldn't have if you hadn't suddenly whirled me about like some stupid dervish."

"I can hear the gossip now," he said, ignoring her. "You are doubtless with child, my child, and your fainting exhibition was due to your condition."

"That is absurd," she said, her teeth clicking together.

"It most certainly is, but your performance . . . Oh, damnation, why couldn't you have collapsed with that Plummer ass?"

Diana didn't reply, and Lyonel, his tongue wrapped about more lovely words, paused and looked at her closely.

She had become alarmingly pale. He'd done it again. He said more to himself than to her, "Why must I cut up at you every time I see you?"

"I don't know."

"I'm sorry, Diana. Please, rest now."

"You are leaving again?"

He frowned. "No, I will stay. If I do leave, I promise to come back. You must, I suppose, have someone available to vent your spleen upon."

He leaned down and lightly kissed her pale cheek. "Sleep, you little twit."

"Lyonel?"

"Hmmm?"

"Do you really think of me as a sister?"

That brought him up short. "I wouldn't know. I don't have a sister. That is, I did have a sister, but she died when she was just a child."

"You don't still feel guilty, do you?"

"Yes. How can I not feel guilty?"

"Your guilt doesn't show in your insults."

"I am made of stern stuff, Diana. Sleep now."

Oddly enough, she was asleep within ten minutes.

As for Lyonel, he kicked a chair in the drawing room. "You want me to what?" he said to Lucia, his eye on the hapless chair that now lay on its side.

9

Better to trip with the feet than with the tongue.

ZENO OF CITIUM

"I said," Lucia repeated, wondering at the cause of Lyonel's sudden loss of control, "that as soon as Diana is fit, we will go to your estate in Yorkshire. You should take care, my chair and your foot are most valuable."

"That is absurd," he said.

"Really, Lyonel, your clumsiness isn't at all absurd. I have never seen you clumsy before. As for my chair, it belonged to my grandmother and—"

"It's ugly and I wasn't clumsy. I kicked it. What is absurd is your idea of using me as Diana's nursemaid at *my* estate. If the chit needs the country air, I will escort the both of you to *your* estate in Yorkshire. You know very well, Lucia, what everyone would say if we went to Ashton Hall." He paused a moment when she said nothing, then continued, "Ah, you are really up to it this time, are you not? The parson's mousetrap for me, isn't that right? I am sorry not to oblige you, Lucia. I have no intention of marrying . . . anyone."

"Why did you thrash Diana?"

"Because she was eavesdropping and I caught her at it. Her upbringing leaves much to be desired." His eyebrows lowered. "So she told you, did she?"

"No," Lucia said mildly, "I eavesdropped."

He raised his eyes upward. "The Almighty save me from meddlesome women."

"What did she hear? Whom were you with?"

As there was no reply from upward, Lyon turned his eyes toward Lucia. "I was giving my ultimatums to Charlotte, if you would know the truth. Dear Diana got quite an earful."

"Ah."

"Yes, ah," said Lyon. "Is there anything else you would like to know? I would spare you the indignity of eavesdropping in the future."

"Actually, yes. I have wondered why Charlotte played you false before she was safely married to you."

"I asked her that. She just gave me a look and said she'd been stupid."

"Interesting. You know, it is most odd," said Lucia thoughtfully after a moment. Lyon waited impatiently, knowing he wouldn't like what she was thinking. "I have no idea what Diana wants to do with her life."

That was unexpected, but Lyon had learned to be wary when Lucia slid so easily from one subject to the next. He shrugged. "She is a young lady, ripe for marriage. Why should she want anything differently than most ladies want? A husband, a family. Isn't that why her father sent her to London? To find a husband?"

"Yes, but he had the good sense not to tell Diana that was his plan."

"She doesn't want a husband? A rich one? Come, Lucia, that notion is most difficult to knead into bread."

"If Charlotte knew how much influence her actions had on you, my boy, I fancy she would be most surprised. Probably very pleased that she could bring Lord Saint Leven to this pass. You have become a cynic, Lyonel. It is not at all flattering."

Lyon yawned.

"You need to have your ears cuffed, my boy."

Anything but my manhood, Lyonel started to say. He grinned at her. "Dear Lucia, forgive me. You were saying?"

"I was wondering what Diana wants to do with her life. She is truly not at all interested in marriage. If I bring it up, she quickly finds something to do or some other subject to talk about." That wasn't exactly true, but she wanted to see Lyonel's reaction.

"Perhaps she is just young for her age." Not physically young, though. "Very well, what is she interested in, Lucia?"

"I am not certain. Knowledge, experiences . . . I believe she views marriage as lacking in both those elements. Sort of the end rather than a beginning. A ride to the guillotine in a trumbril, perhaps."

"That is immense foolishness. Why, I—"

"I know, my boy. You wanted a wife, a home, children. I believe that you could teach her that a marriage based on love and respect is the most incredible experience a human being can have. Life is so deuced short. When one is young, it seems it will go on forever. Ah, well, I suppose you will do as you please."

"Leave her be. Leave me be."

"I received a letter from Lucien Savarol this morning."

"So?"

"I am not so certain I should tell Diana of it just yet. It might upset her."

"More of your damned plots? Oh, very well, why should the chit be upset?"

"Lucien has remarried. A widow from St. Thomas. She has a grown son. No, I shan't tell her."

"If she isn't a selfish brat, she will be pleased that her father has found someone else."

"Her father suggests—and I well imagine that it is his new wife's idea—that Diana remain here a while longer. He asks me directly about her matrimonial prospects."

"As you have said, she isn't at all interested, which is a relief, since she appears to attract all the wrong sort. Take Plummer, for example. Good Lord, what an idiot! Then there is Mortimer Fortesque, I shudder to think of him and that fool cousin of his—"

"You don't have to recite all their names, my boy. Just look about at all the posies. Lord Brackenridge has roses sent from his hothouse in Surrey each day."

"Brackenridge! Surely you will discourage that poseur. He wants nothing more than a mother for his four children, a housekeeper, and someone to warm his bed. Why, he would treat her like a damned brood mare."

"But he already has four children, as you said."

"He wouldn't be able to keep his hands off Diana. You know as well as I that once he got her in bed, he would—" He broke off, furious with himself.

"Perhaps," said Lucia, studying this reaction with great interest. "But he is most assiduous in his attentions."

"Diana isn't a fool. For her sake, keep the man away, Lucia."

"If she returns home, I wonder what will happen to her?"

"Surely there are appropriate gentlemen, even there, if the chit ever decides to test the waters. Now, Lucia, I am off. Diana is sleeping. I will be back this afternoon to see her.''

''Where are you off to?''

He gave her a nasty grin, wanting to poke a hole in her blasted confidence. ''I think I shall pay a visit to my mistress. I have not been overly assiduous lately in my, er, attentions.''

''I hope you will not catch some vile disease.''

''I am not a fool, Lucia.''

''About Diana convalescing in the country—''

''Do as you please, Lucia, just leave me out of it.''

She watched him stride from her drawing room. She was not at all cast down. Indeed, she was fascinated with his contorted efforts at remaining immune to Diana. She would, she decided, grinning shamelessly, leave him out of it, at least for the moment.

Lyonel did visit Lois and was sweetly received. He took her to bed immediately and found to his relief that his body responded as it should, evidently receiving no paralyzing messages from his brain. He gave her a bracelet and prepared to leave.

''My lord?''

He was buttoning his shirt. ''Hmm?''

''I have missed you. Could you not remain with me awhile? I have been a bit lonely.''

''No,'' he said, pulling on his coat, not without some difficulty. ''I'm sorry, Lois, but a relative of mine is ill. I have promised to visit her.''

''Miss Savarol?''

More meddlesome women, he thought. ''Yes,'' he said evenly. ''How did you know?''

''My maid. Her cousin is a parlor maid in the March-panes' household. She heard the lady speaking of it.''

"And what report did you hear?"

"That Miss Savarol fainted in your arms in the middle
of the ballroom. That her illness seemed most strange."

Evidently Lois hadn't received an update from her maid.

Lyon could easily guess everyone's initial reaction. He
supposed when he'd mentioned to Diana that gossip could
begin that she was with child, he had known it as a real
possibility. Charlotte was indeed on her way to Cornwall,
so she couldn't be responsible, though he imagined it
wasn't beyond her to add some damaging speculation before she left. He sighed, wishing the aristocracy had something positive to discuss rather than possible fellow-human
failings. Then again, he could not but be aware that anyone with a grain of perception could see the tension between him and Diana. The devil, should he wear a placard
announcing that the wretched tension between them had
nothing to do with sex? On the heels of that thought, he
knew he was lying to himself, and he cursed softly.

"The girl, Miss Savarol, was very ill. She was lucky
she didn't go into pneumonia. She is now on the mend. Do
pass that along to your maid."

Lois regarded her lover and protector. She liked him.
He was generous and he was kind. He knew a woman's
body and enjoyed a woman's pleasure. Had he seduced
this Miss Savarol? She didn't as yet understand him well
enough to know if he was that sort of man, but she
doubted it. He certainly possessed the masculine charms to
bring a woman about to his thinking if that was his
purpose. She said, knowing it an impertinence, "Then she
isn't with child."

"As I said, she nearly contracted pneumonia. I would
prefer that you not gossip, Lois. It does not please me."

He'd spoken softly, gently, but Lois wasn't fooled. He

was angry. He cared for this Miss Savarol. "No, my lord, I won't, not anymore. Please forgive me."

Lyon wondered in that moment how he would react if Diana spoke to him in that sweet, apologetic tone, her eyes slightly lowered, showing her respect for him, her deference. I should live so long, he thought.

"Very well," he said. He strode to the bed, eyed her plentiful breasts one final time, and lightly kissed her cheek. "I will see you soon, my dear."

His body had responded nicely, he thought as he strolled down the street some minutes later. But unwanted flashes of Diana's beautiful buttocks had leapt into his mind. And the movement of his own hand and fingers caressing her . . . and her thighs, slightly parted, giving him access to . . .

"Damned twit," he said, and walked faster, to keep pace with his rather erratic breathing.

He discovered quickly that there was no need to mention that Diana's illness had been in her chest and not the result of a babe in her womb. Her admirers, those constant visitors with all their damned posies, had already seen to it. He smiled sourly to himself.

"I will not go," Diana said firmly to Lucia. "I do not need to recuperate in the country, much less at Lyon's estate."

Now it was Lyon's turn to eavesdrop. He stood listening outside Diana's bedchamber door. It did not occur to him, even for an instant, to remove himself from that door. It was odd, but he was at once relieved and disappointed that she was refusing to go to the country. He heard Lucia's voice, but could only make out something about his, Lyon's, concern for her.

"The last thing Lyon wants is to have to drag me off to

his estate," Diana continued in a louder voice. "It was not his fault that I caught a rather nasty chill. Aunt, he doesn't like me, truly he doesn't. He wants nothing to do with me."

That, strangely, angered him. Of course she knew that he had stayed hours beside her bed, sweating, worrying, wishing he could take her place, breathe for her, take her in his arms to warm her? He strode into the bedchamber without a knock to see Diana, propped up against three pillows, her cheeks flushed.

"That is not exactly true," he said. "Leave her be, Lucia. She will just make herself ill again if you keep nagging at her."

"What isn't exactly true?" Lucia asked.

"That I dislike her."

"Would you please stop talking around me, Lyon? I am here, you know."

"Very well. I don't dislike you, Diana. However, you know as well as I do that it would be most unwise for me to be your host at my estate. Lucia is meddling."

"I have no intention of going to your estate. If you think I should enjoy you as a host, you are sorely mistaken. I am going home."

"You are going no place until you are well again."

"I will be perfectly myself again by next Monday. Lucia, you will please find me a chaperone for my trip home? You did promise."

"I find that 'perfectly myself' is a most odd contradiction in your case, Diana."

"Oh, be quiet!"

Lyon was quiet. He continued to upset her, and now wasn't the time. He didn't want her ill again.

To his surprise, Lucia capitulated. "Very well, my

dear. If you must insist upon returning to your father, I shall make the arrangements.''

"Lucia, I am not certain that—''

"Shut up, Lyon! It is not any of your affair!''

"It certainly is,'' he said. Then, to his own immense chagrin and surprise, he added, ''I shall be accompanying you. And you will stay in bed for as long as Dr. McComber tells you to. I don't want to have to nurse you aboard some idiot ship.''

Lucia said not a word. Diana stared at him as if he'd gained three extra kings in his deck of cards.

"Oh, for heaven's sake,'' he said, throwing up his hands, ''I might as well accede to Oliver Mendenhall's wishes. I will go there, see to my inherited plantation, and then come home. That is all there is to it.''

"Of course,'' said Lucia in her blandest voice.

"I also find that London doesn't much amuse me at present. A brief change of scene will be beneficial. You know, Lucia. New experiences, new knowledge.''

"What about your little amour?'' Diana said, her voice laced with mockery. ''She no longer amuses you?''

"Not a single new experience,'' said Lyon.

"How very tedious, for both of you.''

"Really, Diana, a lady doesn't know about such things!''

"Aunt, what you mean is I should be willing to accept such awful behavior from gentlemen and keep my mouth closed? Pretend even that gentlemen don't indulge in such behavior?''

"Exactly,'' said Lyon. ''But I am beginning to despair of your behavior. Now, look at yourself. You're flushed again. For heaven's sake, stop getting so excited.'' His inadvertent words immediately brought images of Diana, naked, moaning in his arms, those endless beautiful legs of hers again slightly parted, and he flushed. He said, furious at himself, ''As for this so-called awful behavior from gentlemen, I would suggest that ladies indulge their lust just as freely.''

''Well, I haven't!''

''Doubtless you will. As soon as you manage to trap an unsuspecting gentleman, you—''. He broke off, took a deep breath, but before he could continue more calmly, Diana said, her color high, ''Trap a gentleman! Why would a self-respecting female want to trap one of you fools? If the gentlemen I have met thus far are a fair example—and that includes you, my lord—I should rather become fish bait.''

He managed now to find that calm voice, once so much a part of him and sadly in absence since Diana's arrival. He even managed to look amused. ''Fish bait? But of course you are right. Do forgive me for ranting at you. Get the chit well, Lucia. I will accompany her back to her father.''

As he strode from the bedchamber, he heard her mutter to Lucia, ''Good heavens, Aunt, I don't even know what lust is.''

He smiled, he couldn't help himself. He toyed with the idea of teaching Diana all about lust. ''I am not yet completely lost,'' he said to himself.

Lyonel spent the next several days getting his affairs in order. His stay in the West Indies would probably keep him from England for a good three or four months. He wanted nothing to go wrong in his absence. Perhaps he would be gone longer; better to plan for all contingencies.

As for Diana, after three days she was allowed to receive visitors in the drawing room with Lucia her watch-dog. To each gentleman who came to see her, she sweetly informed him that she was returning home. Not another posie came from Brackenridge upon that announcement.

When the ladies visited, they seemed most interested in her symptoms and subsequent diagnosis. Unlike Lucia, she wondered why they should be so downcast that she should have suffered such a nasty illness.

"I tell you, Mabel," said Lady Doncaster as they took their leave, "there is something between the girl and Lord Saint Leven. One has but to look at them when they are together. Did you not hear that he will accompany her back to the West Indies?"

"She'll be in the family way soon enough, I wager," said Mabel. "I would also wager that when she and Lord Saint Leven return to England, doubtless as husband and wife, she will be carrying a child on her shoulder."

Meanwhile at White's, the Earl of March was saying gently to a furious Lyon, "You see, Lyon, the tabbies really would rather believe Charlotte, her rendition is far more titillating than the truth. Surely you know this, old fellow. Why am I wasting my valuable insights?"

"It is most unfair to Miss Savarol," said Lyon, mouthing the sentiment, but deep down thinking it was more unfair to him.

"Look at the caliber of gentlemen pursuing her. Unfortunately, many gentlemen are also tabbies."

"I told her in no uncertain terms that none of them would do. She is not stupid, you know, Julian. Indeed, she felt not a whit of anything for any of them."

"Why are you returning with her?"

"I don't know. I opened my mouth and said the words. I really don't know."

Julian could have ventured a fairly accurate guess, but he held his peace, saying only, "When do you intend to depart?"

"If Diana continues her recovery at such an impressive clip, I should say we can leave next week. Lucia is busily lining up a family to chaperone on the voyage.'' He grinned at Julian. ''Perhaps upon my return I shall find you no longer a bachelor.''

''I doubt that most sincerely,'' said the Earl of March. He rather thought Miss Diana Savarol a most delightful female. He guessed his friend's bachelor days were numbered. As for himself, there was no shining star on his horizon.

Diana looked through the carriage window at the bustle of Plymouth. She had landed at Southampton at her arrival in England. Plymouth, on the other hand, was more exciting, more alive, more earthy, she supposed, like Road Town harbor. There was constant noise and movement. Sweaty, vigorous human smells, and the salty air filled her nostrils.

''We are to meet Lord and Lady Tomlinson here at the Drake,'' said Lyon, opening the carriage door when they halted.

''Yes, I know.''

He helped her down, thinking she still looked just a bit peaked. ''You need to gain flesh,'' he said, his eyes roving over her. Unfortunately they stopped their brief journey at her bosom.

''Not there,'' she said, her voice acid. ''I never lose flesh there.''

He grinned. ''Thank heaven for something.'' Her eyes lost their greenness and became a stark gray. He raised his hand in surrender, forestalling a comment undoubtedly destined to burn his ears.

''Come along, let's see if your chaperones have arrived.''

Odd, Diana thought as she trailed him into the century-old inn, but she was already missing Lucia. Even the dour Grumber she missed. She pictured Didier, looking so very leonine as he sat at the piano pounding out a waltz, his long, narrow foot tapping to the beat. The old monk—he was a rock.

"I beg your pardon?"

She came closer when she heard Lyon's incredulous words to the innkeeper.

"I said, milord, that Milord Tomlinson sent a message that they would be late."

"How late?"

"Hopeful the message said, milord, to be here late Wednesday night."

"The boat sails on Thursday," said Lyon. "First tide in the morning."

The innkeeper spread his hands.

"Perhaps they will arrive tomorrow, Lyon," said Diana.

He was frowning, wondering what the devil to do.

"Come, now, surely you don't think we should simply give up and return to London?"

"Do you and your wife still wish a room, milord?"

"She is not my wife," said Lyon.

"Ah," said the innkeeper. He eyed the young lady and began to draw some most interesting conclusions.

"Look here," Lyon began, growing angry.

"No, 'tis not important," said Diana, touching his forearm.

He was still frowning as he turned away from the innkeeper. "I suppose we will simply wait," he said finally. "It would be ridiculous to return to London when they might arrive in time. Also, I don't wish to give rise to any more gossip."

"I am your cousin, of sorts. As a relative, surely you can escort me places without tongues wagging."

"Your naïveté never ceases to amaze me." He turned

back to the innkeeper before Diana could retort. "Very well. Two bedchambers and a private dining room."

"My regrets, milord. But we haven't one available."

"I understood that you would," Lyon said at his most imperious.

"My apologies, milord. But a Captain Rafael Carstairs requested the private parlor."

Lyon turned to Diana. "Are you willing to dine in your room, alone?"

She shrugged.

"Very well. See that a maid is sent to Miss Savarol's bedchamber."

It wasn't until ten minutes later that Diana discovered their bedchambers were adjoining. She was uncertain what to do. Obviously the innkeeper believed them to be closer than they were. Ha! That was a ludicrous thought! Lyon, drat him, had left the inn, doubtless to go exploring and enjoy himself.

She was tired, she admitted. She dismissed the young maid and lay on the bed. She was asleep within five minutes.

Lyon stood in the now open doorway between their bedchambers. The room was shadowy in the late-afternoon light, but he could clearly see Diana's outline on her bed. Damn the innkeeper, he thought. He saw no hope for it, and quietly walked to her bed.

"Diana."

She was lying on her back, her head turned away from him on the pillow, one arm raised above her head. She didn't stir.

He gently shook her shoulder. "Diana. Time to wake up. Come on, my girl."

She heard his voice, low and gentle, and sighed softly. "Lyon," she said.

He jerked his hand off her shoulder and straightened. What the devil was she dreaming about? He said more loudly, "Diana, it's time to wake up."

She opened her eyes, blinked several times, and stretched with luxuriant thoroughness. Lyon's eyes went to her breasts, and he gulped and stepped back.

"What time is it?"

"Late afternoon. About six o'clock. I have found a snug little place to eat dinner on Crammer Street, just a couple of minutes from here. If you would like, we can eat there and you won't have to remain imprisoned in your room."

She gave him a dazzling smile. "That is very nice of you. Give me five minutes to rearrange myself."

"I am not at all nice," he said. "Just hungry, and you are my responsibility until I hand you over to the Tomlinsons. I will await you downstairs."

He had effectively wiped out the gentle voice she had heard. He was back to being himself. She wished she understood him but decided quickly that it wasn't worth her effort.

Lyon was a man of few words that evening, even withdrawn, and after a while, Diana gave up her attempts at civil conversation. She was one of very few females present in the small eatery, but Lyonel's forbidding expression kept any interested men at their distance.

They weren't, many of them, gentlemen. Seamen, sailors, merchants for the most part. But she didn't care. She ate her stewed beef with great enthusiasm and successfully chased her green peas about her plate with a fork.

Lyonel knew he'd made a mistake. The devil, he'd known it the minute the damned words had popped out of his mouth. He never should have agreed to take her back. He eyed her from across the small dining table, watching her make a game of catching the damned peas.

She's utterly guileless, he thought, then immediately drew himself up. No, no woman was guileless. He had learned his lesson; he just had to keep repeating that lesson to himself, evidently.

He walked quickly back to the Drake, forcing Diana to skip to keep up with him. He heard her mutter something, imagined accurately that it was an insult on his antecedents, and kept walking. He left her at her bedchamber door.

"You were exceedingly tedious company," Diana said as he turned to leave her without a word.

"Keep your door locked," he said over his shoulder.

"Which door?"

"Both, though you haven't a fear of me."

"I would be a faintheart if I feared you," she said, walked into her bedchamber, and slammed the door behind her.

Damned twit.

Diana, more weary than she'd believed, awoke very late the next morning. Indeed, she soon realized, it was nearly noon. She looked toward the adjoining door. She pulled on her dressing gown and knocked on the door. No answer. She turned the knob and found that the door was unlocked. She peered in. The room was empty. She returned to her room, wondering what to do. To her relief a maid soon arrived with a covered tray.

"Lord Saint Leven asked that you remain in your room," the girl recited.

Oh, he did, did he? Well, she would see about that!

"He also asked that I give you this book. For your enjoyment, his lordship said."

Diana took the book and found it a lurid novel. Her eyes lit up. Well, the afternoon should pass quickly enough.

She bathed, ate, then settled herself into the one chair to

indulge in fantasies. She was giggling with delight when the heroine fainted in the second chapter.

There was a knock on the adjoining door at precisely five o'clock.

"Come," she called.

"Hello, Diana," said Lyon, coming into her room. "You are well amused, I trust?"

"It is most engrossing. The heroine has just succumbed again to the vapors."

"I selected it because it is one of Lucia's favorite authors. She doesn't want anyone to know, but she much enjoys this stuff."

Diana had nothing to say about that. She knew Lucia would be aghast that Lyon knew about her reading.

She sighed. "I miss her."

"I as well. I have loved her since the day when I was four years old and she pulled me out of a tree, kissed the scrape on my elbow, and didn't tell my father of my escapade."

"I cannot imagine you being four years old."

"I was a remarkable child."

"How have you amused yourself today, my lord?"

"My lord? Well, my lord has explored Plymouth, visited ships, and spent time praying in church that the Tomlinsons would arrive in time. Now, if you like, we can have dinner again at the Waving Flag. Unfortunately I did not discover a more refined restaurant."

If Diana entertained hopes that this evening would be more enlivening than the previous, she was doomed to disappointment. Lyon drank more than he should, said very little, and all in all, acted like a man destined for the gallows. Either that, or a brother bound to take his sister to a convent.

She was so furious with him that she didn't try to keep

pace with him on the way back to the Drake. Lyon, a bit tipsy, didn't at first notice that she wasn't beside him until he heard her yell.

He whirled about to see her in the grip of a rough-looking man, two other ruffians laughing and guffawing as they moved in for the kill.

She was struggling with all her might, yelling at the man who was holding her. He saw her elbow punch hard into the man's stomach. He raced back growling with fury when he heard the man shout, "Hold the little trollop, lads! Now, little gal, we're all payers, we are. Stop yer infernal struggling. My Gawd, I want to see me these titties! Lordie!"

"Lyon! Help me!"

10

Record in words one battle of this glorious struggle.

VENANTIUS FORTUNATUS

He had no weapon, but it didn't matter. He leapt into the fray, dragging two of the men off her. He slammed his fist into one man's face, heard the crack of bone, and smiled grimly. He felt an arm grab him about the throat and he was yanked backward. He smelled sweat, foul breath, and cheap ale, and heard growled curses so vile even he was surprised. He sent his elbow back, low, into a man's groin. The curses stopped in a cry of pain.

The man who held Diana was distracted by his partners and loosed his hold. She whirled about and slammed her fist into his throat. He made a disgusting gurgling sound and stumbled backward.

"Kill the damned bloke!"

"Come on, you scum," Lyon yelled, his eyes on the man whose nose he'd broken.

Diana saw one bloody-faced man rush at Lyon, but it was the other one who was coming up behind him, a length of pipe raised in his hand, that made her go cold.

"Lyon! Behind you!"

But Lyon was too late. He spun about, but the pipe struck him solidly on the side of his head. He collapsed where he stood.

"Now, laddies," croaked the man Diana had hit in the throat, "let's show this here little tart a lesson."

"What's going on here? Hold!"

Diana yelled at the top of her lungs when she saw two men coming toward her.

Rafael Carstairs said briefly to Rollo Culpepper, "A damned brawl. There's no hope for it, let's bash some heads."

"Aye, Capt'n," Rollo Culpepper said, his smile wide.

Rafael enjoyed a good fight and he fought dirty. Within moments, two of the men were dragging themselves away, the third was in a moaning heap at his feet, his hands clutching his groin.

He turned to see the young lady on her knees beside the fallen man.

He quickly joined her. He saw soon enough that she was indeed a lady, despite her dishabille. "Are you all right?" he said briefly.

Her eyes were wide and frantic. "Yes, but Lyon . . . Oh, God!"

Rafael dropped to his knees and gingerly felt the growing lump on the gentleman's head. "He took quite a blow. His heart is steady. Where are the two of you staying?"

"At the Drake," she said, her eyes never leaving Lyon's pale face. "Oh, no, I can't believe this."

"Come, now, it's over. He will be fine." With those words, Rafael pulled Lyon up and hauled him over his shoulder. "Rollo, see to the lady. Damn, the gentleman's a load."

"He has a very hard head," Diana said to Rollo Culpepper.

Rollo, no stranger to a fight and its aftermath, recognized shock when he saw it, and quickly said in his most soothing voice, "He put up a good fight, but with the three of those bullies, well, he will have a mighty headache. Who is he?"

"Lyonel Ashton, the Earl of Saint Leven."

Rollo whistled between his teeth. A bloody earl! "Ah, well, my lady, you're not to worry now. Captain Carstairs will see that he's well taken care of."

When they reached the Drake, Rafael shouted at the innkeeper, "Crispin, fetch a sawbones, quickly, there's a good fellow. I'll take his lordship upstairs."

Diana followed in their wake, automatically opening the door to Lyonel's bedchamber. She watched Captain Carstairs gently ease him onto the bed. "Now, let's have a bit of water."

She quickly fetched a cloth and soaked it in the cool water in the basin on the commode. She herself sat beside Lyon and laid the cloth over his forehead.

"Lyon," she whispered, touching her fingertips to the nasty lump on his head. "Please."

"We're sailing in the morning, Capt'n," said Rollo. "We must get back to the *Seawitch*."

"We will wait for the doctor," said Rafael, observing Diana's pale face and shaking hands.

At his words, Diana looked up. "Thank you, both of you. You saved us. It was so awful—" She paused, hearing the voices outside the door.

"The doctor, I fancy, my lady," Rafael said, and moved to the door. "Ah, do come in and see to the gentleman."

Dr. Williamson was drunk, Rafael quickly realized as he watched him move uncertainly toward the bed and lean down.

"Need to bleed him," said Dr. Williamson, giving Lyonel only a cursory glance.

Rafael cursed. "You bounder, you're stinking drunk! What the hell do you mean, he needs to be bled?"

The doctor turned a bleary eye toward Carstairs. "I know what I'm doing, my good man. Get me a basin," he said to Diana.

Diana rose to her full height. She was eye to eye with the doctor. "You are drunk," she said, contempt filling her voice. "You will not touch him."

"Now see here, missie—"

"Get out of here, you bleater!" As Rollo spoke, he firmly took the doctor by the arm and dragged him toward the door.

Diana stood very quietly, watching the ejection. "We are ourselves to sail in the morning," she said. She raised blank eyes to Captain Carstairs. "I don't know what to do."

Rafael could no more stand a woman's distress than the next man. "Where were—are you sailing?"

"To the West Indies. Tortola or St. Thomas."

He blinked at that, and saw a future that would in all likelihood include him. He gave it up without a struggle. "Aboard what ship?"

"I am not certain, no, wait, it is the *Nelson*, a Captain Poutten."

"He's a fool," said Rollo, overhearing this last. "Lord, the man wrecked his last ship, bloody idiot. If I had to serve on his ship, I'd mutiny."

Diana looked from one to the other, helplessly.

"We're sailing to St. Thomas," said Rafael Carstairs, sealing his fate. "I also have an excellent doctor aboard the *Seawitch* to see to his lordship."

Diana's immediate worry was Lyon. "Can you fetch your doctor, Captain?"

"Why don't we simply repair to my ship? My doctor

can take care of Lord Saint Leven.'' He grinned down at her. "If you wish to come with us, we will sail with the tide in the morning."

Diana wanted to throw her arms around his neck. She gave only a moment's guilty thought to the Tomlinsons. She simply didn't care. And, she thought, Captain Carstairs had appeared like Saint George. Who could dismiss the services of such a savior?

"Oh, yes, thank you," she said, relief spilling out of her voice like rain off a roof.

Within fifteen minutes, Captain Carstairs was carrying Lyon out of the inn. Rollo was seeing to their trunks. Diana, who had no money, had gone without a thought to Lyon's stash and removed the required payment for the innkeeper.

Diana, who had sailed all her life, was impressed with the *Seawitch*, a sleek, very modern schooner.

"I normally do not take passengers," said Rafael as he assisted Diana down the companionway, "but there's always a first time for everything. Rollo has given over his cabin. It should be comfortable enough for you. Now, you stay here for the moment. I will send in Dr. Blickford."

The cabin was small but not overwhelmingly so. It was larger than the one she'd sailed to England in. The furnishings were few and simple: a narrow bed, a desk and two chairs, and built-in armoire against one wall, a shelf of books, and other nautical odds and ends.

She had no more time to do anything for at that moment a very small, slight man entered the cabin. He was wearing black breeches and a clean white shirt. His hair was grizzled gray, his eyes a bright blue.

"Well, what have we here? My name's Blickford, my lady. Rollo says your husband got in a rollicking fight and received a smash on his head."

"Yes," said Diana, "yes, he did."

"Now, don't you worry, my lady. A fine, strong young man he appears. He'll be himself in no time at all."

With those bracing words, Dr. Blickford forgot Diana and gave his full attention to the unconscious man on the bunk.

Husband!

Diana stared at his gray head. My God, he thinks we're married! As the haze of shock lifted, she realized now that Captain Carstairs and Rollo as well must have believed them husband and wife. Denials were tripping over themselves on the tip of her tongue, but they remained tripping, for Dr. Blickford turned at the moment of their release and said, "As I said, my lady, he will be all right. Quite a bashing he took, a concussion, I fancy. When he comes out of it, we will have to watch him very carefully. You ever do any nursing?"

She nodded. "Yes, on my father's plantation."

He raised a brow.

"Savarol Plantation on Savarol Island."

"I see," he said. He rose and extended his hand. "My name is Stacy Blickford. Blick to my friends."

She gave him her hand. "And I am Diana Sav—Ashton. Thank you, Doctor."

"Long voyage, my lady. Blick, please."

"Thank you, Blick. And do call me Diana."

The decision was made. She knew in her bones that if she admitted that she and Lyon weren't married, Captain Carstairs would more than likely put them ashore, splendid savior though he was. She couldn't allow it. She told herself that Lyon was very ill and needed Dr. Blickford's care, not some quack who was a drunk. That's what she told herself, very firmly and with ceaseless repetition.

There came a groan from the bed.

Blick turned quickly. "Ah, he's coming about."

If he regains his wits, he will tell them that we aren't married. We will have to return to London.

But Lyon wasn't coming around. The rumbling moan, from deep in his throat, signaled that he was more alive than otherwise, feeling pain, and little more.

To Diana's chagrin, she felt relief that he wasn't as yet regaining his senses. She then felt immense guilt. She started wringing her hands, something she had never done before in her nearly twenty years.

"It's all right, my lady," said Stacy Blickford, gently patting her arm. "He will come about. Ah, here's Neddie with your trunks. This is her ladyship, Neddie. Why don't you stow their trunks over there?"

Neddie grinned, revealing a wide space between his front teeth, ducked his head, and neatly stowed the trunks on the far side of the cabin.

"Now, I shall take my leave. I've got a sick sailor on my hands. I will instruct Neddie to stay close by. When your husband comes around, Neddie will fetch me."

"Thank you, Dr.—Blick," Diana said.

"My pleasure, and don't worry."

"Easily said," Diana said ruefully.

"You young folk haven't been married long, have you?"

"No, not long at all." And we will unmarry as soon as we reach St. Thomas.

"Why don't we get your husband out of his clothes? He would be more comfortable, I wager. Ah, here's Rollo to clear away his things."

"Thank you," Diana said to the first mate as she watched him neatly pile his clothes for removal from the cabin.

"No problem at all, my lady," said Rollo. "I'll be nice and snug with Neddie."

She turned to see Blick easing Lyon out of his coat. Oh,

dear, she thought, consternation flowing through her, the consequences of a grand lie. She heard her own voice say, perfectly calmly, "Yes, he will be more comfortable. Let me help you."

She assisted the doctor with Lyon's coat and shirt. She found herself staring down at his chest. A very manly chest, she thought, and she wanted to giggle, for that description was from one of her romantic novels. When Blick began unfastening his trousers, her courage evaporated. "I feel a bit faint. Do you mind if I sit down?"

"No, of course not," said Blick, not looking at her.

Once Lyon was undressed and under a sheet, Blick straightened. "There, we can find him a nightshirt in the morning when he feels more the thing. Do you feel better now?"

"Yes, certainly," Diana said, eyeing Lyonel's clothing, neatly folded at the end of the bed, then the length of his body under that single blasted sheet.

"Well, you just relax, my lady—"

"Diana, please."

"Very well, Diana. Try to rest, all right? I've moved your husband over just a bit so there is room for you if you wish to lie down."

She nodded, not up to more words. Blick picked up a pile of Rollo's belongings, and the two men took their leave. She was left staring at Lyon's uncovered chest and pale face. His chest was very nice, very solid, covered with dark-brown hair, a bit darker than the hair on his head.

You have certainly done it this time, my girl.

Lyonel moaned a bit, and she sat down beside him. His eyes opened, and he stared at her for a very long time.

"You are all right," she said, gently touching her fingertips to his shoulder. He felt very warm. "You must rest."

She didn't know if he had understood her or not. He closed his eyes again. She gently placed her palm over his heart. The slow, steady beat reassured her.

"Smooth weather, Rollo. Take the wheel, I shall see to our patient."

"Aye, Capt'n," said Rollo, his keen eyes on the endless horizon.

Rafael loved the early morning, the usual silence filled with the activity of his men, the sounds of sea birds squawking overhead, the stiff channel breeze on his face. He made his way to Rollo's erstwhile cabin and quietly tapped on the closed door.

Diana opened it.

"How is your husband, Diana?"

"Blick says that he will drift in and out of consciousness perhaps for several more hours. He seemed to rest comfortably last night."

"And you didn't," Rafael said.

"No, I suppose not. This is all very worrying, you know." He didn't know the half of it, she thought, moving aside so he could enter. He was a large man, of Lyonel's size, broad shoulders, and a handsome face saved from beauty by a stubborn chin and a nose that was just slightly off center. His hair was glossy black and tousled by the wind. His eyes were startling, a pure midnight blue, fanned by thick black lashes that any woman would envy. She prayed he was as sensible and kind a man as he appeared to be. He moved to Lyonel's bunk with silent grace, and Diana wondered if he realized he was the physical epitome of the swashbuckling captains she loved reading about who sailed the West Indies in the last century. She grinned at the thought, wondering if she should swoon like the bleating heroines in the derring-do legends.

Rafael laid the flat of his hand on Lyon's forehead. Cool to the touch. Suddenly, Lyon shouted, "Diana!" and lurched up.

Rafael grasped his bare shoulders and pressed him down. "Easy now, my lord. She is here and you both are quite safe."

"Diana, you little twit, I am going to thrash you!"

Rafael grinned. He made soothing noises and Lyonel quieted. "You have a perfectly normal marriage, I see," said Rafael, standing.

Diana couldn't bear another lie, at least the actual sound of it that could come out of her mouth. She simply nodded, utterly miserable with herself, her head down.

He misunderstood and quickly wiped away his grin. "I'm sorry. I know you're worried. When did Blick see him last?"

"An hour ago."

He nodded. "Blick tells me that your father is Lucien Savarol of Savarol Island. I have had the pleasure of meeting your father. A very gracious gentleman." And a man who wants the French and their damned little emperor six feet under, he added to himself.

"Yes, he is. Lyon has inherited a plantation on Tortola—Mendenhall."

"Oliver Mendenhall?" At her nod, his lips thinned a bit. "That old man was . . . Well, I suppose it doesn't matter now. Now, Diana, it's time for you to have some breakfast. I'll have Neddie bring you something nourishing, and hopefully edible as well."

"Could I also have some water? I would like to bathe and change my clothes."

"Certainly. We must of course keep our water use low, at least until we have a good rain."

"Yes, I know. Thank you, Captain."

"Rafael, please."

"Rafael, Rollo, and Blick. You sound like two peas in a pod and one turnip."

"I'll have to think about that," he said. "The three of us have been together for years."

"You don't have all that many years."

"Behold a man of nearly thirty. Well, twenty-eight, if you wish to be precise. All right, we've known one another for eight years, then. A long time, particularly in our line of work. I see that you lost your wedding ring. Those damned bastards pulled it off your finger? I wish I had known. Did they take anything else?"

Diana was relieved that he'd continued talking, for her own tongue was stuck like glue in her mouth. Her lie had burgeoned into a mighty cloud that threatened to rain on her with typhoon magnitude. She managed to say finally, "No, they didn't."

Her ambiguous reply didn't seem to faze him. Rafael gave her another encouraging pat. He turned in the doorway and said, "Incidentally, most of my men are good fellows and trustworthy. However, some of them might look at you with a grand feast in their minds. If you wish to be on deck, do tell me, Rollo, or Blick so we may escort you."

"I also understand that, Rafael."

Diana found that as she bathed and changed to clean clothes, her eyes went every few seconds to Lyonel. It hadn't occurred to her until that moment when she was standing quite without covering, that there might be a privacy problem. She shook her head. No, Lyon would be reasonable about it. He had to be.

When has he ever been reasonable when she'd been involved? A worrying thought, that.

*   *   *

Lyon thought he heard his mother humming. That was odd because she had died when he was very young. He wondered lazily if he himself was dead and in the hereafter. Then he felt a throbbing pain in his head and opened his eyes.

He wasn't in heaven. He was in a small room. It was a blurred Diana who was humming. She slowly came into focus and he watched her silently as she lifted clothing out of a trunk and placed the things in the drawers of an armoire. What the devil was the little twit doing in his room?

He said, his voice sounding rusty to his own ears, "Diana, what are you doing here? In my room? You know it isn't proper. Kenworthy didn't let you up here, did he?"

She whirled about and hurried to the bunk. "You're awake and sensible! How do you feel, Lyon?"

He thought about that and memory flooded back. "My God, those bastards who attacked us . . . Are you all right? What happened? They didn't harm you?"

"No, no, I am fine."

He frowned. "I guess I'm not. The room is rocking about."

"Well, actually, we're not in a room."

Had he lost his wits from that blow to the head? "Of course we're in a—" He broke off abruptly. "Diana, where the devil are we?"

She swallowed. There was no hope for it. But then again, it was too late. She managed a smile. "Actually, we're aboard the *Seawitch*. This is Rollo's cabin, he's Rafael's first mate, you know."

"No," he said very clearly. "That is impossible. Come clean, my girl. Where are the Tomlinsons? We're aboard the *Nelson* with Captain Poutten."

"Now, Lyon, you mustn't excite yourself. You were

coshed on the head very hard by one of those ruffians. Captain Carstairs saved us. You were quite ill and a quack came to the inn to attend you. He was drunk and wanted to bleed you and we booted him out. There was nothing for it, Lyon, please. Dr. Blickford is attending you.''

''This is absurd!''

''We are on our way to St. Thomas. It was meant to be, Lyon, don't you see?''

He closed his eyes. An awful muddle. A ridiculous muddle. And here he was lying helpless as a damned babe in a damned bunk. In Rollo's bunk. He started to pull himself upright, but he didn't have the strength. He realized at the same time that he was naked and covered only to waist with a sheet. Had Diana . . . ?

He forced himself to calm. ''I trust you have chaperones aboard this vessel?''

Silence.

''Diana?'' He knew deep in his gut what the answer was, but he said nothing. Perhaps he was wrong, perhaps . . .

''Actually, no, if by that you mean another female.''

He came to another realization. The clothes Diana had been removing from a trunk . . . they were her clothes.

''Diana, do you have another cabin?''

''Lyon, why don't I fetch Blick for you? That's Dr. Blickford. He will want to check you over.''

''If you move, I will thrash you.''

''Ha! No, forgive me, I don't want to bait you. Please, Lyon, lie still.''

''Diana, are we sharing this cabin? All the way to the West Indies? For six weeks?''

''Yes.''

''Did you arrange to share your favors with the captain? Is that why he brought me and my . . . doxie aboard?''

She remained unruffled at this insult. ''No. I'm your wife.''

He groaned. Perhaps the boat would sink. Perhaps he would succumb to his wound. Or he could simply throttle Diana. Being a widower wasn't such a bad thought.

"I didn't realize he thought that, not at first. Truly, Captain Carstairs assumed we were husband and wife, as did his doctor. I want to go home, Lyonel. I realized I couldn't tell him the truth. We would have been left ignominiously in Plymouth. It would have—"

"Shut up." He sent his left hand downward to scratch his stomach. "Since you are my dear wife, did you strip me?"

"No! That is, I helped Blick with your upper garments and I got faint before he took off your breeches."

This ingenuous confession made him want to fling off the sheet. "I should thank you for protecting my privacy? Or protecting your maidenly sensibilities?"

"You forget I grew up with slaves. I have seen many of them with little more than loincloths."

He couldn't find words for that. "My head aches and I'm thirsty and hungry."

"I'll see to it at once," she said, and gladly left him to himself. It hadn't been too awful, she thought as she flagged down Neddie and made her requests. She returned to the cabin with a hesitant step, praying that Blick would come quickly. She disliked Lyon's current mood.

She opened the door to see Lyon seated on the edge of the bunk, his essentials covered, thankfully, with the sheet. He looked large and forbidding and altogether splendid.

"I told you to stay still."

"I had to relieve myself."

"Oh. In that case, I am glad I didn't return sooner."

"With your experience, I'm certain it wouldn't bother you at all."

He swung his legs onto the bed. Very muscular manly legs, she thought, and again wanted to giggle.

"Diana," he said very quietly, "this lie, this incredible tale, do you not realize the consequences?"

"There are no bad ones, I think. We will simply unmarry once we arrive at St. Thomas."

He groaned. "Do you not realize what you've done? What you're forcing me to do?"

"It would be nice if you felt forced to be civil to me."

"You are the biggest twit it has been my misfortune to know. I will have to marry you now!"

"That is ridiculous, why—"

Blick knocked on the door and stuck his head in. "Ah, my lord, 'tis awake you are." He paused a moment, very aware of the tension between the two of them. Anger?

Diana made the introductions, feeling tense, and was relieved when Lyon wasn't rude to the doctor.

"Now, let me look at your eyes, my lord. Follow my finger, if you please."

After several more tests, Blick nodded. "You will feel quite fit by tomorrow. Do you wish a bit of laudanum?"

"No," said Lyon. "It is just a dull throb now."

"Very well. Here's Neddie with some food for you. Your wife is an excellent nurse, my lord, and I will leave you now in her capable care."

"I'm glad she is excellent at something," Lyon said.

Blick frowned at that but, after a quick look at Diana, kept his opinions to himself. He wondered if Lord Saint Leven blamed his wife for the ruffians' attack. He said as much to Rafael some minutes later.

"He is probably feeling like the very devil," said Rafael. "You remember, Blick, when I got that bullet through my side? I cursed you for days."

"You were very colorful, 'tis true."

"Well, don't concern yourself further. I will visit our guest in a while. Is Diana over her shock?"

"I don't know," said Blick. "Perhaps you can also provide me with your expert opinion on the lady's state."

"Sarcasm doesn't suit you. You're very poor at it, old fellow. She is lovely, is she not? A pity she's married. A further pity that I don't poach."

"I know, but there are other mermaids in this vast sea."

"Indeed."

"Aside from the addition of a very lovely lady, allow me to point out with straightforward logic that this voyage is not without risk. And now we've two passengers to worry about, one of them a damned earl, a peer of the realm."

"I'll do the worrying, you do the quacking."

"One of these days, Rafael, someone is going to take you apart. And I just might turn my back."

Captain Carstairs merely grinned and began singing a rather dirty ditty.

11

A lion's skin is never cheap.

SEVENTEENTH-CENTURY PROVERB

The conscious Lord Saint Leven was vastly different from the unconscious man Rafael had slung over his shoulder. Rafael saw the intelligence in his eyes, the strength, the character. This man wouldn't like to be in another man's debt. He knew well his own value, but he would accord the same value to another. He wondered what saving this man would cost him. Inevitably something. Rafael shook away his philosophizing, and stepped forward.

He said, extending his hand, "My lord, I am delighted to see you awake and your wits no longer scattered to the winds. I am Rafael Carstairs, captain of the *Seawitch*."

Lyon, who was now leaning back against the pillows of the bunk, clothed in his burgundy dressing gown, nodded as he took the captain's darkly tanned hand. "I understand from Diana that you saved our respective hides. My thanks, Captain."

"He also saved us from a drunk doctor."

"It was fortunate that I was on hand. As for the doctor, he was so foxed I'm surprised he could even speak. It is also fortunate that our destination is St. Thomas."

"So Diana told me. I trust we are not discommoding you overly?"

"Not at all," said Rafael easily. He smiled at Diana. "You see, Diana, all your fretting for naught. I knew your husband would be back to excellent health very quickly. You are looking vastly relieved. It becomes you."

"Yes, vastly, and thank you."

Lyon wasn't blind. He saw the gleaming look of approval in the captain's eyes when he gazed at Diana. Lord, if he did tell him the truth, would he try to seduce her? He imagined that Captain Carstairs had quite a way with the ladies and he would see Diana as fair game were he to discover that he and Diana weren't husband and wife. What to do? And Diana was such an unpredictable chit and so naïve that she made him grit his teeth. Would she succumb to the captain?

He cursed softly.

"Lyon?"

" 'Tis nothing, Diana. Just a slight pain." And you're the source of the pain, damn you. He saw, however, that her look was one of intense worry for him, but again, on a voyage of six weeks, anything could happen between her and that captain. Pity the fellow wasn't at least sixty years old, or was blessed with rotten teeth and a crude manner. But Carstairs wasn't blessed with any of those things. He was about Lyon's age, muscular, lean, and very self-assured. The damned bastard was also handsome. He cursed again, this time silently. It made him feel no better. Perhaps he had a wife tucked away somewhere? No, not likely. After all, Carstairs could have left them; he could have taken all their money. But he hadn't.

Rafael was quite aware of being weighed by Lord Saint Leven, and wondered what conclusion he had reached. He grinned a bit, wondering if the man were also weighing his intentions toward his wife.

"Blick tells me you will be up and about by tomorrow. Indeed, should you wish some fresh air, I can ready a snug spot for you on deck."

"I should like that, Lyon, if you feel up to it," said Diana, unconsciously moving to the bunk. She laid her hand gently on his shoulder. He wanted to give her a look that bespoke his knowledge of her act, but he couldn't, at least not yet. Instead, he laid his own hand over hers and squeezed gently. Her eyes widened, and she gave him a shy, tentative smile.

"Unfortunately, your wife lost her wedding ring," said Rafael. "Did the thugs take anything of yours, my lord?"

"Only my dignity," said Lyon. He gave Diana's suddenly tense hand another squeeze.

Rafael chuckled. "Mine also has known occasional reversals. I try to forget those occasions as quickly as possible."

Damn, Lyon thought again, the captain was likable. He wondered if he were also honorable. Time enough to determine that. He would simply have to keep Diana close. He closed his eyes a moment.

Rafael said quickly, concern evident in his voice, "You are tired, and no wonder. All of us have been trooping in and out of here all morning. I will leave you to rest, my lord. Diana, inform Neddie when you and your husband wish to come up on deck."

"Yes, I shall. Thank you, Rafael."

Rafael!

Lyon added his thanks, in a less-than-enthusiastic voice, to be sure, but the captain didn't appear to notice anything amiss.

Once they were alone again, Lyon said, "You will stay away from that man. He is dangerous."

Diana removed her hand and backed away from the

bunk. "Dangerous? Why, that is absurd. He saved us—you!"

"I mean," Lyon said between clenched teeth, "that he is likely a very charming seducer of females. That, unfortunately, includes you."

"You are ridiculous. He is a gentleman."

"I imagine he will remain mostly a gentleman so long as he believes me to be your husband."

"Ah, so that is why you held your tongue. You are worried about my virtue."

He gave her a sour look. "I don't want you to have your skirts tossed over your head, my dear girl. And you are so silly it is a profound possibility."

Diana looked at him thoughtfully. His face was slightly flushed. Did he think so little of her moral fiber? Her ability to discern when men were honest and when they were not? "So, he is like Monsieur DuPres?"

"No! Well, perhaps, if given the proper opportunity—"

"I did not allow Monsieur DuPres to toss up my skirts. Indeed, I dealt quite well with his pretensions. Why should I allow Rafael to do it? Or any other man, for that matter? And that, unfortunately, includes you."

"I have no intention of seducing you, Diana." He clamped his teeth together and again closed his eyes. "At least until we are married, which we will have to be, somehow."

"Lyon," she said very calmly, "I have no intention of accompanying you to the altar. Most of the time, I want nothing more than to box your ears. I never saw myself married to a man I wanted to kick in the dust."

"I thought it was my manhood that held your interest—at least when it came to kicking."

She just looked at him.

"Listen to me, my girl. You have played the wrong

tune this time. When we arrive in St. Thomas do you possibly believe that Captain Carstairs or any of his crew will not bruit it about that Lord and Lady Saint Leven sailed aboard the *Seawitch*?''

''We could bribe them.''

''And,'' he continued, ignoring that nitwit observation, ''if it is known that we are not married—indeed known that we traveled together without a proper chaperone for you for six weeks—your name will be dragged through the mud. And no father would allow that. He would insist that I make an honest woman of you. I would were I your father.''

''Oh.''

''God save me from foolish women. Do you now understand?''

''I am not without sense, Lyon!''

''That is indeed a surprise to my poor ears.''

''Nor do I believe that you are correct in your assumptions. My father would never insist that I wed a man who couldn't bear my company.''

''What about your bearing my company? Now, I should like to shave and dress. Fetch my gear and some fresh water.''

She gave him a mutinous look.

''You think you would like to bear the title of Trollop of Tortola? Slut of Savarol? And have every sort of man sniffing after you?''

''What would you be called? The Vile Seducer of an Innocent?''

''Not up to alliteration, are you? All right, you're not, then. Diana, men are usually forgiven for their, ah, peccadillos, if they can escape the wrath of fathers. However, I have the misfortune of being an honorable man. I will accept the consequences of your foolishness, as will you.

There is no choice. I trust that you now understand fully. I dislike having to repeat myself. Now, would you please fetch my things for me?''

"I would prefer kicking you in your teeth."

"It is a pleasure to be denied to you."

"I do not like you at all, Lyon."

"It is a pity. For the next six weeks you will have to pretend adoration for your husband, at least in front of others."

"And will you pretend adoration for me?"

He gave her a lecherous grin. "We will see, won't we? Who knows? By the time we reach St. Thomas perhaps you will be with child. Because of you, Diana, we will be sleeping in this cabin. I fully intend to sleep in this bunk. If you don't decide to sleep on the floor, you will be next to me. Who knows what will happen?"

"You are disgusting. You also said you are a gentleman."

"People change when circumstances dictate. Fetch my shaving gear."

"Go to the devil!"

He laughed. "I shall enjoy educating you, my dear. A submissive wife, a gentle helpmeet, a lady who holds her tongue and does not disagree with her lord and master." He paused. "I do hope it will be partially an enjoyable project. In some areas, you certainly are blessed with abundant raw material." His eyes settled on her bosom.

"If you touch me, my lord, I will unman you."

"You tried once and failed."

"I wish Kenworthy were here."

"I told you before we left London that my valet gets vilely ill when he gets within three feet of the water. I shall simply have to make do with you."

"Lucia wouldn't get ill."

"Ah, you wish for her presence now, do you? Let me

tell you something, Diana. Lucia, if she knew our situation, would probably be dancing a jig. A union between us was her wish. Now, fetch my shaving gear.''

At ten o'clock that evening, Lyonel decided he wanted nothing more than oblivion. He again refused laudanum from Blick, for he felt more fatigue than pain. He and Diana had shared a dinner of boiled beef and potatoes in their cabin, and the conversation had dwindled rapidly to tense silence. He knew she was thinking about the single, very narrow bunk, with him in it.

He said nothing, frankly too weary to worry about her missish problems. After Blick took his leave, Lyon very calmly rose and began shrugging out of his dressing gown. He paused a moment at Diana's gasp.

He arched a brow at her over his shoulder, keeping the dressing gown at his waist.

''Excuse me,'' she said, and quickly let herself out of the cabin.

He was lying on his back, a sheet to his chest, his eyes closed when he heard her come in again.

''I shall sleep on the floor.''

''Fine.''

''Will you keep your eyes closed while I disrobe?''

''Yes.''

He was surprising himself, he thought. He was too tired to bait her. He heard the rustle of clothes. He heard a splash of water and imagined her washing her face.

''You may open your eyes now.''

''I don't want to.''

''I will need your blankets.''

''If I get cold during the night, do you expect me to join you on the floor for warmth?''

''I will ask Neddie for more on the morrow. You will simply have to make do tonight.''

He opened his eyes at that. She was on her hands and knees, smoothing out blankets for a makeshift pallet beside the bunk. She was wearing a dressing gown, a pink bit of froth, over her nightgown. Her hair was long and loose down her back. She looked delicious. He closed his eyes again.

He was relieved when she doused the lamp, plunging the cabin into darkness.

He slept soundly. As for Diana, she lay on her back on the dreadful floor, turning first one way and then another, counting the number of nights this would be her bed. When Lyon was well again, she would convince him to take turns. She wondered if that was even a remote possibility. He was the most contrary man.

Lyon awoke early, as was his habit. At first he was disoriented, particularly with the gentle rocking and the sound of breathing very close to him. He gathered his wits, queried his head, found no pain, and leaned up on his elbow. Diana was sprawled on her back, one arm flung over her head, her hair fanned out about her. Six weeks of this, he thought, wanting to groan. His body had already responded to the sight of her and he was cursedly uncomfortable.

He lay quietly for a few minutes longer, then discovered that he needed to relieve himself. He shrugged, hoping for her sake that she stayed asleep for a while longer. She did.

He bathed in the water in the basin. It was cold but he didn't mind that. He welcomed it. Every few minutes, he looked over his shoulder. She slept on, unaware of his predicament. The sleep of the innocent, he thought.

He was dressed and was pulling on his boots when Diana yawned and stretched.

"Good morning," he said, and grinned at the myriad of expressions that crossed her face as she ventured into reality.

She blinked at him, and for a brief instant she gave him the sweetest smile before she got a hold of herself.

"You may have the bunk for a while, if you wish," he said, rising. "I am going up on deck."

He stepped over her and left the cabin.

"Well, that is a relief," she said aloud. "Perhaps he will be a gentleman about this."

The instant the cabin door closed behind him, she scrambled into the bunk. She pulled the sheet to her chin and snuggled down. Her muscles were sore and stiff. The bunk felt like heaven. And the bedclothes smelled like him. She breathed in deeply before she caught herself.

Stop it, you ninny. Sleep was far away, so she forced herself to think about what she would do once they reached St. Thomas. Marry Lyon? She allowed that thought to linger, with all its complexities. Unbidden, she saw herself held over his thighs, her skirts up, his hand on her hips. She began shaking her head. His scent filled her nostrils again, and angry at herself, she rose.

She was brushing her hair when a tap came on the cabin door.

"Yes?"

" 'Tis Blick, Diana. Would you like some breakfast?"

She quickly tied a ribbon about her hair and opened the door, a smile on her lips. "You, sir, are a most versatile man."

"So I've been told, many times. I've already seen your husband. He is sound again. If you would like to come with me now, I'll see that you're fed. I think old Harmon— our cook, you know—is outdoing himself since there is a lady on board to impress. Then, if you like, I'll give you a tour of the ship."

Diana found no fault with that program.

"Do you know much about sailing ships?" Blick asked as they made their way to the poop deck.

She smiled at that. "I have lived all my life in the West Indies, Blick. A schooner is my favorite vessel, so fast and so easily maneuverable. Indeed, a favorite of the pirates some hundred years ago."

He grinned, just a bit uncomfortably. "Well, yes. We can attain speeds of up to fourteen knots, you know, with a fair breeze at our backs."

Diana looked up at the forward wooden mast and the three foresails. "She is beautiful. How many crew?"

"At the present, we have forty men. Her length is ninety feet, so we are not all stumbling over one another. Before Rafael, er, acquired this ship, we were cramped in a much smaller vessel."

What did he mean by that slip? she wondered, but she said nothing.

She saw little of Lyon for the next several hours. Blick introduced her a good dozen of the sailors. The day was bright and warm, sea birds still following them. "Would you like some bread to toss to them?"

"I should enjoy that, yes," she said. "It is one of my favorite pastimes at home. The pelicans, however, become very testy when I exhaust my supply."

Blick chuckled and walked away to ask for the bread.

"Do you sail, Diana?"

She turned at the sound of Lyon's voice. "Of course. Living on an island doesn't give one much opportunity to ride for miles in carriages, you know. In fact, I have my own sailboat. Her name is *Bilbo*."

"Wherever did you get that appellation?"

She smiled, her eyes sparkling. "I haven't thought of that in years. My father told me that when I was three years old, I was fascinated at his talk of bilges and boats. I put the two words together, so he and Dido told me."

"Dido?"

"My nurse, nanny, and a fiery old woman who tells me what to think and what to do, if I let her. She took over running the plantation house after my mother died. Now she does allow me to assist, if I am polite about it and properly serious."

"A slave?"

She stiffened, just a bit, at his tone. "Yes, she is."

"I doubt she is running the plantation house now."

"Why, of course she is. My father has the greatest respect for her." She chuckled. "She also intimidates him a bit, I think."

Lyon realized he'd let his mouth run ahead of his mind. Oh, well, she would find out soon enough. Better for her to have time to accustom herself. "Your father has remarried."

Diana slapped a tendril of hair from her face. "That is not a very funny jest, Lyon."

"It isn't a jest. Lucia received a letter from your father just before we left."

"But she said nothing of it to me."

"She didn't want you made unhappy. Also it appears you have a stepbrother, evidently grown."

"Good morning, my lord. Diana, your bread."

They both turned, each taking bread from Blick. Diana, her face a study in confusion and shock, walked toward the poop deck. She began flinging bits of bread upward.

The birds squawked loudly and flew closer. She heard a curse from a sailor and saw that one of the gulls had relieved himself on the hapless man's head. She wished it had been Lyon, then she could laugh. From the crew she had met, they were dressed well enough and were clean. Of course, if there were not much rain during the voyage, all of them would be as smelly as cow's ears before they reached St. Thomas. She'd heard stories all her life about the cruelty aboard his majesty's ships in the royal navy. These men, however, did not look at all abused.

Lyon tossed his own bread, his eyes on Diana. It didn't really matter now that her father had taken another wife. After all, Diana would be married to him and be herself a wife and no longer a daughter attached to her father's house. I am amazing myself, he thought. I am already used to the idea.

Diana continued tossing bread bits, her mind in a whirl. Her father married! To whom? Why hadn't he written to *her* to explain? And a stepbrother! The last of the bread gone, she wiped her hands on her skirts. She saw that Lyon was talking to Blick. She moved away, careful of the coiled hemp rope just ahead. She raised her face to the sun, looking at the billowing sails.

"We'll not get rid of the blighters easily now," said Rafael, coming to a halt, his feet planted wide apart on the deck.

"They will not come out much farther from land," Diana said.

The rigging creaked overhead and Rafael, out of long habit, cast an expert eye upward. He called out to Rollo, who was at the wheel, "A bit higher in the wind!" He grinned down at Diana. "You're right, of course. What do you think of the *Seawitch*?"

"She is beautiful, save for all the gun ports and cannons. Am I correct? You have ten cannon? Six swivel guns?"

"You've an accurate eye. England is at war, you know. I am not so foolish to venture out without protection."

"I remember my father telling me of the English taking St. Thomas in 1807. Not a shot fired."

"Not a one. The Dutch folded their proverbial tents and left."

Diana smiled. "He also told me the story of the Dutch commander who asked for verification that the English did indeed have overwhelming odds."

"An honorable surrender," said Rafael. "When Napoleon is at last beaten, we will give St. Thomas back. Ah, your husband." He grinned at Lyon. "I suggest you, Lyon, take care with the sun. You'll need at least a week to accustom yourself."

"You're already quite red, Lyon," Diana said, frowning a bit. "I suppose it is better than your previous pallor."

Sharing a small cabin had further disadvantages, Diana discovered that evening. She wasn't at all tired, and as was her habit, she fetched the novel she'd been reading from the armoire.

"Douse the lamp, Diana," said Lyon from the bunk not five minutes later.

As he had the night before, he had kept his eyes closed when she had undressed and bathed. Unfortunately he'd said nothing about sharing the floor. She decided to give him another night to recover from his injury.

"I wish to read awhile. I will move the lamp down here on the floor beside me."

He grunted. Another five minutes later, Diana was enthralled with a particularly exciting scene when he said irritably, "Enough. I can't sleep with that bloody light."

She looked up to see him on his side, looking down at her. "In a bit," she said absently. "Not yet."

"Diana—"

"I shall when I have finished this chapter."

"What are you reading?"

"*The Adventures of Count Milano.*"

He groaned.

"Hush, the hero is in an awful position at this moment."

"Do you call it awful because he is making love to the heroine?"

"Of course not! She is pure and innocent and he wants only to protect her."

"The man sounds like an idiot and a fool. There is no such breed of woman."

"That reeks of Charlotte's Disease, Lyon. One would wish that you would strive for a cure."

"I suppose your count writes bad poetry to the heroine's plucked eyebrows."

"Be quiet."

"You know something," he said after a few more minutes, "I find myself wondering if you didn't arrange this particular plot to suit your fancy."

That caught her attention. "What do you mean? Or will I hate myself for asking?"

"It just occurs to me—since I am still suffering from Charlotte's Disease—that you have neatly engineered me into a corner. You, through your actions, took all choice out of my hands. Perhaps you planned it so you could trap me into marrying you."

Her first reaction to this outrageous nonsense was to hurl her novel at him. She didn't. Instead, she drew a deep breath and said nothing.

"Hit a nerve, did I?"

Her lips tightened, but still she kept silent.

"If you wanted me so very much, my dear Diana, couldn't you at least be honest about it? Was it my hand caressing your quite acceptable bottom? Or perhaps my brilliant dancing that enthralled you? Since you don't yet know anything about my skill as a lover, it can't be that. More likely, it is my wealth."

Very well, she thought. "It was your wealth. Certainly you have nothing else to recommend you."

"You know, I could simply leave you in St. Thomas and sail immediately for England. Leave you to face the music, as it were."

"That, my dear Lyon, would be my fondest hope."

"If I were a bounder that is what I would do."

Diana returned to her novel. She heard him chuckle. She'd let him have his fun. She stopped reading suddenly and dropped her book to the floor beside her. "This is most odd, Lyon," she said thoughtfully.

He grinned. "Indeed it is. We're acting like an old married couple, whereas we could be acting like a young married couple. Would you like to share the bunk with me?"

"I wish you would keep yourself covered."

"You like what you see, Diana?"

He did look splendid, but she wouldn't admit that to him. "You are passable, I suppose." She turned to see his wide, very smug grin. She quickly doused the lamp.

"Tell me, Diana, since we are at least skirting the subject, where did the name Virgin Islands come from?"

"From Columbus, way back toward the end of the fifteenth century. He saw this mass of islands, more than he could or wanted to count. He named them after St. Ursula, who was a virgin, I suppose, and the thousands of maidens who followed her to a martyr's death."

"My God, how awful for the men of Europe! How many thousand are we talking about?"

"Over ten thousand, I believe."

"That probably resulted in dynastic illegitimacies in the thousands."

"Whatever do you mean by that?"

"Well, a man wants to marry a virgin. When she is with his first child, he can be fairly certain that it is his, that his heir carries his blood and not another man's. With the destruction of so many innocents, men would have to make do with what was left. I would imagine that a lot of cuckolding went on.''

"Perhaps you're really not Lord Saint Leven, after all!''

"Hopefully things straightened out in the centuries following the maidens' demise.''

She was silent a long moment, and he could easily imagine her agile mind working quickly. "You know, that is another reason why I don't wish to marry you.''

"Oh?'' He drew out the single word, aware of anticipation.

"Indeed. I have remarked upon your antecedents before. Perhaps because of St. Ursula and the demise of all the virgins, you are truly a bastard. I shouldn't like my children's blood tainted.''

He laughed. "An excellent shot, for a female.''

"Good night, Lyon.''

"Sleep well, Diana.'' He was grinning into the darkness some minutes later. She was right. This was most odd.

And at least for the moment, quite enjoyable.

12

Men are but children of a larger growth.

JOHN DRYDEN

Lyon was impossible, and she wouldn't think about him. He was a cad, a bounder . . . No, she wouldn't think about him.

She breathed in the clean morning air. There was a stiff breeze and the *Seawitch* was slicing through the water, her graceful bow falling and rising in even cadence. Even during her long voyage to England, she hadn't accustomed herself to the endless stretch of ocean. No small islands, barren, lush, flat, or hilly, anywhere in sight, not like at home. It made her feel unbearably alone and quite insignificant. She was standing on the poop deck next to Rollo, who had the wheel. She said, "Is your home port in St. Thomas?"

"No, Montego Bay, Jamaica."

"Then why are we sailing to St. Thomas?"

Rollo looked briefly uncomfortable. "The captain has business there. Actually, well, yes, business, my lady."

Most odd, she thought, seeing his discomfort.

"Please, Rollo, call me Diana."

"Well, yes, Diana. I say, his lordship seems quite recovered now."

Too recovered, she thought, but just nodded. Damned man! They'd been at sea for nearly a week now and the night she'd finally asked Lyon to take his turn on the floor, he'd grabbed his head and begun to moan dramatically.

"That's quite enough," she'd said sharply, frowning at his performance.

He weaved a bit where he stood, then collapsed on the bunk, arms flopping over his head.

"Perhaps I should call Blick. He could dose you with a bottle of laudanum."

He cocked an eye open. "Ah, no, I am a stoic."

"You bear your suffering in noble silence?"

"Yes, and now I must have my well-deserved rest." He sat up, grinning at her. His fingers went to the buttons on his shirt, but his eyes remained on her face, mocking, drawing.

And she'd left, of course, standing in the companionway outside the cabin while he undressed.

She still wasn't used to that wretched floor, she thought now, stretching to ease her stiff muscles.

"I've never been to Jamaica," she said to Rollo.

"If you are unfortunate enough to be attacked by ruffians in St. Thomas, perhaps the captain will take you aboard again."

"I suppose I can smile about it now, just a bit," she said. "We were very lucky that you were there and willing to assist us."

"The capt'n is a fair man," was all Rollo said.

But none of them was smiling toward evening. A storm was blowing up. She was with Lyon when they heard Rafael curse in at least two different languages. Then he gave a series of sharp orders. Several sailors scrambled up the rigging, agile as monkeys, to reef the sails and secure all the lines.

"We will have a night of it, I'm afraid," Rafael said to Diana and Lyon. "I suggest you fasten down any loose items in your cabin, and please, stay below."

And that includes me, Diana thought. She looked at the angry waves slapping against the ship, the darkening sky overhead.

The storm hit at eight o'clock. Diana was sitting on the floor on her nest of blankets when the ship lurched suddenly and she was tossed sideways.

"Diana, are you all right?"

She was grumbling to herself and rubbing her bruised elbow. "No! Should you like to trade places with me?"

"I am not a fool. I think you'd best douse the lamp. I don't want us to set the ship on fire."

She did and stretched out, trying to get comfortable. She wasn't particularly worried about the storm. Living on an island had accustomed her to them. She remembered very clearly the only time she'd been terrified. It was the great hurricane in 1799, so fierce that it had destroyed nearly all their sugarcane, demolished part of the plantation house and killed fourteen slaves. She shuddered, remembering it, and herself, small and frightened, huddled against Dido's stiff skirts, Dido's soft voice soothing her.

Lyon, misunderstanding that shudder, said in an effort to distract her from the storm, "So what happened to the count? The hero of your novel?"

"Oh, him. The brave Count of Milano saved the heroine, saved her father, saved her fortune, and butchered the villain, in a fair fight, of course."

"And clasped her to his manly bosom on the last page?"

"Something like that. Ouch!"

Lyon said after a moment, his voice as bland as the

stewed vegetables they'd eaten for dinner, "Perhaps you'd best join me tonight."

"Don't be absurd!"

"If you like, I will sleep under the covers and you can arrange yourself on top, with your own blankets for cover, naturally."

"Be careful, Lyon, else your true lecherous colors might come to the fore."

"Diana, do not be a twit. I do not wish you to show yourself on the morrow covered with bruises. The captain and his crew will believe that I beat you."

"You could always take the floor."

"Not I. I didn't get us into this impossible mess."

"You are not at all honorable. You are a—"

"Bastard? Arrogant fool? Selfish rake?"

The ship hit a deep trough and she was hurled a good three feet toward the cabin door.

"Enough, come here."

He heard her moving about in the darkness.

"Diana, if I swear I will not touch you, will you please share the bunk with me tonight?"

"I don't trust you."

You're probably very wise not to. "Don't be a missish fool. We will be married, you know. You have already been living in close proximity with me for a week."

She was thinking about it, he knew it. He waited, saying no more.

"I am not going to marry you, Lyon."

That reply was not really unexpected. It came to him suddenly that he'd already accepted the fact that she would be his wife. Strangely, he no longer was fighting the notion. She made him laugh when he didn't want to thrash her. She never bored him and, he admitted, she was lovely. He said mildly, "Very well. All I am asking you to do is keep yourself from being hurt. I swear to keep my hands away from your, er, womanly parts. Come here.''

He heard her snort, then say, ''And I promise to keep my hands away from your manly parts.''

He laughed. ''You have the last word this time. Why don't you take the inside? That way you won't roll off onto the floor. Besides, Diana, I am scared to death of this storm and need your soothing presence beside me.''

''Ha! I don't believe that, but . . . very well.''

She crawled over him, dragging three blankets with her. He didn't move. ''There isn't enough room,'' she said.

He inched closer to the edge of the bunk.

Finally, she was lying on her side, her back to him, wrapped securely in her blankets. She realized after just a few minutes that she was quite used to the even tempo of his breathing. Then the ship lurched again and she felt his arms fly out. He grabbed her about her waist and she struggled to a sitting position.

''Sorry,'' he said. ''I didn't want to end up on the floor. Then the captain and crew just might believe that you beat me.''

''It is a thought,'' she said. ''Would you please remove your hands now?''

''Certainly.''

They settled themselves again.

''Diana?''

''Yes?''

''I don't mean to revolt your finest feelings, but I must turn on my side, else I won't be safe.''

''And you're nearly speechless with fright?''

''Exactly.'' He curled against her back, lightly placing his arm about her waist. She felt his warm breath against her neck. She wished she hadn't braided her hair. At least it would have been some kind of cover.

I won't think about this, she thought, and forced herself to take deep, slow breaths.

As for Lyon, he was sternly informing his lower body not to respond.

Diana awoke several times during the night when the ship heaved in a particularly violent movement. Lyon had her held securely. For the first time in a week, she felt warm enough, and she knew it was from the heat of his body. I will not think about it. I won't let him . . . do what?

Lyon awoke very early the following morning. The ship had returned to its gentle rocking motion. The storm, thank God, had blown itself out and the ship was still in one piece. He realized suddenly that his right hand was beneath the three blankets and was cupping Diana's breast. He could feel the slow upward rise and fall of her breathing. His fingers itched. Her breast filled his hand. His breathing quickened. She felt so soft, her flesh so very warm and inviting even through her linen nightgown. She will be my wife, he thought, staving off the guilt he immediately felt. His fingers curled, just a bit. She moved in her sleep, her body shifting slightly so that her breast eased more fully against his palm.

The Spanish Inquisition should have had this torture, he thought. He felt her nipple respond without her volition. Her breast felt heavy, richly full, and he swallowed convulsively.

She moaned softly and he froze.

Diana felt marvelously warm. She moved slightly, onto her back, and felt the warmth increase. Slowly, she opened her eyes. She was two inches from Lyon's face. He looked as if he were in pain.

She brought her hand up to touch his cheek. "Lyon? Are you all right?"

Then she felt his hand on her breast. Her eyes widened. His face blocked out everything. He kissed her gently.

Oh, dear, she thought, and then she stopped thinking. The insidious warmth seemed to explode low in her belly. Her body arched against him. She wanted more. She wanted . . .

Lyon released her abruptly, cursing vilely. He quickly turned away from her and rose, only to realize that he was quite naked. He grabbed a blanket to cover himself. He was breathing hard, his manhood thrusting outward. He had to keep his back to her. He wouldn't allow her to see the evidence of his lust.

"Turn away, Diana, now."

She obeyed him, her mind in chaos. Was she that inept at kissing? That repellent to him? Stop it, you silly fool! What a perverse creature she was.

"Stay that way or you will have your maidenly sensibilities thoroughly lacerated."

"Why?"

Was that her voice? So high and thin as Harmon's chicken soup?

"Be silent."

Her breast throbbed. Not a hurt kind of throbbing, but a very nice sort of throbbing, and it sent waves of feeling to her belly. She remembered that time when he'd assisted her out of the carriage and carried her. Only this time, the feelings were stronger, more confusing. Her lips were still warm and tingly from his mouth.

Lyon shrugged into his dressing gown. Still, his rampant manhood was in extreme evidence. He quickly sat himself in the chair behind the small desk.

"You can turn over now if you like."

She did. She stared at him thoughtfully, seeing the tension in his eyes, the flush on his tanned cheeks, the rigid set of his shoulders. She didn't realize that her eyes were as soft-looking as creamy butter, vague and a bit dazed, but Lyon did.

"I think," he said very slowly, "that we should have Captain Carstairs marry us today."

All dreamy vagueness disappeared at his words.

"Why?"

"Don't be a fool, Diana! You wouldn't be a virgin if I hadn't fled the bunk."

"Just because you were feeling my womanly parts?"

"Just one womanly part. And, I might add, that one part was nearly enough to send me over the honorable edge. Now, I expect you to be reasonable about this."

He had caressed her breast and kissed her. Was that all that was needed for a man to lose his mind? His control? She discounted her own feelings. In any case, they were long gone. Perhaps she'd just imagined those very odd . . . spurts, or whatever one called them. She decided to feel sorry for him and his male weakness. After all, he'd left her because he'd wanted to be honorable, hadn't he?

"I will be reasonable," she said, easing deeply under her blankets. "You will probably regain your aplomb in a few minutes and regret your words. Now, I am still sleepy." With that dismissal, she turned away from him and closed her eyes.

"Diana, I am going to beat you. Again. Thoroughly."

"Ah, so you have your manly parts under control? Now you will resort to threats?"

He said nothing and she was beginning to relax when she felt him ease beside her on the bunk.

"Lyon!"

"Be quiet. Lie still. It's still very early and both of us might as well get some more sleep."

Small chance of that, he thought.

"Diana?"

"Hmmm?"

"I have large hands. Have you ever noticed?"

"Yes, very manly hands."

That sidetracked him for a moment. "*Manly* hands?"

She giggled. "Yes. That is a favorite word in my novels."

"Very well. Did you also realize that your breast overflows my manly hand?"

"Stop it! You are supposedly a gentleman, a—"

"Very true. And I will also be your husband."

"No!"

"I think I should accustom you to the idea. Accustom you to my touch. I think you much enjoyed my touching you."

She sat up, her fat braid slapping against the side of his face, the blankets held like armor against her chest. Her face was flushed, her expression uncertain.

"My God, you're not afraid of me, are you? My cocky, mouthy Diana? And I, but a mere man?" He paused a moment, then added, "Perhaps a manly man?"

"You are about as amusing as an attack of biliousness."

"That's more like it. Why don't you lie down and let me hold you? You will get used to it."

To his utter surprise, she said not another word, and in the next instant, she snuggled down and lay her cheek against his shoulder. Her hand, fisted, sat atop his chest.

His arm automatically came down and pulled her closer against him. He was smiling, triumph a sweet taste, when she began snoring, loudly, interspersed with equally loud snorts.

"I imagine you can't keep that up for very long," he said. He kissed her forehead and closed his eyes. No, he thought again. Diana would never bore him.

He was right, she thought, striving for another snore. Damn him anyway. Here she was bound against him, his arm firm about her back. She didn't know what to do with her hand. His flesh felt very warm beneath her fingers.

When she couldn't produce another obnoxious sound, she said, with sweet understanding, "I know what it is that troubles you. You miss your little amour. Men, I understand from your precious Charlotte, must relieve themselves in several ways."

He wouldn't let her rile him. Relieve?

"However, I refuse to let you relieve yourself with me."

"You sound like a chamber pot."

The mention of that particular item made her realize that she had a distressing problem of her own. She decided to ignore it.

A few minutes later, he was frowning at her squirming. "What's the matter? Can't you get comfortable?"

This is awful, she thought, but saw no hope for it. She'd managed during the past week to take care of this physical need when he wasn't in the cabin. As for Lyon, she imagined that he, like most the crew, relieved themselves away from the wind off the side of the ship. She sighed. "Lyon, would you please leave the cabin for a while?"

"Be quiet. I'm sleepy."

"You don't understand. I need to . . . Oh, drat, please, just go, for a few minutes."

He began laughing, she felt the deep rumbling in his chest before the sound came from his throat. She lifted her hand from his chest and poked him hard in his stomach. He grunted.

"You tell me you're a gentleman. Prove it."

"All that talk about relieving, huh? When we're married I won't have to leave."

He saw from her face that this was an appalling thought. "Kiss me," he said, "and I'll leave you to the chamber pot."

"I'll bite you instead, you rotter!"

"Perhaps you'd best not yet. I shall have to teach you how to make bites pleasurable. Come now, Diana. You know I can hold out indefinitely. I don't imagine that you can."

"You are a bastard." She leaned down and kissed him quickly, her lips tightly closed.

"There is so much I shall have to teach you." He released her and rose from the bunk.

He gave her a wicked smile before he left the cabin, a blanket wrapped about his waist.

Lyon sat across from Rafael, his leg slung over the arm of his chair, a glass of excellent French brandy in his hand. Rafael, equally relaxed, tossed a card from his hand onto the top of the desk. They were alone in the captain's cabin, a very masculine lair, playing piquet.

"Sorry," said Lyon, and placed his queen of hearts on the ten of hearts.

"I wasn't counting," said Rafael as he frowned at the remaining cards in his hand. "I was never much of a gambler. My brother now, well, never mind about him." No, he didn't want to think about Damien, his twin brother.

Lyon played the jack of clubs, saying as he did so, "By any chance are you related to the Carstairs in Cornwall?"

Rafael looked bored.

"I believe their estates are near to St. Austell."

"I have no relatives, anywhere."

Their play continued in silence.

"It's odd, you know," Lyon said. "I remember meeting a Baron Drago some years ago. He was an older man,

of course, but if my memory serves me, you have something of the look of him.'' Lyon, gazing at Rafael through
his lowered lashes, saw him pale slightly. I've hit upon a
mystery here, he thought, and because he liked Rafael
Carstairs, he shrugged and said, ''I fear if you keep playing
me, you'll lose your ship.''

''I'm sometimes a fool, but not that great a fool,'' said
Rafael, relaxing now, knowing that Lord Saint Leven
wouldn't touch that particular hornet's nest again. ''What
is Diana doing?''

''Last time I saw her, she was teaching one of your
sailors a better way to make some sort of knot.''

Rafael grinned and tossed out another card, only to see
it gobbled up. ''She is charming,'' he said. He watched
Lyon thoughtfully study the remaining cards in his hand.
''I should say, though, that you two should tie the proverbial knot before long.''

Lyon dropped his cards.

''I am not a fool, Lyon,'' Rafael said quietly. ''Nor do I
wish to pry, but you have set yourself something of a
problem.''

''How did you know?'' It didn't occur to Lyon to lie; as
the captain had said, he wasn't a fool.

''Perhaps the wedding ring, or absence of one at first,
then Neddie mentioned to Rollo about blankets piled on
the floor. Also, you and Diana do not seem like lovers.''
He paused a moment, then added deliberately, ''You are
both quite aware of each other, but you are not lovers. At
least not yet.''

''You are observant,'' Lyon said at last. ''I trust no one
else knows of our predicament?''

''No, but Blick is a wily one, probably comes from the
fact that he's the son of a Sussex vicar.''

''Good God,'' Lyon said, distracted. ''A vicar's son?''

"Yes, indeed. He and his father, well, they don't get along, you might say. In any case, he's said nothing to me about the two of you."

"Diana has been so careful about those wretched blankets of hers. Ah, well, 'tis done."

"No, nothing is done. I consider you a friend and Diana as well. As you know, I am acquainted with her father, Lucien Savarol. He may be a West Indian planter, but he is a gentleman and his daughter is a lady. I wish I could advise you, but—"

"You were quite right. I have already determined to marry the chit, but she is the one who refuses. I can't very well force her to wed me."

Rafael leaned back in his chair, crossing his arms over his chest. "Seduce her," he said.

Lyon grinned, then winced. "She would try to unman me, she's already threatened as much. In fact, she tried it once, and thankfully missed, but that is another tale. Don't say it, Rafael, she understands the consequences of not marrying me, at least that's what she says. But she is a guileless creature, if that's possible for a woman to be."

Though sorely tempted, Rafael said nothing to that. "I have discovered, as I am certain you have also, that life is never simple. Unfortunately it is we ourselves who tend to complicate things. I don't suppose that you've noticed how she looks at you, particularly when you are not aware of it. She is not at all indifferent to you. Indeed, I would say that at the very least she desires you. Perhaps, my friend, if you did seduce her, she would come about." He gave Lyon a cocky grin. "I assume that you would be proficient at it."

"Who knows? The chit is driving me insane. Can you imagine living in such close proximity and trying to keep yourself . . . Well, enough. It is not your problem."

"We have about three and a half more weeks before we reach St. Thomas. If the weather holds, that is. Unfortunately on the islands society is so tight-knit, it would be well nigh impossible to wed her there, secretly, without everyone finding out about it. That was your plan, was it not?"

"Yes, if I could get Diana to agree, damn her." Lyon looked down at the cards on the desktop. He picked up an ace and stared at it a moment. "You say she is not indifferent to me?"

"No, she is not. I do know something about women, you know."

"That is what I was afraid of."

"Rest your mind, Lyon. It has never been my habit to poach on another man's preserves. She is yours, not mine."

"Hell," Lyon said, tossing the ace in the air, "I didn't want her to be mine. I didn't want any woman."

"A gentleman does not aspire to dishonor a lady. As I see it, old boy, you haven't a choice."

Lyon cursed.

"Seduce her," Rafael said once again. He saw Lyon tense and wondered if he was thinking about making love to that lovely young woman. "Another game, Lyon? I am feeling more lucky."

"You think I am that far gone, do you?"

Rafael laughed.

13

Waiting for one's pleasures is weary work.

PETRONIUS

Lyonel Ashton, Sixth Earl of Saint Leven, had never before in his life seduced a virgin, a lady virgin, a nineteen-year-old lady virgin who was not, after all, indifferent to him, at least according to Captain Rafael Carstairs.

He decided to try once again to convince her to marry him, silly stubborn girl. He was becoming decidedly tired of her foolish refusal. He found her in Blick's small office, the two of them with their heads together. He felt an alarming spurt of jealousy, recriminations hovering on the tip of his tongue when Diana looked up and smiled at him.

"Lyon! Blick knows so very much about the properties of the plants and herbs on the islands. He is teaching me about plantain. I never knew it could be used successfully for eye inflammation. Did you know that in Africa the juice of the leaves is used for malaria?"

Lyon smiled at her enthusiasm. He felt immensely small over his bout of jealousy. As for Blick, he was looking like a proud, benign parent, and Lyon felt even more foolish at his initial reaction, for Blick was also of the age to be her father. He said easily, "No, I didn't know. Fascinating."

"And then there is the canna lily. It is used for stomach aches. It, however, has deleterious effects, and one must be quite careful."

"I believe Lyon wishes to speak to you, Diana," said Blick, giving her a look of amused affection.

"Oh? What is it you want, Lyon?"

Lyon ground his teeth. "If you can come with me a moment, Diana, I should like to speak to you in private."

Diana cast a look toward the small vial of ground goatweed, to be used as a tisane for purging. "Oh, very well," she said, and Lyon wished he'd kept his mouth closed, indeed wished he'd waited until the evening, when they were alone in their cabin.

"Will you have more time for me this afternoon, Blick?"

"Certainly, Diana, if all the men keep their bones and teeth intact and Harmon doesn't poison them at lunch."

She followed Lyon, waving at Blick over her shoulder. When they reached the deck, Diana immediately walked to the railing and stared out over the endless stretch of water. She was leaning over the rail when spray flew upward. She laughed, wiping her eyes.

"It is magnificent, is it not?" She waved her arms toward the horizon. "But you know, it's as if we're not any place specific. It is the same day in and day out. We could be where we were yesterday for all the change one sees. I guess I still am not used to not seeing land." She sighed. "There are so many islands at home, you know. Landmarks that make you feel that you are someplace definite."

"Yes, I know. You've told me."

She turned to face him. "Forgive me for running on so. What is it you wanted, Lyon?"

He drew in a deep breath. "You are quite tanned. You even have a smattering of freckles across your nose. I want you to marry me. Today, perhaps tomorrow, at least marry me before we arrive at St. Thomas."

"You are quite tanned also, but there are no freckles. No, I won't. Not today, nor tomorrow, not before St. Thomas."

"And that's that?"

She saw that he was quite serious, indeed, he was holding himself up very straight. He looked lovely, she thought vaguely, the stiff ocean breeze tousling his thick chestnut hair. His eyes looked even bluer with his face so tanned. She wanted to touch him, and she did, placing her hand lightly on his shirtsleeve. "Nothing has changed, surely you understand that. My father will protect me. There is no reason for you to, well, to sacrifice yourself through what you yourself have called my blundering."

He looked past her a moment, thinking furiously. Damned little twit! "I don't like your hair braided," he said.

"Since I haven't been able to wash my hair since the storm, it is the only thing to do. I am sorry you find me so repulsive."

He gave her a look of acute dislike. "The good Lord knows you are anything but repulsive. What you are, my girl, is a stubborn witch, and at the moment I am resisting a particularly powerful urge to throttle you."

"There are a number of witnesses, aren't there?"

"If I were to tell them of your singularly stupid stance, I imagine that they would applaud me." He dashed his hand through his hair, making it stand on end. "Look, Diana, there is no going back, surely you must realize that. You spoke of your blunder. Well, it's done and I've accepted the consequences. You must also."

"I don't wish to discuss it further, Lyon. Now, let me

tell you that Harmon is making a special dish for us this evening. Actually, it's for you, to give you an idea of the foods we eat at home.''

He raised a brow at that, accepting her sidestepping for the moment at least.

'' 'Tis a surprise. Are we dining with Rafael and Blick?''

"Probably," he said. "With a special dinner, I have no doubt that we will.''

He watched her walk away, her step firm, in perfect harmony with the swaying deck. The breeze ruffled her skirt, and he swallowed, seeing the clear outline of her legs and hips.

"Very well, Diana. It will just have to be seduction,'' he said to no one in particular, "since you refuse to consider reason.''

The evening began uneventfully, though Diana noticed that Lyon was quiet, which was most unlike him. She wondered briefly if he were still upset with her for refusing to marry him. No, she thought, he must be relieved, not upset. Harmon served them tripe and bean surprise and for several minutes, Lyon just stared at the pile of yams, coco, dumplings and carrots.

"This is a West Indian dish?''

Rafael laughed. "One of their favorites. Been around for the longest time, isn't that right, Diana?''

"Eat up, Lyon. Soak up the sauce with your dumplings. It is civilized, you know.''

Lyon saw to it that Diana drank several glasses of rich red wine. He saw Rafael eyeing him curiously, and merely smiled.

It was close to ten o'clock when he and Diana repaired to their cabin. As was her wont, she prepared what he called her nest on the floor. She hadn't shared the bunk with him since the night of the storm.

"Must you?" he said irritably.

She looked up at him. "Must I what?"

"Continue sleeping on that damned floor."

"Yes, certainly," she said. "You must remember that you were most uncomfortable that one time."

"Uncomfortable? That particular word doesn't come close to what I felt."

"Well, there you are. I refuse, Lyon, to be your little amour on this voyage."

"Perhaps if I promised that you would be my big amour?"

"You are not amusing. Now—" She stopped in her tracks, her eyes widening. He was undressing, in front of her.

"Can you not wait a moment? Then I can leave you."

"No," he said, and continued unbuttoning his shirt. "I told you that you needed to accustom yourself to me. It's about time that you did." He shrugged off his shirt and folded it neatly over the back of the desk chair.

Diana swallowed. "Don't, Lyon."

He merely smiled at her and began unbuttoning his breeches.

"Stop! Oh, you are impossible! I think I shall feed you some goatweed."

"And what is that, pray?"

"A purge," she said, scrambled to her feet, and dashed out of the cabin.

"Too late, my dear," he said quietly to the empty cabin. As he eased himself naked between the sheets, he decided he'd best be careful, particularly after tonight. She just might try that goatweed on him. Then he found himself smiling into the darkness. He fully intended to make his little amour feel sensations she'd never dreamed of before. She would spare not a thought for her goatweed once he'd taught her a woman's pleasure. And she could most certainly cease her ridiculous twaddle about not marrying him.

She came into the cabin, her head down, refusing to glance toward the bunk.

"I am covered, Diana."

His voice was rich with laughter but still she did not look at him.

"Afraid of me, are you?"

"No, damn you! Now, will you keep your eyes closed?"

"All right."

She shot him a wary look, and he yawned.

"Why don't you brush out your hair?"

"No."

Her voice was muffled and he opened his eyes to see her pulling her gown over her head. She turned to look at him and he quickly closed his eyes again. He thought she growled.

He watched her take off her slippers. He waited, aware of his accelerated heartbeat. She stepped out of her one petticoat. She was wearing now only her linen chemise, that endearing garment reaching only to her knees. Lovely legs, lovely hips. As she reached for her nightgown, he sat up in bed, staring at her.

He wanted to laugh, then cry. He groaned instead.

She whipped about, holding her nightgown against her.

"You miserable bounder, you said you would keep your eyes closed!"

"I have been done in by nature," he said, his voice a combination of bemusement and chagrin.

"What are you talking about?"

How many more days? he wondered. "Perhaps," he said thoughtfully, "that is why married gentlemen keep a little amour tucked away. My eyes are now firmly closed, Diana."

He suited action to words. Soon the cabin was plunged into darkness.

"What is this about husbands and tucked-away little amours?"

"I don't think you want me to tell you."

"Perhaps it's best that you don't. You will only make me furious with you, I doubt not."

He sighed deeply.

"Lyon? What is wrong? Your head doesn't still hurt you, does it?"

She sounded genuinely concerned and he smiled painfully. "Why don't you tell me some more about the West Indies?"

"I will tell you a story, a true one, if you will tell me something about yourself."

"Fair enough."

She was silent for a moment, then said, "I told you already that many Quakers settled in the West Indies. Well, one of the most famous was Dr. William Thornton, though perhaps he is still alive. In any case, my father knew him, of course. He practiced medicine, ran a plantation on Tortola, and dabbled with architecture. He is the one who designed the new American capitol building in Washington. There, that is my story for tonight."

Lyon was silent for a moment, then said, "That is interesting. I had no idea. Are there still Quakers in the West Indies?"

"No. Practically all of them were gone nearly a decade before I was born. 'Tis a pity, for they were known for their compassion, and usually they were more temperate than other landholders. Now it is your turn, Lyon. Tell me something about you, not a story."

Why not? he thought. After all, a wife should understand her husband. He settled back, pillowing his head in his arms. "I wanted more than anything in my life to join the army and fight Napoleon. When Napoleon broke the Treaty of Amiens back in '03 I was all of seventeen years old and quite ready to run away to serve my king and find glory. Then my father died. A stupid accident. He was overseeing the cutting down of trees when one of them fell on him." He heard her suck in her breath and quickly added, "He died immediately, I was told. It was tragic and I was saddened, but I was also torn with guilt. You see, for the longest time I was furious at him for dying. I was only a boy, but I knew that I was now the Earl of Saint Leven and there were no brothers behind me to take my place were I to fall in battle. My duty was to my name and to my lineage. So I tucked away dreams of glory and learned from my father's steward how to manage my estates."

"I am sorry, Lyon."

"It is life, Diana. Compromise never killed anyone. It simply hurt for quite a long time."

"I am glad you didn't go into the army. I shouldn't like it if you had been killed."

She wouldn't, would she? Well, that was a proof of sorts of her lack of indifference. "We will never know now."

"How did you come to know Hawk, the Earl of Rothermere? Lucia told me he was in the army, in the Peninsula with Wellington."

"We were boys together, then in school. I remember feeling the liveliest envy of him when he bought his commission and left England. At the time he had an older brother, you see. But with life, one never knows, does one?"

"I suppose that is a profound question."

"No, not really. How do you feel, Diana?"

"Feel? About what?"

"Do you have any physical discomfort?"

"No. What an odd question! I only drank two glasses of wine, Lyon."

"I was thinking about your belly."

"I didn't chew any goatweed either."

"You are being obtuse, my girl."

He heard her turn on her pallet. "I do not understand you."

"Did you have any discomfort yesterday?"

"No, well, not really," she said honestly, wondering what the devil he was talking about.

"Ah." Four more days, he thought. It seemed at the moment like a damned decade. It must be very difficult to be a woman on board a ship, confined in such a small space. He supposed that he might as well try to woo her during the next four days.

"Diana, I truly do not find you at all repellent."

"Thank you."

"It must have been awfully difficult for you in London."

"You mean you now feel sorry for the poor provincial little female thrust into the midst of such illustrious people?"

"I am not insulting you. What I meant was that London ways and London people were different from what you were used to. You did quite well."

"I was very worried about it, indeed, I was chewing my fingernails, but my father told me flatly that he was a gentleman and I was a gentleman's daughter and I should allow no one, not even the Prince Regent, to intimidate me." She chuckled. "Of course I didn't meet the Prince Regent, so I will never know if he would have reduced me to pulp."

"He is most charming to pretty girls. He would have kissed your fingers and praised your eyebrows."

"Actually the only person who intimidated me was Aunt Lucia."

"That old tartar has a kind heart. You mustn't ever forget that. Rest assured that she thinks a great deal of you. After all, she has deemed you worthy enough to marry me."

"Lyon!"

He continued smoothly, "Tell me something, Diana. When I pulled up your skirts and laid my hand to your bare bottom, what did you feel?"

He thought he heard her suck in her breath, but when she spoke, it was calmly enough. "I wanted to murder you, and it hurt."

"What did you feel when I stopped hurting you?"

"Just murder."

"Liar. Do you have any idea what you feel like? You have the softest flesh, the loveliest curve to your—"

"Would you please just be silent!"

"It set my poor masculine brain to thinking. I think Lois, my little amour, you know, was quite aware that I chose her because of her marvelous endowments. Bosomly endowments, that is. But it remains very difficult where you are concerned. Your beautiful bosom or your beautiful backside. I am enamored with both."

"Lyon, you are not flattering me. You are making me very angry. Now, I am sleepy. Be quiet."

"May I have a good-night kiss?"

"If the chamber pot were full, I should be sorely tempted to dash the contents on your head."

"I suppose that means no?"

But Diana didn't reply. She was thinking suddenly about his peculiar questions about any pain in her belly. Her eyes widened in the dark and breath hissed out between her teeth. The wretched man knew it was her monthly flow.

But how? He'd been watching her undress, obviously. Two and a half more weeks of this . . . this chase, with her the cornered fox. Her distress ground to a sudden halt to be replaced with a flash of insight. He had intended to seduce her tonight. She was shaking her head on her single pillow. No, she wouldn't allow that. She couldn't. She had to spike his guns.

"Lyon? Are you still awake?"

"Have you reconsidered my kiss?"

"No. Do you love me, Lyon?"

She could feel his surprise, his chagrin. There, you bounder! But his silence and obvious disarray hurt her. Keep your voice steady, fool. "Shouldn't a gentleman love a lady he wants to marry?"

"It has never before been a necessary ingredient, I doubt."

"Did you love Charlotte? For a while, at least?"

"I saw her through infatuated eyes. I thought her an angel, the essence of innocence and purity. I saw her as the perfect wife, the perfect countess, the perfect mother to my children. Obviously I was a blind fool."

"I am sorry she hurt you, but—"

"It no longer matters, Diana."

"It matters if she has made you a cynical creature who does not trust women."

"I am most fond of women, Diana. I find them quite delightful, in their place."

"And what is that, pray?"

"Several places, actually. On their backs, on their sides, on their stomachs, on—"

"Shut up! I have nothing more to say to you. Lyon, I would not marry you were you the only male on—"

"Please don't finish that trite thought."

"Nor will I let you seduce me. That was your plan for this evening, was it not?"

He'd believed himself a bit more subtle. Ah, well. "Indeed, you are not stupid," he said. "You are many things, my girl, but not stupid. Ignorant, perhaps. Silly and stubborn, certainly. A witch, doubtless. But not stupid."

"I won't let you. Come, let us be friends. You will be free of me soon. Please do not attempt to soil my memory of you."

"Soil? What a repellent notion."

She started to snore loudly.

He laughed. "I should have also said that you are never boring, Diana. We will suit well enough, you will see."

"I will see you to the devil first."

"My dear girl, do you wish that I trot out all my sterling qualities for your inspection?"

More snores answered his query.

Lyon grinned toward her and the snores. "Well, I am most fond of animals and children. I believe during one of your eavesdropping sessions you heard me say that I would be a faithful hound to my wife. It is true. I gamble, but for amusement, that is all. I enjoy the races at Newmarket and Ascot. I am plump in the pocket, which means that you could have most any trinket that pleased you. I am not niggardly. I know that ladies want and expect to be coddled. I would be an excellent coddler."

He could tell that it was becoming more and more difficult for her to continue the loud snores. He grinned and continued.

"I am not a rake, though I have kept a mistress since I came to manhood. Nothing unusual in that. I enjoy sports and promise not to become a fat stoat. I don't believe I shall lose my hair, and my teeth are excellent. Perhaps of interest to you—I am a good lover."

He heard her snore turn into a snort.

"All right, an excellent lover, then. It is just that I am prone to modesty."

The snores stopped suddenly. "Lyon, enough. I don't want or need a coddler. I don't want or need a good or an excellent lover. I simply want to be left alone, to live my life as I wish."

"And what do you wish, Diana?"

"I don't want your trinkets!"

"What do you wish?" he asked again, his voice gentle.

"Your so-called list of sterling qualities was an exercise in amusement. It is not fair of you to demand what it is I want out of life when you recite such drivel to me, expecting me to be somehow impressed with you."

"Ah, you wish me to pry off the lid, so to speak. Very well. I abhor injustice, and that includes the entire slavery issue, something that never really touched me before, but now it does and I'll be damned if I myself will be responsible for the continuation of such an appalling state of affairs." He paused a moment, surprised at himself. His voice had grown deeper, harsher. She was right, he realized. He'd been amusing himself, nothing more. He'd said nothing that really mattered. He could sense that she was listening to him, really listening. "I believe that England has many problems, but we are still the conscience of the world, if you will. A man has dignity in England, and that is important. As for what I want out of my life, I will tell you. I wish to live as contentedly as possible without hurting others. I wish to have children and give them all my care and attention, to make them responsible for themselves and for those who depend upon them, to instill in them a sense of dignity and loyalty and humanity." He stopped and drew a deep breath. Dear God, he'd never before spoken with such passion. Would Diana believe him a fool? An idealistic idiot?

There was a long silence. Finally, he heard her say in a very quiet voice, "I believe you will do all these things,

Lyon. Indeed, I wish you well. You should have added, however, that you are exceedingly stubborn, and when you decide that something must be done, you will move heaven and earth to see that it is.''

''Only when I am certain I am right, Diana.''

''Right from your point of view, certainly.''

''Diana, do not fight me on this. I will make you a good husband.''

''I, however, should make you a deplorable wife. I am not from your precious England, Lyon. My life, my experiences, have made me vastly different from you.''

''What is it that you want?''

''I want to go home and pick up the threads of my life again.''

''You won't be able to. You will no longer have control. Have you so soon forgotten that you now have a stepmother? And a stepbrother? Life, my dear, as you experienced it, will no longer exist. The threads are broken.''

''I will make do. I am still my father's heir.''

''I shouldn't count on that, now that he has a stepson in the house. Dammit, Diana, let me take care of you, let me protect you. I will protect you to the best of my ability.''

She was silent for many moments. ''Lyon, 'tis enough. I don't need any man to protect me. No, hold your tongue. I heard you out. I suppose I am like other women. I do want a husband and children. But for me to consider marriage, I would demand that the man love me, love me and respect me, as me, Diana, not simply as a woman's body in his bed or as a brood mare to produce his children. I should demand that he belong to me as I did to him. And that, my lord earl, is quite beyond you.''

His frustration came to the fore. ''Diana, love doesn't just sprout up in an instant. It is something that can develop between two people; if they care for each other, it—''

"You felt love for Charlotte, if not in an instant, at least very quickly."

He cursed floridly.

"After you have dealt with your inheritance, Lyon, you must return to England. You will find a lady to suit you there. A lady who will be quite willing to accept all that you have to offer. In short, a lady who knows your rules and is quite willing to play by them."

"This is ridiculous," he said, turned over on his side away from her, and set himself to sleep. But his body was rigid, his thoughts in chaos. And he was angry, both with himself and with Diana. He'd let her see a part of him that he wasn't in the habit of showing anyone. And as for her, he disliked experiencing her more and more as a person, as a woman separate from him, a woman who saw things clearly, perhaps too clearly, a woman who refused to bend to his will. Oh, hell.

Well, she had shown herself thoroughly a woman tonight, much to his chagrin. She demanded love, no doubt the romantic sort that he could no longer accept. He drew up his errant thinking at the sound of a sob.

He sprang upright on the bunk. "What the devil is the matter? Diana?"

14

I don't like devils. They vex me and are most unpleasant.

RABELAIS

"Diana?"

Oh, why couldn't he just disappear and leave her alone? He was infuriating.

The sounds were muffled now, and he pictured her with her fist stuffed in her mouth. He eased off the bunk, oblivious of the fact that he was naked, and came down on his knees beside her.

"Come, what is wrong? Are you not feeling well? Is your belly cramping?"

She saw red through her misery. "Must you think everything relates to my being a female? Oh, go away, Lyon!"

He touched his hand to her shoulder and frowned when he felt her flinch. "I will go away after you've told me what's wrong. Answer me. I am uncomfortable when you are silent, since you never are."

"Very well. I am unhappy. I want to be home. I don't want to have to worry about you ravishing me when I am not on my guard. I don't want to be forced to do anything I don't believe is right. There, I have answered you, now go away.''

He sat back on his heels. He wished he could see her face, but the cabin was dark as a pit. He said, very deliberately, ''If you promise to marry me, I will promise not to ravish you.''

She said quickly, too quickly for his ears, ''All right. I promise to marry you once we reach St. Thomas.''

''You are an execrable liar, you know.''

''Damn you, Lyon! What if I were the one to demand marriage? I couldn't force the issue by ravishing you. It isn't fair.''

''Perhaps it isn't fair. However, as a man, I am endowed with more innate good sense than you are. As a man, it is up to me to assist you to reason, to make you see things more clearly—''

He got a fist in his belly with such force that he fell on his rump.

''There is no talking to you, no reasoning with you!'' She jumped at him, pounding his chest.

He grasped her about her waist and pulled her down on top of him. Her legs tangled with his, her breasts were full against his chest, and his body responded instantly. Damn her anyway and her effect on him. He scowled in the dark. ''Do you have cat eyes? I do trust that you were aiming for my chest and not my manhood again.''

He felt her arm raise and quickly grabbed her wrist, bearing it down. He slid his other hand to her bottom, to hold her still against him.

''Let me go.''

''Only if you promise with absolute sincerity to attempt no more damage to my poor body.''

Diana felt him hard against her belly. She felt herself wanting to press against him. It was too much. "I promise."

"Liar. If ever in the future you try to play me false, I shall know it."

"I am not Charlotte!"

He rolled her over onto her back and quickly brought his leg over hers. Now he could see the faint shadow of her face. "I wish I could see you better. I wish I could tie you down. I wish that you weren't being so very womanly at this time."

He lowered his face and kissed her. He first landed on her nose, then her cheek. When he found her mouth, she tried to bite him.

"Leave me be, Lyon."

Her voice sounded thin as air. She was frightened. Of himself or of her own feelings? His opinion of himself and his prowess dictated that she was afraid of herself.

"You're naked, damn you!" Her hand fell away from his back as if scalded.

"Yes, and I wish you were as well. A pity. You already knew I was naked. Your hands have been all over me."

He released her and rose. "No more crying, Diana. Go to sleep and try not to dream about my demise. It won't happen."

"No," she said very low, " 'tis my demise you want."

"Don't be more of an idiot than you have been." He gingerly stepped around her and eased back into the bunk.

"I should like it vastly if you would cease flaunting your body in front of me."

Lyon knew she couldn't see him, at least not specifically. "Flaunting my body? I have never before heard of a man being accused of that. But no matter. Will I wear you down if I keep flaunting? Will you be able to keep your hands off me?"

He laughed deeply at the fairly accurate picture of Diana grinding her teeth in rage.

"Shall I teach you how to flaunt, Diana? Of course, women seem to do it naturally, but perhaps you would like lessons? I could advertise myself as a Flaunter Extraordinaire if ever I find myself in a financial quandary. What do you think?"

"I am delighted that you find your own wit so amusing. But then again, you are your own best audience."

He leaned his elbows on his knees, cupping his chin in his hands. "Did I ever tell you about a little bitch I had as a boy? As in a female dog, I meant to say. I didn't? Well, my dear, her name was Chloe, a silly name perhaps, but it suited her mongrel breeding. I found her nearly starved in a ditch, and saved her hide. Was she ecstatic about my saving her? Oh, no, she wouldn't bring herself to trust me. Every time I tried affection, she bit my hand. A most ungrateful bitch, wouldn't you say?"

"A very smart bitch!"

"Well, in any case, taming her became my ardent goal. She continued to snarl and bite at the touch of my hand on her until I finally brought her to my bed. I would talk to her at night, in the dark, much the same as we do every evening. After a week or so, I discovered that she had moved from the foot of the bed to its middle. Not long after that, I found her snuggling against my chest. Then she was licking my face. She loved me to scratch her ears and her tail would wag with pleasure."

"Are you through yet?"

"No. To my boy's delight, she became my devoted pet, following me everywhere, listening to me with profound interest each time I spoke. It was most gratifying."

Lyon paused, waiting for the blast of Diana's cannon.

"Do you not appreciate the parallel?"

"I have never bitten your hand, to the best of my recollection," she said finally, and Lyon was certain he heard suppressed laughter in her voice. She was back on an even keel. And he was still beset with the same problem.

"Do you trust me, Diana?"

"I might perhaps learn to if you were to scratch my elbows."

"Would your tail wag with pleasure?"

Her pillow struck his face. "Now, now," he chided her, "a nest is not complete without its pillow. Here." He tossed it back. "Where was I?"

"Lyon, you did not find me starving in a ditch. I am not a bitch to be tamed."

"Most women are."

"You are showing classic symptoms of your Charlotte's Disease again."

"Am I? Perhaps you have a point. Well, I will consider it. Now, can you go to sleep without falling into tears again?"

"You are a wretched clod, Lyonel Ashton!"

"Ah, more compliments. I fear to expire from your verbal bounty."

As for Diana, she decided she was safe from his assault for four more days and nights. Her brain was fertile. She would come up with something. It was odd, but it gave her little pleasure to thwart him, not really.

The damned arrogant beast. A bitch to be tamed, was she?

The weather held fair, the wind steady. The *Seawitch* glided toward St. Thomas in record time.

"Not long at all now," Rafael said to Diana, who had

taken a turn at the giant wheel. "A bit higher in the wind," he added.

"She responds so beautifully," Diana said, raising her face higher to see the sails swell more fully. "Not at all like my little sloop."

"You are an excellent sailor, for a female."

She frowned at that and saw his wicked grin. "You and Lyon," she said.

"A compliment, I take it. Blick tells me that you have ravished his poor brain of all knowledge. You appear to be a woman of many talents, Diana."

She smiled at him, abstracted, for the *Seawitch* heeled sharply at that moment. She straightened the wheel, realizing that her muscles were sore from controlling the ship's course.

"I am certain your husband must agree," he added deliberately.

Her brows lowered. "Lyon is, well, he is most . . . Ah, look, Rafael, a frigate bird! Look at that long forked tail. We are nearing home."

"A pity."

"A pity what?"

"That you didn't finish that undoubtedly fascinating thought about your *husband*."

He knows, she realized. He knows. But how? Had Lyon told him the truth? Was that his new ploy? Her monthly flow had ended several days before, but Lyon had made no attempt to seduce her. She wished she knew what he was up to, but she refused to let Rafael draw her into showing her feelings. Or perhaps Lyon had simply decided she wasn't worth his trouble or his continued blandishments. Perhaps he no longer sought the honorable path. She was being a nodcock, she thought, shaking her head. After all, his honorable path wasn't hers.

"I should love to wash my hair," she said. "Do you think you could produce some rain for us?"

"Likely. Look yon, toward the east. I should say we'll have enough rain fall to fill an extra barrel for your hair."

"By evening?"

"Yes, I think so. Now, give me the wheel before your arms become useless sticks. Like most females, the *Seawitch* needs a strong hand upon occasion. Actually, most of the time." He gave her a rakish grin, but she found herself wondering if he weren't utterly serious. Did he dislike women for some reason and was forcing himself to be kind to her because of Lyon? Could Charlotte's Disease be that prevalent?

"I think, Captain Carstairs, that you will probably meet a violent end. At the hands of a woman."

To her surprise, he reacted to her simple jest with thinned lips and his expression grew so grim that it frightened her. Then he smiled, but the smile didn't reach his eyes. "That, my Lady, is a distinct possibility."

She left him in complete disarray. She would never understand men.

She found Lyon perched on a thick coiled rope talking to Rollo. He was obviously enjoying himself. She observed him a moment, unnoticed. He wasn't so darkly tanned as Rollo—or Rafael, for that matter—but to her jaundiced eye, he looked beautiful. His shirtsleeves were rolled up and she looked at his forearms. He had, she decided, a manly tan and very strong manly muscles. She shook herself. She was being silly and perverse. Lyon saw her at that moment and paused in his speech.

Rollo stared, taken aback by the intense hunger he saw in the earl's eyes. He said a bit nervously, "Your lady is here. I shall see you later, my lord."

"You are a beautiful creature," Lyon said as she approached him, "despite the freckles that are proliferating at a great rate." He stretched out, leaning back on his elbows. "Stay there, if you please, Diana. I am hot and you are blocking out the sun."

"I want to talk to you, Lyon."

"Behold a man who awaits your every utterance with utmost attention."

"Be serious!"

"Why?"

"Lyon, Rafael knows. I demand to know if you told him."

"Told him what, Diana? That instead of being my loving wife you are my panting mistress?"

Diana slapped down her skirts at a gust of wind. Sighing, she sat down beside him. She didn't look at him. He enjoyed her profile for several moments. Damn her, he even admired the shape of her small ears.

"Yes," she said at last, turning to face him, "that is what I meant. Is your plan to add the poor captain to your campaign?"

"Is that what Rafael told you?"

"No, from his tone, I just knew that he knew."

"Actually, Rafael spoke to me some time ago. The man isn't a fool, Diana. I shouldn't be surprised if both Rollo and Blick also were aware of our . . . situation."

Diana picked up the end of the rope and began practicing some knots. Her fingers were long and nimble. He thought of her fingers stroking his body, caressing him, holding him . . . He wished he could groan.

"For some inexplicable reason," he continued thoughtfully, swallowing both the images and the groan, "they seem to hold you in some esteem, thus their show of respect for you even though you sleep with me."

"I don't sleep with you, Lyon."

"Close enough. Three feet of distance isn't much, is it?"

"It is enough for a continent."

He chuckled. "You know, it has been a long time since I was this relaxed. A sea voyage, I think, is a great restorative."

She said in a nasty voice, "Restorative from what? Overindulgence with your little amour?"

"Jealousy, my dear? It pleases me, I suppose, though I do grow tired of the game."

"I am playing no game, Lyon."

"Are you not? Well, perhaps you aren't. I have decided that you are likely right. Why should I care, after all, if you are ostracized by your close-knit little society? If you are called trollop, whore, or slut? I shall endeavor to escape your father's ire, I think, conduct my business, and return home. What you will do is your business."

"You are finally showing signs of intelligence," she said, but her tone lacked conviction. Indeed, to his sensitive ears, she sounded upset, perhaps bereft. Excellent, he thought. Deliberately he raised his hand and lightly stroked his fingertips over her ear. She grew very still, then jerked away from him.

"You know, Diana," he said thoughtfully, watching her closely, "it might be to your best advantage to gain some experience before you are hurled as a labeled trollop among the males. Perhaps if one of them touched your ear as I just did, you could learn not to react so strongly. You mustn't show interest, you know, or pleasure, as you just did with me."

"If I could manage it, I would hurl you overboard." She jumped to her feet, slapped down her billowing skirts once more, and turned away. She heard his mocking, quite satisfied laughter follow her.

It rained several hours later, just as Rafael had predicted. Diana scratched her scalp impatiently, hoping there would be enough rainwater for a good scrubbing. She ate her dinner alone in the cabin, then asked Neddie to fetch her a tub.

When the warm water steamed upward from the wooden tub, she raised a smiling face to Neddie. "Are the captain and my husband still at dinner?"

"I believe they are playing cards, my lady. I brought them a bottle of brandy."

Diana just smiled. Neddie stoutly refused to call her Diana.

"Thank you," she said.

Once alone, she unbraided her hair in record time, removed her clothing, and stepped into the tub. As she sank down, she gave a heartfelt sigh of sheer pleasure. She washed her hair with lavender-scented soap, her favorite, then washed it again. "I am human again," she said to herself.

"Indeed, a most delightful female human, I should say."

Water splashed over the sides of the tub as she jerked upright, her eyes flying to his face.

"How dare you! Get out, Lyon!"

"Your hair is quite long and thick. I cannot see a bit of you, more's the pity."

He was standing over her, his hands on his hips. There was a gleam in his blue eyes that made her feel the oddest sensations. She gulped, unconsciously covering her breasts with her hands, even though they were hidden through a thick vail of wet hair. "Please," she said, her voice shaking, "please, just leave."

"No."

He sat down in the chair at the desk and put his feet on

the desktop. He looked completely at his ease. "I have been waiting for some rain."

"I suspect you need to bathe as well!"

"I did. A group of us stripped on deck and cavorted about. We used soap, but it wasn't as sweet-smelling as yours. A manly soap, I suppose you would call it. It was a most exhilarating experience. Since you were avoiding me, I had no worry that you would wander up and surprise us."

Diana eyed the thick towels on the floor, three feet beyond her reach. "You are supposed to be playing cards with Rafael."

"Not a chance."

"Neddie said he took you a bottle of brandy."

"I left it with Rafael."

"You are not a gentleman, Lyon."

"No, perhaps not, but I am a determined man, Diana. You know, my dear, if I look closely enough, I can see the white swell of your breasts."

She howled, and he laughed.

"Are you not flaunting yourself for me?"

"Lyon, get out!"

"You are growing repetitive, Diana. Should you like me to join you? I could manage it, I think. Picture yourself wrapped around me."

She could picture it, and that made her furious with him and with herself. "Lyon, I will surely do something awful to you if you do not leave, now."

"Visions of goatweed?"

"You've been waiting for this, haven't you?"

"Well, I do prefer to make love when my partner is clean and sweet as fresh summer grass. Is that lavender? Very nice." Her eyebrows were lowered, but he merely looked amused. "You see, I fully intend to kiss every inch of you. I should prefer it, of course, if your hair were dry, but I shall make do. Now, isn't the water growing a bit chilly? Aren't you becoming a bit wrinkled from your overlong stay?''

She was becoming shriveled—hang the temperature of the water. She had to get control of this ridiculous situation. She calmly began cupping water in her hands and pour it on her hair. Then she gathered up her hair and began wringing it out. From where he was sitting, she didn't think he could see her, at least not clearly. She wound her hair about her head, twisted it so it would stay in place for a little while, then with no warning, she hurled the sponge and the bar of lavender soap at him.

She didn't look to see how true her aim was, just leapt out of the tub and grabbed for the towel. She didn't turn to face him until she was well and thoroughly covered.

He was wiping his face, and he was frowning.

She laughed.

''No,'' he said quietly to her, ''you won't ever bore me, Diana.''

''Well, you bore me! Now will you leave, Lyon? Your sport is well over.''

''I did see a flash of beautiful white,'' he said, and sighed dramatically. He picked up the sponge and wiped the soap from his face. ''You are either an excellent shot or very lucky. Which is it?''

Luck, she thought, but said, ''I am good at many things.''

''Tonight, I will test your claim.''

She stood in the middle of the cabin, a thick towel wrapped securely about her, regarding him in stony silence. What to do? He looked in complete control. Worse, he looked determined.

Suddenly, her eyes glittered as she recalled his mocking conversation of the afternoon. Why not use it against him?

She assumed what she thought to be a seductive pose. "You know, Lyon, I have always found you a lovely specimen of manhood." She slowly licked her tongue over her lower lip. Did he stiffen? "Perhaps I should let you give me lessons. You did offer, did you not? There are many men, you know, in the West Indies, lonely men who find me beautiful, who want me, who would give me great pleasure once I knew what it was all about. I think perhaps I should like to sample what they have to offer. What matter if you are the first? You certainly will not be the last."

She allowed the towel to slip, careful that it didn't fall below her breasts. Her lashes were lowered, but she was aware of his every expression. He looked uncertain. She wanted to laugh in his face, knowing that he was thinking of Charlotte and wondering. Yes, wondering. Distrustful bastard.

"Perhaps you could tell me also how not to conceive a child. If I ever did decide to be a mother, I should like to decide upon who to make the father. Did I tell you about Jonathan Crowley? Ah, what a handsome man he is; not good enough for me, of course, but I could certainly enjoy him without marriage, could I not?" She gave a delicate shudder and let the towel slip a bit lower. Thank goodness she was so well-endowed, else the wretched towel would have been at her waist three minutes ago. She saw that she had him well and fairly hooked now. He looked furious. He was pale. His hands were fisted. He looked rigid as a statue.

"Just think of all the comparisons I shall be able to make. I do promise to use you as the standard, Lyon. You tell me how virile you are. Perhaps in a year or two I can write and tell you just how well you compare to my other, er, partners. Come, you haven't moved. Cannot I have my first experience now? After all, the sooner I get rid of my virginity, the sooner I can move on to more elusive and perhaps more fascinating prey.''

Lyon didn't move. He watched that tongue of hers glide over her lips. It aroused him, but he ignored it. He wanted to strangle her. Another Charlotte, that's what she was, and just when he was beginning to believe her different. She changed her stance slightly, beckoning him as would a seasoned harlot. Her wet hair streamed about her face, over her shoulders. It should have made her look less seductive, but it didn't.

"You know, Lyon, the thought of being some husband's faithful hound is most boring. No, I shouldn't like that at all.''

That did it. He bounded from the chair, toppling it, and clutched the edges of the desk until his knuckles showed white. "You little slut! The devil, I wouldn't marry you, I wouldn't touch you . . . You are just like the others, aren't you? A bitch in heat! Take your virginity and peddle it elsewhere.'' He smacked his palm to his forehead. "How much does it take for me to learn? I must be the stupidest man alive.''

He strode from the cabin, not looking back.

Diana grinned, then quivered at the loud slamming of the door. She'd won, hadn't she? He wouldn't bother her anymore. No.

She methodically dried herself and donned her nightgown. She sat on the bunk and began to comb through the snarls in her hair. She had won, it was all for the best. She'd given him a marvelous performance. And he'd believed it. Had she been that good? Or had he simply wanted to believe that she was like his precious Charlotte?

Well, it was done. He would leave her alone.

Why did she feel suddenly as if she'd ruined something very precious?

Why did she feel as though she'd lost rather than won?

He doesn't love you, idiot. It is for the best. Damn and blast his silly honor. Well, it was no longer a question of honor or sacrifice. It was no longer a question of anything.

She didn't fall asleep for a very long time.

Lyon didn't return to the cabin that night.

15

A hungry man is an angry man.

J. HOWELL,
PROVERBS

"Lyon, you look as awful as my pet cat who ate the wrong rat and died. Poor bounder, his name was LeBeau. Pity, I was really quite fond of him." Rafael had had a cat whose name was LeBeau, but he'd died of old age and in splendid comfort in his box at the foot of eight-year-old Rafael's bed. He stared at Lyon. The earl looked ghastly.

"Same to you, Rafael," Lyon said at last.

"You need to shave and change your clothes. You look like you've slept in them."

"I have."

"Trouble in paradise? I had the distinct feeling last night that . . . Well, no matter. Anything I can do? I still have that bottle of brandy."

"She's a bitch and has about as much moral fiber as the rat your cat died of."

Rafael whistled.

"Hell, you'd best stay away from her, Rafael, else she'll probably try to get your pants off you." He realized suddenly that it was grossly inappropriate to speak of a lady . . . Lady, ha! "Oh, just forget it."

Lyon stalked away, his hands shoved in his pockets, his head bowed. There couldn't be a more miserable bastard alive anywhere. He waited to return to the cabin until he was certain Diana wouldn't be there.

He avoided her successfully for the rest of the day.

Over dinner that evening, Rafael found himself looking from Diana to Lyon and back again. Neither of them spoke to the other. What the devil had happened?

The captain sipped at his wine. "What did you do all day, Diana?"

"Nothing important," she said, not looking up from her still-full plate.

The ship heaved gently to port and her fork slid to the floor. Lyon and Diana leaned over at the same time and bumped heads. They both jerked back as if scalded. They both rubbed their heads.

Rollo retrieved the fork for her. Diana thanked him in a stifled voice.

"I trust you are feeling just the thing, Diana," Rafael said.

"Of course. Why do you ask, Rafael?"

Rafael just shook his head, but he was aware that Lyon was looking at him, alarm in his eyes for a brief moment.

Diana excused herself a few minutes later and fled to the cabin. As for Lyon, he remained at the captain's table until Rollo and Blick had bid their good nights.

"Why did you ask her that?" Lyon asked without preamble.

Rafael sat back in his chair and regarded the Earl of Saint Leven. "No reason, really," he said finally, as if bored. "She ate scarcely a bite and after what Neddie had told me, well . . .'' He stopped and began fiddling with a piece of bread.

''What did Neddie tell you?''

''Oh, just that he heard her crying in your cabin. He was worried, but didn't have the nerve to disturb her. Even though he was raised by a gin-swilling mother, he still is very sensitive to the female of the species.''

''Damn her! That conniving little bitch hasn't a thing to cry about!''

Rafael arched a black brow, but said nothing.

Lyon cursed quite floridly. Rafael turned away to hide his unholy grin. He said finally when Lyon had completed a particularly colorful curse, ''It is none of my business what goes on between the two of you. We will, however, be arriving in St. Thomas in a matter of days. I would estimate that Lucien Savarol will be reunited with his daughter within three days after that. Not a very long time to get things accomplished, I should say.''

''There is nothing at all to be accomplished,'' Lyon said in the coldest voice Rafael had heard from him. ''Not now.''

Lord, Rafael thought, the earl's voice could freeze the wine in its glass. He rose and said in his most bored drawl, ''Well, no matter. It is probably just as well that you've discovered the two of you won't suit. What if you were married before you found out you detest each other? As for Diana Savarol, I shouldn't imagine her father will kick her off his plantation or his island, for that matter.''

Lyon didn't say a word.

Rafael rose from his chair and walked toward his cabin door. He said over his shoulder in a regretful voice, '' 'Tis a pity that I am not a marrying man. She is a lovely girl. Who knows? I still have several days. Since you are no longer interested, indeed, seem to hold her in the greatest aversion, perhaps I—''

''Damn you, Carstairs! You touch her and I'll nail your hide to the mast.''

''Which mast?''

''Both.''

''Well, I shall have to consider that, won't I?'' He was grinning as he left for his cabin.

Lyon returned to the cabin when fatigue overtook him. There was nearly a full moon tonight and he could see her clearly, secure in her little nest on the floor, fast asleep. The sleep of the innocent, he thought viciously.

In a very short time, he lay on top of the covers, naked, his thoughts in a tangle. He could hear her even breathing. His final thought before he fell asleep was, Why not enjoy her body before he left her? She had offered herself to him, after all. Yes, why not? Then let her seduce all the other men in the Virgin Islands. He wouldn't care.

He didn't act on his decision, not for two more days.

''We're almost home,'' Diana said, her eyes glittering with excitement. Lyon was standing behind her, his eyes on her body. He must be losing his mind. He said nothing.

She seemed to have forgotten for the moment that they weren't speaking to each other. ''Look yon, see what I told you. All the islands. Some are barren as a desert, but others, they are so beautiful. Green, lush, with marvelous freshwater streams. And all the flowers, so vivid and beautiful they make you stare.''

Lyon continued quiet, but he looked. So this is what Columbus saw. It felt oddly safe to see land on all sides of the ship. And Diana was right, it suddenly felt as if they were indeed someplace definite. Not just insignificant beings floundering on an endless ocean.

It was very warm, and the water of the Caribbean was vastly different from the Atlantic. The water was myriad shades of blue. He watched pelicans plunge into the sea searching for food. And countless frigate birds. He was fascinated.

He said suddenly, not looking at her, "I have decided to accept your offer."

"What offer?"

"I will initiate you into lovemaking this evening. No, not really lovemaking," he corrected, "sex, pure and simple sex."

She gulped. Oh, dear. She drew a deep breath and slowly turned to face him. She gave him what she hoped was a siren's smile. "Will you really, Lyon? I am not so certain that I wish you to be the first. I have been with Rafael for many days now and I find him most virile, very manly."

"I thought I was the only manly man you knew," he said, his voice no longer so harshly determined.

Her damned seductive smile stayed in place, and she shrugged. "I suppose I have already begun to enlarge my horizons, so to speak."

His feelings were very simple and straightforward at that moment. He wanted to thrash her. "Not just yet," he said, his brows lowered. It was on the tip of his tongue to tell her that if she slept in the cabin this night, he fully intended to take her, willing or not. He kept the promise to himself. He could just see her trudging to Rafael's cabin and building her damned nest on his floor, curse her.

Instead, he gave her a bored salute and left her.

I've won, Diana thought, staring after him. He wants nothing to do with me now that I've convinced him I am just like his precious Charlotte.

She turned back to the rail and tried to recall her excitement on being so very near to home.

Only a day and a half from St. Thomas, she thought, settling herself for sleep that evening. She looked forward to seeing her father again. As for her new stepmother and stepbrother, she refused to think about them for the moment. Where was Lyon?

Probably sleeping on deck.

She fell into a light sleep.

Lyon smiled into the darkness toward the sound of her even breathing. He was naked, he was ready, and he was determined. He refused to think about what he was doing. No, if the chit wanted to be a whore, he would give her her first lessons. He wondered briefly how long it would take him to sell the Mendenhall plantation. And free the slaves? Certainly, it wouldn't be difficult.

Lyon eased down beside her, her face clear from the light of the full moon that streamed through the porthole.

He looked at her face and paused. She looked so very innocent, trusting. The sheet was down at her feet and she was only in her nightgown. Excellent, he thought. He moved closer and very slowly began untying the three ribbons down the front of her nightgown. She stirred, flinging one arm over her head.

Very gently, he pulled back her nightgown and stared down at her breasts. He swallowed painfully. She is so beautifully white, he thought, studying her in the soft moonlight, so very white and her nipples a soft pink. So very full. His fingers itched. He leaned down and took her nipple in his mouth. God, she tasted so sweet, so soft.

He jumped when he heard her moan softly.

He released her a moment and looked up at her face. She was still sleeping, doubtless an erotic dream, he thought, delighted. He set himself back to his pleasurable work. He cupped a breast, feeling its weight in his hand, and barely managed to stifle a groan. No man had ever touched her breasts, caressed them.

Soon he wanted more. He glanced down at the length of her at the nightgown and knew there was no hope for it. Slowly, he eased it up to her waist.

He sucked in his breath. Long white legs, elegantly slender, but his attention was quickly on the rich dark-blond curls between her thighs, and the flat belly above. He groaned, unable to help himself, his manhood throbbing and painfully hard. He laid his hand over her and felt the heat of her woman's flesh. He closed his eyes a moment, his fingers seeing for him.

It was her own moan that awoke her. Diana blinked, expecting darkness and seeing the cascading moonlight from the porthole. She felt nearly frantic, and frowned, but just for an instant. Then she felt his hot mouth touching her, his fingers searching her, and lurched upward.

"Lyon!"

"Hush," he said, not raising his head. His tongue found her then and she felt as though she were a quiescent ember being brought to flame.

The intense feelings were swamping her, spinning her mind out of control, pushing her body to respond, but she knew this wasn't right, it wasn't . . . She moaned, then suddenly came to her senses, what few there were left.

"No, damn you!" She jerked away, smashing her fist against his naked shoulder. "No!"

"Very well, if that's the way you want it. But you did offer, just remember that!" Lyon came up to his knees, jerked her legs apart, and flung himself down over her.

She felt his manhood against her, pushing, seeking. His

weight held her down. She felt his mouth against her cheek, then against her mouth.

"Please, Lyon," she gasped against his open mouth.

"The invitation was yours, my pet," he said. "Don't fight me, Diana." He forced her legs wider and she felt his fingers stroke down her belly, caressing her until he found her. She felt his fingertip enter her body and felt her own dampness. She shuddered. She felt his fingers opening her, then his manhood slowly entering her body.

She began fighting him in earnest, but she couldn't dislodge him. His breathing was ragged and he looked down at her as he pressed forward, slowly, very slowly.

"Lyon, please."

"Are you begging me? You did want me inside you, didn't you, Diana? I won't hurt you . . . slowly, you're opening for me. Feel me, Diana, I'm inside you."

Suddenly there was a loud banging on the cabin door. Lyon froze over her.

"Lyon! Diana! Quickly, dress yourselves!"

It was Rollo's voice, harsh and commanding.

He wanted to yell, yet he couldn't move, his body stunned with the feel of her. He felt himself pressing against her maidenhead. Just a bit longer, a bit further.

"Now! We're going to be attacked!"

Lyon jerked out of her and came to his feet. He was breathing hard, long, painful breaths.

Attacked! What the devil did that mean? No, it was Diana who was under attack. Lyon shook his head and automatically reached for his britches.

"Hurry!" Rollo shouted.

"Get your clothes on, Diana."

She scrambled to her feet, threw off her rumpled nightgown, and grabbed for her underthings.

Lyon shouted, "We're coming, Rollo!"

They heard his pounding footsteps retreat. They became aware of the sound of dozens of running feet overhead.

"My God, what the devil is going on?"

There was no answer to his question. He was pulling on his boots, forcing himself to calm.

Diana wasn't thinking at all. She couldn't bear to. She didn't bother with her petticoat, just jerked her gown over her chemise.

"Come," Lyon said as she was slipping her bare feet into her slippers.

They raced down the companionway, up the steps, and through the hatch to the deck. They were met by Rafael. He said very calmly, "There are two French men-of-war about three hundred yards from our starboard. They've spotted us, blast this full moon. I don't want you two aboard when the fighting starts. You could be killed; worse, if they take us, you would be captured. See the island off our port?" He pointed to the small lump of land whose outline they could see clearly in the moonlight. " 'Tis not more than a quarter of a mile. I trust both of you are swimmers. I want you to dive over now and swim to the island. Once this is over I will return for you. Diana, Lyon, my luck to you both. Come along now."

They followed him in a silent daze to the bow of the ship.

"Good luck, Rafael," Diana said, eased her legs over the rail, and gracefully dived into the water.

"Take care," Lyon said, clasped Rafael's hand, and followed Diana over the side.

The water was a shock, but a moment later, it felt warm. Diana saw Lyon's head break the surface, called out to him, then began to swim in firm, controlled strokes toward the island.

Lyon realized quickly enough that he wasn't as good a

swimmer as Diana, but he was strong and he kept pace with her. Just as they reached the surf, they heard the loud booming sound of cannons.

"Oh, no," Diana said softly, turning about to look out to sea. "Lyon do you believe Rafael will save the *Seawitch*?"

"If any man can, he will. Come, let's get to shore."

They both collapsed on the sand just beyond the surf line, each of them breathing hard. There were more cannon blasts and gunfire and they saw water billowing upward in the distance around the *Seawitch*.

"If Rafael is smart, he'll cut loose and run."

"If they haven't already surrounded him," Diana said. "There have been so few French ships in this area. I don't understand this. Why are they here?"

"I have this feeling that Rafael isn't your average merchant captain," Lyon said. "There is a mystery surrounding that man and his voyage to St. Thomas."

Suddenly, the immediate fear over, Diana turned to look at Lyon. His hair was plastered against his head, his clothes clinging to his body. She watched him pull off his boots.

"It would appear," she said slowly, "that my virtue was saved by the French."

He looked over at her, wriggling his toes in the sand. "Let us say that you are still a half-virgin, at least for the present."

She could feel him inside of her, pressing, and she jerked at the vivid image. She sat down on the sand and lowered her head between her knees.

"I hope we are on one of your paradise islands and not the barren sort. Do you happen to know where we are? Which island?"

"No, at least not yet. Perhaps in the morning I will recognize something."

Lyon got to his feet and looked around. "I suppose we should do something. Make a shelter." Suddenly a raindrop hit his nose. "Rain," he said blankly. "Bloody hell!"

The moon was suddenly obscured. Diana raised her face and felt the rain begin to clean away the saltwater. "I hope it storms hard. It just might save Rafael and the *Seawitch*. Yes, shelter."

They walked away from the water, then Lyon paused, reality hitting. "I haven't the foggiest notion of how to survive on an island."

The rain was coming down in sheets now.

Diana said, "First of all, go down the beach a bit, take off your clothes and wash off. Your clothes too, else they'll feel miserable and stiff when they are dry."

He nodded and walked away from her. Diana waited until he had turned a bend around the beach, then stripped off her clothes. She washed her hair and her body in the warm, pulsing rain. Like Lyon's tongue and mouth and fingers and his . . . Stop it, you silly fool! She grabbed up her clothes and rinsed them out. She hated to put on the wet chemise and gown, but there was no chance she would parade about in front of Lyon without a stitch on. She was picking up her sodden slippers when he returned.

"Now what?"

"It's too dark to gather palm fronds for a shelter. Let's try to find some thick foliage to protect us from the worst of it for the rest of the night. We need to sleep."

"Perhaps there are people on this island."

"Perhaps," she agreed. She wouldn't tell him yet, but if there were no fresh water on the island, they would be in a sorry condition indeed, and in a very short time.

They made their way inland and soon found a tangle of growth that kept the most of the rain from them.

"At least we won't freeze to death," Diana said as she eased herself down. She hated the wet clothes, the clammy feeling. Lyon came down beside her, leaning his back against what Diana called a manchineel tree. "Just don't touch the leaves, Lyon. They cause blistering."

"I'm surprised you told me."

"If you did rub the leaves, I would just have to listen to your complaints. Besides, you wouldn't be able to help me."

"Such warmth and caring," he said, and sighed. The branches and leaves were so thick overhead that only an occasional raindrop came through. "This is most bizarre. Alone with you of all people on a desert island . . ."

"You are most lucky that it isn't a desert island! So far I have seen abundant coconut palms and some sugar-apple trees. We won't starve. Furthermore, Lyon, if you weren't with me, I wouldn't place your chances for survival very high."

Surprisingly, he agreed. "I wish now that I had read *Robinson Crusoe* after the precocious age of eight. I don't remember a thing."

"It will be all right," she said firmly. "Rafael will escape the French, what with the storm. He will come back for us in no time at all."

"If for no other reason than to have you grateful to him to get you in his bed."

She sucked in her breath. "Unlike you, my lord, Rafael is a gentleman."

He laughed and raindrops fell on their faces from the disturbed leaves above their heads.

"Let's try to get some sleep. I hope there are no creatures about to nibble on us?"

"Do you hear that chirping sound? That's a coqui. A tree frog. He doesn't do nibbling. There is nothing awful to frighten you, I promise."

"You sound like my old nanny telling me that there were no monsters in the night to eat little boys. Good night. I need my strength to accept your directions on survival."

He thought she muttered a curse, but he couldn't make it out. He grinned, thinking yet again that never in his wildest dreams had he pictured himself in such a strange situation.

"Beware the iguana, Lyon."

He started. "What the hell is that?"

"Iguanas look like monsters, but they're more afraid of you than the other way around. There aren't many of them around now."

"Now that you've provided fodder for my dreams, I'll thank you to keep your mouth closed."

He awoke once during the long night, found Diana snuggled against him, and smiled. He pulled her close. Before he found sleep again, he was very aware of every foreign sound, aware of the dense growth all around them.

This is not at all the place for an English earl, he thought.

16

Base and squalid things have no appeal for men of noble virtue.

SENECA

"My God! What the hell is that?"

Lyon was eye to eye with a ferret-sized creature. It was repulsive, and to wake up so, it was a shock.

Diana jerked awake, felt Lyon as tense as a bowstring, and laughed when she saw what had startled him.

"It's only a mongoose," she said, still laughing, buffeting him on his shoulder. She watched the mongoose scurry away. "He was imported by early settlers to keep down the rats who destroyed the sugarcane. He's not so popular anymore as he's too prolific and eats everything in sight."

"Thank you," he said politely. "I don't believe how green everything is. I feel like I've been grown over during the night with green."

"Could be with the heavy rain." She sat up beside him. "Well, my front is dry but my back feels dreadful." She stretched. "Once in the sun, though, we'll be dry within thirty minutes."

"Your back is dryer than mine, I'll wager, since you were using me for your nest."

He looked over at his once-fine leather boots. Even they looked damp and green. He was sore, clammy from a wet backside, and still off-balance from his encounter with that mongoose. He watched Diana rise and stretch, quite thoroughly this time. His body, without his permission, reacted immediately. "Damn you," he muttered.

She stared down at him. "I have said nothing untoward. Are you always such a curmudgeon in the morning?"

He rose and shook off the excess foliage that clung to his clothes. "That is the stupidest thing I've heard you say. For God's sake, our situation is hardly commonplace. I just hope I don't look as dreadful as you do." He stalked off to relieve himself.

Diana stared after him. "I would sail away and leave you here if I could," she said after his retreating back.

That brought a snort, but nothing else. Diana took care of her own needs, then made her way back to the beach. Lyon was already there, his face raised to the bright early-morning sun.

"The first thing to do after breakfast is to make ourselves some hats," she said. "The sun here will roast you like a fowl."

He didn't reply, merely looked out at the water. "Under other circumstances I would say this is the most beautiful sight I've ever seen. The water is crystal blue—at least I think that's what the color is. And the beach, my God, the sand is white." He leaned down and took a handful of sand, letting the grains fall from between his fingers. "Just look, Diana, it's truly white."

She smiled, delighted that he loved her home. Her smile fell away quickly enough. Damn him, he'd tried to ravish her!

"After you are over your raptures, find a rock. We will have coconut for breakfast. Perhaps later I can find some cassava—it's a root I can grind into flour and make some flat bread.''

As she ate her coconut meat, she busily planned what they would do. Unbidden, after she'd thought about the shelter they'd build, the image of Lyon, naked, covering her, came starkly into her mind. She could feel his fingers parting her, his mouth on her. She closed her eyes. At least she knew well enough that she looked perfectly awful. Surely he wouldn't be interested in repeating his ravaging. Unconsciously, she began untangling her hair with her fingers.

Lyon, amused, sat back and watched her. "I've never before eaten coconut. It is quite tasty. You look wonderful, Diana."

"Ha!"

Lyon leaned back, supporting himself on his elbows. "I just assumed that you wanted to make yourself presentable for me. With your hair untangled, you can lie on top of me and make your hair my blanket, along with your body.''

She jumped to her feet. Hands on her hips, she frowned down at him. "I do not understand how you can even think about such things in light of where we are.''

"Why were you trying to fix your hair, if not to seduce me? I've given you a taste of sex and doubtless now you'll be the one to attack me.''

She had no answer to that and simply turned around. She said over her shoulder, "I am going to make myself a hat. If you wish to make yourself one, come along.''

Within an hour, they had fashioned primitive hats from palm fronds. "I suggest you keep your shirt on, Lyon. The sun will bake you.''

"I just wanted to flaunt myself for you. Without words, are you? Well, then, back to business. Do you have any idea where we might be?''

"I've been trying to figure that out. We can't be too-far from Virgin Gorda."

"A fat virgin?"

She giggled. "Isn't that marvelous? Actually that island used to be the capital long ago before it was moved to Tortola. The name is due to the shape, which, as you can imagine, is quite large in the middle. As for exactly where we are, I truly cannot be certain. As for people living here, Lyon, I shouldn't pin your hopes on it."

"No, I shan't. I wonder how large the island is."

"We can explore later. Perhaps I will see something I recognize from another vantage point."

"All right, my dear. What is next thing on our list of things to do?"

He learned about guavaberries, a starchy fruit they would have to bake before they could eat it. Diana found the cassava and dug up the roots with a stick.

And all around them was lush beauty and so many bright flowers that Lyon gave up on remembering their names. "There is a turtledove," Diana said, pointing up at the low branch of what Lyon recalled was a cycad tree at a sleek bird with white wingtips. "The island of Tortola is named after it."

"It's the flowers I find truly amazing," he said. He plucked a scarlet hibiscus and gave it to Diana. Obligingly, she tucked it over her left ear.

"Very beautiful," he said, his fingertips lightly caressing her cheek. Before she could jerk away from him, he added, "Is my face as red as yours?"

"Yes. Keep your hat on. This afternoon we must stay in the shade."

Lyon hadn't the foggiest notion of how to produce a fire. He watched, fascinated, as Diana managed to produce a spark from the sticks she was rubbing together. She leaned her head down and gently blew on the spark, then fanned it gently with her hand. "There," she said, sitting back on her heels. "Now I can make us a marvelous lunch!"

They constructed a small stone oven of sorts. Lyon wove palm fronds together the way she had shown him, and watched Diana pound the cassava root into flour.

"Water," she said suddenly. "The time has come, Lyon. We've got to find some fresh water."

He just stared at her a long moment. They'd drunk the milk from the coconut earlier. "I hadn't thought of that," he said slowly, the implications rising in his mind with alarming accuracy.

They collected hollow coconut shells and went inland. "We must look very carefully," she said, pushing a branch of a tree out of her way. "Let's take some of this fruit. It's mango and quite good just as it is."

"Why must we look carefully?"

"If we find fresh water, it is very likely that it will be surrounded by so much foliage that we won't at first see it."

The island rose only very slightly, but the humidity and the struggle through the dense undergrowth left them quickly winded. They found a pond fifteen minutes later. It was the most beautiful spot Lyon had ever seen. Vivid pink oleanders and scarlet hibiscus were everywhere, and the brightest greens he had ever witnessed surrounded the small pool.

It didn't look at all stagnant, which surprised him. "Can we also bathe here?"

"Yes, certainly. It is fresh because it usually rains in the afternoon."

"Will you bathe with me? Think of the fun we could have."

"Go to the devil, Lyon."

"Let's get our water, then I am going to strip and wallow in that pool."

She wanted to also and eyed it wistfully. She looked up to see him shrugging out of his shirt, then peeling off his britches. She turned quickly around waiting until she heard a splash and a groan of pleasure.

"I've died and gone to heaven," he said, grinning at her. "Look, Diana, keep on your chemise. Come on, I swear not to ravish you."

"There is so much more we have to do," she began.

"And all the time in the world to do it. Come on." With those words, he turned and swam to the other side of the pool.

Diana slipped off her gown and jumped into the water. It wasn't deep, just barely over her head in the middle. She kicked off the sandy bottom. "Ah," she said with great satisfaction when her head cleared the water.

He watched her unbraid her hair and fan it out around her. She looked happy and carefree as a child. He felt something change deep inside him. It was a very warm, a very expanding feeling. "It was that coconut I ate," he said to himself. "It's making me bilious."

"Did you say something?"

He wanted to swim to her and wrap her hair around him. But he had promised, more fool he. He said instead, "The name 'Virgin Gorda' is delightful. Are there others as intriguing?"

She swam toward him, stretched out, and found that her feet touched bottom. "Well, there's Beef Island and Peter Island. Not terribly enchanting. How about Dead Chest or Ginger Island?"

"Virgin Gorda will remain my favorite. What is the Spanish word for slender or thin?"

"Why?"

He grinned at her. I want to find a suitable nickname for you, my dear."

"In that case I shan't tell you! Besides, you told me I wasn't a complete virgin anymore."

At that moment, he actually felt again his manhood pressing briefly against her maidenhead. He shuddered, his eyes closing. He felt the tightness of her, the warmth. "You're virgin enough," he said, and he sounded as if he were in pain.

"Lyon?"

"Leave it, Diana. Do your survival accomplishments include the making of soap?"

She shook her head regretfully. "We haven't the means or the ingredients. However, if you get a handful of sand from the bottom, you can scrub with it."

He disappeared underwater. She watched him sand his chest, his neck, then his thick hair. "Shall I sand your hair for you?"

She shook her head, mute. He was so beautiful. She wanted to touch him, his chest, his face, feel the texture of his hair.

She went on the attack, the verbal attack to cover her lapse. "For a London dandy, you're taking all this surprisingly well."

"I am, aren't I? However, if pirates land, I shan't be able to protect you."

"There have been no pirates for nearly a hundred years."

"Will you tell me pirate tales at night around a campfire?"

"The ones I know would probably keep both of us awake. Now, my lord earl, it is time we got ourselves together." She swam back and prepared to climb onto the bank. She swiveled about to face him. "Lyon, you will turn your back please."

"No."

She frowned at him, but it did no good. He merely grinned at her, the vision of the unrepentant. She climbed out with very little grace.

"Lovely."

She whirled around, and again he felt that tightening feeling. Her chemise came only to above her knees and her wet hair streamed over her shoulders and down her back. "You have beautiful legs. As for the rest of you, I can still see your white bottom and—"

"Stop it!" She grabbed her gown and retreated behind a frangipani shrub.

She couldn't bear to put her gown on over her wet chemise. She peeked around between the trees and saw Lyon climb out of the pool. She quickly closed her eyes, slipped out of her chemise in record time, and was fastening her gown before he could have moved.

"A pity."

She looked up to see him standing in front of her, clothed only in his britches. "What is a pity?"

"Had I been but a moment quicker, mine eyes would have seen all the glory."

She grinned, unable to help herself. She began wringing out her long hair. A few minutes later, she braided it.

They found a shortcut back to their temporary home. Diana made some flat cassava bread to go with the guavas for their lunch.

"I think I'll keep you around," Lyon said, patted his stomach, and leaned back against a palm tree.

"Thank you. At least now you've got the right idea. We must stay in the shade until late afternoon. Nap if you wish."

"How about finishing off your virginity instead? I think I could summon up the energy."

"It's cool in the shade, not more than eighty degrees, I'd say. But in the sun—"

"Not going to answer me, huh? I can't interest you in a little dalliance? After all, you did assure me that you—"

"Lyon, I lied."

"What about this time?"

Diana eyed him with growing anger. He was lying on his back, the very picture of indolence, his palm-frond hat pillowing his head against the palm trunk. His white shirt was unbuttoned to his waist, his arms crossed over his chest. Damn him, even his bare feet were lovely, long, narrow, but reddened from the sun. Well, nothing manly about sunburned feet.

"What about?" he repeated, slanting her a look.

"Never mind," she said abruptly, now regretting the temporary softness of her brain.

"Perhaps you'll tell me later, tonight, when it's dark and the romantic moon is shining down on us. I can sing to you, quote poetry to your long eyelashes, and—"

"I'm going to collect seashells."

"No, Diana, stay in the shade. I'll take my nap and leave you in peace." He closed his eyes.

She heard his breathing even into sleep. As if he didn't have a care in the world.

What had happened to Rafael and the *Seawitch*? She prayed he had escaped the French. If he hadn't, she and Lyon could remain here for a very long time. And that would prove impossible. She sighed and settled herself for her own nap.

"If I knew where we were exactly," she said that evening as they sat in front of their small fire, "we could perhaps construct a boat or something and go somewhere."

"You know how to make a boat?"

"Well, I've seen it done, but—"

"But?"

"No, I can't. We could lash some logs together, I'm not quite certain with what, and make a raft."

"But we haven't a knife to cut your logs."

"No, we haven't. Well, we'll just have to build a signal fire, then. A pity that there really isn't a high point anywhere on the island." They'd explored the island in the late afternoon. It was depressingly small, shaped roughly like a mango. Diana couldn't find a landmark she recognized from any vantage point.

"Would you like some more breadfruit?"

"I'm stuffed, thank you."

"Did you know that the breadfruit was brought from the Hawaiian islands by Fletcher Christian?"

"Who the devil is that?"

"The man responsible for a mutiny against a very bad captain by the name of Bligh. From the stories I've heard about him they should have made him walk the plank. He survived the *Bounty* mutiny to sail again. He might still be alive and well and sailing about, for all I know."

"What's this about walking the plank?"

"A particularly nasty punishment the pirates invented. You see, they would strip the man naked, cut him up a bit so he was bleeding, then force him to walk down this stretch of board and jump into the sea. The sharks were waiting. That was the point."

"And you call this place civilized?"

"It was a long time ago, Lyon."

"You know something, Diana, even with your speed in building a fire, it would take us some time to make that signal fire visible to a passing ship. Worse than that, our only hope is that small rise at the northern end of the island. Someone would have to be looking for us to see any fire we built there."

"I know. I guess we'll just have to hope that Rafael comes back for us."

"If he can, he will." He grinned over the fire at her. "Otherwise, you and I will grow old and crotchety together on our own private island."

She said nothing to that and sat back, looking toward the gentle white-capped surf. It was a beautiful, clean night; then again, it was usually this way in the West Indies. "At least we don't have to worry about hurricanes this time of year."

"Thank you for reassuring me," Lyon said dryly. "I guess we wouldn't reach a very advanced age."

"Probably not. Look at the stars, Lyon. Have you ever seen such a sight in the English skies?"

"Brilliant as diamonds and so close you could reach out and caress them?"

"I suppose you could put it that way."

"I'm randy as a goat. How else should I say it?"

"Stop it, Lyon."

"Why?"

"Very well. I lied. There, I've said it."

"This is a routine that is growing boring, Diana. Once more, lied about what in particular?"

"I lied about wanting to be . . . abandoned. I don't want to be a trollop. I don't want to have men pawing me, ever. I want to remain a half-virgin. I would have preferred being a whole virgin, but what's done is done."

Lyon simply stared at her. He didn't doubt her. He felt like a complete fool. If he hadn't wanted to believe that she was like Charlotte, he would have seen through it in a minute. The glowing embers cast shadows on her face, and he wished he could see her expressive eyes more clearly.

"All that was nonsense? An act to keep me away from

you? To make me so furious that I wouldn't want to touch you?''

''That's right. It worked for a while, until you got furious in the other direction, so to speak.'' She raised her face and looked at him clearly. ''I don't want to be forced, Lyon. Not by any man. I want to stay myself.''

''That's impossible. Now.''

She sucked in her breath at his wretched complacency. She tried for contempt and managed a weak sneer. ''Is this the behavior of a London gentleman? To force a woman? I thought you earls only did that to helpless females dependent on you. Maids, farm girls—''

''Don't be a damned fool, Diana! Never have I taken advantage of a female dependent on me.''

''You were going to force me. What is your excuse for that?''

He shrugged and doused the feeling of guilt. ''I don't have one. But now I do. Please dampen the idiotic woman's logic and listen to me. You and I, my dear girl, are alone together on an island. When we are rescued, we will be soon enough with your father. Now, you have no choice but to accept me as your husband. None at all.'' He paused, then said, ''Something just bit me!''

''A mosquito, I guess. I thought there would be more of them, but we're lucky. On some islands they are everywhere. I could make us up something from mud and wild basil, but it's more noxious than an occasional bite.''

''There's something else, my dear,'' he said, harking back. ''When and if we are rescued, I doubt we'll be wearing much. Already my britches are the worse for wear. As for your gown, I suggest that you simply remove it and go about in your chemise, else it won't last out the next three days. Do you wish to be stark-naked when help arrives?''

There were rips in the gown and two seams had parted. He was right. "You don't have a chemise," she said.

"No." He grinned, and in the dim firelight she could see his white teeth gleaming. "But I suppose you need to accustom yourself to my body. Perhaps it will make you more reasonable."

"Why is it that men seemingly have no modesty?"

"Because we have a natural tendency to flaunt? All right, we just don't, that's all. Besides, I think I should like to have a tan all over."

"Lyon, I don't like you."

"Ah, my heart overflows with your sweet words. I think I shall go to sleep now. If you get cold, feel free to come to me for warmth. I shall try, at least now, to contain my randiness."

"Thank you."

"Lord, I wish I had a brandy. It's really the only thing I miss."

She giggled. "Do you know that we make wine from sugar apples? It is our Christmas wine."

"I know, you've watched it made, but you can't quite manage it. Right?"

"Forgive me."

"I should also like to clean my teeth."

"Hmmm. You know, perhaps there is some white root on our island. We could grind it up and rub our teeth with it. Mixed with water, it also makes an excellent mouthwash. We'll find some tomorrow."

Our island. He smiled a bit at that.

17

'Tis safest in matrimony to begin with a little aversion.

RICHARD SHERIDAN

"Oh, dear," Diana said blankly, staring. Well, at least Lyon wasn't strutting about naked, but the small breech-cloth he'd fashioned out of the sleeves of his white shirt would enlighten the most dim-witted female mind. His legs were long and muscular, sprinkled with dark-brown hair, and when he turned his back, she could see the line of his buttocks, lean and hard. She could just imagine what she would see if Lyon ran and jumped. She gulped and pounded a stone on a hapless coconut. It cracked open with a satisfying splat.

"I will not look at you! You are ridiculous. Wretched bounder. Arrogant—"

"All that?"

She was on her knees, wearing only her white chemise, which wasn't quite so white now. She looked up the length of him and knew such a rush of *that* kind of warmth she nearly choked on the piece of coconut she was chewing.

Lyon came down to his haunches in front of her. "Don't

you like my male attire? I am endeavoring to spare your maidenly, or rather semimaidenly, sensibilities.''

She began grinding the cassava root, viciously.

''You look rather enticing yourself, Diana. We're both tanning nicely. A pity that I can't convince you to sun with me—like Adam and Eve. Are there any fig leaves in the Virgin Islands?''

''Go away and do something useful.''

''I've been trying, but those fish are elusive. You know something else? Fish are cruel. No, it's true. They can see me and I can see them and they're laughing at me.'' He gave his makeshift spear a rueful look. ''I haven't got the hang of it yet and they know it. They swim very close, just to mock me. You would think that with all my varied skills, I could manage to catch something after a day's practice.''

''Keep trying.''

''If I succeed, I must tell you that I have no intention of scaling the creature.''

''Faintheart. Dandy.''

Lyon scratched his belly. ''Why are you in such a snit? We've a shelter of sorts. Plenty of fresh water. Enough food for the next hundred years and even our own private bathtub. God willing, we might even have fresh fish for our dinner.''

''You tan easily,'' she said, and to his amused ears, it sounded like an accusation.

He just grinned at her and continued scratching his bare belly. ''Thank you, ma'am.'' He saw that her eyes were on his scratching fingers and added, ''You know, it's this bloody sand. It gets into everything.'' Still grinning, now more devilishly, he began to scratch his hip. ''I find myself wondering about lovemaking on the sand. Surely it couldn't be all that pleasant. Why, just think of all that sand getting into—"

"Lyon! Go away!"

He stood and her eyes followed his lithe motion. Rot him for that evil, knowing smile. He patted the top of her suddenly lowered head and strolled off, whistling and carrying his silly spear at a jaunty angle.

Diana frowned after him. She was peevish, and there was no reason for it. Not really. It was just that . . . Admit it, you want him, desire him. Either that or she was cursed with some strange island disease. Or perhaps she was cursed with Lyon's Disease.

She sighed. But he doesn't love you. Charlotte ruined all that. He was just a randy male specimen. He'd admitted that, too many times, himself.

She was shaping the flat loaf of cassava bread when she heard his shout of triumph. She straightened, whirling about. She saw him waving his spear toward her, a wriggling fish impaled on its tip.

"This one isn't laughing now," he shouted.

She crossed her fingers, for there were so many poisonous fish in the Caribbean. He strode toward her burnished and beautiful as a pagan God. He was saved from that ultimate comparison by the cocky and quite unholy grin on his face.

"Thank God," she said, eyeing the fish. "It's a grouper. Quite edible and quite good. And nearly enough for two."

He gave her a mock bow and handed the spear, fish and all, to her.

"Did you see any nurse sharks, Lyon?"

"I was careful to keep my toes out of the crevices in the reef, just as you told me."

"Good. They do nibble if they are offered something so delectable as toes.".

"You want to swim with me? Maybe we could find an octopus or a barracuda."

She would like to swim, but she looked at the fish and knew if it weren't cooked quickly, it would rot. She sighed. "A woman's work," she said. "I am chained to my cooking pot, or at least I would be if I had one."

"A little conversation then while you perform that ghoulish task." He sat down beside her on a palm frond, to protect himself from the omnipresent sand, and crossed his legs. She coshed the fish on the head, rendering it quite dead, then picked up another bit of sharp stone. He looked pained. "If I watch this process, I doubt I will be able to eat it."

She gave him a scornful look. "You will get used to it quickly enough. Fish are food, not pets."

"That sounds like a truism from a parent. How are you going to cook it?"

"I'll rub it with some coconut milk, wrap it in palm fronds, and bake it in the embers."

She paused suddenly and looked over at him, her expression thoughtful. "Every time I think about where we are, or where we aren't, I still can't believe it. Castaway with you, of all people, an English earl! It isn't quite like waltzing in a ballroom in London, is it? Or tooling your grays about in Piccadilly?"

Lyon stretched out on his back, pillowing his head on his arms. "A unique experience, certainly. A prewedding trip, so to speak. You must admit, Diana, that few couples have such an interesting opportunity to get to know each other in such odd and various ways."

She found herself looking at his body. The swirls of hair on his chest looked soft and quite tempting. And his flat belly, well . . . She gulped, her eyes briefly straying to the bulge beneath his ridiculous breechcloth.

"Don't you agree?"

She jerked. "Wh-what?"

He opened his eyes and looked at her flushed face. He gave her a very knowing smile. "Are you ready for me now, my dear?"

"I don't know what you're talking about. I suppose you're going to snooze now that you've provided our dinner."

"I need to garner my strength," he said in the blandest voice imaginable.

"Lyon!"

"Don't bleat, Diana."

"I'm not," she said, this time her voice nearly a screech.

"Look, a man who's worth his salt finishes what he begins. And I believe, my dear girl, that you've a wish that I do finish what I started. Tell the truth now."

"We're not married! I've been taught that one doesn't do that until one is married."

"I recall offering you Rafael's services. As a captain he could have tied our knot."

She was rubbing coconut milk distractedly over the scaled grouper. He watched her, amusement growing.

"I've never deflowered a virgin before."

She rubbed more furiously.

"I really should finish since I've only managed to loosen the flower from the stalk, so to speak."

"That is a ridiculous metaphor. I am not an oleander."

"True. Perhaps the sun is addling what few brains I have left. Give me some of that coconut milk. I can feel my nose and surely that isn't right." He rubbed his nose, with the white milk, then lay back again, bending one leg at the knee. Her eyes followed the line of that leg. "After all, here I am proposing not only marriage to you, but also offering you my body.''

''Which is not worth all that much!''

He came up on his elbows and looked down at himself. ''You have no faith, Diana. That can be changed in a flash of interest. I can easily become a man of quite noble proportions. Forgive my lack of modesty, but I believe truth is called for here.''

She sat up on her heels, the smell of fish in her nostrils, and closed her eyes.

''You are provoking.''

''Did I give you no pleasure at all?''

She wanted to fling the fish at him. No, it was their dinner, and she didn't want it to get sand all over it. Oh, dear, sand . . . everywhere. ''No,'' she said. ''What would you expect if I forced you? To enjoy yourself immensely?''

He stretched out on his back again, spread-eagled, his arms out. ''I'm yours. Force me.''

''My body is a temple,'' she said inanely, harking back to Dido's off-repeated lecture when Diana had started her monthly flow at the age of thirteen.

''Behold an ardent worshiper. Incidentally, that is the most amazing thought. Do women really think like that? Lord, you make yourself sound like a holy relic.''

''Isn't it you damned men who want a woman to protect herself? To be chaste and virtuous?''

''You have no worries. You will be. Except with me, your soon-to-be husband.''

''And what about you, Lyon? Will you continue with your little amours.''

''I do wish you would attend me, Diana. Don't you remember? As a husband, I will be the most faithful of hounds. Shall I begin sniffing around your chemise?''

She quickly finished wrapping the grouper in layers of

palm fronds, and shoved it in among the glowing embers. She got to her feet. "I am going to find some conch. Some queen conch to be specific. Since your contribution to dinner isn't all that impressive, perhaps I can make some conch steaks."

"A woman with ambition. That pleases me. Now, as I said, my dear, I shall sleep now and garner my strength."

She could never remain angry with him long, she thought as she walked along the beach, her toes in the warm surf. He made her laugh. It would be rather nice to spend one's life with a man who made one laugh.

"Oh, dear," she said to a circling pelican, "I am losing what little sense I have left."

She made her decision late that afternoon. She left Lyon swearing as he tried to hone a rock to make a sharper spear tip. She made her way to the small pool, stripped off her chemise, and jumped in. She bathed, then washed her hair, spending ten minutes to rinse out all the sand.

When she returned to the beach, he was weaving together some more palm fronds for thatch on their shelter. It covered them, nothing else. She prayed it wouldn't rain hard, else they'd be left under collapsed fronds.

"You're getting quite proficient at that," she said, her voice a bit thin, for she was seeing him now with new and very determined eyes.

"Yes," he said absently, not looking up.

Her new eyes became a bit impatient. She'd even gotten the tangles out of her hair and carefully positioned a scarlet hibiscus over her ear. He could at least look and show his interest.

"You know," he said after a moment, still not looking up, "I dearly wish for a deck of cards. Any ideas?"

Yes, she had some ideas, but they had nothing to do

with any wretched cards. "We could mark some small rocks, I suppose, and make dice."

"What a brilliant—" His voice broke off as he looked up at her. "Lord, woman, you look good enough to eat. Better than that grouper even."

She'd gotten her wish, but found that all of a sudden she could think of nothing to say.

"This I do believe is your example of flaunting. Am I correct, sweetheart?"

Sweetheart? His voice was so smooth, the bees would mistake him for honey.

"I'm not sure," she said, relieved that she could say that much. She felt as if she were on display, a discomfiting feeling that she didn't like. To her combined chagrin and relief, Lyon merely nodded and rose.

"I do believe I'm bored. I think I'll swim a bit before dinner. See you later, Diana."

"I hope a stingray gets you," she called after him. "One barb from its tail and you'll howl like a banshee!"

Lyon didn't reply, nor did he turn around. He was grinning, a triumphant, satisfied male grin. He finally had her where he wanted her. She'd finally decided to accept him, all of him.

He hummed a sailor's ditty he'd learned from Rollo. It was about a female pirate who found her errant husband in a bordello in St. Thomas and stabbed him. He wondered if the story were true.

"The grouper isn't bad at all," Diana said, licking her fingers. "But the conch steak is awful. It's so tough my teeth feel like they'll pop out."

"Pop out? You mean like your bosom? What an awesome thought."

Her immediate thought was to yell at him, but she

stopped herself. He expected her to be embarrassed, to berate him for his drawing comments. Instead, she tried for a flirting smile. It wasn't much of one, but it was a start. "You mean that you find my bosom awesome, Lyon?"

He looked momentarily startled, and she was pleased. But it wasn't to last.

"Well," he said, tossing fish bones over his shoulder, "I'm not certain if awesome is the correct word. I do remember that your breasts more than fill my hands. And my hands, as you've noticed, are quite large." He held them up in front of him, cupping them.

She slouched forward, out of habit.

He had the bad grace to laugh. "That helps very little, my dear girl. You cannot make those lovely attributes disappear, thank the good Lord."

"What about you?"

"One look, one I-suppose-I'm-interested look, and you'll see soon enough."

"Lyon," she said, her voice thin, bordering on invisible.

He sat forward suddenly and took her hand in his. "I enjoy fencing with you. Perhaps in several decades from now, you'll be able to carry it to the finish line."

She blurted out, her eyes on his brown hand holding hers, "Hawk and Frances love each other to distraction!"

"Yes, they do," he said, lightly stroking her hand. "But it wasn't always so. Like us, in a sense, they were forced to wed each other. Frances, bless her imagination, disguised herself as a dowd, and Hawk, the blind idiot, didn't see through her disguise. When he at last saw her as the beauty she really is, the fun began."

"And you did? Saw through her disguise, I mean?"

"Yes. I was quite insightful in those days."

"You mean pre-Charlotte days?"

"If you will. Now perhaps I see things and people even more clearly. It's a beautiful evening, isn't it? I believe I'll take my constitutional." With those words, he rose and strolled away.

Diana stared after him. What game was he playing? On the heels of that thought, she began to wonder if he simply wasn't interested anymore.

It was dark and still, even the coquis and the bananaquits quiet. Diana slowly turned onto her back, careful not to disarrange the palm fronds beneath her. She tried to think of her father, of her new stepmother, but Lyon filled her mind. And her body. Her skin felt itchy, as if it were stretched too tightly over her bones. And there was that ache between her thighs that made her squirm. Where was he? Taking his wretched constitutional, she mouthed with silent sarcasm.

It was all she could do not to get up and go find him. And then do what?

She flung her arm over her eyes to shut out the moonlight and forced herself to take deep breaths.

"Diana."

His voice was quiet, yet commanding. Slowly, she moved her arm and opened her eyes. Her breathing quickened as she came up on her elbows. He was standing just outside their shelter, the moonlight streaming over his body. He was quite naked.

"Take off the chemise."

His voice remained gentle, no lurking amusement. She drew a deep breath and very slowly lifted the chemise over her head and tossed it beside her.

"I've given you enough time, have I not? You want me now."

"Yes."

Was that her voice? Wistful and filled with longing?

"I want you to remember this moment, Diana. Just as I want you to forget that evening on the *Seawitch*. This is the first time we will come together. When we are old and crotchety, we will still come together, but this is the first time and it is magic." At least he prayed it would resemble magic. He was so randy, so much in need of her, he just didn't know.

She thought, I haven't even touched him and yet his manhood is swelled and thrusting out from his belly. She tried to imagine how she would feel with him fully inside her.

"Yes," she said, "this is magic, but I am afraid all the same."

"By the time I come into you, you will feel only desire, I swear it."

Still he hadn't moved. He was waiting, waiting for her to invite him to her. There would be no question of forcing this time.

"You will be my husband."

Lyon realized of course that she was stating a fact that she had finally accepted. He wished he weren't so obvious, but there was nothing he could do about it. He wanted her so much he hurt. But then again, he'd hurt for so long, what did a few more minutes matter?

"Yes, I will be your husband. I will take care of you, Diana, protect you, and probably fight with you until the day I leave this earth. I will try to make you happy."

"And will you love me?"

There, it was said. Her words hovered between them.

"If I do not come to love you, I will be most astounded at my shallowness. I am most fond of you, I find you delightful, and I will come to trust you, surely. It must be enough for both of us for the present. I will not lie to you, Diana.''

She was silent for a long moment. Finally, she said, ''Do you think I am beautiful?''

He trembled and she saw it. His voice was thick and harsh. ''I think you are the most exquisite creature imaginable.''

''You are too.''

He smiled. ''I want to touch you now, Diana. I want to kiss every inch of you. I want to love you and caress you until you are silly with it.''

''All right,'' she said, and lay back. ''Can I do those things to you?''

Lyon wondered if he could control himself. She could have no idea as yet how desperate a man could be. The thought of her kissing him, touching him . . . He wouldn't hurt her. He had been so certain he could control himself before she'd taken her chemise off. ''I don't know if that would be such a good idea this time.''

He drew a deep breath and stepped toward her. He eased down beside her, not touching her yet, just looking into her eyes. They were dark, luminous, filled with moonlight and anticipation. He could feel the warmth from her body.

He leaned over her and very lightly kissed her mouth. He felt her hand come up and gently touch his bare shoulder. He kissed her more deeply. Her fingers tightened.

Very gently, he placed his open palm against her breast. He felt her body leap, felt her sharp intake of breath. He recited Latin declensions to himself. Merciful heavens, he should have relieved his need before coming to her. He drew back, striving desperately for control.

''Lyon?''

''It's you, Diana, you are presenting me with a problem. You see, I want you too much. Just touching your breast is driving me beyond reason." He felt her quiver with his words, and quickly lifted his hand from her breast.

"I don't understand."

Too much innocence, he thought, looking down at her widened eyes, seeing the confusion in their depths.

"I want to come inside you. Now. I hurt so much I want to howl at the moon."

"All right." To his consternation, those long legs of hers parted.

He groaned. Merciful heavens, he wanted to go slowly, give her pleasure, but without his permission, his hand slid over her belly and cupped her, his fingertips pressing inward to find her.

Diana froze. She heard his harsh breathing, felt him looking down at her even as his fingers pressed and stroked. She wanted in that instant to run, to escape, to be free of him and herself, to remain unchanged.

"You're becoming wet."

"Oh, no," she gasped, and her thighs closed tightly, capturing his hand between them.

She felt his fingers gently parting her; then, before she could react, one finger slowly slipped inside her. She couldn't stop her body's reaction. She was throbbing, convulsing about his finger as it went deeper.

"Lyon, oh . . ."

"Yes, sweetheart. It's all right. You're doing fine. With any luck at all we shall soon be in the same boat, so to speak."

He leaned down and kissed her again. His tongue slipped between her parted lips, just as his finger was inside her. She felt his manhood pressing urgently against her thigh.

He felt her maidenhead. He pressed gently, but the thin

barrier held. He would spill his seed, he knew it. And he wanted desperately to be inside her.

"Diana, listen to me. I must come into you now or I will leave you. Do you understand?"

His finger was inside her, gently probing, and his voice was harsh against her cheek, his breathing sharp, as though he were in pain. She didn't understand, but she knew she could help him. "Yes, Lyon," she heard herself saying softly. She gently clutched his shoulders, drawing him closer.

He eased his finger out of her, felt her suck in her breath, and gently moved over her, parting her legs wide as he eased between them.

"Bend your knees." He cupped her face between his hands. "I want to see your face when I come inside you."

He reared back slightly, and she felt his manhood straining against her. Then he was inside her, gently pressing forward. Her eyes were wide upon his face and she saw his intense concentration. She had never imagined such a feeling, such warmth. She wasn't the least bit afraid, not now.

Suddenly, she stiffened, and the gentle feelings disappeared in a rush of pain. He would rend her, tear her. "No, Lyon, please, it hurts."

"Diana, sweetheart . . . Oh, dammit!"

He thrust forward, plunging through her maidenhead, and she cried out, her body bucking in pain. She couldn't dislodge him. He was deep inside her, a part of her now.

He held her face between his hands. His breathing was harsh, but he filled her now. "Hold still." He forced himself to stay quiet. He eased his body over her and began kissing her. "Feel me, Diana. Get used to me. Do you still hurt?"

"A little."

"It will ease," he said, but he heard the tears in her voice and felt her pain, and he hated himself for doing this to her. He hadn't intended it to be this way, but it was simply too much. He felt like a selfish pig, a . . .

"You are so deep inside me. I can feel you throbbing. It is the strangest feeling."

That did it. He groaned harshly, pulled himself back, then thrust forward wildly. He threw back his head, his back arching as he drove deep again, touching her womb, and he spilled himself within her.

He heard her moan, a soft, helpless sound that struck him to his very soul. Some magic you've wrought, you randy bastard.

He came down over her, bearing his weight on his elbows, and tried not to move, but she was so small, so tight around him. He kissed her mouth and tasted the salt of her tears. "I am sorry, so very sorry for hurting you, Diana."

The pain was fading, but she felt stretched to bursting and she was wet. "Will you stay as you are?"

"What?"

"Will you stay inside me all night?"

He wanted to laugh at that, but he felt himself harden and knew that possessing her once was only the beginning.

"Would you mind?"

"If it stops hurting, no, I shouldn't mind. It is all just very odd."

He supposed that odd was accurate enough, since she hadn't experienced pleasure.

"I am very wet."

He felt himself jerk inside her and drew a deep breath. "You are wet with me, this time. With my seed."

"What do you mean, 'this time'?"

"My dearest girl, it is my pleasurable responsibility to

ensure that when I come inside you, you will, ah, well, not be dry, I guess. It makes everything easier. You were ready for me, I should say, it is just that I rushed you.''

He eased out of her, feeling her flinch as he did so, and stretched out beside her. ''You want to know what we're going to do now?''

She gave him a wary look.

He grinned and came to his feet. ''You stay there, Diana. I shall be back in a moment.''

''Where are you going?''

''Just stay still.''

She didn't want to stay still. She felt sticky, tender, and sore. Worse, she felt herself throbbing with feelings that didn't want to go away.

''Don't move, Diana,'' she heard him call from a few feet away.

18

Success is dependent on effort.

SOPHOCLES

After a few minutes, she came up on her elbows. "Lyon?"

"Here I am. Don't move."

He came down on his knees beside her. He was holding half a coconut shell filled with fresh water and his breech-cloth. He dampened it, smiled at her, reaching out his hand.

"Oh, dear, you can't mean to . . . Lyon. I can surely do that myself."

"Hush," he said. He gently pulled her legs apart. He bent her knees and she felt dreadfully exposed. She gulped, trying to bring her thighs together.

He looked up at her face. "Diana, think of me as your husband now. All right? It is your duty to obey me. Now hold still."

She felt the wet cloth touching her. She closed her eyes tightly, with the absurd thought that if she couldn't see what he was doing, neither could he.

The cool wet cloth felt marvelously nice, she had to

admit, as well as the slight pressure of his hand against her. She felt the building of that warm, aching sensation and unconsciously moved against his hand.

Lyon felt her reaction and looked at her face. Her head was turned slightly, her eyes closed tightly. He smiled to himself. "Diana, I'm going to tell you something and I don't want you to be worried about it."

She kept her eyes firmly closed. "What?"

"When I came into you, broke through your maidenhead, you bled. It isn't much, and it won't happen again, but that's why I wanted to bathe you. I didn't want you to be worried or frightened. There, all done."

She tried to close her legs, but he was firmly planted between them. "Lyon," she said, her voice thin with embarrassment.

"I wish it were daylight."

"Lyon!"

"Just a moment ago you wanted me to touch you. You were pressing up against me. Now I will see to your pleasure, Diana."

She felt his fingers gently parting her, felt him ease down between her legs. When she felt his breath against her, she froze, her eyes wide on his bent head.

"What are you doing?"

He kissed the damp curls. "I'm learning you," he said, and lowered his head again. He really didn't believe he could bring her to a woman's pleasure, not this time, but at least he could begin to accustom her to him, accustom her to her own body and its exquisite responses.

Diana couldn't believe what he was doing. It was too much. Surely he couldn't . . . She suddenly saw him doing this to other women, to those little amours of his, and she felt such a violent wave of jealousy and rage that she jerked away from him, scrambling back out of reach.

Lyon was stunned for a moment, his voice bewildered. "Did I hurt you?"

"No, but you can't do that to me. It cannot . . . Well, It cannot be right or proper."

He wanted to laugh at her outrage, but didn't, of course. He kept his voice low and soothing, yet stern. "You belong to me, Diana. I can and will do to you what I know will please you."

"That doesn't please me. It's awful and embarrassing and you do it to everyone!"

Her accusation hurled itself at his head, waded through his confusion, and finally penetrated. "Ah," he said, his voice filled with deep pleasure, "you're jealous."

"I will not let you paw me like you have done to all your other little amours."

"My mouth is more intimate than my coming inside you?"

"Yes! You talk with your mouth."

"That is certainly a fact I can't refute. You are being silly." He heard her jerky breathing and sighed. "Let's get some sleep. Come here now. I swear to keep my mouth closed, both on words and on you."

True to what he'd said, he didn't speak again. He stretched out on his palm fronds and closed his eyes. He needed time. Perhaps tomorrow he could forgo his breech-cloth and fold away her chemise. He found himself praying that Rafael would take his time returning.

Diana eyed him with annoyance and with chagrin, but she didn't move.

"Very well, you're making me go back on my word. You could at least thank me, Diana. I did give you my body."

"I don't suppose you bled?"

"No," he said, and laughed. "Only virgins and semivirgins bleed."

"It isn't fair. I think a man should come to his marriage as chaste and virginal as his wife. I don't think I want to marry you, Lyon."

"If he did, I doubt much would get done."

"You men like to control things, you—"

"That's quite enough, my girl. Listen to me now because I mean every word. The die has been cast. You do belong to me. You will marry me. There is no going back." Suddenly, his voice lightened. "Who knows? I might have got you with child."

"No!"

"I shall try my best to ensure that you are pregnant before we are rescued."

"I won't do it."

"You, my dear, will have nothing to say about it. Neither will I, for that matter. I can but try and try, and you, dear girl, can but receive and receive."

She heard the determination in his voice. She said, a touch of bitterness in her voice, "I am well and truly caught now, am I not? Just because I'm a woman and you are a man—"

"Very true." He added, amusement in his voice, "Just think, Diana, our child could both catch a fish and scale it."

"In England?"

He sighed. It was something to think about. "We will work something out," he said finally. "Now, come here. I want to hold you. I want to fall asleep with you in my arms. Just promise me you won't snore."

She didn't respond to his provocation. "This is all most

odd," she said, more to herself than to him. She snuggled beside him and rested her cheek on his shoulder. She felt him lifting her hair and spreading it over his chest. "Very nice," he said. "Finally I have my blanket."

Diana laid her hand very lightly on his chest. She felt his heartbeat increase. He tried to hold himself in check.

"This is difficult," he said, removing her hand.

I am no longer innocent, she thought, knowing that if she looked down his body she would see his response.

"What do you want me to do?"

He laughed at that, a painful sound. "You are too sore to let me do what will cure me."

She ducked her head under his chin.

"Tell me a story to distract me."

And to distract herself, she thought, searching her mind. She told him about the Arawak Indians, long ago very peaceful inhabitants of the Virgin Islands who were destroyed, eaten, in fact, by the Carib Indians. "The Caribs ate everyone they could get into their pepper pots—Spanish, English, and French explorers, soldiers and settlers. They're almost all gone now."

"With our luck," Lyon said in a sleepy voice, "the only two of them left are here, on our island."

"You can protect us. You have a marvelous spear."

He groaned at that.

Lyon awoke to the sweet sound of Diana's voice. He smiled, coming up on his elbows. She was not ten feet away, on her knees in front of a small fire, making something for their breakfast. She was wearing her chemise. He came up behind her silently, leaned down, and wrapped his arms around her. He lifted her hair and kissed her ear.

She stiffened, then relaxed, leaning back against his belly.

"You were sleeping so soundly, I didn't want to disturb you."

His hands came around to cup her breasts.

"I am more disturbed now than any man has a right to be."

His gentle caressing motion made her body flare. He came down on his knees and slowly turned her to face him. "Good morning," he said, and kissed her.

His hands tangled in her hair, rubbing her back, moving ever downward until he was molding her hips. He was rigid and pulsing against her belly.

"Do you know what I want to do?"

"Yes, you are being very obvious, Lyon."

She felt him pulling up her chemise, then his bare hands were on her thighs, moving slowly upward to caress her hips. She felt his fingers ease between her thighs. "You, sweetheart, are also obvious, if a man knows where to feel."

She could feel his finger easing into her easily, for she was moist and eager. She heard a soft moan, felt that moan deep in her throat as Lyon kissed her.

"I don't have enough hands," he said, his voice fierce. He closed his eyes a moment at the heat of her. "Your breasts," he began, then released her an instant. He pulled her chemise over her head and tossed it on the sand. He held her away from him and looked at her. Her breasts were heaving, her nipples taut. He drew a deep breath, jumped to his feet, and grasped her under her arms.

"Come along. It's time you found that lovemaking is even more enjoyable than making cassava bread." He lifted her, and without thought, she wrapped her legs about his flanks. He kissed her mouth, her chin, pressed her head back to get to her throat and breasts. Her hair hung loose down her back, reaching nearly to the sandy beach.

"You are so beautiful," he said, his hot breath on her breast. "And your taste, Diana . . ."

She was gasping, feeling so urgent that she didn't know what to do. Her fingers kneaded his arms frantically. "Oh, dear, Lyon," she whispered.

The loud boom of a cannon came like a crack of thunder. Her legs tightened about him and she tried to focus her eyes on his face. She heard him curse, floridly.

He eased her down his body. "I don't believe it," Lyon said, gulping in huge drafts of air, his hands still stroking up and down her back, tangling in her hair.

There was another loud crack.

"A cannon," she said.

"Yes, Rafael returning for us, damn his eyes!"

"The signal fire," she managed.

Lyon released her, bent down, and retrieved her chemise. "Put it on."

They got the signal fire going, Lyon using his breech-cloth to fan it into smoke swirls.

The *Seawitch* came into view.

They watched in silence as a boat was lowered over the side of the ship.

"Time to dress," Lyon said.

Diana nodded, mute. She was looking at his breechcloth beside the fire. It was stained with blood, her blood. She quickly tossed it into the fire, then turned to fetch her gown.

Rafael lowered his spyglass, a wicked smile on his lips. His timing was horrible, he thought, and wondered if Lyon would burn his ears. He frowned at his body's reaction to seeing them clasped together, Diana's long, slender legs wrapped around Lyon, her glorious hair streaming down her arched back.

They looked none the worse for wear from their ordeal. Ordeal, ha! It looked as if Lyon had succeeded very well.

"Can you see anything, Capt'n? Are they here on Calypso Island?"

"Yes," said Rafael, turing to Rollo. "They're here on Calypso. Our castaways look quite healthy. Lower the boat, Rollo, and let's get them aboard." When Rollo turned away to obey his command, he raised his spyglass again. He saw Diana toss something in a fire, saw her turn and follow a naked Lyon to their shelter.

"It feels most odd to be wearing all these clothes again," Diana said as she finished fastening the buttons on her gown. "And shoes! How dreadfully uncomfortable!"

They were alone in their cabin. Lyon grunted in agreement as he tugged on his boots.

"Fancy that," Diana continued. "We were on Calypso Island, just a mile from Reefer's Island. There are a few inhabitants there, descendants of pirates, so I've been told."

"As ferocious as the Carib Indians?"

"Ah, no. They've calmed down remarkably, indeed—" There was a knock on the cabin door.

"Dinner in the captain's cabin," Neddie said through the door.

"We'll be right along," Lyonel said. He smiled at Diana. "You've missed a couple of buttons. Hold still." He wanted to pull the wretched gown off her and throw her on the bunk, but Rafael was waiting. "Later," he said.

"Later what?"

"You'll see, love."

She flushed and ducked her head. He obligingly kissed the nape of her neck.

"No cassava bread, I see," said Lyon when they were seated at Rafael's table.

"Diana took good care of you," Rafael said.

"She did indeed," said Lyon, his voice bland. He jumped when she kicked his shin beneath the table.

"I don't think I'll need to examine either of you," said Blick. "I have to admit that I was a bit worried when the two of you went overboard."

"I helped Lyon to shore," said Diana.

"She helped me more than you can imagine. Rafael, tell us about the attack. We couldn't see much in the storm."

Rafael thoughtfully chewed on a piece of bread. "The English are much better sailors than the French. We got one of them broadside, then slipped past the other two before they could figure out what had happened. Also, I gave dutiful thanks to heaven for that blessed storm."

Diana said, "I was very surprised. There haven't been many French war ships in the Caribbean in years, or so I thought."

"Perhaps they thought I was a special prize," Rafael said. "More wine, my dear?"

"Why?" Diana asked, tenacious. "What is in the hold of this ship?"

"Just furnishings, cloth and housewares for local planters. Incidentally, we'll reach Road Town tomorrow. Your father will be there to greet you, Diana. And you, Lyon."

"I thought you were bound for St. Thomas?"

"I was and I went. I sent a message to your father."

Diana sent an agonized look to Lyon.

He didn't answer that look until they were in their cabin an hour later. "We can have Rafael marry us now," he said without preamble, "or we can wait. Which do you prefer?"

Diana paced the cabin. "I don't know. I can't be pregnant. It was only one time. You don't have to worry that—"

"You silly female! We're not getting married just because you could or could not be with child. We're getting married because we have no other choice. Now, enough. Again, which do you prefer?"

"I want to go home."

Lyon sighed. "Why are you so against marriage to me?"

She said without hesitation, "Because you don't love me. Because as soon as you settle your inheritance, you'll want to return to England. I hate England. It's cold and foggy and awful and—"

"So, you see yourself living with your father, stepmother, and stepbrother until you're old and creaky? An unmarried daughter isn't a pleasant thing to be, so I've heard. Is that what you want?"

How many times must he have this same ridiculous conversation, counter her arguments?

"What I want is some time. I don't want to be forced into anything, Lyon. Can't you understand that?"

He clasped her arms none too gently and shook her. "Now you will listen to me, Diana Savarol. I have had quite enough of your perseverating. For heaven's sake, it's not as if I were a troll or a fortune-hunter or a libertine. I am quite good husband material. And I am a good lover, an excellent lover. Now that we've gotten rid of your virginity, I will prove it to you."

He bent his head down and kissed her, roughly and

quite thoroughly. His male attack surprised him, for it wasn't his style. But she made him so furious . . . He eased, gently running his tongue over her lower lip. "You are beautiful and sweet and I want you, Diana. I will be a good husband, you will see."

"All right," she said, and wrapped her arms about his waist.

He didn't ask her what she meant. It didn't seem important, not now. "I liked it better when I didn't have to spend an hour getting both of us out of our clothes." He was breathing hard, and he was surprised at the nearly painful desire she evoked in him. "Diana," he said, and his fingers were on the buttons of her gown, working feverishly. She helped him, or tried to.

"Ah," he said. She was standing naked in front of him and he couldn't get enough of her. He slowly reached out his hands and lifted her breasts. She quivered and brought her own hands up to cover herself. "Oh, no," he said, and smiled down at her. "No, don't hide yourself." He caressed her gently, marveling at how exquisite she looked. He saw that she'd closed her eyes. "Come closer. I want you to feel me against you."

"I don't know, Lyon, it's—"

"It's what, sweetheart?" His warm breath filled her mouth and she knew she was being silly. And she did desire him. She felt the warm, very delightful ache low in her belly and wondered . . . "Lyon? I feel very strange." His hand left her breast and glided over her stomach, downward until his fingers were probing through the curls between her thighs.

"Here?"

She sucked in her breath. "Yes."

"Good."

He lifted her in his arms and carried her to their narrow

bunk. He laid her on her back and stood over her a moment, looking at her. "Thank God for light," he said.

Diana found that her gaze went immediately to his belly and lower. "Oh, dear," she said. His manhood was thrust forward and it looked smooth and hard and alive.

She reached out her hand and lightly touched her fingertips to him. He flinched and she jerked her hand back.

Lyon very much wanted her to touch him, but he sincerely doubted that he could control himself if she did. And tonight was very important. If he could give her a woman's pleasure, he knew she would no longer fight him about their inevitable marriage. She wouldn't be able to reconcile sex between them without the sanctity of marriage. If he had to use sex to control her, then he would do so. So be it, he thought. He eased down on his side beside her. "Hello," he said, not touching her with his hands.

She smiled up at him shyly.

"I love the tanned parts of you. They frame the white parts most enticingly."

"The same is true of you, Lyon."

"You finally looked at me, did you? I'm not such a terrible beast, am I? I am made for you, you know. My own theory is that God created woman first, then decided that she needed a mate to laugh with her, to fetch for her, to fill her with his own body."

"I trust you won't say that to any of the Methodists you will meet." She felt his manhood pressing against her thigh, and her leg jerked a bit, rubbing against him.

She raised her hand to his cheek. "You are a beautiful man, Lyon. I think I want you to kiss me now."

He did. She tasted of the sweet wine they'd drunk at

dinner and of herself. Of Diana. Life stretched before him with pleasant horizons. "You are very special to me and I want to make you happy."

There were no more words between them. He went slowly until Diana, wanting more, lurched up against him.

Still he held back. He wanted her to have everything, to learn tonight the pleasure he would give her the rest of his life. When he gently eased his finger inside her, he wanted to howl with his own pleasure at her warmth, her enthusiasm, her own need of him. He began to caress her softly swelled woman's flesh and her desire flowed over him.

"That's it," he said into her mouth. "Move against my fingers. What do you feel, Diana?"

"I feel urgent," she gasped. "It just keeps getting stronger."

He felt her tensing, knew that she was hovering on the edge, and lifted his fingers.

Her eyes flew open and her disappointment made him smile. "Hush," he said. "You will like this much better." He eased down her body, parting her legs to come between them. He smiled at her as he lifted her hips. When his mouth closed over her, she stiffened for a brief instant, then cried out.

He held her firmly, feeling the spasm overwhelm her. He knew it was the first time, her first time, and he felt so proud, so triumphant that he forgot his own need. She was filled with passion. All for him. When he felt her climax ease, he came into her, swiftly, fully, driving deep.

Her arms went about his back, and he kissed her, knowing she tasted herself on his mouth. "So sweet, Diana, so sweet."

And he was gone, his body exploding, his mind reeling, and she took his groans into her mouth.

Diana held tight, her mind emptied just as her body was filled with him. She'd never imagined, never guessed . . . She sighed, kissing his chin, his throat.

"I'll marry you," she said between kisses.

"I thought you just might," Lyon said. He eased off her, bringing her with him onto her side. She fell asleep, her cheek pressed against his chest, her legs tangled with his.

Dim morning light came through the porthole when Diana, her voice accusing, said, "Just what did you mean by that, Lyon?"

He moaned in his sleep, his hand stroking down her side to her hip.

"Lyon!"

He cocked an eye open to see Diana leaning over him, her eyes narrowed, her beautiful hair framing her face and flowing over his chest. "Kiss me," he said.

"I want to know what you meant," she said, but she kissed him.

"Meant by what?" His hand was stroking her buttocks.

"That you thought I would marry you."

His mind finally wound itself back to the previous night and he remembered his self-satisfying words. He gave her a triumphant masculine grin. His fingers eased between her thighs to touch her. "I meant, dear one, that once I gave you pleasure, you would be mine. Forever. Helpless in my net, like one of your groupers."

Diana wanted to tell him that he was a halfwitted gargoyle of questionable antecedents, but his fingers were driving her wild. And he knew it. She tried for outrage, but couldn't find a drop.

"Lyon," she said on a soft wail.

"I know, Diana. I know."

*   *   *

Captain Rafael Carstairs of the *Seawitch* married Lyonel Ashton, Earl of Saint Leven, to Diana Savarol, spinster, that morning with every man on board witnessing the event.

"You may kiss your bride," Rafael said at last, and Lyon, grinning fatuously, took Diana into his arms. He heard the shouts of the men as his lips touched hers.

"Finally caught," he said against her mouth.

"Like a grouper."

19

Those who go overseas find a change of climate, not a change of soul.

HORACE

Lyon's first view of Road Town left him silent. He supposed he had fantasized some sort of tropical paradise with natives wandering about looking happy, a profusion of flowers and lush foliage, larking colorful birds everywhere, and gleaming white buildings.

Reality wasn't quite so kind. Tortola itself was a long, mountainous island—quite beautiful, really—but its capital was as grim a sight as he'd ever seen. Scores of men, both black and white, swarmed over the docks; piled wooden crates were everywhere, both outgoing goods and incoming, he supposed. It was dreadfully hot, with no beautiful trees or flowers or anything else to shade. From the *Seawitch* he could smell the odors of the outdoor market, fish, primarily, rotting under that hot sun. Haphazard wooden buildings crowded behind the docks. It was appalling. He swallowed, looking down at Diana, who was now waving wildly toward shore.

"There's my father," she cried, leaning over the railing. "See, Lyon, the tall man, the one with the twinkle in his eye—"

Lyon laughed. "Careful, else you'll be swimming to shore."

"No, really, he's the most handsome man in the West Indies. You will like him, I swear. Oh, dear, those must be my new relatives with him," she continued, shading her eyes and straining. "It's two ladies, Lyon. I thought I had a new stepbrother."

"One looks quite young," Lyon said. "I think your father's spotted us, my dear. There's no longer a twinkle in his eyes. Am I in danger of fatherly wrath?"

"Since we're married, I suppose he will put up with you with good grace." She punched his arm, grinning.

Patricia Driscoll stood between her father-in-law, Lucien Savarol, and her mother-in-law, Deborah Savarol, watching the *Seawitch* navigate through the deep calm water of the harbor.

Patricia's muslin gown was cool, but not cool enough standing in the high heat of the day. She wished she could wander into the shade, but she knew that Papa Lucien wanted them all to stand here showing enthusiasm for his daughter and her husband. She would have preferred that her new sister-in-law remain in England, so that she would have been able to go to London. Daniel, her husband of three months, wanted desperately to go to England, and she did as well, although her motives were vastly different from her young husband's. He would change, she was determined that he should, and when they finally managed to go, it would be in style. She dreamed of the parties, the very fine and fancy people she would meet who would believe her charming. Lucien Savarol was one of the richest planters in the West Indies. If he could be brought around, she would have her wish.

"It is all very odd," said Deborah Driscoll Savarol to her new husband. "Cast overboard during a storm and a battle. Captain Carstairs seemed very certain they were all right. Yes, most odd indeed.''

"Yes, you've said that," said Lucien mildly, but his eyes were narrowed with worry. God, the past week had been hell, the not knowing if Diana were still alive. And Carstairs telling him that she was married. His Diana married! That in itself was such a surprise that he was speechless for many minutes. And to an English earl, no less.

Suddenly, the *Seawitch* drew close so Lucien could see his daughter waving at him from the deck. Her beautiful hair was flying wildly around her face and streaming down her back. She looked as excited as he felt. And there was a man standing next to her. A tall man, slender, but he could not make out the man's features. Her husband, he thought, feeling an unaccountable tightening in his gut.

"How untidy she appears," said Deborah, frowning slightly into the bright sunlight. "All that hair flying about.''

"She looks beautiful," said Lucien. "Just like her mo—'' He broke off. Deborah didn't like to be reminded of his first wife, the exquisite Lily. Her portrait was now in his study, banished from the drawing room.

The docking seemed to take forever. Lyon smiled indulgently at Diana, who was flittering about and chattering nervously. "That must be his new wife," she said. "But who is that girl? I do wish I could see their faces—their bonnets are so wide! I hope they are nice. What if they don't like me? Who is that girl, Lyon? Where is my new stepbrother?''

"Patience, my dear.''

Some ten minutes later, Diana surged down the gangplank and threw herself into her father's arms. "I'm home, Papa, I'm home.''

Lucien didn't want to release her. He'd been so very

afraid for her. He drew back and gently touched his finger-tips to her face. "This man staring at us is your husband, my dear?"

Diana started a moment, then said gaily, "Yes. Lyon, come and meet your new father-in-law."

Introductions were made all around. Deborah offered a powdered cheek to her new daughter, which Diana dutifully pecked.

"And this is Patricia Driscoll, my new daughter-in-law," said Deborah. "Unfortunately Daniel couldn't come with us. Lucien had some very important work for him to do on Savarol."

"Ah, well, such a pity," Diana said. They were saved by Rafael Carstairs.

"They are just as I told you, sir," he said to Lucien Savarol. "They're fit and tanned and healthy. I knew Diana must know enough about living on an island so they wouldn't starve." He made brief greetings to Mrs. Savarol and Mrs. Driscoll.

"Yes," said Patricia to Diana, "you poor thing, you're dreadfully tanned. It will take weeks to make that awful brown fade. You've even got freckles."

Diana blinked. She looked at Patricia's very white face, not a freckle to be seen. "I doubt it," she said only. Was she her stepsister-in-law? It was most confusing.

The three men moved a bit off to the side, discussing what, Diana could not imagine. Manly things, she supposed, her lips curling slightly with amusement. There was no doubt that Lyon was a manly man, she thought, flushing slightly as she pictured him naked as a pagan walking toward her.

"Well, you are home," said Deborah.

"Yes, and it is marvelous to be here, at last. Although our week on that island was most amusing. I didn't realize we were on Calypso Island. I was all turned around, you see. But here I am chattering on too much. I suppose we are going to Savarol Island?''

"That is what your father wishes," said Deborah. "I do not have an extra bonnet with me. Don't you have something in your trunks? You did not lose your trunks, did you?''

"No, they'll be unloaded in a moment, I imagine. But I don't want a bonnet. To be warm again, it is something I dreamed about in London.''

"And you are married. Your father was very surprised when Captain Carstairs told him.''

Diana was relieved to no end that Rafael had protected them. He'd said to them, a wicked twinkle in his dark eyes, "Never would I face a father and tell him his daughter seduced a man and that man wasn't her husband.''

"He is an earl, I understand.''

"Yes, Lyonel Ashton, Earl of Saint Leven. He probably has quite a few other Christian names, but I don't know what they are. The English peers seem to dote on names. The more names the more consequence, I suppose.''

"He is very handsome," said Patricia.

"How odd," said Deborah.

Diana didn't know what her stepmother was referring to, so she said nothing. She wasn't certain yet what to make of her new stepmother and sister-in-law. Deborah was small, pleasingly plump, her blue eyes intelligent, her light-brown hair pulled in a severe knot at the nape of her neck. Her pale-green muslin gown was fashionable. As for Patricia, she couldn't seem to take her eyes off Lyon. She was as small as her mother-in-law, but very slender. Her eyes were a dark blue, her hair a very light brown. Her chin was pointed, making Diana think of a fox. She brought her attention back to her new stepmother.

"You are nineteen," said Deborah.

"Yes, I will be twenty at the end of the year."

"Goodness," said Patricia, "it is fortunate that you could marry! I married Daniel three months ago and I am just turned eighteen."

Diana grinned at this guileless pronouncement. "I never felt like I was on the shelf, as the English put it so quaintly, if that is what you mean. Indeed, I am surprised myself that I am married." She snapped her mouth closed on that ambiguous bit of information.

She wished the men would leave off their talk. "Is everyone well?" she asked.

"Who? Oh, my son, you mean. Daniel is an amazing young man, never ill, always so charming and helpful. Yes, he is of great assistance to your father. Lucien is most fond of him, yes, most fond."

"And the servants? Dido? Has she missed me?"

Deborah slapped a fly off her sleeve. "That miserable old woman! I have had nothing but problems with her. One more and I'll have her whipped."

"I beg your pardon?" Diana's voice was icy, her body suddenly very quiet.

"It's quite true, you know," said Patricia. "For a slave she is much above herself."

Deborah looked Diana over, her nose elevated. "She is a slave, Diana, nothing more, just as Patricia said. She was allowed far too much license. There was no mistress in the house and she took advantage and—"

"I was the mistress."

"You? Hardly. An unmarried girl can hardly be considered a mistress."

If Diana weren't so furious, she would have laughed. Not considered a mistress, was she? Deborah could speak to Lyon about that! She said calmly, "Dido, Leah, Tania,

Moira, all of them are my friends. Dido raised me after my mother died. She is loyal, intelligent, and loving.''

Deborah shrugged. She didn't want to get into an argument with her stepdaughter, at least not now. Thank God the girl was married. She should be rid of her soon enough. She hoped the earl was rich. Her hopes were for her own son. Dear Daniel had had a rough time of it, what with their expenses these past few years after Brock had died. Now, at least, Daniel would certainly become Lucien's heir, now that his precious daughter was taken care of.

Diana added in a conciliatory tone, seeing that Deborah had retreated, ''She is also bossy and strict. Much like mothers everywhere, I suspect.''

''We'll see,'' said Deborah. Diana noticed that her lips were thinned with displeasure. Not at all attractive, she thought. Where had her father met this woman? Why had he married her?

She saw her father finally shake Rafael's hand and turn back toward them. His eyes were twinkling, she thought. She felt a rush of love. Then she looked at Lyon, and the rush of feeling was far more basic.

They left immediately for Savarol Island on her father's thirty-foot sloop. Dorian was at the tiller and Diana gave him a gay greeting and a hug. The ladies were settled on a padded bench beneath a tarp canopy. Diana fidgeted as she watched Lyon and her father move toward the bow, their heads close in conversation.

''You have married my daughter,'' said Lucien Savarol as he studied his new son-in-law. He was a handsome man, but Lucien knew that looks meant very little. He also seemed intelligent and articulate as well. Thank God he wasn't some sort of fop. As for his character, he had no intention of allowing Diana to leave Savarol Island with him until he was certain the man was good enough for her.

"I have that honor, yes. I shall try, sir, to make her happy."

"I believe you are related to Lady Cranston? Lucia?"

"Yes, and she informs me that Diana and I meet somewhere back on the family tree. Have you ever met Lucia?"

"No, I haven't. We have, of course, corresponded somewhat erratically over the years. I was in England some twelve years ago, but she was at her estate in Yorkshire at the time. Near Escrick, I believe?"

"Yes. I also have an estate there. Diana has visited the area and enjoyed herself, I believe."

The two men were silent for a moment. The only sounds were of the slapping sails, the ever-present gulls squawking overhead, the splash of the waves against the sides of the sloop. If Lyon listened carefully, he could hear the voices of the women, but could not make out their words. He wondered how Diana was doing with her new relatives.

Lucien continued, pointing to starboard, "Savarol Island lies about two more hours east. It's a small island, blessed with ample fresh water and fine soil for sugar. My grandfather changed the name of the island in a fit of immortality, I suppose. It was called Breadfruit Island before. We are, thank God, very nearly self-sufficient."

"You love it here in the West Indies," Lyon said.

Lucien nodded, and said after a moment, "So does my daughter. I understand that you inherited Mendenhall plantation on Tortola. Forgive me for bringing you directly away before you could visit your new holdings, but there are . . . problems at home that I must attend to. It will give you an opportunity to learn something about growing sugar and plantation life before you go to Mendenhall, and to see Diana's home."

"I thought the cutting of sugarcane was in the spring," Lyon said mildly.

"Yes, it is our busiest season. You see, we are a community in a very real sense, which means, naturally, that there are always concerns, problems, whatever. Ah, look back at Tortola, Lyon."

Lyon obeyed. Sugarcane fields and cotton fields seemed to climb the mountains themselves. It was an impressive sight, and he momentarily forgot the squalor of the dock area of Road Town. He found himself wondering at that moment how Lucien Savarol would react to the sight of the dock areas in London.

"Your wedding was in London? I could get very little from Captain Carstairs," he added, "and believe me, I did try."

Lyon paused for just a moment. He owed this man honesty. "Actually, no, we weren't married in London. We were married by Captain Carstairs, yesterday."

To Lyon's surprise, Lucien Savarol simply stared at him for a moment, then threw back his head and laughed deeply.

"I beg your pardon, sir?"

"Forgive me, my boy. You see, I couldn't imagine my Diana succumbing so quickly, though you seem a man whose character is as strong as hers. However . . . Well, perhaps you will wish to tell me about it."

"She had refused to marry me, if you wish to know the truth. Indeed, I was simply to escort her back here, but I was coshed on the head in Plymouth and the two of us were saved by Captain Carstairs. He and his crew assumed we were married, and by the time I regained my wits, we were at sea. There weren't, of course, any other passengers on board to act as chaperone. Neither of us had a choice. But as I said, I am fond of her as I believe she is of me."

Lucien stared toward Savarol Island, not in sight yet,

but he could feel its pull. "Perhaps," he said mildly, "it would be best if my wife didn't know the actual circumstances."

"As you wish, sir."

"I could tell by the way she looked at you that she does not hold you in dislike. However, Diana . . . Well, she is a most independent girl. I had very little hope that she would find a gentleman in England to suit her. Do you love my daughter?"

"As I said, sir, I am fond of her. I will be faithful to her and protect her to the best of my ability. She will lack for nothing, nothing material, at any rate." And I will give her passion for as long as I am on this earth. But one didn't say that to a father.

This, Lyon thought with some amusement, was the parental interview. He liked Lucien Savarol. Time enough to tell Diana's father that he had no intention of owning one hundred souls.

Lucien asked him about the war and they discussed Napoleon's ill-fated Russian campaign. When Savarol Island came into view, Lyon realize that this was truly a paradise. The island was not large, not more than six miles in length and several miles wide. In the middle, there was a string of gentle hills, their sloping sides covered in sugarcane. The great house, as Diana had told him once that the plantation owners called their homes, was set upon a hill on the northern end of the island. It was a stone English manor house, rising two stories, its balconies covered with the most colorful flowers he had yet seen.

"The house was begun by my grandfather and finished by my father," said Lucien. "The stone is from our own quarry, and my father spent a fortune furnishing the place with proper English wares."

"It is very impressive," said Lyon, and meant it.

* * *

"Well, what do you think?"

Lyon looked about the bedchamber with its high ceilings, floor-to-ceiling French doors, white walls, and spartan furnishings, and shook his head. "This is your room?" At her complacent nod, he added, "Not a frill or a pink ruffle to be seen."

"The walls are stone, so it is cool inside." She walked to the French windows and opened them. "Here is the balcony, Lyon. I tend my own flowers, as you see."

Lyon followed her onto the wide balcony that stretched beyond the corner of the plantation house. Her balcony was a profusion of the most beautiful flowers he'd ever seen, and beyond was the Caribbean, with its brilliant shades of blue.

"I tend them myself," said Diana. "Dido swore to me that she would take good care of them while I was gone. She did."

Lyon breathed in the clean salt smell of the Caribbean. There were no cane fields, indeed, nothing in this direction, just the gentle slope of the hill down to the white beach. Indeed, it was only some two hundred feet to the sea, and the sound of the waves was muffled here.

"I like openness," she added slowly. She grinned up at him. "And I don't like pink ruffles."

He pictured her for a moment in the fog of London, huddled before a fireplace, and swallowed painfully. She was like a beautiful jewel here, in this lush setting. He wondered what the devil he was going to do.

"You saw the wide veranda in the front of the house. We eat most of our meals there. It's blessedly cool, always a breeze from the water. I do hope Deborah doesn't insist upon dining in the formal room. It can be—" She broke off and yanked at his coat sleeve. "You are miles away, Lyon. What are you thinking?"

"About the bed," he said quickly, turning back into her bedchamber. "Let me see if it suits me."

Before Diana could react, he grabbed her about the thighs and tossed her over his shoulder. He eased her down onto her back on the wide bed. He came down over her, clasped her hands in one of his, and drew them over her head. "I've missed you," he said, and kissed her. She was tense and silent beneath him, but he was patient. He felt the moment she began to respond to him. Her lips parted and she arched upward.

He released her hands and balanced himself on his elbows over her. He looked down at her, smiling.

"I survived the parental interview. Am I not due some sort of a reward?"

She clasped his face between her hands and brought his head down. "Yes," she said, and kissed him. She felt him pressing against her belly, hard and probing. She stroked her hands down his back, feeling him shudder.

"Baby! Hot water for you and—"

Dido came to a skittering halt in the doorway. Never had she thought to see her young mistress in such a position. On her back with a man on top of her. Oh, dear, oh, dear.

"Hello," Diana said, peeking around Lyon's shoulder, her face as red as Dido's was black. Lyon rolled off her and came to his feet beside the bed.

Dido shook her head. "Heah in the middle of de day with your man all over you! Shameless, lovie! A good figure of a man, though, and handsome as a dog. Well, you straighten yourself, missie, and take your bath now. Your new stepmammy wants her vittles in an hour. No fooling around wid him—no, indeed. You wait to night-time like a lady should."

Lyon was enjoying himself once his body accepted the

fact that it was to be denied for the moment. Dido was the
scrawniest scrap of humanity he'd ever seen. She was
dressed in a plain gray gown, and her hair was scraped
back from her face in a skinny bun. He'd met her briefly
upon their arrival, watched her clasp Diana to her meager
bosom, and tell her exactly everything that had occurred in
her absence, all without taking a breath. Yet she was a
slave. He shook his head and stepped forward. "Let me
help you, Dido."

"Go along with you, master! You going to bathe wid
my baby here? Not enough room, but you young 'uns . . .
Well I remember my Orial, quite a man dat one was—yes,
indeed."

"Yes, I think I will," Lyon said, taking the steaming
buckets of water from her old veiny hands. "She needs a
good scrubbing, you know. Come along, my dear."

Lyon was being outrageous and Dido seemed to enjoy
this cavalier treatment. Diana scrambled off the bed and
slapped down her gown.

"Come here, baby, and let me get you out of dat fancy
dress."

"Oh, no, Dido. That's my responsibility."

Dido chuckled and wagged an arthritic finger at him.
"Naughty, you are, young master! Randy as a mountain
goat, you young fellers. You take care of my baby, you
hear?"

"I hear," said Lyon.

The old woman took herself off, still chuckling. "Her
highness is in a pelter," Dido added, pausing in the
doorway. "You don't wanna rile herself moh. You hear?"

"Yes, I hear," Diana said, repeating Lyon.

When the door closed behind the old slave, Diana turned
on her husband. "Lyon, you should be ashamed of
yourself."

"She's a funny old duck. You were lucky to have her with you while you were growing up."

"Yes," Diana said, serious now, "yes, I was. I am worried, though. Deborah said something about Dido being above herself and taking the whip to her. I won't allow that, Lyon."

"Of course not." He eased down into a wing chair that faced the tub, stretched his long legs out in front of him, and leaned his head back. "Bathe, Diana. I need to rest awhile."

"You didn't want to rest just a few minutes ago!"

He cocked an eye at her. "I must have forgotten. Lord, I have the strangest feeling, in fact, I think I must be dreaming. I see myself on a sugar plantation in the West Indies. This quite appetizing young lady is prancing about in front of me, and do you know what? I do believe she is going to strip off her clothes, just for my pleasure."

"Close your eyes, you buffoon! And I don't prance, I am not a horse."

He obligingly closed his eyes, at least for a couple of minutes. He opened them to see Diana step into the tub. His body responded instantly. He decided it was the beautiful tan contrasted with her white breasts, her hips, and belly. She turned her head toward him at that moment, and their eyes met.

"Lyon," she began, and made a furtive attempt to cover her breasts.

"Into the tub, sweetheart, or you will go without a bath." But his eyes dropped from her face to the nest of dark-blond curls between her thighs. He swallowed and moaned, as if in pain.

The sides of the copper tub were high and he couldn't see anything but her tanned shoulders.

"Well," she said, rubbing jasmine soap on her arms, "what do you think of everything?"

"I'm still in a state of shock. It is so vastly different here. I understand now how strange London must have been for you. You did very well there, Diana."

She was washing her face and didn't reply.

He steepled his fingers and tapped them thoughtfully together. "Did you truly like Yorkshire?"

She rinsed her face and looked over at him. "Yes, I did. It's wild and beautiful." She suddenly realized where this question was leading and added quickly, "But, Lyon, it's cold there—"

"It was quite warm, really, and the sun was hot. I will admit that it can be dismal in winter, but the snow is beautiful, turning the moors white."

"I've never seen snow."

"The pond on my estate freezes over. You can learn how to ice-skate. There are a lot of things you've never seen or done."

"The same is true of you too."

"Yes." He rose and began to undress.

She climbed out of the tub in a few moments and quickly wrapped herself in a large towel. Lyon was standing there, in the middle of her bedchamber, beautifully naked, smiling at her.

"You are so tanned, expect for your—"

"Yes?" he prodded when she ground to a halt.

"Please bathe, Lyon, we mustn't be late for dinner. Her highness might get in a snit."

He didn't want to, but he forced himself to think about the hours after dinner. The hours after dinner for many years to come.

"I'll give you a complete tour of the plantation tomorrow. You can meet all my friends. My father owns a stallion that even you won't despise. He's half-wild, a Barb, and his name is Salvation."

"You must be kidding!"

"No, and I don't understand that name any more than you do. I asked Father, but the man who sold him the stallion died before he could find out." Her pulse calmed a bit when he was finally in her tub. His knees stuck up and she laughed.

"I am interested in meeting this new stepbrother of yours," he said, sponging himself.

"I hope he isn't like her highness. You know, prim and proper and stiff." Or like Patricia, she added silently.

"Or stoop-shouldered, dressed in black broadcloth, and toting a Bible under his arm?"

"Evidently, his father was a Quaker. Oh, dear. Deborah wanted to lecture me on our sail over from Tortola. It was hurting her to keep her opinions to herself. I doubt she will be able to hold in her strictures much longer. Poor Father. I grew up with him telling me how gay and charming my mother was."

"Who knows?" Lyon said, giving her a lecherous grin. "Perhaps our good Deborah is untamed in bed."

Diana doubted that sincerely, now that she knew more about bed.

As for Daniel Driscoll, he was not, they soon were to see, at all what either of them expected.

20

Not every truth is palatable.

BEAUMARCHAIS

Daniel Driscoll was a giant of a man. A gentle giant, Diana soon discovered, despite the square, very stubborn-looking jaw and shoulders, and arms so massive and heavily muscled they strained the evening coat he was wearing. Making clothes for her stepbrother was not an easy task, she imagined, unable to do more at the moment than simply stare at him.

After introductions were genially made, Daniel took Diana's hand in his huge ones and gave her a gentle smile. "I always wanted a little sister. You are beautiful. You look very happy."

His voice was deep and slow, and his eyes, a very light blue, twinkled at her. His mother and wife looked like midgets next to him, and Diana, in her newly discovered knowledge of marriage, wondered, slightly appalled, how he could make love to Patricia without squashing her.

"And I have never had a brother. I am delighted to have one now. And yes, I am happy." She grinned. "I would

be your *little* sister even if I were older than you." He
showed even white teeth as he smiled, and though she
knew objectively that he was too rugged to be termed
objectively handsome, there was such gentleness, such
kindness in his face, that it didn't matter. She felt an odd
surge of protectiveness toward him, which, she supposed,
was ridiculous, given his sheer physical power.

"I've always wanted to go to England," Daniel said to
Lyon. He towered a good five inches over the earl, and his
massive shoulders blocked him from Diana's view for a
moment. She wondered, stifling a giggle, how Lyon felt
about being a *little* brother-in-law.

"Yes, well, certainly," Deborah cut in, her voice sharp.
"It is just that you don't wish to go to England for the
right reasons, Daniel. Surely, you must see that everything
is changed now. You must—"

"Yes, Mother." Daniel Driscoll merely smiled indulgently down at his mother from his great height, and Diana
wondered how many times this particular strain of conversation occurred. She had a feeling that there was great
strength of character beneath this calm-speaking man. But
she was curious and was relieved when Lyon, bringing his
gaze back to his new stepbrother-in-law, asked, "Why do
you wish to go to England?"

"I wish to be a physician," Daniel said simply. "Have
you ever heard of Dr. John Lettsom? No, well, he is a
Quaker, still alive, I believe, and living in London. He
was born here in the West Indies, on Little Jost Van Dyke
Island. An amazing man, really, and an excellent doctor.
I—"

"Now, Daniel," Deborah said quickly, placing her hand
on her son's arm, "don't run on so. You do not wish to
bore his lordship." She gave Lyon an arch look. "My son

hasn't yet realized that his place is here, running Savarol plantation. This idea of his is just a young man's fancy.''

"Sickness is disgusting," said Patricia, "and doctors are poor folk with nothing to show for all their labors. Why, just think of that doctor you worked with in St. Thomas, Daniel. He was so poor he could barely take care of his wife and family.''

Daniel merely regarded his new wife from his great height, his face showing nothing. "Dr. Gustavus is a good man," he said only, his voice as impassive as his expression.

Lucien Savarol shook his head at his wife to forestall further comments. "We will eat on the veranda," he said.

"But, Lucien—"

"On the veranda," Lucien repeated firmly. "Lyon is not used to the heat and there's hardly a breath of air in the dining room.''

The veranda was on the second floor, some thirty feet long and ten feet in width. There was a railing and a roof and comfortable furniture. It was an odd feeling, Lyon thought as he seated Diana in a tall-backed wicker chair, to be dressed as fine as any English gathering and to be seated outside, the sounds of birds and the sea in the distance. He had wondered as he'd dressed in his evening clothes whether he would be roasted alive, and he greeted the cool evening breeze with gratitude. He stared silently a moment at the beautiful prospect before him. The well-scythed lawn was bordered with palm trees, red bullet trees, a name he'd never heard until Diana had mentioned it upon their arrival, mahogany trees, and masses of bougainvillea.

The servants—no, slaves, he amended to himself—walked silently, their bare feet making no sound on the mahogany floors. They were clean, wearing simple muslin trousers or dresses. The women wore bright-colored scarves about their heads.

"That, Lyon," Diana said, "is poached fish with herbed avocado sauce. And here are crab backs."

She watched his face as he tasted the dishes and smiled happily when he nodded. "Do try some sweet-potato casserole. You might not like the taste, it is very different, but—"

"It is most unusual," Lyon said, and chewed. "Nearly as tasty as your roasted breadfruit, my dear."

"Oh," said Patricia, "I had forgotten that you were marooned together on an island! An English earl. How vastly romantic! You ate breadfruit?"

"Yes," said Diana. "And I made cassava bread, though this English earl thought the root looked disgusting, and then the English earl finally managed to spear a grouper for one dinner. We found a pool of fresh water, so that was no problem."

"You were lucky, my boy," said Lucien, "to be with Diana."

"An understatement, sir."

Diana said to Daniel, "I did not know Dr. Lettsom was still alive and in London. My father has told me he is an extraordinary gentleman. We had an excellent physician on board the *Seawitch*. His name was Blick, and he took care of Lyon."

"Yes," continued Lyon. "He took his medical training in Scotland, in Edinburgh, I believe. A fine man, and dedicated. He also taught your daughter all about goatweed, sir."

"Beware, my lord husband, or you'll find yourself at an impasse."

"Tell me of London society," Patricia said, her voice high and a bit shrill.

Daniel, who had been listening closely, now lowered his head and began to eat with stolid concentration.

Diana, after a quick drawing look at her husband, said, "Most fascinating. There was this one lady, her name was Charlotte, Lady Danvers. She had a way of making men quite mad."

Lyon, copying Daniel, merely forked down some stewed kidneys.

"Now, I was staying with Lady Lucia Cranston. A martinet and most fond of Lyon here. I personally believed that—"

"You clumsy idiot!"

Diana gasped to see Deborah slap Moira's face, hard.

"You have ruined my gown, you stupid girl!"

She raised her hand to hit the thin black face yet again, when Lucien said, "Enough, Deborah. 'Tis just a bit of wine. Your dress isn't at all ruined."

Deborah was breathing hard, her eyes narrowed with frustration and anger. "She did it on purpose," she cried. "I will not have it!"

"Nonsense," said Diana sharply. "Moira, please fetch Mrs. Savarol some water. The wine will wash out quite easily."

"You have no say! You are not mistress here!"

Diana was ready to spring at Deborah's throat. She felt Lyon's hand on her wrist. She heard her father say, his voice calm and mild, "I had intended to have a toast to my new son-in-law. And I shall as soon as you have some more wine, my dear."

Deborah subsided. Patricia giggled nervously. Daniel merely continued eating.

"Calm, sweetheart," Lyon said quietly.

"I cannot allow her to—"

"Later, Diana." She had rarely heard that stern tone from him before, and it stopped her.

Lucien began speaking of the repairs in the boiling house, and after a few moments, Diana managed to reply sensibly. From the corner of her eye, she saw Deborah grab a cloth from Moira and dab angrily at the stain on her gown. There was no expression whatsoever on Moira's thin face. *What has she been doing?* Diana wondered. She felt awash with sudden helplessness. *How could her father have married such a mean-spirited woman?*

She speared a bite of coconut fruitcake and chewed it furiously. When her father raised his glass, her mouth was full.

"To my son-in-law, Lyonel Ashton. My lord, welcome to my family."

"Thank you, sir."

Daniel sent a thoughtful gaze to Lyon and raised his glass.

"Yes, to you, my lord," Patricia said, her voice so sweet and winning, Diana could only stare at her. *How could she flirt with Lyon with her own husband sitting beside her?*

Diana had no opportunity to speak alone with her father. There was a new piano in the drawing room downstairs and Patricia played for them. Quite well, actually, Diana was forced to admit. She herself was yawning mightily after tea, and her father, smiling at her, told her to take herself to bed. He bid her and Lyon good night on the second-floor landing, Deborah at his side.

"I am glad to have you home," he said, and gently kissed her cheek. He stood looking down at her for a long moment, saying nothing, and Diana fancied that he was somehow sad. She wanted only to rid him of that sadness and said lightly, sending a sloe-eyed look toward Lyon,

"He is not a bad husband, Father, stubborn and autocratic perhaps, but not exactly unmanageable."

"Daniel is right," Lucien said. "You do look happy. Good night, my dear."

Lyon quietly closed the bedchamber door and leaned against it, folding his arms over his chest.

He watched Diana prowl toward the French windows and jerk them open. Balmy night air swirled into the room.

"She is mistress here, Diana."

Diana whirled about, her face flushed with renewed anger. "She struck Moira! And for what? Nothing, that's what!"

"What does it matter? Moira is a slave, a possession, a piece of property."

"Don't you condescend to me, Lyonel Ashton! Or use that sarcastic tone. She is a human being with feelings! I know that your poor servants in your precious England are many times treated awfully! I can just imagine how your darling Charlotte treats her servants."

"Are you quite through being snide?"

Diana walked to the armoire and smashed her fist against the pale oak door. "Ow," she muttered, and rubbed her hand.

"Do you feel better?"

"No. I wish it were Deborah's face."

"You are quite fierce, aren't you?"

"I would rather be fierce than act so righteously superior!"

"It is not an act, sweetheart."

She heard the humor in his voice, but refused to acknowledge it. She began unfastening the buttons at her bodice. She was so rough that one button popped off and went flying across the floor.

Lyon looked at her a moment longer, shrugged, and

pushed away from the door. They undressed in silence. He watched his wife snatch her nightgown from the armoire and carry it with her behind a screen.

"That is a waste," he called.

Lyon stretched out naked on the cool sheet, his arms above his head. He could hear the sweet song of a nightingale and the muted hissing of the waves. In a few minutes, he would kiss away her upset and love her thoroughly. His member grew enthusiastic at the thought, and he grinned. Moonlight flooded into the room. The flowers smelled sweet. And he was randy as a boy.

"What are you doing, Diana?"

"I am sewing together my nightgown," she called out, her voice nasty.

When she finally emerged, she doused the one lamp and walked slowly toward the bed, her body silhouetted in the shaft of clean moonlight.

"I'm tired," she said, sitting on the far edge of the bed.

"Your bed is somewhat short. I'm not at all tired."

"The bed is just fine for me, and you should be."

"Shut up and come here."

"You have no modesty at all." She inched away from him.

He grabbed a nightgowned shoulder, and as she jumped off the bed and he didn't release the delicate lawn, it tore cleanly, from throat to foot.

"Oh!"

Lyon lay back on the bed. "I told you the gown was a waste. I fancy that is one item of clothing you will have no need for, for at least the next thirty years. Come here, sweetheart. You are in a foul humor and you shouldn't be. You have me, after all."

"You are good for very little."

"I beg your pardon, madam?"

"Did you tell my father the truth? About us?"

"Yes. He deserved to know. An honorable man always deserves the truth."

"Does he know that you intend to drag me back to England?"

"We didn't discuss that."

She was still clutching the nightgown in front of her. Her hair was loose and flowing about her shoulders, the way he liked it.

"I don't know what to do."

"I will tell you what you're going to do at this moment. You are going to drop that nightgown and show me your beautiful body. Then you are going to leap into my arms, wrap yourself around me, and let me kiss every inch of you."

She looked at him, suspicion, uncertainty, and if he weren't mistaken, a bit of interest in her eyes. He grinned. "Every inch," he said, his voice low.

"I never thought an English gentleman—and English earl, for heaven's sake—would speak in such a manner."

"I am just a man, Diana. I save my peerage for the realm, and my gentlemanliness for my clubs."

"Will you get me with child?"

That bald question took him aback, but just for a moment. "Yes, I will do my best. We will make a battalion of children, if you wish." He wanted to add that she could possibly already be carrying his child, but he didn't. He also remembered the awful time Frances had had birthing her child. He paused, but just for a moment. "Come, Diana."

He held out his hand to her, palm up. She looked at his strong hand, the long, blunt-tipped fingers. She felt a shiver run through her. She thought him exquisite. She had never believed she would find a man she would think exquisite. She sighed and climbed onto the bed beside him.

"I don't like the canopy," she said, feeling his hand gently slide from her waist down her hip to her thigh.

"Let us remove it, then."

He leaned over her and studied her face in the moonlight. Lightly, he touched his finger to her lips, slowly tracing their outline.

"Did you like the crab backs?"

"Oh, yes, immensely."

He brought his leg over hers and she felt the crinkly hair slide along her thighs. His hand lightly cupped her breast, lifting it, weighing it in his palm.

"Did you like the shrimp casserole?"

"Most tasty."

A fingertip brushed against her nipple. He was looking down at her intently, his eyes following his finger.

"Do you like me?"

His eyes gleamed. "You are the tastiest of all," he said, and kissed her. "Open your mouth, Diana."

She obeyed him and felt his tongue lightly touch hers. A shaft of pure pleasure skittered down her body, and her hips jerked upward.

"Ah, yes," he said, and deepened his kiss. His hand moved downward, coming to rest on her thigh.

"Open your legs."

She opened her eyes and looked up at him. His gaze was intense and the movement of his fingers was driving her mad. "Will you touch me?" Was that her voice, she wondered vaguely, so high and thin as turtle soup without the turtle?

"You mean like this?"

His fingers gently parted her, and the slight pressure on her woman's flesh made her gasp. She couldn't look away from him and knew that everything she was feeling was written clearly on her face for him to see. She felt embarrassed and urgent.

"And like this?" He slipped a long finger inside her.

"Lyon!"

His eyes were closed a moment, a look of intensity on his face. What was he feeling? His finger was moving in and out of her, and she felt herself stretching, yielding.

She was panting, wanting, aching.

"Bend your legs, Diana. I want to come into you now."

He eased over her, pressing himself against her, now touching his damp fingers to her face, fingers damp with her.

"You are very nice," he said, nibbling on her earlobe. He reared up and she felt him guiding himself into her. Slowly, he eased inside her, and without thinking, she raised her hips to bring him deeper.

He came his full length into her; she looked up at his face and saw strain there, and something like pain. He lowered his body and she felt him pressing against her, and the sensation built like a raging fire.

"I never thought my body would be—" she began, and moaned as his fingers came between their bodies and found her. "Lyon," she gasped.

"Yes," he said, gaining a bit of control. "Yes, Diana, let me see your pleasure."

She whirled out of control, her body heaving, her back arching back, mewling cries bursting from her throat.

"You are so beautiful." His control snapped and he surged into her, feeling the aftershocks of her climax, the tightening of her muscles about him, driving him wild. He gave it up and gave himself to her.

*   *   *

Lyon stood quietly on the balcony smoking a long thin cheroot. It was just a few minutes before dawn, he thought, gazing toward the lazy white-capped waves that seemed to melt onto the white sand. He'd been told by Captain Carstairs that some men felt the pull of the tropics deep in their souls. Lyon didn't know if his soul was involved, but he did feel something akin to a pull within him. Standing alone in this magnificent setting, it was easy to forget that in but a few hours, black men and women would be toiling beneath a hot sun, black men and women owned by a white man.

He cursed softly. What a damnable situation. He turned slightly to look back into the bedchamber. He could see Diana lying on her side, her beautiful hair tangled wildly on the pillow, only a sheet covering her. She was his wife, his responsibility. And this was her home. He cursed again and inhaled deeply.

Suddenly, his attention was caught by a shadowy movement near a mahogany tree below. He took a step closer to the balcony railing and strained to see more clearly. He saw a woman emerge, her movements furtive and quick. She was covered by a long cloak.

This was interesting, he thought, and stood very still.

Her pace broke at the distinctive call of a turtledove. She paused, raised her head, and her cloak fell back a bit. He could make out long hair, loose, and thought it was Patricia Driscoll.

Then he saw a man behind her. But he was in the shadows and Lyon couldn't make out who he was. The only thing he was certain of was that it wasn't Daniel. What the devil was she doing out here? He watched her hug the man, then hurry away, toward the back of the house. A back entrance, he imagined. Where was Daniel?

The sky lightened, it seemed, from one moment to the

next. He saw clearly the thatched huts in the valley to his right where the slaves lived. Their own small village, Diana had told him, complete with their own gardens. At the opposite side of the great house was the overseer's house, where he had lived until six months ago with a black girl who had borne him three children. It occurred to him that Patricia could have been coming from the direction of the overseer's house and that the man had been the overseer, Grainger. Perhaps he would recognize him when he met Grainger today.

He saw red. A betrayed man's cynicism rose in force. A betrayed man's rage. Women, he thought, lying, dishonest cheats, all of them. Here Patricia Driscoll had been married to Daniel for only three months and already she was playing him for the fool, the cuckold. Just as Charlotte had done to him, without even three months on her plate, hell, without even a marriage ceremony on her damned plate! God, was there no end to a woman's treachery?

He heard a soft moan at that moment coming from the bed, and he frowned. His dear wife for how many days now?

He ground out the cheroot on the stone at his feet and walked purposefully toward the bed. Women needed to be kept on a tight rein to keep them honest. Women needed to be mastered. He pulled the sheet off Diana. She didn't wake, but turned onto her back, flinging her arms wide. He grasped her ankles and pulled her legs apart. He came over her and with one powerful thrust entered her body.

She cried out, suddenly coming awake.

"Lyon!"

"Hold still." She was tight, unyielding, not ready for him. He could feel himself stretching her unnaturally. He felt her hands pushing at his shoulders, heard her harsh breathing. He was hurting her, but he didn't stop. He felt her body quivering, not from desire, felt her shrinking from him.

He cursed, thrust deep, holding her hips still in his hands.

He moaned his release and fell over her.

Diana bit her lower lip, but she couldn't stop the tears from sliding down her cheeks.

Lyon came to his senses. He felt dazed. He pulled out of her, easily now, since she was wet with his seed. He rose from the bed and looked down at her. The bedchamber was bathed in early-morning light.

He saw her tears, but she made no sound. She lay as he had left her, her legs sprawled wide. She was staring up at him, her eyes clouded, filled with confusion, with hurt.

"Why did you do that?"

His mind refused to work.

"Why did you hurt me like that?"

"You are a woman, and like all women, you—" He broke off, his mind torn by what he had done, what he had thought, the ease by which the rage buried inside him had burst out.

"Do something with yourself," he said, his eyes going down her body. He felt himself flinch at the sight of the bloodstains on her thighs. Blood and his seed.

He had raped her. Raped his own wife, torn her. He felt sick, the betrayed man's rage dead as cold ashes. He'd done it because he'd thought Patricia Driscoll was betraying her husband.

He quickly turned away from her and pulled on his trousers.

"I am going to swim in the sea," he said over his shoulder, and nearly ran from the bedchamber.

Diana didn't move until she heard Dido's quick steps nearing her bedchamber.

*   *   *

Patricia looked at Lyonel Ashton, Earl of Saint Leven. How had the self-righteous prig of a sister-in-law managed to trap him? And here she was, stuck with Daniel Driscoll, a young man she'd believed would rescue her from the awful genteel poverty of her aunt's house in Charlotte Amalie, a stupid man who wanted to be a physician, a man who wasn't particularly interested in her.

If she'd had the chance to go to London, it would have been to capture the earl. Wealth and position. It was what she deserved. Not an oaf like Daniel Driscoll.

She listened with half an ear to her father-in-law talking to the earl. "You should be here when the cane is cut and processed. It is bedlam. You know, Lyon, that we make sugar, molasses, and rum, of course. The most of the rum goes north, to the United States. If you like, Diana will show you about the plantation and explain things to you. She knows as much as I do about growing sugar. Diana?"

Diana raised her head and very slowly and deliberately placed her bread on her plate beside a slice of uneaten pineapple. "Yes, Father?"

Lucien gave his daughter a quizzing look. "Would you like to give your husband a tour of the island? He can ride Egremont."

Lyon started at the name. "Egremont, sir?"

"Why, yes, my boy. I know it is the name of one of your famous racing dukes in England. A small joke, I suppose."

Lyon forced a smile. "I should like you to, Diana," he said.

Lucien, of course, took his daughter's acquiescence for granted. "Excellent. I will be meeting with Theo Grainger. Our overseer," he added to Lyon. "A good man, knows the estate and can be trusted."

Like hell he can be trusted, Lyon thought. He wanted to meet the overseer. He looked at Patricia, perhaps seeking a clue, but read nothing in her expression. As for Deborah Savarol, she was markedly quiet this morning.

"Very well," Diana said. "Where is Daniel?"

"There was a sick slave," Patricia said, her voice the epitome of scorn.

Millie, a very substantial black woman, appeared at that moment. "Mr. Grainger here to see you, massa."

"Thank you, Millie. If you will excuse me?"

"I am ready, Diana," Lyon said, and rose.

"I have been riding your mare, Diana," Patricia said as Diana also rose. "She is something of a brute, isn't she?"

Diana paled, then flushed. "No, she is not."

Lyon watched her rush upstairs to change into her riding clothes. He walked slowly toward the library. He wanted to meet the overseer.

"This is my home," Diana was saying to herself as she swiftly changed her clothes. "My home, my mare. If Patricia has hurt Tanis, I will tear her hair out. As for you, my dearest husband, I will make you very sorry for what you did."

21

As always, I am bearable at one moment, unbearable the next.

GOETHE

"My God! Look at her flank!"

Lyon looked. Tanis, Diana's mare, had had a riding crop slammed into her, hard and repeatedly.

He loved horses, and this unnecessary cruelty appalled and angered him. "That bitch," he said, gently stroking his gloved hand over the mare's flank.

"Yes," said Diana. "I shall speak to her about this, you may be certain!" Diana recalled at that moment that she wasn't at all on good terms with her husband. She said, her voice distant as she flipped her hand toward another stall, "Egremont is over there, Lyon. Salvation is in the next stall. I do believe that Egremont will probably suit you better—he's the more vicious and unpredictable."

Lyon merely arched a brow at her, but her words hit the mark. He strolled over to regard the huge black stallion with an appreciative eye. "You are quite right, Diana," he said, his voice quiet, "this fellow is a brute."

He watched Diana speak to the stable boys, then she turned back to him. "Do you wish Father's saddle or the Spanish?"

He looked himself and selected the Spanish saddle. It was made of the finest leather and intricately tooled. He stepped back and let the boy, Jessie, saddle the stallion. Diana was acting more normally now, he thought, until she remembered that she shouldn't. He wanted very much to apologize to her, to make her understand that . . . That what, you fool? He had been vicious and unpredictable and an utter bastard.

"Diana," he said abruptly, once they were astride their mounts, "what do you think of the overseer, Grainger?"

Diana was in the midst of planning retribution for Patricia, her anger at her husband momentarily forgotten. "What?"

"Grainger. What do you think of him?"

She shrugged. "As Father said, Grainger knows his business, he doesn't brutalize the slaves, and he is trustworthy. He's been on Savarol thirteen years now. I'll never forget when he came, it was on the first day of January at the turn of the century."

Lyon pictured Grainger in his mind. He had met the man briefly an hour before and drawn his own conclusions. Though not tall, he was built like a boxer, massively muscled, swarthy of complexion, and pleasant in his manner, at least to Lucien Savarol and to him, the Earl of Saint Leven. But Lyon was seeing him as Patricia Driscoll's lover. The man had a fleshy mouth, and Lyon thought again, frowning slightly, he wasn't a young man. Forty, if he was a day. But then again, one never knew with women. His lips thinned at the thought, then he realized that he was again falling into the trap and pulled himself up. Diana wasn't Charlotte nor was she Patricia Driscoll, and he had hurt her.

He paused a moment, gently turning Egremont to follow Diana's mare down a winding path away from the great house. The great stallion quivered with power beneath him.

"What do you think of Patricia?"

She looked at him briefly over her shoulder. "She is a vicious idiot." And her expression said clearly that he and Patricia were one of a kind.

"If she hadn't harmed your horse, what would you think of her?"

"Not much more than I think of you at this moment."

"Diana, about this morning—" He stalled.

Diana said, "Since you despise us so much for owning slaves, I will spare you a visit to their village. I will show you the boiling house."

"Very well," he said mildly. He listened to her speak of how the gangs of men and women worked the long rows of sugarcane, cutting the stalks with sharp machetes called "bills." The stalks were piled onto four-pronged carriers on the backs of mules or into donkey carts. Little boys drove the animals and carts to the mill. She showed him the animal treadmill that stood on a slight elevation so that the cane juice could run from the rollers down a trough to a big copper receiver. This would be, she said, released directly down into the clarifier inside the boiling house.

Lyon thought a clarifier sounded like it purified the cane juice, but her clipped voice didn't invite questions, at least to his mind, so he held his tongue. At least she was talking to him.

"How does one make rum?" he asked finally, pulling his stallion close to her mare. Her scent wafted to his nostrils and he closed his eyes a moment.

"It's made from molasses. We have three cisterns filled with molasses—that's a by-product of the sugar, you know— enough for estate use and to export north." She pointed out the rum stillhouse, built near the molasses cisterns, telling him about the big wooden vats called butts that held up to one thousand gallons of fermenting mash each.

He listened closely, or tried to, but her voice was a monotone, detached, with no interest in it. She was furious with him and he couldn't blame her. He sighed, wondering at himself for his utter loss of control. He'd acted like a bedlamite. It was an appalling thought to realize that the debacle with Charlotte had affected him so deeply. In the light of day, he knew, oh, yes, he knew that Diana was nothing like his erstwhile fiancée, but still, he'd been like a bull enraged by the red cloak when he'd seen Patricia coming from her lover. He sighed, wondering how the devil he was to mend his fences with his young wife. He was aware of the blistering sun overhead, the overwhelming smell of the fermenting mash as they neared the stillhouse, and the constant movement of dozens of black men and women.

"You should be around here during the spring. Your nose would rot off with the smell."

Some humor, he thought. "You appear to know everyone," he said, watching her wave to yet another black, calling out his name.

"Of course. I grew up with them. Do you know the name of everyone who works in your employ? You grew up with them, did you not?"

"What is that?" Lyon asked, ignoring her sarcasm.

"Those are pewter worms."

"I beg your pardon?"

"Hollow pipes made of pewter. They coil around, downward in a spiral shaped like a huge spring. See? They're suspended in a cistern of cold water. When the hot vapors run down the worms they condense—and out comes rum. It's a pity you will not be here to see the process."

"I shall be somewhere, I suppose."

"Yes, but not here.

She was not going to make it easy for him, of course. He said finally, "If I am not here, neither will you be."

"I wouldn't be too certain of that," Diana flung back at him, and nudged Tanis' sleek sides. He followed her through a narrow path in a cane field. The field ended only a hundred yards or so from the sea. Diana rode down the beach, then drew to a halt. "There is our dock. When we're ready to ship, we load hogsheads into moses boats— they're small dinghies that are rowed out to sailing schooners."

"I see."

"You probably don't, but it doesn't matter."

"You are a patient instructor, Diana."

She gave him a look at that. "I suppose I could tie you down and beat the information into you. Perhaps you would understand that approach."

"I am sorry I forced you this morning."

Angry color surged over her face. "Forced? Is that what you call your despicable behavior? I hope you come to a bad end, Lyon. You deserve it!"

He watched her gallop down the beach. He didn't follow her. He sat still on Egremont's back and stared up the slopes of the three hills of Savarol Island. Row after row of sugarcane climbed and wound around the gentle slopes. So many souls needed to work the rows. He was rather relieved that he wasn't here during harvest time. He could picture Grainger whipping those sweating black backs when Lucien wasn't around. Then plowing Patricia in the middle of the night when Daniel was sleeping.

What the devil was he to do? He'd mucked up things with Diana, after swearing to her father that he would protect her, take care of her. The sun beat down on him

and he dismounted, tying Egremont to the branch of a
white cedar. He stripped off his clothes and dashed into the
turquoise water. He dived forward, feeling the brief shock
of cool water close over his head. The bottom was sandy
and firm, the water now like a tepid bath. He imagined
himself diving into the cold, muddy waters of the Thames
and laughed. A pelican dived expertly into the water some
twenty feet from him, emerging with a wriggling fish in its
long beak.

"Congratulations, old fellow!"

He flipped onto his back and floated for a while. The
sun beat upon his face but the water kept him cool. He
could hear nothing, see nothing except that same circling
pelican and the brilliant blue sky. He decided he would
simply have to seduce Diana, treat her very gently, prove
to her that he wasn't a maniac from Bedlam. As for
Patricia, well, he supposed he would just have to wait and
see. Perhaps he could drop some none-too-subtle comments in that girl's ears, let her know that he knew her
secret. Or he could tell Lucien.

Of course he had no real proof. He had seen her, had
seen the shadow of a man, knew that they were coming
from the overseer's house. The man hadn't been black, of
that he was certain. There were no other white men on the
island, save himself and Lucien. At least none that he
knew of yet. He could hear himself now saying to Lucien
Savarol, "I saw your daughter-in-law just before dawn
with her lover, though I didn't see his face or her face and
didn't see them committing adultery, actually."

Damnation.

He turned over and touched his feet to the sandy bottom. He swam back until the water came only to his waist,
then stood and walked through the gently tumbling surf.
He didn't see Patricia until he was out of the water,
shaking himself like a wet mongrel.

"Good morning, my lord," she called to him, her voice high.

He stopped dead in his tracks. He eyed his clothes. They were neatly piled near Egremont, some thirty feet away. He was perfectly naked. The sun was in his eyes and he shaded them with his hand.

"You are now married, Patricia," he called back to her. "However, I am not your husband. I believe you should take yourself off until I clothe myself."

She laughed merrily. He was the most beautiful man she'd ever seen, she thought, unable to tear her eyes away. Not that she'd seen all that many men, of course. She realized suddenly that Daniel was very likely somewhere near, and pulled her gaze away. "I will see you at lunch, my lord! Not as much of you, of course!" She laughed, mounted an old swaybacked nag, and cantered off down the beach.

Lyon stood quietly, looking after her for a moment. He saw her bring her riding crop on the poor animal's flank, and flinched. Life, he decided while he pulled on his clothes, wasn't simple, even in this paradise. More than one person, and things invariably got mucked up.

He didn't see Tanis in the stable when he returned with Egremont. He wondered if Diana would follow the plan of avoiding him now. He returned to the great house to find Lucien in his library with another white man, one Lyon hadn't seen before.

"Hello, Lyon. Do come in, my boy. Charles Swanson, my bookkeeper; my son-in-law, Lord Saint Leven."

Swanson looked like the young vicar in Escrick, Lyon thought. Narrow-shouldered, slight of build, pale-gray eyes, and strangely enough, very white-skinned, as if his face never saw the sun.

"My lord," said Charles Swanson, "it is a pleasure."

His voice was deep and rich, again like the vicar's in Escrick.

Lyon shook the man's hand. The slender bones felt like a woman's in his strong grasp.

"Charles, here, keeps all our accounts in order," said Lucien. "Not an easy task, I assure you."

Lyon wondered briefly where the man lived. In the overseer's house? Could he have been the one he saw early this morning? No, for heaven's sake, he thought, that was ridiculous. The young man looked like an aesthete and somewhat effeminate. He wouldn't have been surprised to see him in a monk's cowl rather than breeches and a white shirt, or hunched over old scholarly volumes in a musky library.

"Did Diana give you a tour, Lyon?"

He wanted to tell Lucien that his daughter had given him a monotonous little speech and then the boot, but he merely nodded.

"Did she also swim with you?"

"No. I believe she wanted to see some of her friends." He smiled. "She deserted me."

Lucien heard nothing amiss in his son-in-law's voice. "I have told Charles that you have inherited Mendenhall plantation on Tortola. He is acquainted with the attorney for the Mendenhall estate, Mr. Edward Bemis."

"Mr. Bemis has seen to everything, my lord," said Charles. "He is a competent gentleman, and honorable. He, ah, knows that you have arrived and are here on Savarol Island."

"Does he, now?" Lyon said. "I imagine that I will meet him soon enough. Perhaps next week, once I learn a bit about plantation life and its workings."

Charles bowed his head in acknowledgment.

"Well, my boy, why don't we join the ladies? It's time for luncheon and I, for one, am ravenous."

They left Charles Swanson at the desk, poring over ledgers. "Where does he live?" Lyon asked once they were alone.

"He has a small house near Grainger's," Lucien said. "Why?"

Lyon shrugged. "I just wondered. How long has he been in your employ?"

"Not long. Just four months. He came highly recommended from Jamaica. Worked for the Barretts, you know, at Greenwood." Lucien paused a moment. "A strange man in some ways. He avoids the sun like the plague and his only request is that he go to Tortola every week. As for his glowing description of Edward Bemis, well—" Lucien shrugged. "Who knows?"

Who knows, indeed? thought Lyonel. "Your home is magnificent," he said as they walked up the wide mahogany stairs to the second floor.

"I know. You could transplant it to England, could you not?"

"No," Lyon said as they came onto the veranda. "Its proper setting is here in paradise."

All three ladies were seated at the long table. Diana had changed into a cool muslin gown of soft pink. She avoided Lyon's eyes. As for Patricia, she was eyeing the earl with a knowing look that made him flush a bit. Deborah was frowning toward the black girl Moira.

"My dear," Lucien said, leaning down to kiss his wife lightly on her powdered cheek.

Lyon, watching this, strolled to Diana, and said, "My love." He kissed her cheek, and as he straightened, he saw the glint of anger in her eyes. He grinned. "I told your father you'd deserted me."

"Yes," said Patricia. "He was swimming—alone—when I found him."

"Where is Daniel?" Lyon said quickly, aware that Diana was now frowning from him to Patricia.

Patricia gave a petulant shrug. "Likely he is tending a sick slave. There is always something wrong with them. I do hope he washes well before he joins us."

"You may serve the luncheon now," Deborah said.

"Yes, missis," said Moira, scurrying away.

"Impudent little fool," Deborah said under her breath. Lucien had told her in no uncertain terms the previous night that she wasn't to abuse the house slaves, and for many moments she'd simply stared at him, unable to find words to defend herself. In the end, she'd said nothing, merely nodded, her head bowed.

Diana was thinking; Lyon swam naked. She stared a moment at Patricia, who was eyeing Lyon hungrily, at least to her mind. Damnable man!

Daniel arrived a few moments later, apologizing for his lateness, spreading his warmth to everyone at the table, even to his wife, who most likely didn't deserve it, Lyon thought.

"I keep forgetting how big you are, Daniel," Diana said, grinning at him. "You make the veranda shrink."

"The curse of my life," he said. "Mother has always wondered how I could become such an oak. She believes me a changeling." He said easily to Lucien, "Thomas had a nasty cut from a machete, sir. Fortunately he didn't wait to tell me. Hopefully there will be no infection."

"Thank you, Daniel. Ah, braised rabbit in molasses. It is one of Diana's favorites, Lyon."

"Just so long as it's not mongoose in molasses," Lyon said. "I awoke on our deserted island to see one of the fellows staring me in the eye. It was most disconcerting, particularly when Diana just laughed at me."

Conversation at the table was pleasant until Patricia

asked, "Tell me about your wedding in London. Was it a grand affair? Was the Prince Regent present?"

Diana's fingers tightened about her fork and she shot an agonized look toward her husband.

Lyon said easily, "Actually, we weren't married in London. We decided it would be more romantic to be married at sea. Captain Carstairs did the honors."

"Well!" This from Deborah. "Are you certain the man has the authority?"

"If he didn't, then Diana and I are living in sin," Lyon said.

"Just when did he perform this ceremony?"

"The children are married, Deborah," Lucien said, finality in his voice. "That is quite enough."

"But why didn't you marry in London?"

"Obviously because they didn't wish to," Daniel said in a repressive voice to his wife.

Lyon added, looking briefly toward his very silent wife, "Diana wanted to come home. There wasn't time to plan a formal wedding."

Deborah obviously wasn't satisfied, but she held her tongue.

"Delicious," Lyonel said. "What is this, Diana?"

"Yams and molasses."

"If it sits long enough on my plate will the molasses become rum?"

"I explained rum making to you."

"True enough," Lyon said. "I'd forgotten about the worms." No response, not even a slight smile. She'd lost her sense of humor. He'd make things right again, after luncheon.

"Diana, I want to talk to you."

She was seated on her balcony, staring out to sea, her body still, her expression thoughtful.

"Diana?"

"Yes? What do you want, Lyon?"

"I want you."

"I see. And if I say no, will it matter to you?"

"I should like to speak to you about that."

"Short of jumping over the railing, there is little I can do to stop you."

He sighed and moved to stand beside her, his elbows on the railings. He inhaled the sweet scented air. Without turning, he said, "I suppose I can make excuses—they'll sound bloody weak to your ears, of course—but I would like to tell you the truth." He paused, still not turning to face her.

"I suppose I could fling you over the balcony."

He turned at that, leaning back, his elbows balanced on the railing. He grinned at her. "You could try. I believe I should enjoy your efforts."

"Talk, my lord."

"Very well. I was awake very early this morning, before dawn, in fact. I was standing out here, smoking a cheroot. I saw Patricia coming from Grainger's house and he was with her. She was wearing a long cloak and I couldn't see her clearly, but I could tell she was white and young. All I could think about was that she was betraying her husband, she was betraying Daniel, a fine man, and they'd been married such a short time. She became Charlotte to me. I was enraged. I went crazy. I took out that rage on you. I apologize for it. I mean that, Diana. I hope you will forgive me for hurting you."

She sat still as a stone, watching him. His words played over and over in her mind. It was odd, but she'd imagined that something had triggered his memories of Charlotte and driven him to hurt her, a woman, the betrayer.

"It is difficult to accept."

"Which part?"

"That Patricia would betray Daniel with Grainger. He's not a young man, Lyon. Are you certain what you saw?"

"Completely. Actually, I didn't see the man clearly, simply that he was white. I do not believe that Charles Swanson is a seducer, at least he doesn't seem the sort."

"No, not Charles, I think. Are you equally certain it was Patricia?"

He paused a moment. "You mean, did I see her face clearly? No, not really, but who else could it have been? Certainly it wasn't you."

"No, it wasn't me. What are you going to do?"

"Nothing at the moment, I don't believe. What I'm trying to do is to get you to forgive me. What do you say, sweetheart? Another chance for the bedlamite?"

"She should be whipped."

"Yes, I suppose so. I don't wish Daniel to be hurt, and yet—"

"She will continue until she is discovered? And his hurt is inevitable?"

"Just as mine was, yes. I was a lucky devil, though. I discovered Charlotte's perfidy before we were married."

"What would you have done if you had discovered it after the wedding?"

Lyon stared at a blood red bougainvillea. "I don't know," he said finally. "I truly don't know."

"Would you come with me, Lyon?"

He arched a thick brow. "Where?"

"A private place. A place I spent a lot of time while I was growing up when I was upset about something or wanted to think. I would like to show it to you."

"Do you mean to cosh me on the head and bury my body?"

"No."

"Let's go, by all means."

It was siesta time and there was no one about. They saddled their own horses and Lyon followed her past the cane fields to a rocky, forested area at the southern tip of the island. She said nothing, merely click-clicked Tanis up a narrow, overgrown trail. "We are here," she said, turning in her saddle.

Lyon stared around. They were nowhere, as far as he could see.

"It's a cave," she said as she dismounted.

His eyes lit up. He hadn't imagined anything of the sort on a Caribbean island. The cave had a narrow, low entrance, but once inside, it magically became a huge room, with great stalagmites and stalactites touching in several places. Diana lit a lantern near the entrance.

"I have never brought anyone here before. I have found some bones and jugs that are very old. Probably of the Arawak Indians, though I cannot be certain. Also, I haven't explored the entire cave. There is a passage, but it is too narrow for me to squeeze through. I haven't found another entrance."

"Thank you for bringing me here." His voice sounded disembodied, rumbling, coming back to him even as he spoke.

"I brought you here to forgive you properly."

He began to laugh. It sounded demonic and he stopped abruptly. "Spread that blanket, sweetheart, and I will show you the depths of my . . . Well, you will see."

"Yes," she said, grinning at him, her hand lightly stroking over his chest, "yes, knowing you as I do, I most certainly shall."

"It is chilly in here, Diana. Let's put the blanket near the entrance. You look exquisite with the sun shining on your body."

He stood in front of her for several moments, not touching her, merely looking at her. Then he began to strip off her clothes, very slowly, stroking each inch of her as it was uncovered, then he laid her on the blanket. He stood over her, still fully dressed, and stared down at her. He loved the whiteness of her breasts and belly and the golden tan of her legs and shoulders. He came down on his knees. Lightly, he reached out his hand and circled a nipple.

"Lyon," she whispered, "I feel embarrassed. You are fully clothed."

"Yes," he said, and leaned down to kiss her nipple and take it into his mouth. He laid his hand lightly on her flat belly. He felt the muscles tighten and his fingers moved downward to tangle in the whorl of dark-blond curls. He found her, moist, swelled, and smiled at her. "I have decided to keep you. You are not cold, are you?"

She felt his fingers caress and probe and stroke. Her hips lifted. "Lyon."

A finger gently eased inside her. Her muscles clenched and she watched him close his eyes a moment. He was feeling her, learning her. It was intensely erotic and she moaned softly. "Please, your clothes."

"I can't, not yet." He opened his eyes. His finger deepened.

"Lyon!" She jerked upward.

Quickly, he opened his britches and lifted her onto him, impaling her, feeling himself so deep that he nearly lost control. Her legs tightened around his flanks, her back arched back against his arms. He kissed her deeply, feeling her take more of him, offering him all of her. He watched her face as he lifted her and lowered her on him. When his fingers found her, her eyes opened wide, and she cried out and he took that cry into his mouth. He was kissing her deeply when she reached her climax. She nearly toppled both of them in her frenzy.

As she quieted, he held her close, kissing her temple, smoothing her hair, stroking her back, even as his manhood throbbed and pulsed, demanding release inside her.

"Diana?"

She gave him a dazed, sated look.

"On your back, love."

He didn't leave her, but carefully lowered her. Then he was astride her, driving deeply, feeling her legs tightly clasp his hips. And it was she, this time, who watched his face at the moment of his release.

"This is very strange," she said, hugging his clothed body tightly against her.

"You are magnificent."

"I suppose that you are also." She lightly nipped his earlobe with her teeth. "You never took off your clothes. I feel terribly exposed."

"You are, and I love it. Your pleasure . . . it moves me, Diana. It makes me feel like I have been given a gift that is as rare and unique as you are yourself."

"But you don't love me, do you, Lyon?"

He was silent. She felt his body stiffen slightly.

"No, it is all right. I don't love you either." That was a lie, but she didn't want his pity. She felt him pull out of her and flinched just a bit.

"Did I hurt you?"

She said honestly, "I am still a bit sore from your . . . well, your deed of this morning."

"Deed? You are kind. Let me help you dress."

They left the cave after a bit of exploring. "It has a name?" he asked as they emerged into the late-afternoon sunlight.

"I call it Smuggler's Cave. Silly, of course, but not too bad for a ten-year-old girl."

"Why don't we call it the Trysting Cave?"

"You are a man with very limited thoughts, Lyon!"

"Yes, ma'am. Otherwise known as a randy goat."

"And I am a randy ewe?"

"There is nothing sheepish about you, Diana." He tossed her into her saddle. "I hear a turtledove."

"Yes, there in the frangipani. See him?"

"I see him. He's alone."

She gave him a slow, very satisfied smile. "He won't be for very long. His voice is sweet and seductive."

Lyon click-clicked Egremont. They rode side by side. "Perhaps," he said, smiling at her, "you will now tell me the truth about clarifiers and worms?"

She laughed, a sweet sound, and lightly punched his shoulder.

"I am forgiven?"

Since she loved him, it would be nearly beyond her not to forgive him. "Your way of apologizing was most . . . thorough."

He let it go at that. He imagined it would take her some time to forget what he had done.

"Look, Lyon! The turtledove—he is no longer alone."

Nor am I, he thought, extremely pleased.

22

Heavens, with you I must look after myself!

PLAUTUS

Diana and Patricia stood in the shade of a cascading bougainvillea at the edge of the croquet grounds behind the great house. It was late the following morning, and the sun was climbing high in the sky. Diana experienced a small flash of memory of her mother whenever she was here. She could hear light laughter, smell a strange elusive scent. She felt a moment of overwhelming sadness, but was brought quickly back to the here and now by Patricia's sharp voice.

"What is it you want, Diana?"

"I want to know why you abused my mare."

"*Your* mare? I was under the impression that everything belonged to your father."

"Tanis is mine. But it wouldn't matter, in any case. Why would you hurt a helpless animal?"

"I told you, the mare is a brute."

Perhaps, Diana thought, if she weren't seeing Patricia with new eyes, she would be more tolerant, more patient. As it was, she wanted to throttle the girl. To betray

Daniel, kind, gentle Daniel, it was too much. Good heavens, Patricia was only eighteen and but a few months married. Hadn't the infamous Charlotte been only eighteen when she betrayed Lyon?

"Tanis is spirited," Diana said finally, bringing herself back to the subject at hand. "Her spirit is something to be encouraged, not something to be broken. You will not ride her again, ever."

"You are no longer mistress here, *my lady,* as Deborah told you. Nor do I take orders from you. When you leave, as you will, I shall do exactly as I please."

"If I leave, my mare will go with me, you may be certain of that!"

"Your mare is large enough for Daniel to ride. I doubt that you will take the animal anywhere."

Frustrated, Diana could only stare at her sister-in-law.

"Daniel would never abuse an animal or anyone weaker than he."

"Daniel is too soft," Patricia said with a shrug.

"You believe him soft because he is kind?"

Patricia didn't reply. Her mouth pouted; she looked like a sullen child.

"Why, then, did you marry him?"

"That, dear Diana, is none of your affair. Now, if you are quite through trying to boss me about, I have things to do."

"What things? From what I've observed, you do nothing at all, save live off my father's bounty."

"I am a lady." She waved her hand negligently at the croquet hoops. "I am also becoming quite proficient at this silly game."

Diana laughed.

"You bitch! Shut up! I *am* a lady!"

"What you are, Patricia, is spoiled and thoughtless. Stay away from Tanis. And stay away from my husband."

Patricia's eyes gleamed. "I saw him, you know, quite naked, coming out of the sea. He is very tanned save for his . . . If you hadn't been so very close perhaps—" She gave Diana a particularly coquettish smile. "Well, who knows what he would have done?"

Why hadn't she kept her mouth shut? Diana knew that Patricia had honed in quite accurately on her weakness. Had she sounded jealous? Evidently so. Patricia wasn't stupid. A lady, was she! She repeated, her voice calmer now, "Stay away from Lyon."

"We'll just have to see about that, won't we? After all, I am younger than you and not so dreadfully brown." Patricia gave her a drawing smile, raised her parasol, and strolled away.

I am not at all good at confrontations, Diana thought, depressed. I should have slapped her and stomped her in the ground. She sighed deeply, trying to remember what Savarol was like before the advent of Deborah and Patricia. Endlessly peaceful, that's what it had been. Perhaps a bit boring as well. How she wished now for just one day of boredom.

"You won't win with dat one, missis," said Dido, slipping into the garden from behind a frangipani tree.

"Still eavesdropping, Dido? It is not well done of you. And no, she buried me quite nicely."

Dido patted her arm. "You go away soon with dat handsome man of yours. You forget all dis nonsense."

"And what will happen to all my friends if I leave?" Diana said, her voice harsh as the sun overhead.

"It's your daddy dat's responsible. Maybe he made a big mistake with the new missis. Maybe she fooled him good. Now you stop your worrying and find dat man of yours. You make de love with dat young stallion. Dat make you smile again."

Dido was right. It certainly would make her smile—like a dazed idiot. His power over her was frightening, particularly since he could make her as docile and soft as the morning dew with but a touch. She wondered idly if she held any of that power over him. Perhaps a bit, but as he'd told her, he was a man, and a man was quite forward and simple in that regard. No, not much power at all. After all, he didn't love her.

"I have to make things right again, Dido," she said, nodded to the old woman, and walked back to the great house.

She spent an hour penning a letter to Lucia, giving her an abbreviated version of her adventures since leaving London. She wasn't really surprised to feel Lyonel's strong hands on her shoulders, kneading her flesh gently, knowing her and her reaction to him.

"Lucia?" he said, and she could hear the amusement in his voice. "Did you tell her you made an honest man of me?" He leaned down and nibbled on her ear.

"Have I?" she asked, turning around in her chair to face him. He was wearing buckskin britches and a loose white shirt that was open at the neck. His throat was strong and brown, the visible hair on his chest thick and curling. She wanted to touch him.

He looked like a planter, not a London gentleman. He looked tanned and tough and strong. She felt a spurt of warmth deep in her belly, felt herself quiver.

He saw it. He gave her a lazy, very satisfied smile, and his hands came around her throat to lightly stroke the pulse in her neck.

"Have I what?" he said, his voice as seductive as the turtledove's.

She didn't have the faintest idea what he was talking about, and she refused to humiliate herself by asking. She said instead, "I had a most dissatisfying confrontation with dear Patricia."

"Did you plant your fist in her face?"

"No. She did me in."

His hands became quiet. "I don't believe that," he said slowly. "In my experience, you're like a terrier who never gives up. I have the wounds to prove it."

"She talked about seeing you naked and how you were tanned everywhere but your . . . well, and what you would probably have done if I hadn't been close by. All that in the same breath that she was a lady!"

He laughed.

"Jealous, little one?"

She pulled away from his bewitching hands and rose, twitching at her skirts. "It is not funny."

"Perhaps not," he said mildly. "You didn't accuse her of anything, did you?"

"No," she said, her voice miserable. "I don't know what to do, Lyon."

"It's siesta time. Let me kiss you and love you until you howl with pleasure."

"What about you? Will you howl with pleasure?"

"No howling." He grinned at her. "The manly thing to do is to groan and thrust deep while I kiss your breasts and caress you with my fingers."

She turned red.

"Ah, Diana, you please me immensely." He drew her against him and pressed her face against his shoulder. "We will figure out something, sweetheart. Try not to worry yourself overly about it. I do have some ideas, you know, at least with regard to Daniel."

"What are they?" Her voice was muffled against the warm flesh of his shoulder. She loved his scent, and breathed deeply, burrowing closer.

"I am a wealthy man. I think that Daniel and his wife should go to England. I have a feeling that Daniel would be happy as a lark were he able to study medicine. He seems quite oblivious of mundane things, more's the pity."

His hands stroked down her back, lower still, to cup her buttocks, and lifted her against him. "I want you," he said, nipping at her earlobe. "Of course, since I am such a simple being, you must know that."

He was hard against her belly. "Yes," she said. "I know you are simple, you've told me that enough."

"Doesn't it make you pleased with yourself?"

There came a loud cry. He released her suddenly, spinning around. "What the devil!"

He strode to their bedchamber door, Diana at his heels. He flung it open and stopped, staring at Deborah, who was standing over Moira. The black girl was cowering at her feet, her arms covering her head.

"Shut up, you stupid fool!"

Diana met Deborah's eyes. She was stunned at the fury she read there. The older woman's bosom was heaving.

"What do you want?" Deborah nearly shouted at Diana and Lyon.

"Stay put, Diana." Lyon calmly walked to Deborah and wrested the riding whip from her right hand.

"Why?" he said, towering over her.

Deborah knew, had known instantly, that she'd made a bad mistake. She drew herself up to her diminutive size. "She is impertinent and I will see her sold, immediately."

Moira was blubbering, the sobs louder now that Diana and Lyon were here.

Diana, impetuous of nature, found herself standing perfectly still, her brain working quickly. Moira was the only slave Deborah abused. Certainly she'd spoken of Dido's impertinence, but never had Diana seen her do anything but frown slightly when Dido clothed herself in her bossy manner. She asked quite calmly, "What did Moira do, Deborah? Perhaps his lordship and I can assist you."

Lyon's expression didn't change. His volatile and impassioned Diana, speaking so softly, so reasonably?

"It is none of your affair, miss! I will speak to your father. The little slut will be off Savarol Island by the end of the week."

"Why?"

Deborah shot Lyon a sideways look. "She is unmanageable," she said only. She stretched out her hand and Lyon placed the whip on her palm. "I didn't touch her with this, although God knows she deserves it."

"Moira," Diana said to the still-sobbing girl, "go to the kitchen and refresh yourself. And stop that infernal noise!"

"Yes, missis."

Diana, purely by chance, saw Moira's face. She saw her shoot a venomous look at Deborah. That look was also . . . smug, triumphant. Because she and Lyon had protected her? Somehow Diana didn't think so. A mystery, then. One day of boredom, she thought again. Just one day without the eddies and tensions.

"We will see you at dinner, Deborah," Diana said. "Lyon, you wished to read Lucia's letter, did you not?"

"What? Oh, yes, certainly, my dear."

Once Lyon had closed their bedchamber door behind him, he said abruptly, "All right, what was that all about?"

"There is something going on that I don't understand. Deborah hates Moira, and not because she's slothful or incompetent. And Moira looked smug, pleased with herself, Lyon, I am certain of it. There is something strange happening here." She paused, sighing.

"Moira is a very pretty girl," Lyon said.

"Well, yes, that's true. What of it?"

"Perhaps nothing, perhaps everything. Now, my dear wife, where were we?"

She gave him a look that made his body tighten, but didn't answer him, not then anyway.

He didn't speak until they were naked on their bed, Lyon over her.

"Diana, look at me. I want to see your expression when I come inside you."

Her mouth opened on a cry when he drove into her, fully, deeply.

"Diana, don't move!" His voice was ragged, his large body quivering. "Merciful heavens, you make me delirious, woman."

It seemed to become more powerful, more intense each time, Diana was thinking vaguely. When he pulled out of her, she clutched at his shoulders, but he only shook his head. When his mouth found her, caressed her, his tongue stroking her, she knew that if he were to stop, she would shatter into a thousand fragments. "Lyon!"

"Yes, sweetheart. Come along, now. Let go for me."

She did, and he reveled in it. When he thrust into her again, the feelings she thought exhausted revived, and she stared at him, amazed at herself. He grinned, though it looked somewhat painful.

She thought the words were in her mind, but when she opened her eyes, so difficult at the moment because she felt as if she never wanted to move anything again, she saw him looking thoughtfully down at her.

He kissed her lightly on the tip of her nose, then her cheek and ear. "You taste like sweat, sex, and Diana."

"Faithful as a hound, Lyon?"

His grin became a laugh. "If you keep the hearth so very warm and inviting, yes, this hound will never budge an inch."

"And if I weren't so . . . well, so . . ."

"Responsive? Perhaps eager is the appropriate word for a well-bred miss and a lady. And if you weren't so . . . well, I would just have to teach you, slowly and with great patience. But then again, you have always desired my mouth, have you not?"

She buffeted him on his shoulder. "You're sweaty."

"So are you. I wish your tub were large enough for the both of us. Tell you what, Diana, let's go swimming tonight. All right?"

"Yes," she said, her eyes gleaming, "all right." And with no Patricia about, she added silently.

It was after midnight. The great house was quiet and dark. They walked hand in hand toward the sea, laughing softly, speaking nonsense. The sky overhead was brilliant with stars and a three-quarter moon, the scent of the flowers less overwhelming as they neared the sea. A fresh breeze ruffled their hair.

Diana said in a drawling voice, "Lyon, I am not wearing anything beneath my gown."

He groaned and tightened his hold on her hand, hurrying her forward. She laughed in delight.

"I feel like we're back on Calypso Island."

"I do hope there is no one about," Diana said. "Just think of your embarrassment!"

"What about you? I have need of only one fig leaf, whereas you, my dear wife—"

He broke off instantly at the sound of Diana's indrawn breath.

"What is it, what's the—" Then he saw. A body, lying sprawled beside an oleander. It was a woman, curled up on her side, unmoving.

The woman was black. Lyon dropped to his knees and

turned her over. It was Moira. Quite dead, a narrow hemp rope still about her neck. Her eyes were open, her tongue bulging from her mouth. He quickly removed his shirt and covered her. He picked up her wrist. She was still warm. Her killer had done his work quite recently.

He rose and turned to his still wife. "Diana, we're going back to the house now." She didn't reply and he clasped her shoulders, shaking her slightly. "Diana!"

She said in a stiff little voice, "I am all right, Lyon." Her jaw worked spasmodically. "Moira?"

"Yes, someone strangled her. There is nothing we can do for her. Come along now."

Lucien was still staring straight ahead, his expression blank. Moira's body had been taken to her family's house in the village. Right now, men were combing the area. The family were seated silently, in shock, in the drawing room.

"You heard nothing?"

Her father's voice sounded so strangely detached.

Lyon said, "No, not a thing. We were going for a swim when we came upon her."

"Nothing like this had ever happened," Lucien said, looking at the assembled faces as if searching for an answer. "We've had fights, certainly, particularly after the harvest when the rum is flowing. But this . . . What kind of man would do this?"

A man? Diana wondered. Why not a woman? Moira wasn't all that strong. A woman could have come up behind her and hooked the rope around her neck and drawn it tight, tighter . . . She shuddered and closed her eyes. She saw Deborah standing over Moira, that riding crop in her hand, enraged with the girl. She felt Lyon's hand on her shoulder, gently pressing, reassuring.

"What was she doing out there, alone?"

Patricia gave an odd little giggle. "Meeting someone. It's obvious, isn't it? She was meeting her lover and he killed her."

"You're overwrought," Daniel said, stroking his wife's hand. "Sir," he continued to Lucien, "there is nothing more we can do tonight. Patricia needs to rest."

"Yes," Lucien said to all of them, "we will discuss this in the morning."

How could anyone sleep? Diana wondered silently as she walked beside Lyon up the stairs. There was a murderer about. Moira, was, had been, only fifteen years old.

"Hang on," Lyon said close to her ear.

He held her that night while she shivered from reaction. "I remember when she was born, even though I was only four years old. I can remember my mother saying it was a difficult birth. Moira's mother's name is Mary. She is a fine seamstress. Oh, God who and why, Lyon?"

"We will find out, Diana," he said over and over. He was remembering starkly Diana's impression of the black girl's expression the day before. To Deborah. And Deborah hated the girl.

Sleep was difficult, even if there had been nothing but the silence of the night. They could hear the intermittent wailing coming from the slave village. On and on it went.

The following morning, after breakfast, the family adjourned to the drawing room. Grainger and Charles Swanson were there, both men looking as exhausted as the family. Lucien stood by his large mahogany desk, his long fingers drumming its surface.

"Your findings, Grainger," he said, nodding to his overseer.

"I had a detail of a dozen men. We searched the area thoroughly. There was no one about, but then again, one couldn't expect a murderer to lurk nearby. Nor did we find anything helpful. The hemp rope—it could have come from anywhere. Not at all uncommon.''

Charles Swanson cleared his throat and gave his report. "I spent hours in the village, questioning the girl's family. There was a young black, name of Bob, but he was obviously distressed at the girl's death.''

"Murder,'' Diana corrected.

"Well, yes, murder. I don't believe he had anything to do with it. There is no motive.''

"Surely you don't believe him,'' Deborah cried. "They're all liars and now afraid. He killed her, there is no other way.''

"Bob has an alibi,'' said Charles Swanson to Deborah Savarol. "He didn't leave his hut last night, not for a minute.''

Discussions continued. Diana found herself looking at each face, studying each expression. She kept coming back to Deborah.

Dido came into the room, sidling toward Lucien.

Yes?'' he asked impatiently.

"A white man is here, massa. A Mr. Edward Bemis.''

"Edward!'' Charles Swanson cried out, then paled at his outburst. "He is a friend, of course. I had no idea he was coming here. I thought he would wait for his lordship to return to Tortola—''

"Yes, certainly, Charles,'' said Lucien, cutting his bookkeeper off. "Show the gentleman in, Dido.''

Edward Bemis indeed looked the gentleman, Lyon thought, studying the tall, lean-built, immaculately dressed man as he came into the drawing room. He wouldn't have looked at all out of place on St. James's. His hair was blond, his face tanned and a bit too wrinkled for his age, doubtless from years spent in the Caribbean sun. It seemed as though his eyes, a clear pale blue, had been faded by that same sun just as his skin had been darkened. He looked to be in his mid-thirties. What was the man doing here? And his appearance was so very timely.

Introductions were made. Lyon didn't like the way the man looked at Diana, but when Bemis offered his hand to Lyon, he shook it.

"My lord," Bemis said, and Lyon nodded. Bemis turned. "Ah, Daniel, a lovely prize you've captured."

So Bemis knew Daniel, did he? From where? St. Thomas? Did Daniel look a bit embarrassed? Lyon wasn't certain. When Daniel responded, it was with his usual slow, kind voice. "Yes, indeed, Mr. Bemis. You do remember Patricia, do you not?"

"How could I not?" He took Patricia's hand and gallantly kissed her wrist. "The loveliest young lady in all of Charlotte Amalie." He turned his eyes to Diana, but was careful in his manner. "A long time, my lady," he said.

"Yes," Diana said. "A very long time."

Finally, Lucien cleared his throat and motioned Edward Bemis to be seated. "We are all here, Bemis, because we've had a tragedy. One of our slaves, a girl named Moira, was strangled last night."

"Good God!"

"By her lover," said Patricia.

"Who is this lover?" asked Bemis.

"A slave by the name of Bob," Deborah said swiftly.

"That isn't true, at least according to Charles," said Lyon slowly. "It is a mystery," he added, his eyes on Edward Bemis. The man looked mildly interested, nothing more. After all, Lyon thought, what was one black life to him? Had he really just arrived on Savarol Island?

"Why are you here, Bemis?" Lucien said.

"To meet with his lordship," said Edward politely.

"There are decisions to be made, and since he is here, in the West Indies, I didn't feel it appropriate for me to make them."

"What decisions?" Lyon asked.

"I, ah, feel that we should discuss them in private, my lord." A rich dandy, Edward Bemis was thinking. A man who would soon return to his soft life in England and leave him in control. Excellent, just excellent. He couldn't have planned it better had he been able to.

Unfortunately, he soon discovered that he'd misjudged his man.

It was an hour later. Diana, Lyon, and Edward Bemis were seated on the veranda, sipping cool lemonade.

Edward said in a nicely balanced voice, between condescension and flattery, "Perhaps I could speak with his lordship for a bit, my lady?"

"If it is about Mendenhall plantation, my wife is very much involved," Lyon said shortly. "What is it?"

Bemis cleared his throat. He didn't like it, but after all, Diana Savarol was the daughter of a planter. "As you know, my lord, England outlawed the buying of slaves some years ago."

"Yes, I know."

"Well, in any case, it has made things difficult for planters, English planters. Labor, abundant labor, is necessary to grow sugar profitably. I have discovered that I can buy slaves for Mendenhall from the Portuguese. They took over England's role. It will cost us more, but—"

"I see," Lyon said, cutting him off. "You wish me to authorize you to break the law?"

Edward Bemis flushed. "Well, if you wish to put it that way—"

"Is it not the way it is?"

"Yes, that's the way it is," Diana said. "Why would you think that Lord Saint Leven would go along with this, Mr. Bemis?"

"Profit," said Bemis succinctly. "Your now-dead relative, Oliver Mendenhall, would have approved it, my lord. Indeed, he did purchase some dozen slaves several years ago from the Portuguese. Why, I remember after the Hodge affair, he was infuriated, he—"

Diana turned to Lyon and said quietly, "Back some years ago, in 1807, I believe, a planter on Tortola by the name of Arthur Hodge of Estate Bellevue, was actually tried for murdering one of his slaves. I'll never forget the slave's name—Prosper—like a character from Shakespeare."

"Good God," said Lyon. "What had the man done?"

Diana's voice rose in fury. "He had the gall to eat a mango that had fallen from a tree he was supposed to watch. Hodge beat him to death."

Edward Bemis said sharply, "It was a miscarriage of justice! Just because the English were writhing in guilt about slavery, while knowing nothing about the West Indian economy—"

"Hodge was hung, just behind the jail in Road Town," Diana said.

"The whole point was that even though the slave was the planter's property, he was still, first and foremost, a man."

"Yes," Bemis agreed. "Nonsense, of course. The black beggars aren't really human, they have no feelings, they—"

"I daresay that Moira didn't at all like being strangled," Lyon said smoothly. He raised his hand to cut Bemis off. "I will not authorize you to break English law and purchase more slaves from the Portuguese. I will come to Tortola to Mendenhall plantation next week. I wish to evaluate the workings of the plantation here on Savarol first."

Edward Bemis could only stare at the Earl of Saint Leven. In his vast experience, greed ruled, and absentee English owners gave him free rein to do just as he pleased, just so long as they received money. He said slowly, "There are now only ninety-seven slaves on the plantation, my lord. Some of them are old and quite useless. The women have bred too many females. They work, indeed they do, but not as quickly as the men, nor do they have the endurance men have. Without new blood, the plantation will not be able to compete. You will lose your inheritance. Planters are losing vast sums every year now."

"It seems excessively wise not to abuse any slaves, doesn't it, Mr. Bemis?" Lyon rose from his wicker chair. "Will you be staying here at Savarol, Mr. Bemis?"

"If it is all right with Mr. Savarol, yes, I should like to. I have no wish to put you out, my lady, or Mrs. Savarol. I shall stay with Charles Swanson."

Lyon looked at him with surprise, studying him more closely. Unlike Charles Swanson, he didn't seem at all effeminate. His imagination was running amok. Perhaps they were simply friends. He said easily, "Have you known Mr. Swanson long?"

"Oh, yes, Charles and I go back a long way. He grew up in England, then came out to St. Thomas. I met him there some years ago. I spoke to Mr. Savarol when he was in Tortola seeking a new bookkeeper. Thus Charles came here." He shrugged, gave a charming smile to Diana, nodded to Lyon, and took his leave.

"He is not a nice man," Diana said.

"No," Lyon said slowly, "I don't believe that he is. But he is straightforward, isn't he?"

"What do you mean?"

But Lyon merely shook his head.

Still, even realizing that Edward Bemis wasn't a nice

man, it came as quite a shock to Diana, returning from her Trysting Cave the following afternoon, to hear furious shouting. She drew up Tanis at the edge of a small clearing, in the shade of a mahogany tree. She saw Edward Bemis arguing with Charles Swanson. Anger flowed between the two men. Whatever was going on? Why were they behaving in such a manner?"

She heard Bemis say quite clearly, "I heard, damn you! Do you think I'm deaf? Even though you live on this backwater island, I know!"

Charles Swanson said something Diana couldn't hear, but whatever he did say enraged Bemis.

"You ungrateful bastard!"

She saw Bemis strike Charles. The bookkeeper tumbled to the ground, holding his jaw. Bemis shook his fist at him, muttered something Diana couldn't hear, then stalked away, back toward the great house.

For an instant, she considered showing herself. No, she thought, no. Charles Swanson was getting up now. He looked fine. Very quietly, she guided her mare back into the trees.

23

What is the use of running when we are not on the right road?

GERMAN PROVERB

Lucien Savarol was tired and irritated, though his face didn't show these emotions. His weariness was from a night without sleep, his irritation from the damnable mess that swirled around him, a mess he didn't understand, a mess that was affecting every soul on his island. He felt helpless and didn't know which way to turn. At the moment, he was seated across the chess table from Lyon, seemingly concentrating on his next move. They were alone in Lucien's study, a branch of candles their only light.

Lucien finally moved his king's knight to the king bishop five square.

Lyon looked up at him, cocking his head in question.

"I fear your knight is not in defensible position there, sir."

Lucien merely shook his head, his voice rueful. "Forgive me, my boy, I suppose my mind is too many thoughts away from our game. You play well."

"My father taught me. He was a fine player, much

better than I.'' Lyon looked up at the painting of the first Mrs. Savarol. ''Diana has the look of her. A very beautiful woman, sir.''

''Yes, she was. Her name was Lily. There has not been a day in my life that I haven't missed her. She died birthing my son. He died as well. Had she been in London, attended by a physician there, she would have lived. When will you return to England, with Diana?''

Lyon said slowly, ''Does Diana have her build, sir?''

''I don't know. I am not her husband. My Lily was narrow, and I should have known she would need special care. I was a fool and I am still paying for it. She, of course, paid the highest price for my stupidity.''

Lyon remembered again the awful scare with Frances. Her English physician wouldn't have saved her. No, it was Lucia who would be present when Diana birthed their babe. ''To the best of my knowledge Diana is not yet with child. I am truly sorry for what happened.''

''Get Diana away from here.''

''There is the question of Mendenhall plantation. You know that I have a difficult time with slavery. Frankly, I still do not know what to do. There is one thing certain, though: I do not trust Edward Bemis.'' Nor anyone else on this bloody island, he added silently.

Lucien shrugged. ''He is much the same as the other attorneys in the West Indies. They're a special breed, Lyon. They start out as overseers, and if they're smart and cunning and their masters leave, they can become attorneys. They're a necessary evil, since owners do go back to England. I expect he was delighted at your inheritance—an English earl who wouldn't have interest in the plantation save for its profits. But you have thrown him. He fully expected you to be like the other English owners, as I said, greedy and uncaring about anything save the profits he sends them.''

"I have no need of income from Mendenhall."

"And you despise me, I suppose, because I own slaves? Have owned slaves all my life?"

Lyon said slowly, thoughtfully, "I did, before I met you, despite Diana's assurances that you were the kindest man she'd ever known, myself included. Now, I have seen that there is no abuse, no cruelty. But the fact remains, sir, they are property. Human beings shouldn't be property."

Lucien picked up his doomed king's knight, fingering the smooth white carved marble between his fingers. "Lily played chess very well, as does Diana. But that isn't the point." He sighed, dropping the chess piece onto the board. "I have lived all my life in the West Indies. Irrevocable change is coming. How soon, I don't know. If slavery is abolished next year, even five years from now, I am not certain that Savarol plantation will continue to exist. In that, Bemis is correct. Already, planters throughout the Caribbean are losing everything. The sugar market is steadily dropping every year. But you see, Lyon, slavery is still an economic necessity. When it is not, then slavery will cease by itself. I have searched for answers, but I cannot find them. Nothing is simple, I fear."

Lyon was silent. He studied his father-in-law in the dim candlelight. He realized quite clearly that he wouldn't want to be in Lucien Savarol's place. No, nothing was simple.

"That is the main reason I forced Diana to go to London."

"I beg your pardon?"

"I forced Diana to go to Lucia. I knew that eventually everything would fail here. I wanted her to marry an Englishman who would keep her safe and away from the West Indies. I would swear on my last breath that no slave revolt would ever occur here." He gave a pained smile. "Of course, I have been severely wrong of late in my judgments. You will have to decide what you will do with Mendenhall, Lyon.''

"I know. It is difficult to concentrate with all the trouble we're having here.''

"Yes." Lucien added in a calm voice, "Deborah appeared to hate Moira. Oh, yes, don't look so surprised, my boy. I heard about the screaming match and the riding crop you took from my wife. There is little that happens here that doesn't come to my ears. Did she strangle Moira? I really don't know. I pray, of course, that she did not. I pray she is not capable of such a thing, but how much does one know about another? Really know?''

I know now that I would trust Diana with my life. "You're tired, sir.''

"Indeed I am. Shall I get rid of Bemis for you?''

"No," Lyon said slowly. "I should like to watch him a bit. He and Charles Swanson seem to be on bad terms. Diana told me she came upon them quite by accident this afternoon in the throes of a vicious argument. Evidently Bemis struck Swanson.''

Tell him about Patricia and Grainger. But he couldn't. At least not yet. "Surprising, I should say, given their years of supposed friendship.''

"Well, there is one thing I didn't know about. Perhaps there are others. One of the government men on Tortola recommended Charles Swanson to me. My former bookkeeper was an incompetent, cruel imbecile. He was here for but a short time. His predecessor died of old age, competent to his last day. To date, Swanson seems like a gift from heaven. A fight between him and Bemis? I suppose I am not surprised, not really." Lucien Savarol rose from his chair. "I grant you the game, Lyon. Now I'd best find my bed before I fall asleep like a senile old man on the stairs.''

Lyon thoughtfully followed his father-in-law up the stairs, watched him enter his bedchamber, then slowly walked to his own. He set the branch on a table beside the armoire. There was no movement from the bed. He stripped off his clothes and slipped between the sheets.

Diana was naked. Had she fallen asleep waiting for him? It was an exceedingly pleasant thought. The night was warm. He slowly pulled the sheet down until it pooled at her feet. She was sprawled on her back, her legs slightly parted, one arm flung over her head. She looked incredibly beautiful to him. He felt the now-familiar surge of desire for her, deep, swirling feelings that seemed to grow stronger by the day. He'd assumed those feelings were rooted in honest, straightforward lust, but he was beginning to wonder. The feelings were growing more and more powerful.

She mumbled something in her sleep.

The candlelight sent a soft glow over her body.

He slowly eased to the foot of the bed. He grasped her ankles and gently eased her legs up, bending them at the knees. He then spread her legs wide and stared down at her. The candlelight was soft and gentle, but he knew if it were the harshest light, he would still find her exquisite. He eased himself between her widespread legs. Lightly, he touched his fingers to her, reveling in her soft woman's flesh, the delicate pink flush of her.

She moaned something unintelligible and moved slightly. He held her legs firm until she quieted. "Diana," he said very softly, "I have never seen a woman as beautiful as you." He explored her, his fingertips light as a butterfly's wings, and when he felt the dampness, the building heat, his need was so great he thought he would surely lose control. But he continued stroking her, caressing her, tangling his fingers in the soft dark-blond hair. When he eased his finger inside her, he knew she was ready for

him, her body responding fully without her mind's awareness. He smiled painfully at his enthusiastic member. No,
he wanted first to bring her to pleasure, to watch her eyes
as she came awake racked with the sensation he would
give her. He leaned down, his mouth coming over her.
She was hot, her woman's flesh swelled.

Her hips moved upward in his hands.

He eased his arms beneath her thighs and lifted her.

She moaned and thrashed her head from side to side.

His mouth was deep and hot.

Wake up, Diana, wake up and feel what is happening to
you.

She did, with an alarmed jerk. "Lyon!"

He raised his head and splayed his hand over her belly
to hold her still. "Hush, love. Enjoy."

She did. When she felt his hand gently come over her
mouth to muffle her cries, she felt freed and gave herself
to her pleasure.

He came over her then, and she felt his fingers parting
her and he was thrusting deeply and powerfully into her
body. She welcomed him, her mind in chaos, her body
equally out of control. And again she cried out, into his
mouth, and in turn took his groans as he spilled himself
deep inside her.

Lyon couldn't have moved had his life depended on it.
His heart was racing fast as the wind. He buried his face in
the pillow beside hers, trying to recover. Never before had
he felt such depth of feeling, and it seemed to linger,
pulling him deeper, chaining him to her, and oddly, he
didn't mind. To his stunned surprise, he felt himself harden
within her, and this time he moved slowly, savoring her
heat, the tightness of her about him.

"Would you come with me again, Diana?"

She looked at his taut features, heard the deep, harsh

words, and nodded, mute. "Lyon," she moaned softly when his fingers found her.

"It is all over for me," Lyon said some minutes later. It took all his strength to raise himself on his elbows over her. "And I don't care. I can't believe this, Diana."

"You were looking at me, weren't you?"

He gave her a very male, very cocky grin. "Lord, yes. You're malleable, sweetheart, when you're asleep. Of course, I took the hint when I found you charmingly naked in our bed. An invitation I couldn't resist."

"I was warm, that is all."

"Little liar. No, I take that back. You were more than warm, you nearly burned me."

"Lyon!" She squeezed his shoulder, felt his warm flesh, so smooth, and stroked her hands over his back.

"Go back to sleep and moan for me and perhaps I shall find it within myself to pleasure you again."

She laughed, unfortunately for him, and he slid off her onto his side. "I'm a sweaty mess," she said.

"As in messy, from me?"

"You are becoming more outrageous by the day—night, rather." She made to get up, but he held her arm. "A moment, Diana."

She turned to face him. "Why? I wish to bathe."

"Lie down a moment."

She obeyed him. "Why?"

He was staring at her belly, and she shifted in some embarrassment beneath his intent gaze. "I am not quite certain what I should be looking at." He splayed his hand over her belly, his fingertips not reaching her pelvic bones. "I have large hands," he said more to himself than to her. "I think our babe can grow comfortably in your belly. But your father is right. When you are with child, we are returning to England."

"He spoke of my mother, didn't he?"

"Yes, and he is terrified that you also could die in childbirth. Needless to say, I shan't allow it."

"I am a big clumsy giant compared to my mother, at least that's what Dido has always told me."

Lyon, still intent on her very lovely belly, didn't answer.

"He still misses her so. Poor Father."

Lyon leaned down and kissed her stomach. "Too tired to even moan for me?"

"Yes. I am beyond anything like that, husband."

He sighed. "Married to a cold woman. Just my blasted luck."

She sent her fist at his shoulder and he obligingly grunted.

"And a shrew."

She punched him again, and he grabbed her hand and rolled on top of her. "Get off me, you brute! You're heavy and sweaty."

"You weren't complaining just a few minutes ago. Indeed, if I close my eyes, I can still hear the echoes of your abandoned yells. Not that I minded covering your mouth, sweetheart."

She suddenly relaxed her body and closed her arms around his back. She buried her face against his shoulder. "I disliked you so very much, in London, at first. I thought you were a dandy and an arrogant, conceited boor. Remember the first time you carried me to the front steps? I felt the strangest sensations and thought I had a stomach-ache or that I was hungry, or something. Did you know then what I felt for you?"

He gave her his special knowing, very masculine grin. "Yes, you were charming. As I recall, it took all my wits and control to keep from throwing you on Lucia's front steps and having my evil way with you. Your breasts . . .

ah, they were a mighty temptation. So cocky and innocent you were.''

''Then you had the gall to beat me.''

His hand cupped over her, his fingertips stroking her lightly. ''That,'' he said, his voice deep, ''you deserved. Our courtship was a bit unusual, I suppose. Incidentally, when I first met you, I thought you were a silly, arrogant little twit. I wanted nothing to do with you.''

''Now,'' she said with smiling satisfaction, ''now, you have everything to do with me.''

''The good Lord knows that! You know what I would like to do? Go for a swim. With any luck at all, we won't stumble over another body.''

His humor sounded a bit strained to her sensitive ears, but she managed to say easily enough, ''Yes, let's.''

There were no bodies to be found that night. They swam in the cool sea, played until they were exhausted. He was holding her against him, her wet hair wrapped about him like a blanket. ''Diana,'' he said quietly, not looking at her, ''we shall have to go home soon.''

He felt her stiffen.

''Home to England. I have an idea about Mendenhall. Once it is settled, we will return. I swear to you, though, that we will come back to Savarol for visits. And we will stay in London only when you wish to. My estate near Escrick will please you. You enjoyed the moors and the heather, remember? And there are Frances and Hawk.''

She said nothing for many moments. He felt her legs wrap around his hips. Finally, ''Can we take my mare back to England with us?''

Lyon felt as though Atlas and his worldly weight had both fallen from his shoulders. ''Yes, certainly. We can breed her if you like with Flying Davie from Hawk's stable, and have a lot of little Tanises.''

"You are a nice man, Lyon," she said, and kissed him.

"Yes, I am. Are you only just now coming to that conclusion?" He dunked her beneath the water when she didn't answer immediately. She came up, sputtering and laughing. "I take it all back . . . you are a brute."

"But I am your brute," he said, and dunked her again. He felt her arms go about his legs and he went under.

They walked back toward the great house, covered with their dressing gowns. Lyon paused a moment and gently lifted her face. He studied her features for a long time, saying nothing. He kissed her.

"You taste like salt."

"As do you."

"As I said earlier, it is all over with me. All the suspicions, all my notions of women as the betrayers. Charlotte's Disease is a thing of the past. I love you, Diana."

She blinked up at him, unable to quite believe him. She felt her heart thudding in strong, hurried beats.

"It's true. I think it's because you are so very exquisite with your legs wide apart, lying on your back, moaning wild little cries in your sleep."

Still, she stared up at him, silent.

He clasped her head between his hands and kissed her deeply. "Even though you are salty and wet and dreadfully tanned, I still love you."

A deep shudder went through her. "All right," she whispered finally. "All right."

"Excellent," he said, took her hand, and led her back to the great house.

She was nearly asleep in their bed when she heard him say softly, "You said it aloud, you know, that afternoon in our cave."

Said what? she wondered, her mind too fuzzy to think straight.

"I knew then that it wouldn't be fair or just not to return your affection."

"Hmmm," she managed. She remembered now that she'd told him she loved him. She evidently hadn't just thought it then.

She fell asleep smiling. Her husband would be a handful, of that she had no doubt. He was strong-willed and stubborn. They would argue and yell at each other, and love. They would have children, and with any luck life would be good.

Oddly, Lyon was thinking along the same lines. Life, he decided as he drifted into sleep, would never be boring.

Not with Diana. Diana Ashton, Countess of Saint Leven. A nice sound, that.

Diana was given ample evidence of his stubbornness the following morning. He said, "I am going to Tortola, to visit Mendenhall. As I told you, I have something of an idea. I wish to see exactly how things stand before I act."

"All I need is fifteen minutes to pack a valise," she said.

"No, you are staying here."

And that is supposed to be that? she wondered, staring silently at him for a moment. He tells me he loves me and then gives me orders?

I will act reasonably about this, she decided. "Lyon, you know nothing of Tortola or of anything. You need me to be with you."

"I'm going with Bemis," he said shortly.

"Lyon, you are being ridiculous and too stubborn for words! Of course I am coming with you."

"I will not argue with you. You are not coming, and that's an end to it."

She opened her mouth, further arguments—quite good ones actually—already formed, but he forestalled her.

"No, Diana. I want you to stay here, safe."

"Safe! Now that is excellent male logic. Have you forgotten so readily that Moira was strangled? Murdered by someone, and we haven't the faintest idea who did it?"

"I will also add that I wish you to be in your father's company at all times. I expect you to take care. I have forgotten nothing."

"I am going with you."

His eyes darkened. He said slowly, as if she were a dim-witted child, "I am your husband and you will obey me. You are remaining here on Savarol. I should be back in two or three days."

She argued with him, she couldn't help herself, but he was immovable. Finally, furious with him, she shouted, "Go, then! I hope the boat springs a leak. I hope you end up by yourself on another Calypso Island, alone!"

"Ah, my loving wife," he said, tight-lipped.

He left just after breakfast, Bemis with him. Diana watched him stride toward the stable, Bemis beside him, from her balcony, and cursed softly. "Idiot man."

Her eyes widened with fury when she saw Patricia, skirts flying, race after the men. She saw Lyon turn and speak with her. Patricia, laughing, stopped, then waved good-bye.

It is not fair that a man can tell me what to do and what not to do just because he is married to me. Not fair at all. Her major failed argument with him was that she didn't trust Bemis, and he'd merely given her that arrogant stare of his.

But she didn't trust Edward Bemis. She didn't trust anybody.

Her father spoke to her from her bedchamber door. "Diana, my dear, would you like to come with me to the fields? Grainger has told me there are problems, particularly with Bob, the young man in love with Moira. He is upset and making crazy accusations. Evidently the other slaves are listening to him.''

At least her father trusted her and valued her opinions.

They rode with Grainger to the fields within the hour. She felt a stirring of worry at the sight of the small knot of slaves, obviously talking about Moira.

She heard Bob speaking loudly, "Dis man, Bemis," he was saying. "Bastard, dat man."

And several other men agreeing.

"You see, sir," said Grainger, drawing his horse to a halt. "I hesitate to use the whip, but—"

"Of course you won't," said Lucien. "Diana, you and Grainger stay here. I will handle this."

Diana watched her father ride to the group of slaves and casually dismount. She saw Bob's face darken with confusion at her father's words. She wanted to ride closer, to hear what he was saying, but Grainger said softly, "No, Miss Diana. Leave him to deal with it. The slaves trust him implicitly, you know that."

"And do they not trust you?"

"Yes, but not to the same degree. I have accepted that."

"Who do you think strangled Moira?"

Grainger shrugged. "I don't know. If I did, I should certainly let it be known."

"You don't think it was one of the slaves?" Diana persisted.

"I would be very surprised."

Diana watched her father closely for many moments, watching him gesticulate to make a point. "You know," she said slowly, not looking at the overseer, "nothing like this ever happened until all the new people came."

"That is true." He paused a moment to flick a fly from his horse's mane. "That, of course, includes your husband."

"That is fair," she said after a moment, cooling her instant fury at his comment. "However, my husband was with me, and I assure you I had nothing to do with it."

Grainger sighed. "I meant no insult, truly, it is just that what has happened is so beyond anything we've ever had to deal with. I feel like a man caught in a house that is on fire and I'm staying to warm my hands."

"And I don't like the fact that my husband accompanied Edward Bemis alone to Mendenhall plantation."

"Your husband, Miss Diana," he said with a grin, "is well able to take care of himself."

"Even around a snake?"

"Bemis is many things, a snake included, but he isn't stupid. No harm will come to your husband."

If only she could be certain. Stubborn, arrogant man. The slaves were dispersing. Her father rejoined them just as Daniel rode up to join them.

"What is happening?" he asked in his deep, calm voice.

"Daniel! Oh, it is Moira, you know. The men are upset, not that I blame them. We must do something."

"I wish your father had spoken to me," Daniel said. "I could have spoken to the men."

"Perhaps," Diana said.

"All is well now," Lucien said, reining in Salvation. He looked a moment at Daniel and grinned. "My boy, the horse is going to collapse under your weight." Indeed, the old stallion, looked ready to drop. "Why won't you ride Egremont? He's up to your weight."

Daniel merely smiled and shook his head. "He makes me nervous," was all he would say.

"Trade with me, Daniel," Diana said, laughing.

He was so good-natured, she thought, watching him climb onto Tanis. "Now your feet don't touch the ground."

Daniel gently scratched behind Tanis' ears. "Sir," he

said after a moment to Lucien, "one of the women is ill in the village."

"Who?" asked Grainger.

"Old Granny Gates. It's her heart, I doubt not, and there is little I can do, she is very old, but—" He shrugged, his voice trailing off.

"You will ease her with your presence," Lucien said. "Go on, Daniel, and see to her. Keep her family with her."

At dinner that evening, Diana thought that Deborah was uncommonly disturbed. Not that she was a bitch to any of the servants, Diana thought, but she was tense, saying little. Oh, Father, she thought unhappily, what have you done?

As for Patricia, she was giggling, playing the coquette to every male at the dinner table, Diana's father included. They were all there, save for Bemis and Lyon.

Daniel was his usual quiet self; Charles Swanson, with little encouragement from Patricia, was telling highly embroidered tales of his years on St. Thomas.

And here I am missing my wretched husband, Diana thought, barely tasting one of her favorite dishes, saltfish patties.

Dido arrived at the table, a wide smile on her weathered face. "A surprise for da massa," she announced, and set a small plate of sweet-potato pone in front of Lucien Savarol.

"What have I done, Dido?" he asked, smiling at the beaming old woman.

"You tell dat boy, Bob, dat you find the bad man. And you will, massa. Bob, he believe dat you will. He grateful."

"One hopes you are right," said Diana, looking fondly at the sweet-potato pone, her appetite magically returned.

Her father grinned at her and passed her the plate. "I am stuffed, my dear. Go ahead."

"Really, Lucien, it was prepared for you," Deborah said with a frown toward Diana.

"Like father like daughter," Lucien said. "The child has begged it off my plate since the advanced age of four. Isn't that so, Diana?"

"Indeed it is. However, I am willing to share."

"Oh, no!" Patricia flushed slightly, then smiled at the table at large. "It is most fattening, Diana. Surely, as a lady—"

"My little sister is perfect," said Daniel. "As much as I love my food, I won't even demand a bite."

Diana laughed and forked down the exquisitely prepared dish, savoring each bite.

"I really wish you would share with your father," Deborah said again.

Lucien gave his wife a puzzled look, then turned to Charles as he began another amusing story.

Daniel finished off his dinner. Grainger sat back in his chair, his hands folded over his stomach. He looked tired and older suddenly, Diana thought. She wished she could think of something to say that would make things better, but there were no words forthcoming.

An hour later, Diana was yawning, unable to prevent it.

Her father smiled at her. "Time to go to your bed, my dear."

She shook her head. "I don't know why I am so tired."

"Come, Diana, I will see you to your room," Deborah said, rising from her chair.

Diana yawned again. She felt as though there were heavy weights tied to her feet. Every step was an effort. Her mind felt like mush. Deborah said nothing, merely entered Diana's bedchamber with her and helped her undress for bed.

"I don't know what is wrong with me," Diana said, weaving toward the bed.

Her last thought before she fell asleep was that Deborah was looking uncommonly severe. How very odd.

The next morning she felt sluggish, as if she had overindulged in the heavy estate rum. She'd only done that once, when she was twelve years old. Her father hadn't punished her, merely smiled at her and said what she was now feeling was punishment enough.

Her head throbbed. It was an effort to dress herself. Only Patricia was at the table when she came out onto the veranda.

"Did you sleep well?"

Was there sarcasm in Patricia's voice? Diana shook her head. "I suppose so," she said, and seated herself.

She wanted to see to household matters, but she didn't have the energy. It seemed, even to her not-very-objective eye, that Deborah was dealing with things efficiently.

She dragged herself to her bedchamber after lunch and fell into a deep sleep.

"What is this, love?"

She heard a man's voice, quietly talking to her. She felt a man's mouth kissing her.

"Lyon?"

He was frowning down at her. "Wake up, love. It's late. You've missed your dinner."

She forced her eyes to open. "You're back," she said, touching her fingertips to his cheek.

"Yes, of course I am. I missed you and hurried. You're right, I should have taken you with me, then at least I would have had you on hand to cure my bouts of distraction."

"What about Mendenhall?" Talking was such an effort. Keeping her eyes focused was an equal effort.

"My decision wasn't particularly difficult. I brought Bemis back with me, to arrange things. He doesn't yet know what I plan. It involves your father. Diana, how long have you felt so tired?"

She heard the worry in his voice and smiled up at him. "Since dinner, last night. I couldn't keep my eyes open. You said I missed dinner. What time is it?"

"Nearly ten-thirty."

"But that's crazy!"

She felt his hand on her forehead. She was cool to his touch. He sat perfectly silent for many moments. Then he felt fury flow through him. He was wondering if she had been drugged. Dear God, why?

She felt one of his hands slide beneath her thighs. "What are you doing?"

"I think you and I are going for a swim."

"All right."

"If I dunk you enough, I suspect it will clear your head."

The cool evening water did indeed bring her about. They stayed in the water nearly an hour. Lyon practiced restraint. He'd missed her terribly and had felt guilty most of his trip because they'd parted in anger. Then he'd felt rage at what he'd seen at Mendenhall plantation.

"I did leave you here because I wanted you to be safe. I'm a bloody fool."

He cursed floridly.

Diana, clearheaded now, wrapped her arms about his neck and kissed the pulse in his throat.

"Don't tempt me, woman."

"Why not?"

"Because," he said and frowned over her head. A wave knocked them forward at that moment, and they went under in a welter of arms and legs.

"Because why?" Diana asked when they'd emerged.

"Because," he said thoughtfully, cupping her chin in his hand, "if I'm not mistaken, someone drugged you."

She gaped up at him.

"I left you here safe and someone drugged you."

"That's insane!"

"Yes," Lyon said slowly, "yes, it is."

"But—"

"I want you to tell me exactly what you ate and drank at dinner last night. And today."

She did. When she'd finished, Lyon took her hand and led her out of the water. Slowly, he toweled her off and handed her her dressing gown.

"Very interesting," he said only. "That sweet-potato pone, no one else ate any of it?"

She shook her head. "No, as I said, Dido had prepared it for my father, but he insisted I eat it. I did."

They walked back toward the house.

"Lyon?"

"Yes, love?"

"What is going on here?"

"If I don't find out quickly," he said finally, "you and I are leaving."

Lyon, the next morning over breakfast, took the bull by the proverbial horns.

He attacked.

24

No gods assail us; we are mortals fighting with mortals.

VIRGIL

Lyon gazed around the breakfast table, his expression bland. The last person to arrive was Patricia, yawning as innocently as a child.

"I'm glad you're back, Lyon," Lucien said. "Your visit was quite a short one, my boy."

"I saw what I needed to see," Lyon said, then added with a slight smile. "And I missed my wife."

He paused a moment, staring at every face at the table. He saw Dido standing by the veranda door. He said clearly, "When I returned last evening, Diana was asleep. It appears that's all she had been doing since dinner evening before last. It is also quite clear to me that she had been drugged."

"Good God! Surely—" Lucien broke off, staring at his daughter. "Are you all right, my dear?"

"Yes, Papa. Now I am."

There were other exclamations. Lyon waited until everyone had made a response, then continued. "It was probably the sweet-potato pone that was drugged. Diana told me it was a dish prepared especially for you, sir. You gave the dish to Diana. She was the only one who ate it.''

"Impossible!"

"Utterly ridiculous!"

Lyon heard the women—odd how they sounded nearly alike, almost as if . . . He shook his head, but his eyes, for the moment, were on Dido. The old woman started, and he would have sworn that her black face paled. She took a step forward, then retreated again. He would speak to her after breakfast.

Lyon continued thoughtfully, "Either it was a very long-lasting drug, or she was fed more of it at breakfast yesterday, or perhaps at lunch. I have little knowledge of drugs used here in the West Indies. Perhaps Daniel can tell us."

Daniel was staring at Diana, shaking his head slowly from side to side.

"Daniel?"

"Huh? Oh, yes, the drug. There are several that have long-lasting effects. Yes, several. Are you all right, Diana?"

She looked at his concerned face, felt his slow, gentle voice wash over her. "Do not worry, Daniel. I survived."

Deborah said sharply, "It is also possible that she had a fever. Indeed, it is more likely than drugs, for heaven's sake. Daniel will also tell you that there are many such illnesses that last a day or so."

"That is true," said Daniel. "There is one in particular that makes one very lethargic for twenty-four hours or so."

Lyon wanted desperately to grasp at that straw. "She had no fever last night when I returned."

"There is no fever," Daniel said. "Just the extreme weariness and a ferocious headache."

"I see," said Lucien. He couldn't help himself. His eyes went to his wife's, and he searched her face. There was something in her eyes, something she didn't want him to see, to know about. He frowned and sipped at his coffee.

"You know," he said, looking from his son-in-law around the table, "I have a violent dislike of mysteries. Dido, I would like to speak to you after breakfast. In my study."

"Yes, massa."

"I should like to be present, sir," said Lyon.

Lucien nodded, then said, "You returned very quickly, Lyon. Did Bemis show you everything?"

"I showed him all he wished to see," said Edward Bemis. He sounded vaguely put out. "His lordship toured the plantation house, the slave compound, but scarcely looked at the fields. He spoke to the overseer and several of the slaves."

"Your telling is accurate," said Lyon, a bit of irony in his voice. "So far as it goes," he added mildly.

Lucien started to ask Lyon what conclusions he had drawn, but held his tongue. Obviously Lyon hadn't confided in Bemis. He would wait until they were alone. He prayed the boy hadn't come up with some sort of fantastic scheme to free the slaves that wouldn't have a prayer of working. It had been tried before. Failure, always failure.

Lucien Savarol sat at his desk in his study. Lyon and Diana stood together by the French doors. Dido was wringing her arthritic hands, facing him across his desk.

"The sweet-potato pone, Dido. Who prepared it? Who could have drugged the dish? A dish, I will add, that was prepared especially for me, and not my daughter."

"Lila," Dido said. "But da missis and da young missis came in the kitchens. I didn't see them do nothing."

"Bring me Lila, Dido."

Lila, a massive black woman with a round face and a rather vacant expression, could tell them nothing. Both Deborah and Patricia had visited the kitchens. Was this uncommon? Lucien asked her. No, evidently it wasn't. Save perhaps for Patricia. The young missis rarely came into the kitchen.

"Damn," Lucien said when the three of them were alone again. He chanced to see his daughter give her husband a questioning look.

"What is it, Diana?"

"Something we should have told you sooner, Papa. Lyon—"

Lyon shrugged. "Yes, it is time all the cards are on the table. Sir, several nights ago, I awoke early. I was smoking a cheroot on the balcony. It was just before dawn. I saw a woman—I am nearly certain it was Patricia—coming from the direction of Grainger's house. He was with her, at least I am nearly certain it was Grainger. I didn't know at the time that Charles Swanson, another white man, was here on the island."

Lucien Savarol toyed with a carved wooden letter opener until with a vicious gesture he broke it in two, flipping over the inkpot. Black ink spread on the papers on his desk. "That is interesting, to be sure. However, the question is why would Patricia want to drug me?" He cursed and rose abruptly. Diana knew the instant he realized the other possibility. Lucien turned slowly and in a very pensive voice said, "Could it have been Deborah?"

"I don't think so, sir. I see your point, of course. Then she would have had a reason to drug your food."

"But she is Papa's wife!"

"I will add that Patricia is Daniel's wife," said Lucien.
"We appear to be at something of an impasse."

Now was not the time, Lyon decided, to tell his father-
in-law of his plan. Besides, he wished to think it through
more thoroughly.

"Let's go visit the slave village," Lyon said to Diana.

"That is a good idea," Lucien said. "Perhaps, just
perhaps, someone will tell Diana something."

That wasn't Lyon's reason for visiting the village, but
he only nodded.

Daniel was in the village, attending to a woman who
had cut her arm. "Nothing much," Daniel said by way of
greeting. "But a slash like this needs immediate attention." He patted the black woman's hand and continued
with his bandaging.

"Introduce me to the slaves, Diana."

She cocked her head at him, then nodded. They spent
the next couple of hours touring the village, Lyon asking
questions. Granny Gates had died the previous night, and
they paid their respects. They were both sweating freely
under the fierce sun.

"Let's go swimming," Lyon said, wiping the perspiration from his brow.

Diana led him to the far end of the island. The beach
sand was an odd pink color, the water the palest turquoise.
Palm trees crowded onto the beach.

"Did I ever tell you about palm trees, Lyon?"

"No, and I am prepared to be fascinated."

"Are you now, my lord? Well, they are so close to the
water, you see, because that is the only way they can get to
other places. A coconut falls and perhaps is swept out with
the tide. I am not certain of the number of days the
coconut can last in the sea, but it must be ample. When the
coconut comes to shore on another island, it plants itself, I

guess you could say. I am not really a naturalist, so I can't tell you the process. And that is why there are palm trees everywhere.''

"Just as I thought. Fascinating." He cupped her chin in his palm and kissed her. "Will you roast me a breadfruit for lunch? Just like on Calypso Island?''

She smiled up at him. She was wearing only her chemise and it was clinging to her body, damp and revealing. She'd tied her hair up with a ribbon, and strands had escaped, framing her face. As for Lyon, he was naked.

His stomach growled at that moment.

"I suppose I shall have to do something for you, my lord.''

"I can think of a number of things, but I am hungry.''

They picked mangoes and ate them as they sprawled under a palm tree. "Now, you very stubborn man, tell me about your trip.''

"You're no longer peeved with me?''

"Yes, but there is nothing I can do about it.'' She added handsomely, "I also decided to forgive you because you are just a man. You have occasional lapses into manly foolishness. I shall be tolerant.''

"Why do I think that life as I have known it is over?''

She poked him in the ribs. He closed his arms around her and pulled her close. "Tell me your adventures, Lyon.''

"It was a simple necessity, not an adventure. Road Town is a god-awful place except for the government buildings and wealthy planters' homes. But you already know that. Bemis hired two horses and we rode to Mendenhall. As you probably also know, it's in the hills and the road, if you can call it that, was washed out because of recent rains.'' Lyon paused a moment, his eyes clouding with obviously distasteful memories.

"It was what I expected, I guess, but even so, I suppose

I was praying it would be more like Savarol. The great house was inhabited by the overseer, a greasy individual by the name of Torrence. He has bad teeth, incidentally. He wasn't expecting me, of course. I'd made certain that Bemis didn't have the opportunity to give him warning. The house was a pigsty. We found him in bed with one of the slaves, a girl who could have been no more than thirteen or fourteen years old. As for the ninety or so slaves on the plantation, they were kept like animals. There was filth everywhere. I saw lash marks on several backs, including women. Torrence, of course, talked a mile a minute, assuring me that everything would be much better just as soon as I made decisions about the plantation, and on and on. I didn't smash my fist into his face, though the temptation was great. My impression was that Bemis and Torrence have been having a merry time until the new owner came to Tortola. That I surprised them wasn't to their liking. I have never seen Bemis so tight-lipped. There is something else. I had this inescapable feeling that I would have had my toes cocked up for me had I not been married to you."

"Lyon, no!"

"Oh, yes, love. You see, with my death, you would inherit, so it would gain them nothing to do away with me. Bemis finally ran out of excuses on our return trip to Savarol last night. I held my tongue, acted the bored aristocrat to his satisfaction, I believe. I further think that Torrence believes I will allow things to continue as they are. As your father says, most overseers and attorneys are used to absentee owners who care only for a profit."

"What are you going to do?"

He grinned at her, leaning toward her to wipe mango juice off her chin with his fingertips. "Not just yet, Diana. I wish a couple more days to think it all through." He didn't add that his plan couldn't succeed without her father's involvement and agreement.

"I am your wife!"

"Lord, that's true." He gave her a lecherous smile and closed his hand over her thigh. "I believe it's time to treat you like a wife. I suppose you missed my man's body sorely?"

"Ha!" But her eyes roved down his body to his manhood. It swelled beneath her interested look.

She reached out her hand and touched him. He throbbed and swelled. Her eyes flew to his face. His look was one of amusement and . . . intensity. "You feel very odd, Lyon. Hard but soft-feeling, like velvet, I think." Her fingers closed around him, and to her immense delight, he groaned.

"Lyon," she said softly, her eyes on him and her moving fingers. "You know how you love me sometimes?"

"No. How do I love you sometimes?"

"You . . . Well, you know. Your mouth, you . . . Oh stop being such a dreadful tease!"

"Ah, that is the way I wish to love you all the time now I know you won't turn red with embarrassment."

She flushed slightly. "Well, would it give you the same pleasure were I to kiss you there?"

"Diana," he said, his voice deep and fervent, "it would make me want to expire with pleasure."

"Ah," she said, vastly pleased.

He watched her lower her head, felt her soft lips on his belly, felt her hand push him onto his back. He lightly touched his hand to her head. When her lips lightly brushed his manhood, he thought he would explode. He sucked in his breath in a hiss.

"I like the way you taste," she said, and he felt her

warm breath caressing him. It was nearly too much. "Am I doing this all right, Lyon?"

"Sweetheart, if you do what you are doing much more, both of us will regret it."

She raised her head a moment and grinned at him. "I shall just have to see, won't I?"

She was between his legs, her hair, now loose from its ribbon, flowing over his belly and thighs.

When he could bear it no longer, he tugged at her hair until she released him. "Come here, woman."

She eased up over his body, took his face between her hands, and kissed him deeply. "Now," she said with satisfaction, "now you know what a man tastes like."

"I much prefer you." He flipped her onto her back and she sprawled in the sand, her sweet laughter washing over him.

Diana wondered vaguely many minutes later how the feelings could just keep getting stronger and wilder. Her heart was finally slowing from its mad gallop and she felt as sated and sleepy as an animal lying in the sun.

"Lyon?" She ran her fingers through his thick hair.

"Ummm?"

He sounded as sleepy as she felt. "I just wanted to tell you something."

"What?"

"Your very manly bottom is going to get sun-roasted if you don't move."

He raised himself on his elbows over her.

"I suppose there is now sand everywhere . . . and in everything."

She pushed at his chest, laughing. They swam out to the reef and back again. She didn't want to return to the house. She didn't want to lose the magic and return to reality.

Reality at the moment was too frightening.

Lyon guessed the direction of her thinking. He patted her cheek. "It will be all right. Everything will be resolved soon."

He questioned her about Grainger on their ride back to the house.

"As I told you once, he has been here on Savarol for thirteen years. I was very young when he arrived. He has never been very talkative. My father told me once that he'd lost his wife and had come from Jamaica here to escape, only he found peace here and stayed. He has always been kind to me, a bit gruff, but kind. I remember one Christmas he made me a doll from sugarcane." Diana paused, smiling at the memory. "I ate her. I would dislike it intensely, Lyon, were he responsible for all that is happening here."

Lyon had seen Grainger in quite another light, through a veil of distrust for a man whose job it was to keep human beings in line. And the man had seduced Patricia. Not very honorable.

He sighed. Or had Patricia, that little coquette, seduced him? He said, his voice pensive, "I should dislike seeing Daniel hurt."

"I too."

They parted at the house, Lyon taking the horses to the stables so Diana could have the bathtub first.

"Don't you look like a dowd!"

"Hello, Patricia. How very nice to see you. Of course it's always a pleasure to see you. Your conversation is always so very gracious and enlightening."

The two girls faced each other on the landing, Diana giving Patricia an amused look.

"You think you are so much better than I am, don't you? Just look at you."

"I will, in a few minutes, after you have finished with your compliments."

"Deborah says your face will look like old leather if you continue in your hoyden's ways."

Diana obligingly touched her fingers to her cheek. "I do believe I can already feel my skin cracking. Are you through now, Patricia?"

"He won't stay with you, he won't. He is a gentleman, and a gentleman wants a lady, not some frowzy trollop."

"This he you're talking about . . . my husband, I suppose?"

"I would wager he didn't just visit Mendenhall when he was on Tortola."

"This is most curious," Diana said, fisting her hand at her side. She had an overwhelming desire to slap Patricia, hard. "I do wonder at odd times, you know, why you dislike me so very much."

"Because you've always had everything you wanted. It's not fair, you don't deserve anything."

"At least," Diana said very softly, "I do not play my husband false."

Patricia sucked in her breath. "You liar! Liar!" She grasped her muslin skirt and raced down the stairs, her soft brown curls slapping against her face.

Oh, why, Diana scolded herself, why couldn't you have just kept your mouth shut?

Because the girl is obnoxious, that's why.

Diana decided she should find out where exactly Patricia had come from. Had she been desperately poor growing up? Was this the reason for her unwholesome behavior? Poor Daniel.

*   *   *

Charles Swanson wasn't at the dinner table that evening. Lucien waited an extra ten minutes, but the man didn't put in an appearance.

"Odd," said Deborah. "We will dine."

"I haven't seen him since early this afternoon," Grainger said.

Edward Bemis merely shrugged. "The last time I saw him, he was working in the study."

There was tension so thick at the table that Diana fancied she could practically see it. If she could have seen it, she imagined the tension would look like thick gray swamp mud. She'd heard there were crocodiles in Jamaica in the swamps there. She shuddered, not really tasting the shrimp and coconut.

Edward Bemis was preoccupied, and said little. Daniel, as was his wont, forked down his dinner with good appetite, merely smiling at Diana when she remarked on his giant's body needing sustenance.

Patricia was sullen; Deborah, like Diana, seemed to sense undercurrents of something not at all pleasant.

Lyon, in odd moments, found himself wondering what Savarol had been like before the advent of the wives. And Bemis, of course. God, he detested the man.

Who had drugged Diana?

Who had strangled Moira?

She'd been buried the day he'd been on Tortola. Diana hadn't said anything about it and he supposed she'd been sleeping during the funeral. Why not test the waters? he thought.

"I understand Moira was buried yesterday?"

Lucien said, a frown marring his wide forehead, "Yes, the poor child. Grainger and I decided that our people shouldn't work. Unfortunately, we have no preacher here. I said the service."

"She was just a slave," Patricia said under her breath, but Lyon heard her, as did Daniel.

"That is quite enough," Daniel said in the firmest voice Lyon had ever heard from him. It was about time, Lyon thought, that the young man gave his wife the back of his hand.

Dido placed another huge platter in the middle of the table.

"That," said Diana with great pleasure, "is Lila's one-pot delight."

"What is it?" Lyon asked.

"Well, those little black things staring at you are raisins. The other ingredients are equally harmless."

Lyon gamely forked down a big bite. He tasted bacon, potatoes, carrots, and other things he couldn't readily identify.

"We will change the dining habits of the London aristocracy," he said, smiling at his wife.

"No, my dear girl, "Lucien said. "Don't even think it. Lila remains here, with me."

"Perhaps I should have her teach me how to prepare some dishes before we leave."

"You, in the kitchen?"

"Why not, Patricia? After all, I've been told that you occasionally visit the kitchen yourself."

Daniel raised his head from the one-pot delight. "Oh? When was this?"

Lyon squeezed Diana's thigh.

"Just something I heard, Daniel," she said, forcing lightness in her voice.

Bemis said, "My lord, surely you and I should have a discussion."

"Ah," said Lyon.

"About Mendenhall," Bemis said, a definite edge to his voice. "Torrence is most concerned."

"I think he is wise to be concerned. Perhaps we should discuss Mendenhall at that. Tomorrow, I think."

Bemis looked as though he would say something more, but at that moment there was a yell from the grounds.

"My God, what now?" Lucien tossed his napkin on his plate and shoved back his chair."

They heard running steps toward the house and another yell.

Diana thought she knew the reason for that yell. She closed her eyes a moment, not moving.

25

There's small choice in rotten apples.

SHAKESPEARE

Charles Swanson was dead. Shot through the head. He'd been dead for some time. His body was cold. He'd been stuffed beneath some bougainvillea at the eastern edge of the front grounds.

One of the gardeners had found him and promptly vomited up his dinner.

They searched the area, but found no trace of Swanson's murderer. A gun was found some ten feet from the body. It belonged to Lucien. Its place was empty in the gun case.

There was utter silence in the great house.

"My God," Lucien said again, his eyes on his hands clasped on his lap. Diana wanted to go to him, but Lyon gently tugged at her hand and shook his head. Deborah walked softly up behind his chair and laid her hand on his shoulder.

We are all here, Diana thought, sitting here, silent and helpless. Edward Bemis looked the worst of any of them. He appeared to have aged a decade. His hands were shaking badly. When Lyon handed him a brandy, he said nothing, but grasped the goblet and downed the contents in one gulp.

Patricia began sobbing softly and Daniel, so very gently, took her in his arms and began rocking her as if she were a child. She seemed a child pressed against his huge body.

Diana watched Deborah move away finally from her father and seat herself in a wing chair in the far corner of the drawing room. Her eyes stared blankly ahead and she was still as a stone. She was mumbling something under her breath, and only garbled sounds came to Diana's ears.

Lyon said slowly to Lucien, "I believe, sir, that it is our responsibility to discover who has done this."

Lucien had never felt so weary in his life. His body felt weighted down and his brain numb. He nodded slowly. "Go ahead, my boy."

"Very well," Lyon said. His eyes went to each face. "I believe," he continued, "that each of us should account for his or her time since this morning. I think Mr. Savarol said that he saw Swanson this morning at ten o'clock. Is that right, sir?"

"Yes," said Lucien. "That is correct."

"Did anyone see him alive after that time?"

Grainger nodded. "Yes, I saw him early this afternoon. In the study, about one o'clock I think it was."

"No one saw him after early afternoon?"

No one had, or rather, no one admitted to having seen Charles Swanson.

"Then we will assume that he was killed between one o'clock and six o'clock. Did anyone hear anything that resembled a gunshot?"

No one had.

"All right, then. I shall begin with my own whereabouts." Lyon spoke slowly, concisely.

". . . and after swimming, Diana and I returned to the house about five o'clock. Of course, my wife and I give each other alibis. It is unfortunate, but no one saw us after we left the village. About what time was that, Diana?"

"Three-thirty, I think."

Lucien Savarol had no witness to account for much of his time. He'd worked alone in the study, then walked to the mango grove, to think about things, he said. What things? Diana wondered, but she remained silent.

Everyone had seen someone during the day and early evening, but no one could account for every minute. Even Grainger, normally surrounded by slaves during the day, had been alone for several hours, writing letters in his house, he said.

They sat and stared at one another.

Lucien sighed deeply. "What now, Lyon?"

It disturbed Lyon that Lucien Savarol seemed so very removed, so willing to hand the responsibility to him. Was it Deborah he was thinking about?

"We will need to bury Charles Swanson. Bemis, does he have relatives? You and he were friends, after all."

"No," said Bemis, "there is no family."

"There is something I should like to know, Mr. Bemis," Diana said suddenly, her voice clear and firm. "I saw you and Charles arguing. I saw you strike Charles."

All eyes went to Bemis, who had turned perfectly white. If looks could have killed, Diana, Lyon thought, would be dead meat.

"Yes, Bemis. Can you please explain that?" Lucien said.

Bemis got himself together, but Diana saw his control was hanging by a thread.

"It was . . . personal," he said finally. "It has nothing to do with his death. Nothing."

"I think you can be more specific," Deborah said abruptly, rising from her chair. "What do you mean by personal?"

Bemis shook his head. "It is none of your business. My God, he was my friend!" He jumped to his feet. "Do you understand me? He was my friend! Did you see him! His head was nearly blown off. My God!" He rushed from the drawing room, slamming the heavy door behind him.

No one said anything for many moments.

"Well," said Deborah.

"Well, indeed," agreed Lucien.

A lovers' quarrel? Lyon said nothing. Perhaps it had been Charles Swanson Patricia was meeting and Bemis found out about it. The jealous, castaway lover. But then again, how to account for Moira's death? Surely Bemis had no reason to strangle that poor girl. Or did he? Was it possible that there were two killers? Lyon sighed. They were no further to discovering any answers than when they'd begun.

Before they went their respective ways to bed, Lucien said, "I don't think any of us should ever be alone. Or if any of you have to be alone, take no chances."

Diana said to Lyon as they lay in their bed some time later, "Did you see Deborah's face?"

"Yes. She seemed extraordinarily upset, but she had a firm hold on herself. Perhaps she knew that Patricia was seeing Charles Swanson, and out of anger for her betrayal of Daniel, she killed him."

"But why Moira? Would a woman be strong enough to have strangled Moira?"

"Yes, I think so, if she caught her unawares."

"Deborah hated Moira."

"Yes, it appears so."

"Lyon, I'm afraid."

"I know, Diana. God, I know." He drew her against the length of his body. "I very much want to take you away from here."

"I can't go now. My father—"

"Yes, Lucien. I do believe that Deborah knows something. What it is and whether or not it has any bearing on all of this, I do not know."

"Everything was fine until she came here. She and Patricia and Daniel."

"Yes. There is no getting away from that, is there? God, I wish there were a magistrate here or some way of finding out about everyone's pasts. I was involved in a mystery just once, and not really all that involved. It concerned Frances and Hawk and their racehorses." He told her the story, finishing with the true, outrageous finale. "And Amalie, Hawk's former mistress, saved the day. It must have been an amazing sight to see Amalie jumping onto the villain's back, screeching at the top of her lungs."

Diana laughed in the darkness and Lyon eased a bit. He kissed the tip of her nose, then her smiling mouth.

He felt her smooth palm slide down his chest, and deepened his kiss. When her hand found him, he forgot all the tragedy, the fear, and their helplessness. "Ah, Diana," he said, "you please me more than any woman in my life."

She raised her head and gave him a mock frown. "That is supposed to be some sort of compliment?"

"It is true. And don't I please you more than any other man?"

"Since you are the only one—"

"Then your answer must obviously be a resounding yes."

He eased his body over her, stretched her arms above

her head, and gently clasped her wrists with his hand. He was hard and demanding between her thighs, and she allowed herself to forget, at least for the time being.

"I think," Lyon said some minutes later, deep satisfaction in his voice, "that I just got you with child."

She blinked at that, still recovering. She felt him still deep inside her, felt the wetness of his seed, and wondered if perhaps he weren't right.

"You sound very proud of yourself, husband."

"Certainly pleased that at last I found the right vessel."

"Vessel! You conceited, arrogant—"

He kissed her and to his surprise felt himself growing hard again. "Again, my love?"

"I think so, my lord," she whispered, and drew him tightly against her.

"I always believe that if I make a claim, I should do my best to fulfill it."

"Yes," she said, "that is something I should agree with."

There was pleasure, but it was a desperate pleasure, for both their minds couldn't remain oblivious of the misery that surrounded them.

Diana, on the following morning, didn't at all feel that she was with child. Of course, she had no idea what being with child should feel like, and she smiled to herself. Her smile faded rapidly. She had things to do today and people to speak to. The uncertainty, the fear, was eroding everything.

Usually Deborah was in the cookhouse at this time, overseeing the meals for the day and setting the slaves to their various tasks. At first Diana had felt strange, having another person assume this responsibility. When she and Lyon had returned, Lila had come to her several times, and Diana, in full goodwill, had directed her to Deborah. She thought again that Deborah was efficient, and although curt with the servants, she wasn't cruel.

All save Moira. Who was dead. She seemed to have a running battle with Dido, but upon closer inspection, every insult Deborah hurled at the old woman's head bounced right off. Yet, Diana thought, Dido thought her father had made a mistake. She shook her head, her various and sundry thoughts too chaotic to bear.

Deborah wasn't in the cookhouse.

"Missis already here," said Lila, offering Diana a steaming portion of her famous cho-cho pudding.

Diana made her way back upstairs toward her father's bedchamber. The door was closed. She paused a moment, her hand raised to knock. She heard soft sobbing from within.

Deborah! Crying? Very slowly, Diana turned the knob and pushed the door open.

Deborah was sitting in her father's chair by the French windows, her face in her hands. Her shoulders were shaking.

Silently, Diana walked to her and gently laid her hand on her shoulder. "What is it, Deborah? Can I help?"

Her face was tear-ravaged and her lower lip trembled. Then she got a hold of herself. "What do you want?" Her voice was harsh and raw from her crying.

"I heard you crying. I want to help."

"Ha! You want nothing more than to see me gone. I'll tell you something, miss, your father was miserable when I met him, couldn't forget that mother of yours. I made him happy, I tell you. I made him forget her."

"Is that why you had my mother's portrait removed from the drawing room? To make him happy?"

"She haunted him. I removed it so he could be free of her, finally."

"Why did you hate Moira?"

Deborah sucked in her breath. "So," she said finally, very slowly, "this is why you want to help me. You want your father to believe that I strangled the girl. I will tell you something. I wanted Moira gone. She was stupid and very sly. I couldn't make her realize . . . Oh, it is too much! I didn't want her hurt. I just wanted her gone. That's all. Just gone, from Savarol."

Diana remembered that smug look on Moira's face that day Lyon had taken the riding crop from Deborah. Sly? Yes, smug and sly.

"But why? Did she displease you so mightily?"

Deborah firmly closed her mouth.

Frustrated, Diana changed course. "You know, it is Lyon's idea that Patricia and Daniel return with us to England. Lyon wishes to provide Daniel a substantial allowance so that he may study medicine, as he wishes to."

"No!" Deborah rose abruptly from her chair, her movements clumsy, frantic. "No," she said again, more calmly. "Daniel's place is here, on Savarol Island. With me. Do you understand? You will not interfere."

"And Patricia? She would likely sell her soul to dance at balls in London."

"Patricia is a . . . She is young. She will do as she's bid."

"Daniel is a grown man, Deborah. I daresay he will do as he pleases."

Deborah just shook her head, not looking at Diana. "Leave now, Diana. Just go away."

"Very well. But, Deborah, if you wish to have someone to talk to, I am willing. I really don't hate you, you know. If you make my father happy, then I am happy for him."

The older woman looked as if she would have said something to that, but she didn't. Diana left the bedchamber, gently closing the door behind her. Her expression was thoughtful.

"Missis is upset."

"Yes, Dido, she is. You are obviously the one I learned my eavesdropping from. How long have you been lurking here anyway?"

The old woman gave her a smug look. "Long enough. So much trouble since she and de others come here."

"Dido, tell me about Moira. She'd just come to the great house before I left for England."

"Moira a pretty little girl. Too pretty. Sly, dat one. Missis wanted her gone."

"Surely you're not implying that my father would seduce her!"

"No, not your father. No, not de massa." She nodded toward Deborah's bedchamber door. "I hear dem at night, taking der pleasure. Both of them loud and laughing. Until—" Dido shrugged.

"Until when? Until I came home?"

"Missis worried," Dido said, and shrugged.

Diana watched the old woman carefully flick her feather duster over a precious Chinese vase atop one of her father's favorite tables. Aggravating old woman!

As she walked across the front grounds toward the stables, Diana thought of her father in bed, making love with Deborah. It was embarrassing, since she now knew all about lovemaking. He was her father, after all.

"What is this? A blush on your tanned face?"

She whipped around to see Lyon grinning salaciously down at her. He cupped her chin in his palm. "What thoughts are going around in your head? Are you thinking about me? Thinking about me caressing you and doing all those things that make you howl and cry out and beg me not to stop?"

"Are you quite through with your fantasy?"

"Never. And I love it when you make your voice so sour and tart. Come, Diana, let's go somewhere private, then you'll tell me what you're thinking."

"You won't like it," she said, but fell into step beside him. "I have been a detective this morning."

He stiffened, all retorts and sexual repartee gone in an instant. "You will stop it. As of now. I will not have you taking any chances. In fact, I think it best you be with me all the time, just as your father said. Day and night."

"Don't be silly, Lyon. I heard Deborah crying in her bedchamber. I spoke with her, that's all."

He sighed. "Tell me."

She did, and even told him about the wretchedly secret Dido.

"Deborah is exceedingly upset, Lyon. It must be about all that's happened. She knows something, I am sure of it."

"Possibly. Now, why don't you come with me to see Grainger? I daren't leave you to your own devices. Lord knows what you'd take it in your twit head to do next."

"Surely you don't wish to speak so harshly to the soon-to-be mother of your child?"

He grinned down at her, a triumphant very satisfied male grin. "There is that, isn't there? I have always endeavored to hedge my bets, as they say in the clubs. After lunch, during siesta, I shall pay another visit to my . . . vessel."

She poked him hard in the stomach. "I swear I will not conceive if you continue with such drivel."

"You, my dear, have no control over conception." He paused, looking skyward. "At least I hope you don't."

"Ah ha! So you've heard about talk of voodoo, have you?"

He frowned at her.

"Charms abound, wicked rites and rituals. Dire happenings. You're wise to hold me in the highest respect, my lord."

"I'm wise to hold you beneath me."

She laughed gaily, the awfulness for the moment submerged. At least it was until they reached the overseer's house. Lyon knocked on the whitewashed door. It was a pleasant house, mellow brick, one story, a well-tended garden surrounding it.

"Grainger is probably in the fields or at the stillhouse."

"Or at the mill or in the village." Lyon knocked again. "Grainger!"

They heard a strange shuffling sound, then the door cracked open. Diana sucked in her breath. Grainger looked like misery itself. His clothes were disheveled, his hair on end, his eyes bloodshot.

"Oh, it's you two," he said. "What do you want?"

"I should like to know why you are drunk," said Lyon mildly.

"Swanson's dead, murdered. Isn't that reason enough?"

"His funeral is this afternoon, Grainger," Diana said. "May we come in?"

"No. I don't want either of you here."

"Just one question, then." Lyon paused just an instant. "Why were you meeting Patricia Driscoll? I saw both of you, you know. Before dawn."

Grainger turned pale as a sheet, then he flushed. His face gave away the truth.

Lyon continued, his tone still calm, very mild. "She is young, is she not? Too young to take you for her lover."

"Look, my lord, Miss Diana—" He plowed his fingers through his already rumpled hair. "It was nothing. I was with her, yes. It was nothing. Patricia's lover?" He laughed, a hoarse sound that made gooseflesh rise on Diana's arms.

With those words, he slammed the door in their faces.

"Goodness," said Diana, staring at the closed door.

"Yes," said Lyon thoughtfully.

"Everyone seems to be hiding something."

"Let's speak to your father."

"I hope he is in better shape than Grainger!"

They did not find Lucien alone until after Charles Swanson's funeral. He was buried in the Savarol cemetery, a beautiful spot some two hundred yards from the great house, an area carefully tended and surrounded by a low white wooden fence. He was buried next to Moira. The grave of Diana's mother was set a bit apart, with bougainvillea covering it.

She said in a low voice to her husband, "Once my grandfather died, Father made the decision that the slaves should be buried in the family plot. I remember him saying that without the slaves we wouldn't be here. That's why it's so large."

Two fresh graves, and one of us is a murderer, Diana thought, and shuddered. Lyon's hand closed about her arm.

"Father, may we speak to you?"

Lucien wiped the perspiration from his brow with a beautifully embroidered handkerchief. Deborah must have made it for him, Diana thought. "Certainly," he said.

"Sir," Lyon said as they walked back toward the house, "if you don't mind my asking—"

"Go ahead, my boy."

"Deborah's family. You said her first husband was a Quaker?"

"Yes. Albert Driscoll. He was well-thought-of, but when he died, he didn't leave much to his wife and son. Deborah was living in genteel poverty, I guess you'd call it, when I met her in St. Thomas.''

"And Daniel was working for a doctor?''

Lucien nodded. "Yes, a Dr. Gustavus was his name. A good man from all accounts. He thought highly of Daniel, needless to say."

"And Patricia, Father?"

"Ah, Patricia. Her maiden name is Foster. She was living with an aunt, a Miss Mary Foster, when she met Daniel. She even brought something of a dowry to Daniel. Two thousand pounds. Unfortunately, Deborah needed the bulk of that money to clear her debts. That was just before I'd met her, you understand."

"Did you meet this Miss Foster, sir?"

"Yes, I did. A maiden lady indeed—full of good works, carried herself as if she had a board down her back, had pinched lips. The proverbial, disapproving spinster. Highly religious, of course. One of those intolerant Methodists.''

"Patricia couldn't have been very happy with such a person," Diana said.

"Probably not. As to Patricia's real parents, all I know is that they are dead. Miss Mary Foster took in her niece at a very early age. She ran a boardinghouse in Charlotte Amalie."

"No wonder Patricia longs for gaiety," Lyon said.

"Do you think she is happy with Daniel, Father?"

Lucien paused a moment and plucked a hibiscus. "It was your mother's favorite, Diana," he said. He looked from his daughter to Lyon. "I would have said she was happy as a clam with Daniel, but after what you told me about seeing her with Grainger . . . Well, who knows?"

"Grainger admitted he was with her, but said it was nothing. He was extremely upset."

"I've never known Grainger to lie, and I've known him many years."

"Do you think it's possible that Daniel knows of his wife seeing Grainger?"

"I've said nothing. One hesitates to hurt Daniel, you know."

"Yes, we know," said Lyon.

"Such a large, self-sufficient man. And yet . . ."

"Yes," Diana said. "And yet."

26

By now you will have discovered that women too can be militant.

SOPHOCLES

"Look, Patricia, it is time you and I stopped our infernal arguments. I know you dislike me, and that is your prerogative, but I am afraid. Please, let us talk for a moment."

Patricia regarded Diana from beneath her blue silk parasol. When Diana had come up behind her, she'd known an awful moment of sheer terror. Oh, yes, she was afraid too. She drew a deep breath, calming herself. "What do you want to talk about?"

"About you and Grainger."

Patricia went white.

"I will tell you the truth, Patricia, for there is no more time left to us to keep silent because of each other's sensibilities. Lyon saw you just before dawn one morning, with Grainger. Lyon and I spoke to him. He's very upset, more upset than I've ever seen him, but he swore he wasn't your lover."

Patricia just stared at Diana. Then, suddenly, frighteningly, she laughed. And laughed. "Oh, it is too much! You believe that Grainger and I . . . It is too much!"

She snapped her parasol closed.

"What do you mean? Then why were you with him? And in such secrecy?"

"Mind your own business, Diana. It has nothing to do with anything. Oh, God!"

"Patricia, please. Two people have been killed. I know that you know things that you haven't told. It cannot go on. You must tell the truth."

"The truth," Patricia repeated softly, looking toward the sea. "The truth is a strange monster, isn't it, Diana? One thinks one knows the truth, but then it seems to change and fade and slip through one's fingers. I don't know any truth that would make sense to anyone." She faced Diana, her shoulders drawn back.

Diana felt a brief surge of respect for her. "What do you mean that truth is a strange monster? *Monster?*"

"I meant nothing."

"Do you love Daniel?"

Patricia sucked in her breath. She said nothing, but her fingers were tearing at the lace on the parasol.

"He is a very kind, gentle man. How did you meet him? And Deborah?"

"I met him in Charlotte Amalie, as you know. It was a very short time ago, actually. My aunt, Miss Foster, was ill, and he came with Dr. Gustavus to attend her. As you said, he was very kind. My aunt adored him, and let me tell you, Aunt Mary didn't believe any man worth a sou. And I? Well, I wanted desperately to escape. Daniel was there, and yes, he was ever so kind. I met Deborah soon after that. She appeared very fond of me, yes, very fond."

"But you weren't poor. My father mentioned that you

brought Daniel a dowry of two thousand pounds. That is substantial.''

"I wasn't informed of the money until I told Aunt Mary that Daniel had asked me to marry him.''

"You married him to get your dowry?''

"Oh, how can I expect you to understand? My precious aunt was mean, poor-spirited. I do not know where she got the two thousand pounds. And why she would have saved the money for me, well . . . again, I don't know. She certainly wasn't all that fond of me. I had no choices, not like you have enjoyed all your spoiled life.''

"Choices? I?'' Diana laughed. "Oh, Patricia, so few of us have choices.''

"Why? Are you breeding? Was your husband forced to marry you?''

"No, I am not breeding.'' She remembered Lyon's words and added quietly, "Perhaps I am now, but I wasn't when we married.''

"You should leave this place.''

"Perhaps I shouldn't mention this just yet, but Lyon wishes for you and Daniel to return to England with us. Daniel wants desperately to become a physician. He can receive excellent training in London.''

"Why?''

The single, very cold word drew Diana up short.

"I know you don't like me, despite what you said. You don't think I'm a proper wife for Daniel. You don't know either of us, not really.''

"As for knowing you, I fancy if we do all return to England, that lapse will soon be remedied. However, Deborah doesn't wish for Daniel to leave Savarol. I don't understand why, but she is very adamant.''

"Deborah and Daniel are very close.''

"Yes,'' Diana said. "It will be Daniel's choice, though.''

Patricia raised her parasol and looked blankly at the lace she had shredded. "You should leave," she said again, then walked away swiftly toward the house.

But what about Charles Swanson? Diana wanted to call after her. Was he your lover? But she kept silent. This was their first conversation that wasn't fraught with ill feeling. At least not too much ill feeling.

Diana sighed and started off in search of Lyon.

"You shouldn't be alone, little sister. Lucien told us all quite clearly to stick together."

Diana grinned up at Daniel. "Well, now I'm with you, big brother. No one would dare try anything with you on the scene."

"Probably not. I saw you talking to Patricia. Did she rip up at you?"

Gentle Daniel was also very observant, Diana thought. "No," she said honestly, "not this time."

"What did you talk about?"

"She was telling me how the two of you met."

"I see. Would you care to go riding with me?"

"Yes, I should like that." They walked side by side toward the stables. "It will be a relief to get away for a little while. There is so much tension. Understandable, of course."

"Yes, indeed."

"Patricia also told me about her Aunt Mary."

"Poor woman. She was so very unhappy, you know. I used to think that her religion demanded her unhappiness, but now, I don't think so. Perhaps it was something deep inside her, perhaps she was like a bud that is incapable of blossoming."

Diana smiled at him. "You are immensely understanding, Daniel."

"Sometimes," he said. "Only sometimes."

"You will ride Salvation, won't you?"

"I told you that stallion makes me nervous."

"All right, then, Tanis."

Lyon didn't hesitate. He entered Lucien and Deborah's bedchamber and quietly closed the door behind him. Like Diana, he knew that Deborah was keeping secrets and he couldn't allow it to continue. He had to find out the truth, and he prayed there was something here to lead to something.

He walked to the small writing desk in the corner of the bedchamber. It was Deborah's personal desk. Lucien kept all his papers in the desk in his study. He pulled out the top drawer. There were several letters to Mary Foster that she'd copied. He read them. Nothing, just formal inquiries about her health and general comments about Savarol Island. He carefully replaced the letters. There were other letters, from friends in Charlotte Amalie. In another drawer there were ribbon-tied documents. He read each of them. One was Daniel's birth record. Another, marriage lines between Deborah and her first husband. And a second paper with Deborah and Lucien's marriage lines. There were bills marked paid, many of them years old. Odd that she would keep them. He frowned, seeing that many of them were made out to Dr. Gustavus. "Paid for services" was written on each of them in Deborah's neat hand. The sums were not all that small. Could they all be for his professional services? Had she or Daniel both been so consistently ill? He placed the bills back into the drawer.

In another drawer he found her stationery and quills. Nothing unusual. There was but one other drawer, hidden behind a small panel. He pressed on the panel, but nothing happened. He continued lightly probing with his fingertips

ntil he found a slight indentation. He pressed it and the
anel eased open. The drawer behind the panel was locked.
_yon frowned a moment, then steeled himself. He picked
p a letter opener and forced the small lock. There was a
hick envelope in the drawer. He pulled it out and opened
t. It was filled with carefully cut-out newspaper pages.
The top one was a brief announcement of Patricia and
Daniel's marriage. The second was an announcement of
Deborah's marriage to Lucien Savarol. He placed the two
side and looked at the next.

It was a page from the *Charlotte Amalie Gazette*, and
vas one year old. He read it, then froze.

"Oh, my God," he said softly to the empty room. He'd
rayed he would find something, but this?

"What are you doing here?" Deborah stood in the
doorway, staring at Lyon. She saw the newspaper pages in
is hand and sucked in her breath. "No," she moaned
oftly, wrapping her arms about her. "Oh, no, please."

"What else did you and Patricia talk about?"

Diana turned in Salvation's saddle toward Daniel. She
ouldn't tell him about Grainger, she couldn't hurt him
ike that, despite her passionate speech to Patricia that
here was no more time to spare anyone's feelings. She ran
er tongue over her lips and forced lightness into her
voice. "As I told you, Patricia gave me the story of how
ou two met. It sounded most romantic, Daniel. Love at
irst sight and all that."

"Yes, I suppose it was. It seems like a very long time
go now."

"Goodness, 'tis only four months or so, isn't that right?
You are already seeing yourself as an old married couple?"

Daniel merely smiled at her and dug his heels gently

into Tanis' sides. The mare tossed her head and broke into a canter.

Diana kept pace with him. They stopped for a few minutes at the slave village.

"I don't feel like riding back just yet," Daniel said as he remounted Tanis. "Why don't we go to the end of the island? There's a lovely spot there I'd like you to see. I found it not too long ago. It's special, to me."

"All right," Diana said agreeably. She was silent for several minutes, wondering what to do. Then she said finally, "Daniel, Lyon and I would like for you and Patricia to return to England with us, once all this . . . awfulness is cleared up. You could study medicine there and—"

"You spoke of this to Patricia?"

"Yes, I did. And to your mother as well. There is something I don't understand, though, not really. Deborah seems intent upon keeping you here, with her."

"She is most possessive."

"But surely she understands how very much you wish to help people. She must know how important medicine is to you. Why, just look at how many of our people you've helped."

"Yes, she knows."

"Will you come back to England with us?"

He gave her a very serious look. "You have spoken to many of us, haven't you, little sister? You appear to have found out so very much."

Diana shook her head. "Not really, it's just that . . . Well, it's all so confusing, isn't it? All these terrible things happening. But you didn't answer my question, Daniel."

"Didn't I? Well, soon, perhaps. Yes, soon."

He nudged Tanis ahead and Diana frowned after him.

*   *   *

Lyon said very quietly, "Shall I read these newspaper accounts to you, Deborah?"

She walked like a very old woman toward the French windows, standing there, staring out over the grounds. "God, I tried. I tried so very hard."

"This first one is a year old. It concerns the murder of a young girl in Charlotte Amalie. She was strangled. She was the daughter of a local merchant. It appears to have raised quite a furor. The murderer wasn't found."

He paused a moment, looking at her. She hadn't moved.

He picked up a second newspaper page. "This one is another report of a young girl who was strangled. It is about a year and a half old. Also in Charlotte Amalie. She was a slave. No one appears to have cared too much."

"Stop it!"

"Deborah, why have you kept these gruesome articles?" But he knew the answer. Oh, yes, he knew, and the truth he had sought now made him feel as cold as death.

Deborah slowly turned to face him.

"And those bills you paid to Dr. Gustavus? They were for care of Daniel, were they not?"

"Yes. He knew, you see, and claimed he wanted to help Daniel. He also wanted money."

"And you wanted to get Daniel away from Charlotte Amalie before he was found out? Because surely it was just a matter of time before what he'd done was discovered?"

"Yes. I thought I could control him here on Savarol Island. Oh, God, that little fool, Moira! If only I could have gotten rid of her, once I found out what was going on! If only she'd understood! I warned her, I even threatened her, you remember, the riding crop. But it was too late. She wouldn't listen."

"How many girls did he kill?"

"Five. Over a period of four years. I kept hoping that

Dr. Gustavus would help him. He kept Daniel so close, so close. Daniel didn't know that Dr. Gustavus knew his secret. Only I knew."

"But why Patricia? How could you let him marry her?"

"I thought . . . no, I believed truly that she would change him. He seemed so very fond of her and she of him. I prayed—oh, God how I prayed—it would all cease, that the sickness in his mind would stop. But I soon realized that things were not well with them. It was at that time I met Lucien. No, I didn't marry him for Daniel's sake. I love him."

"But Daniel seems so very normal, so kind and—" He broke off, still grappling with the truth.

"Yes, he does. I never would have guessed, never, and I am his mother. One evening, some four years ago, I was awake when he came in late one night. He'd killed a girl and he was still in the throes of this strange excitement. He told me everything. Then Dr. Gustavus came."

"And Charles Swanson? He was shot, not strangled."

"It was Patricia's fault!"

"She shot him?"

"No, but it was still her fault. I told you that I soon realized all was not well between Daniel and Patricia. Daniel is . . . impotent. Patricia told me. She and Charles Swanson became lovers."

"And Daniel discovered it?"

"Yes."

"And he shot Charles Swanson?"

"Yes."

"It is difficult to accept, Deborah. Surely you have realized that Charles Swanson and Edward Bemis were, well, closer than men should be."

"Patricia knew it too. She wanted to change Charles. And she did, for a brief time at least."

"Daniel must be stopped, Deborah."

"He is my son!"

"Yes, and he must be stopped."

She shuddered and buried her face in her hands. She moaned softly.

Lyon walked to her and put his arms around her. "I am sorry," he said, "truly sorry. Will you speak to Lucien now?"

"He will hate me," she gasped. "He will despise me for bringing madness and death to his island."

"No," Lucien said from the doorway. "I won't despise you, my dear, but Lyon is quite right, you know. Daniel must be stopped."

Lyon met the older man's eyes from across the room. He wondered how much Lucien had heard. He patted Deborah's back and gently eased away from her. "We must find Daniel," he said very gently. "You know that."

"Yes, I know."

Lucien said, "We will speak of this later, Deborah. Come, my boy."

"Daniel, it's my cave! You found my cave!" Diana whirled about to grin hugely at Daniel.

He merely returned her smile as he dismounted from Tanis' back.

"Yes," he said, turning to face her, "I guessed it was your cave. I found camping things and clothes that I figured belonged to you."

Diana also dismounted and tethered Salvation to an oleander bush. "Have you done much exploring?"

"No, I'm much too large to get about."

Diana giggled. "Even I am too large for much exploring."

"You never found another way out?"

She shook her head.

"Shall we go inside?"

"Lead on, big brother!" She shivered and wrapped her arms about her. "I always forget how very cool it is inside." She remembered quite clearly that afternoon she and Lyon had spent here, and unconsciously, she smiled.

"Did you and Patricia speak of other things, Diana?"

She blinked at the unexpected question, but replied readily enough, "No, not really. All this awfulness, Daniel, well, I know that Patricia knows more than she's telling. I'm sorry, but from what she told me today, well—"

"What did she tell you?" His voice echoed strangely about her, very low, very deep.

"Things that didn't make much sense. She spoke of monsters."

"Ah."

"Oh, let's not speak of it, at least for now. Listen, Daniel, can you hear the sound of water? I know there's an underground lake."

"Perhaps you will find it, Diana."

"We haven't the time to hunt for it, I'm afraid."

"My mother isn't well, you know," Daniel said after a moment.

"She is naturally upset."

"Yes, and soon, very soon, she will not be able to keep things quiet. You see, she loves your father."

"What ever are you talking about?"

He stepped close to her and cupped her chin in the palm of one large hand. "You are a beautiful girl, Diana. Perhaps, had I met you before Patricia, things would have been different."

She felt a sudden spurt of alarm. "What do you mean, Daniel?"

"Nothing, I suppose. I do know, though, that there

isn't much left for me to do. The net is drawing tight. It is not like Charlotte Amalie here.''

She was growing colder and colder. She realized suddenly that she and Daniel were alone, in this isolated cave, and no one knew where she was. No, she was being silly. Daniel was just upset, as was everyone else. Had Deborah killed Moira and Charles?

''After you, Diana, it will have to be Patricia. She is not what I thought she would be. She is weak and silly and she betrayed me. With Swanson, and that damned man was a pervert!''

Diana didn't move. His fingers were lightly stroking her jaw. His voice had become oddly singsong.

''And of course, then Lucien and your husband. They must all die. I must protect myself. Surely you understand that? And my poor mother, I must protect her.''

''Let us go now, Daniel. You don't know what you're saying. Please, Daniel.''

''Poor Diana. I am sorry. You are not like the others. They were all so foolish, so cleverly mean to me. You really must face up to things now, you know. I can't bring myself to strangle you. But I must leave you here. I know this was a burial cave a long time ago. You won't be alone in your death.''

She jerked away from him, her heart pounding, and rushed toward the cave entrance.

She was nearly there. Escape. Oh, God.

He caught her about her waist and hauled her back.

She was no match for his strength, but she fought him nonetheless. Her fingernails scored his cheek before he caught her arms behind her back. He jerked her arms upward until she quieted, unable to fight more because of the intense pain.

''Daniel—'' Was that her voice, disembodied, so pitiful?

"Hush, Diana. Don't fight me. You know you can't win. Come, now, I will tie you up, but not tightly. You will get free but not until I've left."

He drew off his belt and bound her hands in front of her. "Sit down, now." When she didn't move, he shoved her down. She felt the hard earth and sharp stones.

"I will leave you light. I am not a monster."

Monster! Patricia knew, or at least she suspected.

"Daniel, you aren't . . . well. Please, I can help you. Lyon can help you, he—"

He threw back his head and laughed. It echoed off the walls of the cave, bouncing back, surrounding her, and she wanted to scream with the terror of it. She watched him bring her lamp near her and light it. He stared at her a moment, not speaking.

He leaned down suddenly and kissed her, hard. "Such a pity. Good-bye, little sister."

She watched him stride to the cave entrance. He looked back at her and shook his head.

She struggled to her feet. She heard a loud scraping sound. She was nearly to the opening when the huge rock slammed over it and she was plunged into darkness.

She screamed, falling back as the earth shook from the impact of the boulder.

She fell to her knees. Silence. She was surrounded by silence and darkness. She looked toward the flickering lamp.

*There is no limit to investigating the truth,
until you discover it.*

CICERO

Lyon stood stockstill in the dim, cool stable. "What?"

"Miss Diana ride with Massa Daniel."

"Oh, God! Where did they go?"

"I don't know."

Lucien looked at Tom, the stable hand, and nodded. "Very well. Lyon, we must round up men, not only to search for Diana, but to find Daniel."

Lyon nodded. He wasn't up to finding words. He felt sick and stupid and blind. And Daniel was with Diana. Would he hurt her? Had something in his mind finally snapped? Was Diana now a threat to him, or another girl he had decided to kill?

"Where is Salvation?"

"Miss Diana ride Salvation. Massa Daniel ride Tanis."

"Of course, I'm not thinking straight." Lucien ran distracted hands through his disheveled hair. "We must go to the village and round up some men to help us. Lyon, you take Egremont, I will go find Grainger."

"Tell the women to stay in the house."

"Yes, of course you're right."

Ten minutes later, Lyon reined in at the slave village. He was told that Diana and Daniel had ridden away a half-hour before. No one knew where they had gone. He organized three dozen men to search. He had to tell them the truth, and when he did, Bob, Moira's lover, stared at him in disbelief, then howled in fury.

Where to look?

"I hear Massa Daniel say something about showing Miss Diana a special place of his," said an old man who was squatting next to a fire.

Lyon left the slave village in an organized uproar. He galloped Egremont back to the great house. Thirty-six men would comb the island, every foot of it. He prayed one of them would find her . . . alive.

Diana stared toward the massive rock that sealed the cave entrance. She was trapped, alone, and she would die here, without ever seeing Lyon again.

She fell to her knees, her mind as numb as her body. She didn't know how long she remained there, her mind blank, when she became aware of a strange raw sound and realized that it was coming from her. Low, ugly sobs. "Shut up, you stupid weak fool!"

Her voice bounced back to her and the sound, although magnified and eerie, made her feel better. She continued aloud, "I will not sit here and wait to die. I won't!"

She looked at the lamp. She guessed she had another hour of light, not much more. Perhaps less. She shivered, more from the cold now than from the deadening terror. "All right, my girl, you will do something. You will find a way out of here."

She rose and walked to the entrance. She set her shoulder against the rock and shoved against it with all her strength. It didn't move. Not that she'd expected it to, not really. She turned her back to it and stared beyond the lamp into the hollow darkness. There was another way out. There had to be. If she didn't believe that, she might as well curl up and wait to be plunged into darkness, for eternity, alone.

She picked up the lamp and walked swiftly toward the back of the cavern. It ended abruptly. This was the north side, the side that was nearest the sea. She'd carefully explored the opposite side of the cave, particularly after she'd discovered that narrow opening. Unfortunately, she hadn't grown any smaller, so she would not be able to squeeze through it. No, she had to search out the more-recessed northern side. She'd avoided it as a child. The ground sloped up at an alarming rate, and she'd fallen once on the loose rocks. "Careful now," she said aloud, and was again reassured by the sound of her own voice.

Nothing. There was nothing save the expanse of slimy walls, treacherous loose rocks, and the stalactites, glittering, wet spears in the dim light.

She forced herself to continue. She hummed softly to herself, trying to think of pleasant things. Oddly enough, it was the wild, untamed moors of Yorkshire she pictured in her mind, the rolling mists that flowed over the harsh ground, forming strange patterns around the roughhewn rocks in the early morning. Oh, God, she wanted so desperately to see Lyon's estate, Ashton Hall.

What if now she would never see it? Never know the pleasure of being mistress of Ashton Hall, Lyon's wife and lover and—

The lamp flickered and she froze. "No! Not yet!"

The light grew steady again, but it was much dimmer now. "No," she said aloud again, and frustrated, frightened, she whirled about and slammed her fist against the cave wall. To her surprise, she felt something give way. She raised the lamp. Her heart began to pound.

Feverishly, she set down the lamp and began digging at the loose dirt against the wall. It came away slowly, but she didn't pause. Suddenly, just as she pulling away a large rock, the lamp went out.

"No!"

She fit her hands about the rock, closed her eyes, and jerked. The rock gave way. She heard it hit the cave floor and tumble down the incline. It rolled and rolled, the sound of it more frightening then she could have imagined.

It was then that she saw a beam of clear sunlight.

Patricia didn't hear him. One moment, she was alone, walking swiftly back toward the great house, the next Daniel had grasped her arm.

Oddly enough, the first words out of her mouth were, "What have you done with Diana?"

"She is dead," Daniel said, his voice deep, calm, sounding so very normal in the bright sunlight. "I really didn't want to kill her, but she was discovering things, too many things. It was just a matter of time and I had her alone. And my mother, she is very close to breaking now. No, I had no choice, and she came with me so willingly. As for you, my dear wife, you will deserve your death."

"You're insane," she whispered, her voice ground nearly away in her fear. "You can't, Daniel, no!"

His grip tightened on her arm and he dragged her inexorably toward the southern end of the front grounds, toward the narrow, very sheer cliff that overlooked the only rocky shore on the island, some thirty feet below.

Patricia screamed, a high, piercing scream. It was the

last thing she did. Daniel's fist slammed into her jaw and she crumbled.

"Oh, my God!"

Lucien grabbed Lyon's arm. "He's got Patricia. Lyon, he's going to the cliffs!"

At least he didn't strangle her immediately, Lyon thought. He shook his head. God, had he strangled Diana? The two men were standing on the second-floor veranda, guns in hand.

"Let's go," Lyon said.

"Don't kill him, Lucien! Don't!"

Lucien touched his wife's arm. "Stay here, Deborah. There's nothing you can do now."

Deborah fell away from him, sobbing wildly.

The men took the stairs two at a time.

Dido, Lila, and the other household slaves stood huddled next to the front door.

"See to your mistress," Lucien said over his shoulder to Dido. "Keep her inside!"

Lyon ran faster than he'd ever done in his life. He would make Daniel tell him where Diana was.

Dear God, she couldn't be dead.

His booted feet pounded the earth. Suddenly, he burst through the thick growth of oleanders. There was Daniel, an unconscious Patricia in his arms, standing only about ten feet from the edge of the cliff.

And there was Grainger, not fifteen feet away from him, pointing a dueling pistol at him.

"Ease her down, Daniel." The overseer's voice calm, strangely detached. "Do as I tell you, boy. Set her down."

"No, Grainger, I can't do that." Daniel's voice sounded strangely apologetic. "She betrayed me, you see. She is like all the others."

Lyon came to an abrupt halt, uncertain what to do.

"Daniel," he called out, "where is Diana?"

Patricia moaned at that moment and began struggling. Daniel eased her to her feet, but kept his arm clamped around her.

"Where is Diana?"

"Dead,"Daniel said. "I didn't want to, Lyon, but I had no choice."

"Release her, Daniel!" Grainger took a step forward, and Lyon wanted to yell for him to stop, for he realized that the overseer was trying to find a better vantage point to get a clearer shot.

Lyon stood stock-still, not wanting to accept Daniel's flat words. No, she couldn't be dead. No!

"She deserves to die, Grainger," Daniel called, crushing Patricia against him until she stopped struggling. "She did betray me, you know, with that little fool, Swanson. She's like all the others. They were all cruel, they didn't care. They laughed at me. And why do you care anyway, Grainger? Did she bed with you too?"

"You damned bastard! She's my daughter!"

In an instant of blank surprise, Daniel eased his hold on Patricia and she slipped downward. His eyes met Grainger's from across the distance.

Grainger fired. The gunshot rent the silence.

Daniel looked down at the red stain that was spreading on his white shirt, covering his chest. He gave a loud growl, leaned down, grabbing Patricia by her hair, and began dragging her toward the cliff edge.

Grainger fired again. Lyon watched Daniel flinch and stagger. Grainger had got him in the middle of the back. And yet he was still standing, still walking.

Patricia was screaming.

"Daniel! Don't!" It was Deborah, running, her skirts held up in her hands. "No, Daniel! It's over. You must stop now. You must come to me. I am your mother, I will protect you. Please, Daniel.''

Daniel turned at the edge of the cliff. Blood covered his chest, droplets falling to the ground.

''Mother?''

Grainger fired again. The shot slammed into Daniel's throat, and his head jerked back.

Still Daniel stood, bewildered, like a lost child, blood spurting from his throat, staring helplessly at Deborah. ''Mother?'' It was a whisper, a soft, bewildered whisper.

''Daniel!''

Patricia struggled and Lyon saw Daniel look down at her. Then he released her. She rolled over onto her stomach, burying her face against the ground.

''You damnable bastard!'' The final shot hit Daniel in the belly. He weaved where he stood, then fell slowly to his knees. There was no sound from him when he rolled over the cliff to the rocks below.

''Daniel!''

Lyon's last sight of Daniel was a vision of red. Blood, so much blood, spurting everywhere, onto Patricia, soaking into the earth. He whispered, very quietly, ''But where is Diana?''

He didn't follow Grainger and Lucien as they ran to the cliff and peered over the edge. He couldn't move.

''Lyon!''

It was her voice, haunting him. He'd failed her miserably. If only . . .

''Lyon! I'm here!''

He turned slowly, unable to make his body react, unable to think. Diana was jumping off Salvation's back. She was a filthy mess, but it didn't matter. She was the most beautiful sight he'd ever seen.

She hurled herself against him, nearly toppling the both

of them. "I saw it all," she sobbed against his neck. "Oh, God, he was . . . helpless."

"He said he'd killed you." He flung the gun away from him and tightened his grip on her until she squeaked.

"No, he trapped me in our cave. I found another way out."

"I never would have found you," Lyon said, "never, until it was too late. God, Diana."

Neither of them was aware of the pandemonium that surrounded them.

Epilogue

No sweet without sweat.

LATIN PROVERB

Ashton Hall, Yorkshire
September 1813

"You ridiculous man! Stop that, Lyon! You are cruel and I shall surely pay you back." Diana giggled and squirmed as he began tickling her.

"Hold still, wench." Lyon was nipping at her earlobe, his fingertips now lightly caressing her ribs. She bucked beneath him until he came over her, pinning her body beneath him.

He pressed his body against hers and felt her answering response.

"Lyon," she whispered, her arms coming about his back.

There were no more words between them.

"We must light a lamp. I can barely make out your self-satisfied, very smug female grin."

"Have you the strength, my lord?"

"No. I feel aged and used up." He pulled away from her and lit the lamp beside their bed. He sank down again, drawing her close.

"You're sweaty as a pig."

"You malign me, woman, after I make you yowl with pleasure?"

She smiled, pressing her lips against his shoulder.

"You are so sweet, Diana, but I imagine that you taste a bit salty yourself. I must investigate further." He ran his tongue along her jaw. "Sweaty as a piglette?"

"You are not gallant. Oh, dear, what is the time? Remember, Frances and Hawk are coming for dinner."

Lyon said something inelegant and Diana grinned. She raised herself on her elbow and peered down into his beloved face. "I love you, my lord."

Lyon grunted. "I think it is my house you love. You merely tolerate me because I am the owner."

"It is beautiful," she said. "I never saw an Elizabethan manor house before. It's also chilly. So I will keep you. You do provide warmth for me at night. And I must admit that Tanis is quite happy here."

"Ha! She is happy because she's been covered by Flying Davie. Just like a mare or a woman . . . satisfy her in bed and she'll be happy anywhere."

"I think there must be some truth to that," she said. "I trust you will never lose your talents."

"Remember when I thrashed your bottom?"

She felt his hand stroke over her buttocks. "I will do anything to save myself," she said, and kissed him fully on his mouth.

There was a light knock on the bedchamber door.

Lyon groaned. "It's probably Kenworthy. We must bathe, I suppose, else Frances and Hawk will know exactly how we've spent our afternoon."

"And morning."

Lyon rose slowly and called toward the door. "Have hot water fetched, Kenworthy."

"It is, uh, here, my lord."

Lyon, because he was quicker, bathed first. He was dressing while Diana hummed to herself in the bathtub.

"Diana?"

"Hmmm?"

"Patricia will be arriving in three weeks or thereabouts."

That drew her up. "How do you know that?"

Lyon waved a letter at her. "I meant to tell you earlier, then you sidetracked me. In any case, she will be coming to us, in London, for the Little Season."

"How is Grainger?"

"According to your father, he is just fine. He and Patricia have gotten quite close. He very much regrets, of course, the fact that he sent her to his wife's sister, Mary Foster, but says that at the time he didn't see any other option. But at least he did send her money and provided her dowry. He is pleased she is coming to us. Your father also writes at great length of our project. Surprisingly enough, it is our project that has drawn Deborah out of her depression."

Daniel, she thought, and she felt the familiar pain. Poor Deborah.

Their project, she thought as she rubbed the lavender-scented soap over her shoulders. "Does Father really believe it will work?"

"Yes, I believe he does. He expected, you know, that I would simply free the slaves and toss them out on their own, to make their own way. He writes that the slave village is now operating quite efficiently again, much expanded now, of course. Deborah herself is directing the school and all the slaves, not just our Mendenhall people, are benefiting."

"And missionaries?"

"Not as yet. Your father is adamant on that score. Since

none of the slaves will be freed until his death, he wants no trouble or unrest in the meanwhile. He writes that five years should prove ample time to prepare all our people to the practical side of being free men and women.''

Lyon paused a moment, looking over at his wife. She was climbing out of the tub. He sucked in his breath. He wondered if the mere sight of her would always move him. Her beautiful hair was pinned up, with a few strands escaping to frame her face. She had no tan now. Her shoulders were as white as her breasts and her soft belly. He forced himself to look away or they wouldn't be downstairs to greet Frances and Hawk.

He said after a moment, "Diana, you are certain this is what you want?"

"As you said, Lyon, it is our project. Yes, I am quite certain."

"You will have no inheritance. Even Savarol Island will be bequeathed to the slaves."

"But I will be the executor. And Deborah also. Besides," she added on a grin, "you are provokingly wealthy. I don't think we will have to worry about our next meal." She shivered suddenly. "My father will live for many more years, Lyon. It bothers me to speak of life after he is gone."

"True." He grinned suddenly. "Your father also writes that Grainger has made him swear not to tell anyone of his plans, else he might find himself dispatched sooner than he would like by a disgruntled slave."

"I devoutly pray that Grainger was jesting!"

"Since your father has written it in an amusing way, I suppose he was jesting. Now, my dear, when do you plan to tell me your very interesting condition?"

Her eyes met his from across the bedchamber. "How did you know? I just come to realize it this morning."

"I am a man of the world."

"Ha! Does that mean a wretched rake?"

"Very well, a faithful hound of the world. You've had no monthly flow, my dear. A husband tends to notice things like that, you know. No interrupted bedding with my wife."

She flushed just a bit and wrapped her towel more firmly about her.

"And neither of us will worry. I will ensure that Lucia is well ensconced with us long before the child is due."

Diana walked over to her husband and sat down on his lap. She wrapped her arms about his neck. "I will keep you, my lord. Yes, I shall."

There was another knock on the door.

"Go away, Kenworthy! Tell the earl and countess to dine alone. We will join them for tea."

Diana thought she heard a giggle from the other side of the door. Lyon did too. He groaned. "Go away, Hawk! Frances, please, remove that fool!"

They heard Hawk say very clearly, "Ah, these newly-weds. Shall we spare their sensibilities, Frances?"

"Go away!"

Diana buried her face against Lyon's throat.

"Shall we dine, Frances? Alone? Ignored by our host and hostess?"

"I fancy we have no choice, Hawk," said Frances.

They heard Hawk say in a loud stage whisper, "It seems to me that they're striving mightily to produce a suitable offspring for one of our progeny. Thank the Lord we have both a boy and a girl, they won't have to worry."

"Or perhaps, husband, since our daughter is a dark bandit like you, we should have another. More choice, you know."

"Ah, I grow an old man in your service, Frances."

They heard Frances laugh, a low, very inviting laugh. Her voice was breathless when she finally called out, "We shall see you two at tea," she called through the door.

They heard her giggle again.

"How long until teatime?" Lyon asked as he began kissing his wife's bare shoulders.

ABOUT THE AUTHOR

CATHERINE COULTER is the bestselling
author of numerous historical romances as well
as of two highly acclaimed contemporary novels
False Pretenses and *Impulse*. She lives in
Northern California with her husband, Anton,
and her cat, Gilley.

λ

27 million Americans can't read a bedtime story to a child.

It's because 27 million adults in this country simply can't read.

Functional illiteracy has reached one out of five Americans. It robs them of even the simplest of human pleasures, like reading a fairy tale to a child.

You can change all this by joining the fight against illiteracy.

Call the Coalition for Literacy at toll-free **1-800-228-8813** and volunteer.

Volunteer Against Illiteracy. The only degree you need is a degree of caring.